The
WATER
DEVIL

ALSO BY JUDITH MERKLE RILEY

In Pursuit of the Green Lion
A Vision of Light
The Serpent Garden
The Oracle Glass
The Master of All Desires

The
WATER
DEVIL

A MARGARET *of* ASHBURY NOVEL

JUDITH
MERKLE
RILEY

THREE RIVERS PRESS • NEW YORK

Copyright © 2007 by Judith Merkle Riley

Reading Group Guide copyright © 2006 by Three Rivers Press, an imprint of the
Crown Publishing Group, a division of Random House, Inc., New York.

Published in the United States by Three Rivers Press, an imprint of the
Crown Publishing Group, a division of Random House, Inc., New York.
www.crownpublishing.com

Three Rivers Press and the Tugboat design are registered
trademarks of Random House, Inc.

Crown Reads colophon is a trademark of Random House, Inc.

Library of Congress Cataloging-in-Publication Data
Riley, Judith Merkle.
The water devil : a Margaret of Ashbury novel / Judith Merkle Riley.—1st ed.
        p.   cm.
1. Margaret of Ashbury (Fictitious character)—Fiction.   2. Great Britain—
History—Edward III, 1327–1377—Fiction.   3. Women healers—Fiction.
3. Women healers—Fiction.   4. Women mystics—Fiction.
5. Forced marriage—Fiction.   I. Title.
        PS3568.I3794W38   2007
     813'.54—dc22   2006015348

ISBN 978-0-307-23789-7

Printed in the United States of America

Design by Karen Minster

10 9 8 7 6 5 4 3 2 1

First Edition

for

STEPHANIE

in celebration of long friendship

ACKNOWLEDGMENTS

As always, I am grateful for the assistance of my daughter, Elizabeth, who read the manuscript, and for the kindly and intelligent support of my agent, Jean Naggar. But, above all, this book owes its second life to the astonishing and wonderful fans of the Margaret series. Thank you, thank you, all of you.

The
WATER
DEVIL

PROLOGUE

I T WAS NOT LONG AFTER CANDLEMAS IN the Year of Our Savior 1362, when I was writing down the cost of pickled fish and flour and thinking them too high, that a Voice came into the inner ear of my mind. "Margaret," it said, "I did not so order the world that you would learn letters to waste them on account rolls. How much better if your accounting was of My glorious works?"

"But Lord," I answered, "You have commanded that wives serve their husbands, and my lord husband hates keeping household accounts."

"Margaret, how do you know that you won't be serving him better by hiring a clerk for the accounts?"

"Full time? Lord, think of the expense. And suppose he's a rogue?"

"Have your steward tell him what to write; then you can review it once a month, as Master Wengrave across the alley does to his great satisfaction."

"But, Lord, You know what happened last time I hired a clerk to write for me."

"Why don't you leave Me to arrange things My own way on occasion, Margaret?"

Now who am I, a sinful mortal being, to disobey Our Lord who is so much higher than everyone, even husbands and other men? So I corked up the inkwell and put down the quill, and looked out the window of the solar, where cold February rain was streaking the glass and the tall, brightly painted houses of the merchants and vintners across the street looked all knobby on account of the many little window panes being round and bubbly. It is good to be rich and looking out of glass, I thought, watching two heavily bundled men taking a dray-cart full of wood into the courtyard of Master Barton the Pepperer's big stone house across the way. There was a time once, when I'd have been dodging between those icy drops, intent on the business of making a living. But here a glowing brazier chased the chill from the chamber, and bright tapestries mocked the gray outside. Below me in the hall, I could hear the thumping and banging of the trestle tables being set up for dinner, and the smell of pickled cabbage and salt fish cooking came sneaking up through the joints in the door like a cat on the prowl. Then there came a knock at the door, not loud, but persistent, accompanied by a distressful cry.

"Mama, mama, come quick. Father is having another fit and says he is going to run away to a monastery where at least he'll be left in peace to contemplate his sins."

"Alison!" I said, running to the door, "whatever did you do to set him off? You know he's working so terribly hard these days. Next month he travels to Kenilworth, and the presentation copy has to be ready."

"It wasn't me, mama," said Alison, standing framed in the doorway, her face pious. "It was Caesar who ate his pen case."

"I *told* you never to let that puppy into his office," I said, speeding down the narrow stairway with Alison behind me.

"Margaret," said my lord husband, standing confused between the gangling hound puppy and the children, "this is absolutely unbearable. Do something!" His office was a chaos, the straw on the floor all heaped and scooped as if someone had been digging in it, the iron bound chests thrown open to reveal piles of tumbled manuscript and books marked at various important places with an oatstraw. There were inkbottles and a quire of paper piled helter-skelter atop the double locked steel box that held the rents and the remainder of the eighty gold moutons he had brought home from Burgundy. There were inkstains on his old ankle length wool surcoat that's split up the middle for riding, and his liripipe, wound round his head like a Turk's turban against the chill, had gone askew with all his heavy thinking, tilting precariously over one dark eyebrow.

"I can't get a thing done here, not a thing!" he said, managing to look damaged and irritated all at once. And yet beneath it, I could also see he was secretly pleased with all the muddle. A house with many children, blazing with life and joy and troubles, so different than the cold, grim manor house of his childhood, the blood and death in foreign places he had just left behind him. His brown eyes lit up as he spied me there, and the tiniest little smile flitted across his face as he looked down at the top of my head. He is very tall and handsome, my lord husband, with his long Norman nose and dark curly hair, and our hearts can speak together when our lips are silent. Just now his heart was saying, Margaret, I was dull and sad here, working on a rainy day, and I needed a little chaos, and to see you, to make it right.

"My treyscher lord," I said, "you have too many worries and burdens. Why don't you hire a copy clerk to help you put together this work?"

"But, my cher Margaret, dear heart, what of the cost?" I could see his mind already working over the excellence of the idea. A good lad to carry his books behind him when he came from the illuminators, to copy his notes in a fair hand, to run and buy that extra bottle of ink or sharpen more quills. It seemed perfect.

"If he did the household accounts as well, the cost of his keep might be considered a reasonable expense," I answered. In this way Nicholas LeClerk, who failed in his University studies from rioting and roistering in taverns, came to eat at our table, and God's commands were obeyed, and my paper left off midway in the accounting of money and instead was given over to the accounting of the mysteries that are concealed in creation, and how I through fate became entangled with one of the strangest ones of all.

four childrens' caps of best wolle   3d. each
1 barrel of pickled sturgeon   £3

3 bushels of wheaten flour at 18d. each from Piers the Miller
   who has cheated in the measure again

IN THE YEAR of our Lord 1360, I, Margaret de Vilers, widowed
and married too often for respectability, having returned from adventures abroad with several excellent pilgrims' badges and my current husband, thought to leave adventuring alone. The whole world
was then at war, our King having gone forth to Reims to claim by
force of arms the Sainte Ampoule of Holy Chrism that was brought
to earth by a dove to anoint French kings, and with it to anoint himself and thus take hold of the crown of France.

The French already had a perfectly good king, who was living in
state in the Tower of London, having failed to provide the extremely
large ransom he felt his kingly dignity required. So it seemed a
promising moment, you understand, and our King decided he must
go, and where the King must go, so must the Duke, and where the
Duke must, so must his chronicler, my lord husband, Sir Gilbert de
Vilers, youngest and most eccentric of the distinguished but impoverished old family into which I had married after a most brief pe-
riod of widowhood. In the words of my former husband, Master
Roger Kendall, who was a Master of the Company of Mercers of
London and very rich if rather old, "When you think of wars and
high talk, Margaret, remember it's all really a matter of money.
Everything usually is." So that is what I think was at the bottom of
everything, even if everyone else does think it was all about a jug of
ointment in a foreign church. So that is where my story begins,
with a war, and all the warriors of England gone abroad in search of
fortune. And it all goes to show that even if you hide peacefully at
home from adventure, adventure will come and find you anyway if
that is how God wants it.

CHAPTER ONE

THE SHOUT OF BUNDLED CHILDREN PLAY-
ing in the musician's gallery echoed through the
dancing chamber in the heart of Leicester Castle,
chief seat of that mighty warlord, the strong right hand and
sage councilor of King Edward the Third, the Duke of Lancaster. Chill air, damp with spring mist, blew in through the
high, unglazed windows, gusted along the shining tiled floor,
and whispered along the gray stone walls, leaving traces of
oozing damp in memory of its passage. The heavy French tapestries that hung on the walls in days of celebration had been
put away, and the chamber given over to homely uses, for
Leicester Castle was a castle of women, of children, of old
men and priests since the day that the King's great expedition
had sailed for France.

A half-year had passed since every available horse, every
uncrippled man, and every unspent farthing had been pressed
into service in King Edward's greatest venture, the final, the
definitive campaign against the ruined French, which was to
end by seeing Edward crowned King of France at Reims. Their
anointed king, foolish, luxury loving King Jean, was a prisoner
in England, captive since the battle of Poitiers; a weak Dauphin
controlled a Paris savaged by disaster and isolated from a kingdom overrun with bandits. Now was the time for Edward to
press his family claims for the throne of France. Only the Duke
had argued against it, this risking everything on one throw of
the dice. Not a game, said the King, we command overwhelm-
ing force. The anointed King of France lives, as does his legal
heir, argued the Duke, and while they live, the natural French

hatred of a foreign king should not be taken lightly. I am no foreign king, but the legal heir, said Edward. Nevertheless, it is a foreign country, our supply lines will be long, it will be winter, and we will have ravaged the countryside. We will take everything with us, countered the King. With the first maps ever used in warfare, he planned the route. Six thousand wagons would carry the supplies. There would be food and tents, forges for arms and horse shoes, hand-mills and ovens for baking bread. There would be collapsible boats for fishing the rivers in Lent, there would be hundreds of clerks and artificers of every trade, sixty hounds and thirty falcon-ers for the King's hunting, and the royal band. Every great captain and petty nobleman who could ride a horse would be with him, and his own four sons. The Duke's advice was swept away in the great plan. Loyal that he was, he stripped his estates, taking horses, knights, tents, clerks, and even his own chronicler, a scholar-knight learned in languages, to record the mighty triumph. Now all over England, women waited, and the dancing-chamber stood echoing, and without music.

On the floor of the chamber, beneath the gallery, Duchess Is-abella's sewing women were at work. Seamstresses in heavy wool gowns clustered around a smoky little fire of green wood built in the great fireplace of the chamber. Yards of plain white linen were spread across their laps as they sewed the endless expanse of hems on a set of sheets. An old woman, nearly blind, recited, or half-chanted, the tale of the false steward, Sir Aldingar, as she spun by touch. At the end of a trestle table set up in the center of the room, a well-dressed dame with scissors addressed another woman who held a knotted cord. On the table, a length of fair linen, as smooth and luminous as baby's skin, was laid out ready for cutting.

"Dame Isabella says they must be cut three inches longer than the old ones, for her daughter grows apace," said the lady with the scissors.

> "He wolde have layne by our comelye queene,
> Her deere worshippe to betraye:

Our queene she was a good woman,
And evermore said him naye,"

sang the old woman in her tuneless voice, as a half-dozen needles
flashed in and out of the sheets in tiny, precise stitches.

"It is the length Dame Petronilla brought from the Mistress of
the Robes," answered the other. Away from the fire, the air fogged
as they spoke.

"Then it cannot be cut whole on the bias on this piece, as she
requested. Are you sure this is the length the Duchess wanted
made up?"

"Sir Aldingar was wrothe in his mind,
With her he was never content,
Till traiterous meanes he colde devyse,
In fyer to have her brent."

"Perhaps she has made an error. It measures short. We must ask
before we cut." Again, they held up the long girl's shift that was
their model, and measured off the inches with knotted string.

"If Dame Petronilla has made an error, *I*, for one, certainly don't
want to be the one to point it out," said the sewing woman.

"Then I'll go look for Dame Katherine myself," said the lady. Laying down her scissors and departing through the open door, she left
the sewing woman to puzzle over the material, wondering just how
it might be pieced in such a way that the different stitching might
never be noticed.

"What do you mean, the piece is too short?" came a sharp voice
through the open door. "Are you accusing me of cutting it off? Oh,
I see, a *mistake*. I do not make mistakes." The needles by the fireside
paused, and the sewing women looked at one another.

"Lady Petronilla," said one. "Why did our good duchess ever make
her assistant to the mistress of the robes?" Rapid footsteps passed by
their little circle, accompanied by a sort of icy breeze which was
not so much a breeze as a feeling of chill. They looked up to see the

back of Dame Petronilla de Vilers's rigid form moving toward the table, the train of her heavy black gown slithering across the tile floor behind her.

"I heard that the Duke dispatched to Dame Isabella from France a list of wives of his knights to whom she should give preference in her household."

"Is Lady de Vilers's husband dead, then?" whispered another seamstress, casting a look at the black dress.

"No, she lost a son, they say."

"She doesn't seem old enough to have lost a son in France."

"No, an infant. Sir Hugo, her husband, was devastated at the news, and when she asked to be sent away from the place where he had died, he used influence to have her sent here, where company could distract her from her loss."

"An infant? And for that she goes all in black? That is much for only an infant."

"Ladies are different from us, I suppose."

"As different as she is from ladies," came the catty, whispered response.

> *"And nowe a fyer was built of wood;*
> *And a stake was made of tree;*
> *And now queene Elinor forth was led,*
> *A sorrowful sight to see. . . ."*

The woman in black looked scornfully at the length of cloth laid out on the table. "You'll have to piece it—or send for more—that was the last length from London in the chest."

"But—but—Lady Isabella wanted it whole, and ready in time for Easter—"

"Then have it ready," said Dame Petronilla, turning abruptly to go. She was just above the medium in height, with hard blue eyes and narrow, even features marred only by a nose slightly flattened and off center, as if it had once been broken. She wore a thick, black wool gown beneath a furlined surcoat of imported black velvet, decorated with dark green silk embroidery. Her heavy, honey blonde hair was braided and coiled tightly beneath a fine white linen veil. It was very fine, very fine indeed. I wonder—thought one of the sewing women, glancing at the beautiful length of linen that lay on the table, the linen that had been taken from storage for Lady Blanche's new Easter shift.

"Don't disturb me again with your incompetence. You have delayed me on my way to my prayers." A heavy gold crucifix, the agonized corpus of silver gilt upon it dabbed with red enamel and fixed with rubies, hung on her bosom. At her waist, beside her purse and the keys with which she was entrusted, hung a black-beaded rosary that ended in yet another cross, this time in silver, heavily tooled and ornamented. Hands folded before her chest, her eyes glittering strangely, she hurried, erect and cold, from the room.

A very holy lady, thought the woman with the scissors. So many hours in prayer. Why, she even brought her own confessor with her from the country. For a moment her eye caught on the light, airy movement of the veil as its owner stepped through the door into the draft that whirled down the passageway. Impossible, she thought. Besides, all white linen looks alike. Forgive me, Lord, it must be envy. It was I who wanted to be named assistant to the Mistress of the Robes; if only my husband had greater rank and preference, the way the de Vilers family has, the honor would have been mine.

CHAPTER TWO

CECILY, WHAT *HAVE* YOU DONE TO YOUR hair? Even the tangles grow tangles. I swear, it promises to eat the comb alive! Mother Sarah, is Peregrine dressed yet?" As Peregrine's infant wail joined his older sister's in sympathy, I felt a tug on my sleeve. The morning sun had just peeped over the horizon and the cold lay like a blanket along the floor. From downstairs came the clatter and crash of pots, the sound of hurrying footsteps, and the first acrid smell of the fire being built up on the kitchen hearth.

"*My* hair's combed, Mama." My second girl, Alison, still pudgy with baby fat at seven and a half, held up a long, silky strand of her strawberry blonde hair for my inspection. Her voice was smug.

"I'm sure that's lovely, dear—"

"That's because yours is all straight—yow! And God made mine curly because it's *better,* that's why!" Cecily squirmed away from the comb as her face turned red with indignation beneath its freckles. Not yet ten, knobby-kneed, rebellious, and as full of troublemaking ideas as an entire sackful of monkeys, she was my oldest, and my despair.

"Hold still, hold still," I said as I attacked her wild, red curls again with the ivory comb. "What's this I see here? A twig? Cecily, you've been climbing again. How will you ever be a lady if you keep climbing trees?"

"I don't *want* to be a lady. I want to be a—a—"

"I don't want to hear that you wish to be a boy because you *can't* be one, and that's that."

"—a *dragon,* so there!"

"Ha! Cecily wants to be all green and scaly and UGly—"

"Girls, girls, that's enough. Alison, is that a grease stain on the front of your good dress? You can't wear it that way. Change to the blue one at once, before you make us late."

"But it's not *pretty*," Alison's wail joined the grief stricken cries of her sister and baby brother. Why is it always so hard to get to church in time for mass? Especially on a feast day like this, Saint Augustine's day in May of the Year of our Lord 1360, when the whole world will be looking with serpents' eyes to see who's lazy enough to come ill clad? You'd think God would grease the way to mass, and make it easier than other things, instead of making the way all thorny with snares. And if it were all meant to be a test of faith like some saint in the desert being tempted, wouldn't it be grander, something like yawning pits and fiery flames, and not just children howling and Mother Sarah losing Peregrine's left shoe? I intended to take that up with God sometime when I wasn't dressing children.

"Your pattens, girls, it's muddy outside—no, not a word. I don't care if it stopped raining last night. I say it's muddy, and muddy it is."

There was a time long ago in our great prosperity, when Cecily and Alison's father was alive, that he arranged to have a poor knight's widow give them lessons in French and manners. But Madame was so stiff and proper she could barely manage to lower herself to teach a mercer's daughters, no matter how great their father's wealth and propriety. And when I remarried after his death, she considered it such a ghastly breach of etiquette that she departed in a cloud of disdain.

The French language, however, seemed to stick with the girls better than Madame did, especially since it is spoken in my new husband's family. I cannot say the same for the manners, which wore away faster than the knees of a little boy's hose. Well, if they can't act like ladies, then let them at least look like ladies, I thought, especially at church on holy days. But already Perkyn had thrown open the heavy front door. I checked them as they went out. Eyes hardly red anymore, and fixed properly on the ground. Steps grave. Clothes clean, hands folded across their stomachs. Peregrine, in

Mother Sarah's arms. Perkyn, solemnly closing the front door and following behind. All in order. Good. Perhaps today, no one would ever know that I had raised a pair of little red-headed terrors.

The last pink shades of dawn were still shining in the muddy puddles that filled the gutter down the center of Thames Street. Mud and wet stones made the uneven paving before the houses treacherous. The air was still fresh and cold, and filled with the rolling sound of the bells of Saint Botolphe's calling the parish to mass. Bundled figures were still hurrying in the direction of church. Praise heaven, we wouldn't be the latest. Halfway there, I turned to check over the household again.

"Put your hood up, Cecily. Alison, don't step in the puddles on purpose. Oh, Lord in Heaven, where's the baby?"

"Coming, coming, my lady. Perkyn's carrying him through the mud. It's too slippery for me. He's had to go slower. See? There he is now." There, rounding the corner into Botolphe's Lane, was my littlest darling, just past two years old, the only heir to the house of de Vilers, pink cheeks shining in the cold, brown curls tucked under his pointed red hat, chattering like a magpie to old Perkyn, who carried him in his arms.

The dark, shadowy narthex was still crowded with people jostling their way into the nave. The smell of wet wool and city mud mingled with the heavy odor of their bodies. Amid the clatter of pattens and the sound of greetings exchanged, I could make out catty women's voices:

"Well, look there, *Lady* Margaret de Vilers. I remember when Mistress Kendall was too good for her. No family at all. Came from nowhere."

"She just goes from scandal to scandal."

"Just look at her there, parading with her servants and that fur-trimmed surcoat. Who does she think she is?" I tried to hurry by, but a large man in pepperer's livery blocked my way. Behind me, the family was packed together by the crowd.

"*I* heard that she'd eloped with her husband's copy clerk, and his body hardly cold." I looked to see who was talking. Through the crowd, I could make out a bobbing white veil—another—a whole cluster of them.

"Disgraceful, I say."

"Some unfrocked monk named Gregory—a worthless loafer and beggar who copied letters in taverns." The white headdress turned, and I caught a glimpse of a red, spiteful face. The cordwainer's wife. No one I'd seen in church in recent memory.

"Gregory? I thought she married Sir Gilbert de Vilers. What happened to the beggar?"

"That's another scandal. He purchased a knighthood with her money and shed his religious name quicker than a snake sheds its skin."

"It was family connections. Mistress Godfrey told me that he was a younger son cast out by his family as a wastrel. Of course, once he got money, they took him back."

"Well, *I* heard that the Duke of Lancaster just dotes on him, though for the life of me, I don't understand why—"

"Sh! She's looking this way. You don't think she overheard, do you?"

"Of course not, dear, she's much too far away."

The problem with holy days, in my opinion, is that they bring out the Sunday sleepers, who think they can raise themselves up in godliness by speaking ill of everyone else. Besides, they have to make up for lost time for all the gossip they missed at the masses they slept through. I gave them a nasty stare as we passed.

We found our spot in the corner near Master Kendall's chantry, where the crawling light from the rising sun through the rose window made patterns on the floor in front of us. Around the stone pillars of the nave, clusters of tradesmen and goodwives conducted business and traded ideas on the pruning of fruit trees, the repair of shoes and harness and such like, while the faint droning of the priest at the altar was lost like the humming of bumblebees in a summer garden. Latecomers scurried past the marble font, hastily blessing themselves and inserting themselves among the press of people as if they had been there all along. I put my thoughts on God, and the noise and bumble vanished. I used to think that one must pray like a priest, or God wouldn't listen, but luckily He taught me otherwise. Lord of the universe, You who are love itself, bring my love home safe. Let the campaign end in France, and bring him back.

Margaret, I don't organize the affairs of nations to please one woman.

Surely, Lord, there is more than one of us.

Margaret, for every person who prays for love and peace, there are a half-dozen who pray for war and glory. What do you think of that?

Is Your Grace mathematical, then? I didn't know You were an accountant, too.

Margaret, there are days I don't know why I put up with the irritation you give me.

Because of my love, Lord. Only You know how I crave to hear his step in the hall, and the sound of his voice calling my name. I want to see him again, so tall and fine in his old green velvet gown, and hear him laugh when he discovers he's forgot a pen stuck behind his ear. It is our secret, Lord, how I feel for the warm spot in the bed where he ought to be. I want to bake and brew in double portions again, and make a face at his horrible puns, and feel him kissing the back of my neck—

"Mother, you're doing it again."

Lord, keep my little ones safe, my fatherless girls, who need Your blessing, my dear baby, his son—

Margaret, you have, on many occasions, already made your wants abundantly clear. As Supreme Judge of All Things, I assure you that you are one of the half-dozen most talkative of My creations. Why don't you attend to Margaret's business, and leave God alone for a bit to do God's business?

But, Lord, I haven't finished praying for my relatives, and neighbors, and old Gammer Kate who sells eggs but her chickens have died, and—

Margaret, has no one yet informed you of the saying that 'short prayer pierces heaven'?

I thought that was a priest's idea, since you, Lord, have an infinite capacity to listen—

A vast sigh, like a wind in all the trees on earth, seemed to spread through the universe.

"Mother," Cecily's voice was urgent as she tugged at my sleeve. "You have to stop. People will see." I opened my eyes. Sure enough, a faint pinkish-orange haze seemed to stand in the room. That meant I was seeing through it, and the glow was all around me. Oh, dear. I thought about the sadness of orphans and the tragedy of sailors who are lost at sea and the grief of heathens who will never hear the Gospels until it started to fade. One can't be too careful if one has this problem, although if the world were a better place, it would be not be considered inappropriate, especially in church. After all, aren't you supposed to talk to God in His own house? But I guess that's not how priests see it. They want to do all the talking themselves.

It is all God's fault anyway. Long ago, in a time of great terror and trouble, God appeared to me in a vision of light, strengthening my heart and giving my hands the gift of healing. Of course, being God, and having a sense of humor somewhat different than ours, He left behind this visible and highly embarrassing sign of grace, which has caused me nothing but trouble since and set me on many of my more outlandish adventures. If Master Kendall had not snatched me from the street to cure his gout, I'm sure I would be dead right now. After all, plenty of people have been burned alive for far less than glowing, and it does rouse up envy in certain circles. Luckily, no one was looking my way. The altar bell had announced the elevation of the Host, and drawn all eyes to the front of the church.

It was as we made our way out to the light of the crowded lane by the church that a man still in spurs, his coarse, heavy face topped by a jeweled beaver hat, jostled up against me, then bowed extravagantly. I nodded, my face cold as ice, and passed by him in a hurry. Where do they come from in war time, these profiteers who think a woman whose husband is abroad must always be seeking nocturnal entertainment? I heard his companion say,

"No luck yet, eh?"

"The ones who pretend to be cold are always hottest, once they're bedded."

"I'd rather have one of the little ones. The Kendall heiresses. I hear they're worth a tidy sum——" But the voices were lost in the crowd. Filthy things. They'd not be beyond a dowry kidnapping. I'll have to make sure myself that the shutters are bolted at night, Mother Sarah can be so forgetful. It's high time Cecily and Alison had their own companion, not just a nursemaid who's getting old and frail. Someone who will keep them from flying away with every idea that flits through their heads. If I could place them in the Duchess's household—but their father, Master Kendall, was not a lord, and they might not be well treated—

"Mother, I heard that man," Cecily's sharp little voice interrupted my thoughts.

"I did, too. Not just Cecily," said Alison. "And he left off the important part. He said we were rich, but he forgot to say I'm pretty."

"And vain!" hissed Cecily.

"I won't have you married against your will," I answered.

"I'm never going to marry at all," announced Cecily.

"Then when you're a dragon, *I'll* marry Damien when he comes home rich from the war with step-grandfather.'

"You will *not*," said Cecily, giving her sister a sharp jab in the ribs with her bony elbow.

"Girls, girls. Quiet. No, Alison, you can't pinch Cecily back again. Everyone is looking at you." With some effort, our little parade was set in motion again, with Mother Sarah between the two girls, who still bounced with indignation, and Peregrine, now seated on the steward's shoulders, pointing at the mules and passersby with a pudgy finger.

"Look, Perkyn, there's a spotty one. I want it. I will have a blue spotty one and a green spotty one, too."

"Roans don't come in blue and green," said the old man, his voice serious.

"Mine will. I will have extras for Cec'y and Alison, but only mine will fly."

"That will be a sight to see," said Perkyn.

At the corner of Thames Street we were halted by the vast household of Sir Robert Haverell, the vintner, coming down St. Mary Hill Lane. Down every lane and alley, people leaving the churches that dotted the City clustered and strolled in their Sunday best. Merchants in the colorful livery of their guilds, their wives in gold chains and fine linen headdresses, strolled surrounded by their servants and children. Carriers and porters in decent brushed russet mingled with Billingsgate fishwives, their coarse gray gowns covered with brightly dyed and embroidered Sunday surcoats. There were even here and there a few knights with their spurred heels, surcoats gleaming with embroidery, although they were those who were too old or lame to have gone abroad on the latest campaign. Bells were calling across the City, from tower to tower, from St. Martin-le-Grand to St. Mary's, St. Margaret's, St. James-in-the-Wall, St. Dunstan's. Deep beneath the clangor you could hear the resonating sound of the great bell at St. Paul's Cathedral. Pausing there at the corner, Sir Robert gave me a formal nod, but his wife spoke.

"Why, good morning, Dame Margaret. Have you word from Sir Gilbert? We have prayed for his good fortune abroad. His patron's glory brings honor to our parish." Ah, yes, I thought, and substantial wine orders. God of commerce, bless you for my false friends. They are better than none at all.

"Papa's coming home soon," announced Peregrine.

"Why, how big his dear little boy has grown. Why, it seems only yesterday you brought him home from abroad with Sir Gilbert. My, you are a big boy."

"Yes, I'm big now. I'm going to have a horse. Grandfather says so."

"And his own horse, too. Why, someday, he'll be a great lord." I could feel Cecily and Alison sizzle behind me.

"Now, my dear, if you're having another grand feast like the one you had when Sir Gilbert returned for France, you must remember us. I'll have my husband reserve the very best—but we do need to know as much ahead as possible! My, that was memorable! People still talk about it, you know. The poetry—how *original*! And your noble father-in-law and his distinguished guests—such an honor! Can we look forward to another visit from them soon?"

"Doubtless," I answered, beginning to feel sour. Unannounced visits are his style, I wanted to say, but I bit my tongue. That dreadful old man thinks my house is his personal town home. He turns everything upside down, eats everything that isn't locked up, terrorizes the children and servants with his shouting, and tries to seduce the housemaids. The only virtue of this campaign is that he is out of the country, along with my husband's irritating older brother Hugo. Would that they would take hold of some Frenchman's castle abroad and stay there! There's no honor I wouldn't wish for them: governor of Calais, a fortress and lands in Aquitaine—just far from here, Lord! And let them take my sister-in-law, that snobbish Dame Petronilla, with them! At least she's mewed up out there at Brokesford until they return—

"Wife," said Sir Robert, nodding agreeably, but not too intimately, at me, "we must be going. Duty, you must understand, Dame Margaret. My burdens draw us from your agreeable company. But do remember us to Sir Gilbert, and tell him our prayers have been with him and all the other heroes of our King's glorious enterprise." With his wife and vast household, he swept off toward his vast stone-and-timber house that stood not unlike our own parish castle near Sommer's Key. Goodness, I thought, his household seems bigger every time I see it. War or peace, the vintners always prosper.

THE NEXT DAY A LETTER, dirty, much traveled, and covered with seals, arrived by common carrier.

"What are you looking at, Mother?" asked Cecily, as Alison danced around demanding that the letter be opened at once, and Peregrine scrubbed across the floor of the solar pushing the lid of an old jug that he was imagining as a horse and rider.

"The seals—they're all melted underneath, as if they'd been pried off and fastened back."

"Papa letter," said Peregrine, not looking up.

"Well, I suppose someone must always read letters from abroad," I said, inspecting the address: To my right trusty and heartily beloved wife, Margaret de Vilers, abiding on Thames Street in London, be this letter delivered in haste.

"What's in it, mama, what's in it, in it, in it?" chanted Alison.

"Hmm. I can't really say. It starts out plain, and then I can't make head nor tail of it. It starts out with 'right trusty and well beloved wife, I recommend me to you and pray this letter finds you and the children well.' Then there's things about the estate at Whithill which I already know well enough, and then he says because of the king's many triumphs he will be occupied in France for a very long time, and then he says he had the good fortune to meet a very learned man outside of Paris—goodness, he doesn't even say where, does that mean something?—and learned of a method for dying and converting plain, coarse hempen cloth into cloth of gold that will interest that wise adviser and companion of his youth, Brother Malachi, and I must take it to him at once and recommend him to that holy man and not be troubled in my mind for he has great hope of God's grace. That's the part I don't understand. It's all Latin mixed with alchemical things. Goodness, when has Gregory ever called Malachi a holy man? They've known each other far too long for that. And now he writes as if Malachi were a stranger, possibly even a hermit far gone in sanctitude. Holy! Why, it's hardly the same Brother Malachi at all! I think he knew the letter would be read."

"I want to go, I WANT to go, take ME!" shouted Alison. But I had already called for Mother Sarah to watch Peregrine.

"Mother, please, please let me come too. I have something important I need to ask Brother Malachi," said Cecily. I was puzzled by the serious look on her face. Usually the girls only want to see Mother Hilde, my dearest friend who lives with Malachi and calls herself his housekeeper these days. That's because Mother Hilde bakes the best honey-seed cakes in all of London, and has the greatest store of fairy-tales of any woman I've ever known. What on earth could Cecily want to ask an alchemist?

"You can go only if you hurry and get ready decently. And you, Alison, only if you behave."

"So there, Cecily, I'm going to Mother Hilde's, too!" exulted Alison as we hurried from the house.

CHAPTER THREE

O UTSIDE THE WALLS OF PARIS, THE King's great army had been encamped for many days. The Bishop of Reims had sealed up the Sainte Ampoule and ordered the city gates closed, a detour through Burgundy had brought the king a bribe of two hundred thousand gold moutons to go away, and now the capture and sack of Paris, which might have cheered everyone up, seemed to be an increasingly remote possibility. For one thing, the French had finished the city wall since the king of England's previous visit; it now encircled all of Paris, high, gray, forbidding. For another, the Dauphin, a useless caitiff, seemed determined to hold onto the throne that would have added such luster to the name of Edward the Third.

The only virtue of this siege, thought Gilbert de Vilers, is that nothing happens, so I can catch up on my writing. Above the walls, through the open flap of his little canvas pavilion, he could make out the old familiar landmarks of his student days; the squat towers of the Bastille, the rows of flat, crenellated towers of Les Tournelles. Farther away stood the peaked, slate roofed towers of the Louvre and Saint-Pol, and towering above all else, the square towers and massive nave of the mighty cathedral of Notre Dame. What a strange, strange thing, he mused, to be on the outside, a "Sir" on his name and his armor hanging beside him on a pole in this cramped tent, instead of wandering inside, lord of the taverns of the left bank, picking quarrels and singing bawdy songs in merry company. They said they were eating cats and rats inside the walls. He knew they'd never give up. Gilbert sighed. Everybody asked his advice, and nobody took it. The only positive thing of the entire campaign was a handy side-fee he'd tucked away for assisting the negotiations with the Burgundians. A piece of luck that, from his previous travels, he'd known the Abbot of St. Michel Archange.

The light was fading as Gilbert wrote,

> "—and then did the most noble and puissant Duke of Lancaster go with heralds before him to the walls of the city of Paris and challenge the Dauphin to single combat, but the latter, being weak and sickly, refused to answer the demands of honor—"

Actually, said Gilbert to himself as he wrote, if I'd been the Dauphin, I wouldn't have come out either. If they lost both King and Dauphin, they wouldn't have a chance. And if they've got even a single spy, they know we're as badly off as they are. We've burned down everything for twenty miles, and what we didn't burn, they did before they retreated into the city. There's no food, there's no fodder, the cart horses are dying and the men are grumbling. We can't last.

"Hsst. Gilbert." Someone, he couldn't tell who, was outside his open tent flap, visible as only a dark shape in the last of the pallid twilight. "Listen, Gilbert, you clot-headed scribbler, get out here." Oh. Father. Gilbert stuck his pen behind his ear, raised one eyebrow, and looked at the dark shape with a quiet, ironic gaze. "Is that any way to look at your *father,* you serpent's tooth?" said the shape.

"My pardon, most worthy and reverend sire," said Gilbert, rising and saluting the old man with studied formality.

"Gilbert, come look at the horses. We've lost two more—"

"Sumpter horses?"

"No, my destriers, dammit. My heart, my blood. Come look. It's something in this accursed French fodder. You pussyfoot around the Duke all the time. Take some advantage from your position, and tell him about my horses. If we stay longer, the Brokesford stud is dead. I have three stallions left, Gilbert. Three, counting the one you've

got. God knows if I'll bring even one of them home sound again."
Gilbert had not seen his father in such a state for the entire campaign, even when he'd lost the eighth archer from the manor and
begun to doubt he'd have enough men for plowing, if they ever got
home. Gilbert rose quickly, threw a heavy, fur-lined cloak over his
stained leather gambeton and wool tunic. Outside, his own horses
were picketed, where his boy was feeding them. His father stopped,
and peered fiercely at the fodder, running it through his fingers and
smelling it. "No, no. This stuff's all right." He eyed the big black destrier whose fodder he'd just inspected. Thin and winter coated, the
stallion rolled his eye and skittered sideways. "Thin, dammit, thin.
But at least his spirit's still there." At this, the boy feeding the horses
snorted. Calling Urgan spirited was flattery indeed; he was bad
tempered and crazy, the best looking and the meanest, most unreli-
able horse the manor possessed. That was why Sir Hubert had decided to lend him to Gilbert for the campaign.

They made their way through the lit fires roasting rabbits, roasting hedgehogs, roasting any small unmentionable creature that had
allowed itself to be caught. Around them archers and pikemen, and
sappers huddled and drank watered French wine. Outside his father's and his older brother Hugo's tents, the last of the Brokesford
stud was picketed. Three men in soft, knee length leather boots,
their heavy, fur-lined cloaks drawn close around them, were gathered around a bloated, dead destrier. Another man, one of the stable hands from Brokesford, knelt at the creature's head.

"My lord!" cried Sir Hubert, sweeping the quilted arming coif
from his white hair and kneeling before the great Duke of Lancaster.

"Rise, rise at once, Sir Hubert," said Henry of Grosmont, Duke
of Lancaster, Earl of Derby, Lincoln, and Leicester, steward of
England, Lord of Bergerac and Beaufort, and second only to the
king himself in power and lands. "Your destrier seems to have died.
What is your opinion?"

"My lord, there's too little fodder, and what we have is going
bad." He paused. The word "retreat" was not in his vocabulary. "If
we stay another week, we will lose the horses."

"That is exactly what I think. But I would rather say, 'another two days.'" said the Duke. He was a shrewd-eyed, sober-headed man of fifty, who had learned through long experience when to take chances and when risk was futile. Now as he paced about the destrier, a handsome dappled gray he had once thought to have for himself, he was making up his mind about something.

"That is my opinion, too," said the Earl of Warwick, one of the commanders who had accompanied the Duke.

"Someone must tell the king that he risks losing in a day what it has taken him twenty years to get," said the Duke quietly. And silently he added to himself, and that someone will have to be me. Your will be done, Lord.

THE FOLLOWING DAY, the archers on the city walls looked out at a sea of churned mud and garbage, spotted here and there with the decaying corpses of horses. Across the low, undulating fields, blackened and ruined, the columns of supply carts, footsoldiers, and mounted cavalry wound into the distance toward Chartres. In the rear, a detachment of horsemen and archers, banners whipping in a curious, icy wind that had sprung up, guarded the last of the supplies from any pursuit that could be mounted from the city. Black clouds were moving across the sky, and the cold wind blew away the sound of the bells of Cathedral of Notre Dame, ringing for the *Te Deum* that was being celebrated beneath its high, shadowy arches.

What an odd wind, thought Gilbert. Just look at how it's piling up those black clouds. I hope the rain won't be heavy. He had a padded arming coif beneath his pointed helmet, the high neck of his thick wool tunic stood between him and the chain mail of his gorget, and a heavy, quilted leather gambeton stood between the tunic and his mailshirt, and still he felt cold. The first drops of rain dampened his long riding surcoat, embroidered with the de Vilers arms, and it clung to the steel breastplate beneath. Damn, it'll have to be polished again, he thought. All best quality armor, bought new from the most expensive armorer in London, and not yet paid for. I should have been a Lombard, he thought briefly. Those bankers make money no matter who wins. Well, I suppose it's lowly, lending out money for a living. But just now, I wouldn't mind being a bit lowlier myself and cozy at home with Margaret. You don't find a banker riding a crazy horse in a rainstorm at the tail end of a retreating army.

On one side of the winding column of carts, pack animals, and men, the stumps of trees were all that remained of a slashed and ruined orchard. On the other side of the road, blackened fields stretched to meet the ruins of a little village. Here and there an old tree, too big for destruction, extended its branches. But as Gilbert watched the toiling column moving into the distance, from the black clouds above came the distant rumble of thunder, and a faraway flash. Then a bright streak of lightning streaked across the sky, and another crashing boom came, much closer this time. Urgan rolled his eyes and flicked his ears back and forth, then paused, quivering all over. Gilbert was about to sink his spurs into him when he heared the gush and felt the icy breath of the hailstorm. A sheet of white descended in front of him, and huge stones pelted down, bigger than pigeons' eggs, clattering on his helmet, battering animals and soldiers to the ground. Lightning, snaking from the sky, seemed to seek out the mounted knights in their wet armor. In front of him, footsoldiers, smashed to their knees by the assault from heaven, held their shields over their heads. There was a hideous "crash" and the mounted knight in front of him was struck dead, together with his horse. But Urgan, with an eerie scream, was on his way, out of control, too crazed to feel the heavy curb bit and fleeing wildly to the shelter of the nearest tree. Beneath its outstretched branches, Gilbert was at last able to pull him to a stop. There was a blinding crash, and Gilbert de Vilers vanished briefly from the world.

"WELL, BROTHER GREGORY, you always wanted to see God; now's your chance." The voice of Godric of Witham, the abbot who had booted him out of the monastery for disputing with his interpretation of Saint Paul's concept of salvation. There had been a few other things, too, but Gilbert had never counted them relevant. What a narrow old man; he could never admit when he was wrong. Worse than father, even.

"I didn't know you were dead," said Gilbert de Vilers, who felt curiously insubstantial at this point.

"Oh, I've been dead for ages. A bit of bad fish six days before Holy Week three years ago. But just take a look at yourself." The former Brother Gregory looked down and saw the tree, blackened and split by lightning. Beneath it lay several dead, drenched archers and Urgan, his bony legs stuck straight out like a set of fire-blackened pokers. Still tangled in his harness, flat and stark, lay a tall looking fellow in full armor, dark hair matted beneath his helmet, several days growth of beard, muddy, drenched surcoat with the de Vilers arms . . .

"Wait just a moment," said Brother Gregory, "that's me." His body's eyes, he noted, were staring open, fixed and dead, in a ghastly stare.

"Villanous looking fellow, isn't he?" said the abbot. "Let me tell you about his sins—intellectual arrogance, snobbery, pride, gluttony—" but Brother Gregory wasn't listening very hard. Godric always *had* been a prig, and besides, his knowledge of Aquinas was practically cursory. Why Brother Gregory himself would have made a better abbot . . .

"I was very fond of that body—" said Brother Gregory.

"But now, not that you deserve it in the least, look up, Brother Gregory." Gilbert looked up. He saw rank upon rank of angels dressed in velvet and cloth of gold, gently waving their irridescent wings like butterflies at rest. Between the angels was a staircase made of light and he knew he was invited to climb it by the sound of enticing music that came from above. He put a foot on the staircase, then looked down at his body in the mud. All around the tree, piles of hailstones that looked almost like heaped snow were melting. A miserable death, in the French mud, undignified by honor, unshriven. He'd always planned on something a little better than that. But the music was more urgent, more inviting now. Brother

Gregory looked up at the shining host of heaven. He thought hard. There was something he was struggling to remember.

"I can't go just now," he said, "Margaret's expecting me. I sent her a letter I'd be home."

Godric the former abbot looked disgusted. "Your earthly vows and promises are void now," he said. "Go up."

"Oh, no, it's more than a promise. Margaret can't do without me. How will she manage? The children—my family. She'll have to go live with them, and they're very hard to get along with. And she must be out of money by now—" Looking up at the golden company, he said, "I really don't mean to be rude. I mean, this was what I always wanted. You know that I prayed for it all my life. But even though it's higher and better, and my soul's desire, well, you see—" He took a step back down the staircase again and looked regretfully at the cold, muddy place below the shattered tree. Would it hurt to jump so far? Suddenly he was surrounded by a blazing white light, and felt a strange warmth moving through him.

"What are You doing that for? Look at what he's doing. Turning his back on Your heaven itself. Can't You see he is unworthy, just as I always told You?" Gilbert could hear the abbot's voice nattering somewhere distant.

"On the contrary, that's exactly why he is worthy," came a vast, vibrating voice in response. "Poor dried up, right-thinking Godric, you stand at the foot of my staircase and still do not understand that I exist in the past, the present, and the future all at one time. Brother Gregory is worthy because even before, he would be this, and when what will be is, he will be yet again otherwise. Could you make such a choice as he has done, holy man? When you have at last learned that there are many paths to the foot of My staircase, I will invite you, too, to mount up it." Abbot Godric looked again and saw a crowd of people climbing up the staircase: priests and nuns, merchants and knights, horse traders and carpenters, fishwives and laundresses and . . .

"There goes Brother Peter—I fasted much more strictly than *him*—and that horrible brewster who served ale on Sundays—"

"Ah, Godric, Godric, you were the most virtuous of virtuous men. But where was love?" answered the Voice.

GILBERT DE VILERS'S DEAD, staring eyes looked up into the frightened face of one of his crossbowmen. He blinked.

"He blinked!" cried the soldier. "A miracle! He lives!"

"Take off my helmet," whispered Gilbert, "I've got the most terrible headache." He saw they'd cleared his foot of the stirrup, pulled off his surcoat, and unbuckled his breastplate. Had the heralds already counted the dead? Had they been stripping his corpse? His leg throbbed. He hoped it wasn't broken. There lay Urgan, his harness covered in mud. "Oh, my God," groaned Gilbert, "father's horse. I'm finished. I'll never live it down." Gray clouds were scudding across the sky, but still it was too bright to look at. He closed his eyes again. "I think my leg's broken," he said. "Send for the surgeon and strip Urgan's harness." Someone put something beneath his head—a saddle blanket by the smell—and he could hear the clatter and grunting as they tried to undo the girths of his heavy war saddle and pull it from beneath the dead animal. How odd to be smelling things again. The blanket, the filthy mud, the charred scent of the tree, all laced through the cold air. Then he heard—a snort. He opened his eyes. Urgan was twitching all over like a slaughtered pig, then thrashing wildly. In a panic the horse scrambled up, spilling the saddle and its lashed-on equipment to the ground with a crash. He turned his head to watch as they ran to catch the bucking destrier's bridle and at the same time avoid his vicious hooves.

"Well, who would have thought it," said Aimery the squire. "As good as new and as mean as ever. But look here—every place that metal touched his coat, there's a big singe mark."

Two miracles, Lord, thought Gilbert as he looked up to the dreary gray sky from the jolting cart where he had been piled with the other injured. Surely, I'm meant to see Margaret again.

KING EDWARD THE THIRD rode out with his advisers to assess the damage. Animals lay dead along the route of march. The little band on horseback stopped to watch as drovers freed a dead ox from his yoke. The army had lost so many draft horses it was no longer mobile. Twelve hundred cavalry mounts were dead. The human toll of the storm was visible everywhere, as the living gathered up the dead. Soldiers and stable hands, smiths and wheelwrights, all those with leather helmets or no helmets at all had been mortally injured. The heralds rode up, reciting the first list of the nobles killed. "So many, so many," said the King. The cold wind blew at his cloak and ruffled his long beard. It had gray in it, the first his advisers had noticed. "It is the will of God," he said. "I will accept the request of the Pope to negotiate a treaty of peace."

On May Day, not far from Chartres, the French clerics and ambassadors met the English warlords to negotiate. Together, delegates of the French and English parties carried the treaty to be signed by the Dauphin in Paris. The gates of the city were thrown open; all the bells were ringing, and the streets hung with tapestry. But King Edward was not there to see the celebration. The crown of France having slipped from his grasp, the King of England rode at full speed with his four sons to the nearest channel port, leaving the Duke of Lancaster to lead the troops back to Calais.

CHAPTER FOUR

THE UPPER WINDOW OF THE LITTLE house on the crowded alley called St. Katherine's Street was open, and Mother Hilde was leaning out of it watering the marigolds in her window box. She was looking even rounder and more cheerful than I saw her last, for spring brings babies, and babies make prosperity for Mother Hilde, who is the cleverest midwife in the whole of London, if not the entire realm. Her sleeves were rolled up, and as she poured the water onto the green leaves and around the roots, I could hear her humming and talking, and though I couldn't make it out, I knew it was for the plants. Mother Hilde talks to cabbages, too, and they are always grand and big, and her roses and beans always prosper like burgesses.

"Why, it's Margaret!" she said, looking down at the street when I called. "And the girls, too! Go right in—the door's unlatched, but Malachi's in back. Don't make a sound. He's got a new process he's been working on for days."

How like the old days, I thought, when Brother Malachi was always sure that next week, next month, next year, the secret of the Philosopher's Stone would be his. There was a time, when I was a poor girl fresh from the country, that I lived with them and was Mother Hilde's apprentice in midwifery, though it isn't respectable to mention these days now that I travel in more elevated circles. It was Master Kendall who lifted me into wealth by marrying me to cure his gout, and also as a joke on his greedy family who were just sitting around waiting to inherit. As for Brother Malachi, whenever he was a real friar, I'll never know, because ever since I've known him he's been the most celebrated alchemist, the most ingenious mind, and the greatest fraud in five kingdoms.

"Mother Hilde," I said, as she joined us in the brightly painted little room that made their "hall," "hasn't Malachi got discouraged yet? The Stone seems very hard to find."

"Discouraged? Oh, no, he's more enthusiastic than ever. He says he's found a new way to cause the black crow to fly from Sol and Luna in a cucurbit. Not that it isn't all beyond me, mind you. Such a mind, such a brilliant mind! Why, it's a gift just to hear him speaking of it—all that wisdom and those long foreign words. So tell me, Alison, I see you looking about the room. Were you thinking of the honey cakes I just might have baked yesterday, and just might have saved, thinking you'd be by?" Alison beamed expectantly, and Cecily looked at her toes. "Both girls shall have one, while I ask your mother about this awful lump right here on my left hand."

"Mother Hilde, really, you should have sent for me sooner," I said as I looked at the stiff, swollen joint.

"Do close the shutters, will you, girls?" called Mother Hilde to my greedy offspring. In the darkened room, the glow always shows, and there's no use exciting the neighbors. I fixed my mind on the Nothing that is greater than nothing, and then the light began to glimmer around the edges of the Nothing. I felt the crackle of powerful light rising in my spine and hands. Taking Mother Hilde's old, gnarled hand between mine, I could feel the heat moving into it, and the knotted joint start to shrink. Orangish pink light filled the room, gilding the faces of the children and transforming ordinary pots and clay jugs into shining, ruddy gold. It glinted on the gaudily painted figures of the zodiac that peered down from between the bright red and green painted ceiling beams of the Malachi the alchemist's curious little hall. It flowed like liquid into the empty spaces, healing and changing. The hand felt softer, now, and the heat that flowed from it was even. I let the light linger a bit, then watched with regret as it faded and the room transformed itself back into an ordinary place. I felt limp with the weakness that follows healing. But this was a little healing, and the weakness would pass in moments. A big one can put me in bed for days. And when I'm pregnant, the light goes inside to aid the child, and I can't do any healing at all, so you see what I mean about God being whimsical.

"Now, how is that hand? Let me see you move it."

"Why, quite as good as new, Margaret," said Mother Hilde, wiggling her gnarled old fingers happily. "There's many a pretty baby I'll yet bring into the world with that hand." She tipped her head on one side and inspected me with her shrewd, old eyes. "Margaret, you're worn down. Too many worries. Here, put your feet on this stool and try some of this. No girls, it's not right for you. It's a tonic I've made, just like currant wine but with a few little inventions of my own. When you are grown-up ladies, then——"The girls looked at each other. "Now, why are you looking at each other like that?"

"They've been having a problem being ladies, lately, Mother Hilde. They think you mean never."

"Nonsense. You shall soon be ladies. Twelve, thirteen, ready to be engaged and wed to some worthy gentleman. You are fortunate to have a fine dowry from your good old father, and a stepfather with connections. Being a lady isn't so bad at all, once you get used to it. And I assure you, it's far better than the alternatives."

The tonic was strange tasting, warming, and made my blood run faster. "Mother Hilde, why didn't you call me? You know that day or night I would come."

"Times seemed different, somehow."

"Different? Nothing's different. Oh——oh, my goodness, did you think it was because——"

"Well, you do have a lot of grand friends since we returned to the City from our trip over the waters."

"Mother Hilde! Those are money-friends and fair-weather friends and downright false friends. Not true friends like you. Oh, the trouble that purchased knighthood has made! Who'd have thought it would tangle things up so?"

"Then you are still the same Margaret after all!"

"Always, always, Mother Hilde," I said as we fell into each other's arms.

"But, Mother Hilde, when is Brother Malachi coming out? I had something important to ask," said Cecily, breaking into our sentimental moment. Mother Hilde went and put her eye to a crack in the door of the back room, Brother Malachi's laboratorium.

"With company here, it's high time he came out, process or no process. Let's see. Cecily, hand me the towel there, I'll take the lid off the pottage kettle and see if the smell will lure him out. He and Sim haven't had a bite since the middle of last night, when they consumed an entire loaf of bread and a couple of salted herrings." But at the very moment the lid was lifted, there was a sudden cry from the back room, and a loud noise, like, "whump!" Mother Hilde and I leapt with the shock of it, and she slammed the lid back on the kettle as if the act of removing it had caused the commotion, and it could all be fixed by putting it back again. The door to the laboratorium burst open, and a dense, stinking cloud billowed into the room. In the midst of the cloud, a round, shortish figure appeared, his pink face blackened with soot, bellowing curses and slapping at sparks on his robe. Behind him, another even shorter figure, an equally sooty, big headed, lopsided youth in a russet tunic, was trying to blow away the smoke by waving his cap at it.

"Sim! Stop that! You'll just stir up the smell," cried Brother Malachi. "Ah, Margaret! Back again! You have just witnessed an historic moment! I've got——" But Mother Hilde was opening the shutters with newfound agility. Wind and smoke battled at the windowsill, and cold gusts of air made the fire under the kettle sway and leap.

"Oh, Malachi, my love, must historic moments always smell bad?" said Mother Hilde, choking and waving her hands in front of her face as if to disperse the stinking cloud. But Malachi, his eyes running, was almost dancing with excitement.

"The black crow! It flew! This latest method has done it! From here it's only a step to the White Stone! When the smoke clears and the crucible cools, we ought to see it lying there. I tell you, this process of Arnold of Villanova is the most lucid, the most clear I have ever worked with——" Suddenly he spied us in the room. Just as in the old days, I had thrown open the door to help disperse the smoke. Cecily, her hands over her nose and mouth, was turning purple in an attempt to keep the smell out by holding her breath, and Alison, her nose pinched between thumb and forefinger, was taking advantage of the confusion to rummage about in search of another honey cake. "Stop that," I whispered fiercely, abandoning the door to grab her by the back of the neck.

"Ah, what's this I see? A party? Margaret, I haven't seen you for ages. Ah, I see the tonic bottle's out." He picked up the earthenware bottle and peered into it. "And this kettle on the fire?" He stooped into the fireplace and lifted the lid. "Why, soup, too. If my olfactory faculties were not entirely drowned by the smell of my experiment, I imagine it might smell good. Food! How could I have forgotten it? My brain needs renewal—I imagine Sim might crave a little something, too, ah, excellent, Hilde, my jewel, how did I ever live without you?" As the smell thinned and vanished, Mother Hilde, her eyes still winking back tears from the acrid smoke, had laid two great wooden bowls of pottage on the little table in the hall, and was engaged in cutting thick slabs from a loaf of heavy brown bread. Malachi poured water in a basin and washed his hands and face, leaving soot on his ears and in a ring beneath his multiple chins, while Sim, his apprentice, contented himself with washing his hands only. Then he settled himself, announcing at intervals, "Splendid, splendid!" while food vanished from the table at an astonishing rate.

"A masterwork, this soup," announced Malachi from his seat on the bench, as a second large bowlful disappeared down his capacious middle. "Hilde, you have surpassed yourself. It must be the garlic. No one but you has a true understanding of garlic. And that bit of pepper from the sausage—outstanding. Yes, what is it, Cecily?" Cecily, having waited until Malachi looked mellow and sated, was now twisting in embarrassment as she tried to make words come out of her. Very softly, hoping I would not overhear, she said:

"Brother Malachi, you can change things into other things, can't you?"

"Why of course," answered Malachi, "that's an alchemist's business."

"Mother said the Philosopher's Stone changes ordinary things into better things, like lead into gold."

"Well, that it does. But I must admit, little Cecily, I haven't quite got it yet." Cecily's face fell in disappointment.

"Then the White Stone isn't *the* Stone?"

"Not yet, not yet, child. The White Stone is just a step required in the process. Not that it isn't wonderful, mind you, but it's not the all-transforming Stone." Mother Hilde, her face wise and silent, cast me a glance. We pretended to be busy, but our ears were tuned for the next question.

"Then when will you get the real Stone? I need you to turn something."

"What kind of something?"

"Brother Malachi, when you get the Philosopher's Stone, can you turn me into a boy?" Brother Malachi sputtered and set down his soup spoon.

"Whatever do you want that for? I always thought you were a perfectly nice girl," he answered tactfully.

"Boys get everything," said Cecily, her voice serious. "They get to ride any horse they want, and travel where they like, and carry a sword to smite down enemies. And—and—they don't have to sit still and *embroider* for just simply hours, and never talk and have ideas, and look at their feet when they're in the street instead of up at things happening, and—and—be *ladies*. I hate it, and I want to be a boy, because it's better." Malachi's round, pink face looked troubled.

"Well, admittedly, being a boy *in general* is essentially better," he said, thoughtfully, "but in specific, not all boys get to do the things you say—and yet, yet—this is a point entirely unconsidered in the texts—how odd that you should bring it up. If being a boy is better, as holy writ assures us, and if the Philosopher's Stone changes all things into their higher forms, then all women could change themselves into men, and there would be no more human race. Now, if God Himself commanded mankind to be fruitful and multiply—to say nothing of other species—and if they all went and turned themselves into males and couldn't, then God's true will would be countermanded. Hmm. So then God would consider men and women equally valuable, although, let us say, different. Strange. Let's think this through another way. I have never seen it written that the Stone can change a woman into a man, and since the Stone is created by God to change lower things into higher things, then that means, goodness—but surely, it's far better to be a man—"

"You mean you can't make me into a boy, even if you get the Stone?" At this, Malachi's face cleared.

"Ha, Cecily. Let's consider it an experiment. *When* I get the Stone, and *if* you still want to be a boy, then we'll try it. If it works, you get your wish, and if it doesn't—"

"Then boys and girls count the same to God, and the whole world is wrong, but I still have to embroider," said Cecily.

"Cecily, you are a sage child. The man who marries you will be terrified," said Brother Malachi.

"Hurry and get that Stone," said Cecily, sighing, "I know I'm going to get very tired of pretending to be a lady until then."

"Well," said Brother Malachi, setting down his soup spoon, "we'll just go in and see if we've got our White Stone. Things ought to be cooled down enough now. I think I've just lost another philosopher's egg, but the precipitate inside ought to be what we're looking for if the ever-wise Arnoldus is right." We watched as he took a deep breath, plunged back into his laboratorium and opened the window into the back garden, then donned his heavy leather gloves. Sim ran in behind him to hand him his rod and touchstone. Despite the fast fading smell, we all crowded round to watch him reach into the heart of the athanor. There in the sandbath sat a blackened, cracked glass vessel made in the shape of an immense egg. "As I thought," said Malachi. "It's ruined. Margaret, you have no idea of the cost of these things. And there's only one glass blower in the entire realm that can make them properly. Ugh. I'm making his fortune. Now—let's see—well, at any rate, it shines—" he prodded the blackened metallic stuff inside the broken egg with his rod. By this time, Cecily was quivering with excitement, and even Mother Hilde and I, hardened by his many previous attempts, held our breaths.

"Everything's smoked up—let's see——" he poked off ash and blackened, crumbly stuff to reveal the metal beneath.

"Looks all ashy and black, like silver tarnish," said Cecily, her voice sad.

"Child, must you be so blunt?" said Malachi. Frowning, he tapped the ash off his rod. "The mercury hasn't vanished the way it was supposed to; it's created some sort of compound. A—blackish, silvery—compound. I wonder if it's good for anything? Let's see, if I reversed the process before the three-headed dragon and calcinated the——"

"Smoke is everywhere. Looks like making hams id here. Whad are those bones on the string? They look like muddon bones." Alison, ever fastidious, was holding her nose, making her voice sound as if she had a bad cold.

"Mutton indeed, they're——"

"Malachi, must you?" I asked. "They're still so innocent."

"Saints' backbones," announced Sim, Malachi's apprentice, in a cheerfully malicious voice. No one knew how old Sim was, including him, except that he didn't seem to grow much and his head was too big for his body. More than twelve, less than twenty, and cynical enough for three old men. "They're all nice and old looking now," he added.

"Margaret, you must understand that there's a world of difference between innocence and gullibility," rumbled Malachi. "Now these, girls, are my stock in trade for my summer business . . ."

"Saint Ursula's martyrs—hundreds of 'em—they'll fetch a pretty penny this summer when we go travelin'." Sim's voice had a froggy sound. Was it due to change sometime? Then he *had* to be more than twelve. Let's see, would that make him about eight when Malachi found him in the street—but then he could have been ten, so if you add on . . .

"They look more like pig's backbones, not mutton," said Cecily in her sharp little voice, peering closely at the strung-up vertebrae. "Will you wrap them up fancy, like the ones in church?"

"—my stock in trade, which is, in truth, faith and hope, without which the human race could not carry on, which these—ah— artifacts—allow people to attain through contemplation—"

"You'll need the money for a new glass egg," observed Cecily. "It's good you can make more of these whenever you like."

"Child, more and more I begin to understand you are your father's daughter—ah, yes, old Master Kendall was a shrewd one, that he was."

"Yes, it's better to make things the way you do to get money. Mama had to sell her ray-robe, the fancy one with the gold embroidery that I liked to try on, and the money stepfather left in the box in the chest is all gone anyway," announced Alison.

"Alison, you stop!" I cried, my calculations of Sim's age rudely interrupted.

"Margaret, if you wish to keep household secrets, you'll need to lock these children in the wardrobe."

"Step-grandfather already did that," said Alison, her face smug.

"I'm not surprised about that, not in the least," said Malachi. "Margaret, I am lamentably short of ready cash in this season, but—"

"I didn't come for a loan, Brother Malachi. I came for this," I said. Reaching into the bosom of my gown, I took out his letter, all crumpled and covered with seals, folded and refolded, and stained with its far traveling. "It's a letter from Gregory that he said to bring to you." Malachi sat down on the tall stool before the athanor, unfolded the letter and peered at it closely.

"Wanna see my *skulls*?" Sim asked Cecily. "They're killed Frenchmen."

"Me, too," said Alison. "Do Frenchmen skulls look like English? Mother Sarah says they've got horns."

"Sim, have you got a mother?" I could hear Cecily ask as the girls followed him to the chest in the corner.

"Never did," he said. "I just *came,* that's all."

"You're lucky, *our* mother wants us to be ladies——" but the voices faded as they dove into the trunk.

Malachi squinted at the letter. He held it several different ways, then sighed, then scratched his head in thought. "Impossible," he muttered, "as usual, Gilbert's out of his mind." Clearly, this would take time. I sat down on the window seat with Mother Hilde, where clean air poured through the open shutters. Birds were at work in the garden, nesting in Mother Hilde's crabapple tree, no doubt. It always was a favorite spot with them.

"You still call him Gregory?" asked Mother Hilde. "So do I, unless I remember. But Malachi knew him in their student days, so he's always called him Gilbert."

"I try to remember not to call him Gregory when I'm in company. He really doesn't want people remembering he was ever at the abbey——there's so much gossip, you know, and now his writing has put him in favor with the Duke——but it *is* the name I first knew him under——"

"Ah well, it's worse with lords. Every time they get new lands, they're my lord something else."

"Certainly not our problem, Mother Hilde."

With a shout, Malachi stood suddenly, his round, pink face alight. "Eureka!" he cried.

"That's Greek," said Mother Hilde, looking pleased. "It means he's happy. Such a brilliant man, such a mind! He's even happy in other languages."

"Margaret," he said, rounding the big brick athanor and approaching the window seat, "this recipe is a hash. I've come to the conclusion the letter is a code. Gilbert wrote it to evade the censors."

"Exactly my thought——but is he all right? Does he say when he'll be home?"

"I'm coming to that, I'm coming to that. The key is alchemical—— that, and certain common turns of phrase based on our long acquaintance. It is a code decodable only by me." Malachi extended the letter and pointed to the recipe. "You see here? Gold stands for the king, and the conversion of the plain cloth to making France ours. Now, here, where the gold precipitates out in solution—that means the king has lost, Margaret, and is coming home. Let's see, full moon in Aries—yes, some disaster, fairly recently—"

"But is Gregory coming home? When? Does he say?"

"Here—let's see. Ah, the devil! He knows I always used to call them Gemini. So rude of him! Hmm, yes. Mercury, the metal of Gemini. With luck, Margaret, he'll be home in late May or early June. Now here's an interesting thing, Margaret—he seems to be saying that even if the army didn't do well, he's made some money. I wonder how? He always was an ingenious chap. Even in marrying you, Margaret. Well, I don't think you have to worry about that box in the chest much longer, except for searching out a new hiding place, where those children can't find it."

But in the midst of joy, another worry stabbed through my mind like a lance. "Malachi? Does he say anything about his older brother and his father returning home, too? Pray God he gets here before them, or it's more than the cash box I'll have to hide. Lord, lord, keep that awful family of his all penned up at Brokesford at least until I've had time alone with him."

CHAPTER FIVE

W HAT ON EARTH IS KEEPING OLD
Peter so long? They saw them feeding here
only yesterday." Impatiently, the Lord of
Brokesford flicked away a fragment of pigeon pie that had
fallen on the worn and greasy bosom of his old leather hunting
coat. The offending remnant of pie was still in his hand; he
avoided further mishaps by downing it at a gulp. Newly returned from France, directly returned to his estates without
incident, and happily returned with all his limbs intact and
both sons living, he felt especially blessed. God had clearly
willed it all, it was obviously a reward for his virtue, and he
felt filled with the contentment that comes from a sense of
righteous deserving.

It was pink dawn, an excellent English dawn and not one of
those dank, inferior, foreign ones such as he had seen entirely
too many of on the march to Calais. From the clouds the night
before, from the signs of the birds, of the stars, it promised
to be fair. English sun, English grass, and English cooking—all
better. He surveyed his little universe with the eye of a man
who knows that he is lord of everything that counts. Cloths had
been spread on the dewy grass of the meadow beside a mean-
dering stream. Arrayed on the cloths were the plentiful dishes
of a hunt breakfast being consumed by Sir Hubert, his family
members, neighbors, and guests. Grooms held the saddled
horses and the impatient hounds. All were waiting for the
return of the old lord's chief huntsman and finest scent hound,
who were trailing the herd of red deer from this, their last
grazing spot, to the place where they now fed. A little tent of

twigs marked the place where the stag had fed, there among the does and fawns. It was this scent that Old Peter and Bruno were following; today they would hunt the stag.

"Ah, this air. There's no better spice for a dish," said Sir William Beaufoy, Sir Hubert's old comrade-in-arms and guest of honor. He had not paid a visit to Brokesford Manor since long before the campaign; indeed, since their last adventure together, a little matter of devising a scheme for ransoming Sir Hubert's youngest, and most ungrateful, son from captivity in France.

"It will do you good to get away from the close air of the court. As for me, I feel a new man when I'm away from that harping shrew with whom I'm forced to dwell." Sir Geoffroi, the old lord's nearest neighbor, helped himself to a large slice of smoked ham as he spoke. At these words, Sir Hugo, eldest son and heir of the Lord of Brokesford, cast a sharp glance at his wife, Lady Petronilla, who had made her views most clear on being forced to retreat from the delights of the Duke's court. She avoided the look, staring coldly into the distance.

Not for Sir Hugo the battered, comfortable old garments of his elders. In the manner of a French aristocrat, he sported a jewel on his black beaver hat and a brown velvet hunting surcoat of the latest cut. His wife, too, had put off her long black gown for a new riding habit in mossy green, and wore a little dagger at her belt beside her hunting horn. Adept with the bow and arrow, she was a woman who loved blood sports, and rode well enough to never miss the "mort," the death of the prey. Jolly her up a little, thought Hugo. Some hunts, a little night sport, and she'll soon be pregnant again. For as long as his brain could fix on anything, he contemplated his loss. Why should everything go to his younger brother's son, just because he'd run off with some woman of the lower orders who bred like a rabbit? Irritating, irritating it was. Petronilla needed to do her duty, and quickly, too. Well, at least he knew now she wasn't barren.

"Surely, there must be some good in this woman. Can she cook?" responded the tactful Sir William.

"Cooking's all very well," responded Sir Geoffroi. "But it all turns to poison in the stomach with the interfering. She interferes with my steward, she interferes with my stable, she knows my business better than I do, according to her. And quarrel with my wife? I tell you there's no end to it. Two mistresses under one roof—a recipe for trouble if I ever heard one. And under the conditions of my brother's will, I can't be rid of her."

"Ah, I see, she's your elder brother's wife?"

"Exactly, and with right to a room, board and keep, two gowns a year, a full supply of candles, freedom of the household, and freedom to interfere to her heart's content! By God, I wish I could wall her up in that room, but then that ghastly lawyer her niece married would be down on me like a wolf on a lamb. Oh, he'd love the excuse to worry me out of my property."

"Lawyers, there's no END to 'em!" Sir Hubert began to shout. "A PLAGUE of lawyers has descended on us, a PLAGUE, I SAY, to EAT HONEST MEN out of HOUSE AND HOME! Their GRASPING HANDS are EVERYWHERE, with their—"

"I do believe I saw otter tracks just over there," interrupted Sir William, gesturing with a cold chicken leg to the reedy bank. Only quick action could distract Sir Hubert from one of his famous fulminations. The trick, his old friend knew, was to stop the early storm clouds before they had blown together. Once at gale force, the storm would cause the budding leaves to shrivel and living creatures to flee. The old lord in a fit of passion might even give up the stag and mount an expedition against the some local justice's house instead. Already, the rustling of field mice and water voles in the grass had stopped. It was time to defy the rules of courtesy for the greater good.

"Otters, no hunt for gentlemen," announced Sir Hugo. "Why, when I was in France, the lords there left them for the peasants to trap." The superior tone in his voice caused his old sire to glare at him. Glaring at him reminded him of the ridiculous French hunting garb his son had affected. And *that* reminded him of his heir's irritating habit of spouting godawful French verse at every rose and female form within ten miles. As far as Sir Hubert of Brokesford was concerned, the entire French invasion had been a disaster—the Brokesford stud stripped, no more than half a dozen suits of rather badly dented armor captured for resale, no ransoms of note, and most unspeakable, the corruption of good English morals with fancy, sickly foreign ideas.

"Otters, hate 'em," growled the Lord of Brokesford. "They got into my fishpond this Lent, and just before I returned on Saint Benet's day they ate the big eel I'd been saving."

"If you ask me," said Sir Roger, a pink-faced, high-living fellow who was "Sir" by courtesy, being the parish priest, "that otter had ten good fingers and went on two feet." Lady Petronilla, Sir Hugo's wife, gave Sir Roger a cold, narrow-eyed stare, which did not escape Sir William's shrewd eye. Hmm, he thought. I think Sir Roger's hit it. She had it cooked up while he was away from home, and blamed the otters. When the cat's away, the mice will play. . . . Here's another place the conversation must be headed off.

"This coppice beyond the meadow here I know is yours, but the woods there beyond the rise, are they all in your demesne, or are they divided between you and your good neighbor here? I've never really had it clear." Sir William gestured again with the remains of the chicken leg.

"Ah, don't probe there, that's a sore spot," said Sir Geoffroi. "There's a fine stand of ancient oaks on the other side that some lawyer from Hertford claims he has bought title to."

"Title indeed. There's no title if the land was not for sale, and it's NOT! Those oaks have been in the family since the first of us was listed in the Domesday book. I tell you, a de Vilers does not sell old oaks to the highest bidder! My grandfather, I say, my very grandfather, tithed six of them for the cathedral roof, and was never the same afterward. Do you think I'd ever see them SOLD to MERCHANTS for their despicable WAREHOUSES? If that shady friar hadn't cast doubts on the title, I swear that LAWYER would not have DARED—"

"Oh, look yonder, isn't that Old Peter I see?" said Sir William, putting a restraining hand on his friend's shoulder. Sure enough, the figure striding from a coppice planted thick with hazel and young oaks was indeed Old Peter, who was not in fact old at all, but merely older than Young Peter, his son, who held a half-dozen greyhounds at the side of the assistant huntsman.

"The stag, by God, he's found him! Humph, this stag, I've been saving him for you. A noble beast. Would that he and the lawyer could change places. THEN we'd have a HUNT!"

THEY APPROACHED THE HERD upwind, but the sound of the dogs sent the deer scattering for the forest. Urged on by their groom, the loosed greyhounds cut off the stag, sending him bounding across the scrub wasteland and into the rolling, newly plowed and seeded fields of the tiny village of Hamsby, the farthest outpost of the Lord of Brokesford's demesne. At the sight of the stag, the little boys posted to keep away the birds fled. Followed by the yelping hounds, the stag darted across the plowed strips, followed by galloping horses that sent the dirt clods flying. Then as quickly as it had come, the traveling disaster passed, save for stragglers called across the wreckage by the horns in the distance. A flock of rooks settled in the churned up dirt, and the little boys ran again to the fields to throw stones at them.

Among the beeches at the edge of the forest, the stag splashed up the stream for a distance to throw the dogs off the scent. The hunt paused until Old Peter's horn from deep among the trees told them the scent had been found again. In the van, the old lord and Sir William crashed through the underbrush and into the deep woods behind Bruno. For centuries here the foresters had culled the lesser trees; in this place nothing but the twisted limbs of ancient oak trees scratched the sky. But the horses had easy footing; beneath the budding, new leafed branches, the ground had been picked clear of every twig and fallen branch by peasants in search of fuel, though it was death to touch the trees themselves. They passed a clearing, cut in two by the stream, here only a brook, and Bruno lost the scent again. Still on the trail of the stag, they rode up the brook and into the forest depths again, while Bruno searched the banks for the lost scent.

"What is this place?" asked Sir William. They had reached the head of the brook, a spring like a deep rocky pond, save at the center, where from an unknowable depth, green water roiled and bubbled as if in a boiling cauldron. Beside the spring, an immense rock stood, with a cord wrapped around it several times. From the cord, bits of rag hung, some bleached white with age. But strangest of all, the spring was located at the end of a kind of house created entirely of the thick, dark trunks of living yew trees planted in two rows the same distance apart as pillars that would support the nave of a great cathedral. The vast age of these dark pillars was unguessable. Their interwoven, eternally green tops formed a heavy, hedge-like roof, denser than thatch. The strange tree-building cast a heavy black shadow that seemed even more eerie among the airy branches and dappled shade of the surrounding oaks. For some reason, it reminded Sir William of a graveyard, and a cold chill went up his spine.

"They say there's a spirit here in the water," said Sir Hubert, lifting his horn to call the rest of the hunt. "Some old nixie called Hretha, who grants wishes. But it also makes excellent beer." From the forest behind them, the calling horns and baying hounds responded, and the first riders crashed out of the woods into the strange clearing.

"Where's Old Peter?"

"We've lost the scent."

"Trust the beast to hide here, of all places," said the Lord of Brokesford manor.

"New rags, new rags, in spite of all I tell them," Sir Roger announced in a disgusted voice, riding his bay cob around the big rock.

"And just what is that?" asked Sir William, his curiosity aroused.

"When the blessed Saint Edburga rested here, this spring opened up in the ground at the very place her head lay. Do you see the ruins of that holy hermitage there? Look closely at the stones, and you will see the representation of her holy martyrdom." Sir William noticed tumbled rocks, cut square, beyond the strange green, tree columned hall. From one of the rocks, the badly worn image of a skull peered back at him. This was no holy hermitage, thought Sir William, taking a deep breath. Something ancient was here. Something pagan. He shuddered and crossed himself. "The hermitage was dedicated to the blessed head of Saint Edburga, but as you see, it has fallen into decay."

"Yes, indeed, that I see. What a pity," said Sir William.

"Only in church will prayers to God almighty and to Saint Edburga be answered, but they persist in making offerings here to some ridiculous pagan water devil, and deny the saint her candles. Folk superstition! Nothing good will come of it!" The hunting priest was indignant. The hounds were busy smelling the ground around the spring. The horses and riders milled about, waiting for the dogs to pick up the stag's trail again.

"What do they want?" asked the visitor. Lady Petronilla had pushed her gray mare closer to the conversation. She, too, knew little of local traditions, for her father's estates were in the south, and she used every excuse possible to avoid long residence at Brokesford.

"Wishes, vain wishes. The rock, they say, is alive. As for the spring, there's an evil spirit there that grants unholy desires. Barren women, especially, come here, though I have threatened them with excommunication. Walk three times around the spring sunwards, and make an offering." Petronilla leaned forward for a better view of the green, boiling depths, her heavily ringed hand clutched deep into her mare's mane. Her breath was hard, and her blue eyes glittered like chips of ice.

"And in what way is the rock alive?" asked Sir William.

"Oh, once a year on Midsummer Night it is said to wade into the water to drink, though no one has ever seen it. Also, it weeps. If it's chipped, they say, it will bleed, but there's a curse on anyone who tries it, so they leave it alone. Those rags are offerings."

"Why, it's nothing but an oversized wishing well. I've half a mind to try it out. Besides, a man can't have too much good luck," said Sir William, half relieved by the explanation. "Sir Hubert, watch this." He fished in the bag at his belt and came up with a quarter farthing.

"Find us that scent; I crave venison tonight," he said, and flipped the shining quarter circle into the water. From the distance, Old Peter's horn sounded. The hounds that had crowded around the horses ran off, yelping, around the fallen stones and into the woods. The first to follow them was Petronilla, spurring her horse away from the waterside as if scalded. Sir Hubert paused only to signal any stragglers with his own horn, then followed the fast vanishing hunt into the forest.

It was not more than an hour before the "mort" was ringing in the afternoon air. One long, three shorts, pause, one long, three shorts again to mark the stag coughing blood from a mortal swordthrust. As the apprentice huntsmen cut a pole to carry home the stag's quarters, the grooms butchered the creature according to unchanging traditional ritual, first cutting off the testicles and tongue, then cutting away the shoulders, then emptying out the liver and entrails. Hounds gobbled the scraps that were fed to them; a new apprentice was "blooded," marked in the stag's gore. Dame Petronilla looked on with glowing eyes, her hand tight on the hilt of her little knife. Red puddled into the earth, red stained the butchers' hands and arms. At last the quarters, strung to the pole, were taken up for the return to the manor kitchen.

Far from the bloody ground, the green water bubbled mindlessly, alone beneath the sheltering arch of the ancient yews, where the birds were silent.

CHAPTER SIX

I N THE MONTH OF MAY, BIRDS SING AND SO do all the street sellers and beggars: the hot pie man sings "hot pies, hot PIES, so fine," right up and down the street, and the blind woman by the church sings, "for the LOVE of CHRIST, a FAR-thing only, have PI-ty" as she rocks back and forth, and wandering down the back alleys where he can be heard by housewives hanging out their wash, the man with the string of dead rats tied by the tail sings the most tunefully of all: "I'm the RAT catcher, I'm the RA-A-A-T catcher." Then there's baa-ing and the clank of milk pails as the goat woman comes with her goats and calls out at our kitchen door for our order, and the singing of the woman who bears duck eggs on her head in a basket, who does a good custom in this neighborhood. I tell you, you can hardly even hear the birds for all the noise. The fine day had brought them all out, birds and human singers and dogs and grunting pigs, and the cacophony all came floating in through the open kitchen shutters, mingling with the busy chicken sound from our little henyard and the sound of Master Wengrave's big sorrel mule braying.

We were baking bread that day, cook, the girls and I, and the kitchen was smelling all fine and yeasty as we uncovered the starter. The girls had big aprons on, rolled over at the top several times and tied up high under their arms; to keep hair out of the baking, they each had their hair rebraided in a single long braid down the back, Alison's smooth, and Cecily's fuzzy. They stood over the big wooden bread troughs, their sleeves rolled up, waiting for cook to turn out the dough into them.

"Alison, don't taste the starter. It will grow inside you, and you'll split."

"Did you ever know anyone who split like that, mama?" asked Alison, who is too fond of ghoulish things for my taste.

"From eating the starter? I'm sure there are lots of greedy girls who've done that. Just look at how it grows in the pan—you wouldn't want that to happen inside you, would you?"

"Then you don't know anyone, do you, mama?" said Cecily, who is horribly hard-headed.

"Don't we have raisins? I want to bake a cake, a sweeeeet one," announced Alison.

"No raisins, no cinnamon, no pepper until father comes home. They're too expensive." The sharp cry of a magpie came in on the breeze from the tree outside the window, followed by a sound almost like a human voice, "treat, treat, treat, treat."

"Oh, there's my wicked pie who flew away when the cage was broken. And he spoke so clearly, too! Now he's learning calls from those bad birds outside. I swear, he's living in the tree just to taunt me." Cook leaned her head out the window and called, "Come to mama. See? I've put out your treat for you. Treat, treat!" Amid a handful of crumbs on the windowsill she laid a tiny sliver of bacon fat. There was a flash of black and white feathers, and the bird settled on the windowsill, strutting up and down and inspecting the company inside with one beady black eye. We held very still, so that he wouldn't think we were going to try to catch him. First he tilted his head, one bright eye on the treat, then he gobbled it up in a flash. "Treat, treat, treat," he called, as he flew up into the green branches outside.

"We has an understanding, that bird and me," said Cook, "he won't come in and I won't catch him. But he's gone to the bad, I say. He lives in that tree like a pirate, flying down to steal anything he wants. He's shameless."

"He has my hair ribbon that I took off in the garden. I just laid it on the bench, and, swish, it was gone like that," said Alison.

"So *that's* where it went," I said. "I thought I told you not to take it off."

"It *fell* off when I was playing ball with Peter Wengrave," said Alison.

"He took it straight up to weave into his nest, I saw it," said Cecily.

"That's not a nest, it's a pile of trash," announced Cook.

"Don't have the men pull it down," said Cecily. "Maybe he's got a family in it."

"A world of wicked magpies hatching up there, what else should we expect these days? The day of the Lord is coming," said Cook, stirring the last batch of dough with her strong right arm. Outside, we could hear a new song being sung in the street by some drunken rowdies. "The King rode out in noble company, a crown for to win—" it began, before it floated away. The news from France, all done into a song. My, the word of the defeat had certainly traveled fast.

"HALT, you mindless sots! Have you contemplated your SINS? Vain singing in place of godly and sober conversation, all is VANITY—" Goodness, spring had even brought out Will the street preacher. And there was only one reason he'd be in our neighborhood. I'll be seeing him at the kitchen door asking for a loan. Sure enough, there were footsteps in the alley and a voice at the open window. The magpie had perched on a branch above him, and was inspecting Will's long, rusty black gown and moth-eaten hat with the ear flaps turned up.

"Ha, bird. You dress in black and white like a Dominican. And like the Dominicans, you are here begging ahead of me. I know you for the vulgar jester you are, bird. Ah, it's a wicked world when lords and burgesses reward jugglers and mountebanks ahead of men of learning." I poked my head out of the window. We'd inherited Will and his endless manuscript on the sins and corruption of the worldly folk of London from Master Kendall, who said it was good to have someone around to keep his head clear by reminding him how others saw him.

"How goes the writing, Master Will?"

"Well enough, well enough. I am revising. I have been too light on lawyers, flatterers, fawners, gossips, and givers of bribes. In the meanwhile, I found myself short of fourpence for ink."

"Come in, come in at the door, Master Will. We're relieved of the burden of vile Mammon these days, but if you've brought your inkhorn, you can pour some out of the inkwell in my husband's office."

"Sir Gilbert not home yet? I hear the army was housed in hovels, eating rats. Perhaps a slice of, hmm, not even a joint of mutton on the fire. Your house is getting to look like my house, Dame Margaret— only larger, of course. It is a sinful world where merchants prosper when men of honor must live like beasts, ah, mm, excellent cheese, this—"

Because Master Will goes all over town telling people to repent, he is a very good bearer of news. While he ate what there was, we heard that the first of the soldiers were already in the city, arrived with the Duke himself, who had come to escort King John from the Tower across the water to Calais, as part of the peace settlement. Then we heard all about the local sins, of which he keeps a good list. Then we heard ensamples of how the low are too high, and the high are too low, which is always interesting. "—and then, in the Cheap, the widow of a gentleman fainted dead away from hunger— thus are the widows of heroes treated in these wicked times!—You know her, I believe: Dame Agatha, that dwells in Fenchurch Street with her sister's husband's family. The man resents her and seats her too low at table. She would rather not eat at all than be seated too low. There's a lady of true gentility! I said to her, said I, think you of Dame Margaret, whom you know and who would make you wel- come, and she said never, when a woman of rank gives her word, it is given. Pride, I say, that goeth before a fall—" Well, goodness. Madame. She certainly hadn't prospered since she'd walked away from giving French lessons.

The girls, I noticed, had become very silent, and occupied them- selves with a great show of kneading the bread.

"Now, about that ink—"

"You'll have it, Master Will," I said, wiping my hands on my apron.

Master Will's tall, raggedy form had scarcely passed out through the kitchen door when the girls lost their sudden and uncharacteristic silence.

"Mama, pleeeeease don't bring Madame back," said Cecily

"She's much too mean, Mama," Alison added.

"She did a very good job of teaching you French, and she's not mean, just firm," I answered.

"She has too many rules. Being a lady is very tiresome," announced Alison.

"Yes, and she says ladies let boys win at games," said Cecily.

"*And* they always let the boy have the biggest piece on the plate," said Alison.

"And she said boys must speak first because they are cleverer than girls, and will grow to be men, and do worldly things. But Peter Wengrave is so slow, he doesn't even know his letters yet, and cries when the master beats him, and I knew my letters long ago," said Cecily.

"And, Mama, there's the fingers," said Alison.

"What fingers?" I asked.

"The fingers to pick things up. First and third for this dish, first and second for that, don't touch with your little finger, and never put fingers in the sauce deeper than this first little bit. There's ever so many rules for fingers. I don't see why being a lady needs fingers and getting the smallest piece. Hands are more sensible."

"Alison, you cannot go through life snatching out the biggest piece of chicken and splattering gravy up to your elbows. You both are in need of a lot more manners than you have."

"Pleeeeease, no more Madame," they chorused. I sighed. More of Madame would be just right. I suppose I just hadn't been firm enough.

"You're in no danger of Madame," I said. "She won't have us."

"Then we don't have to be ladies after all?"

"No, you just have to be ladies anyway."

"We could be pirates instead," suggested Alison.

"Some pirate *you'd* be, stealing sweets——" answered her sister.

"When I'm a pirate king, you'll be just a common sailor, because you don't even *know* what's good to take. You just climb all the time, and sit up in the pear tree dreaming."

"I do *not*——"

"Girls, girls, you haven't kneaded the bread in the trough long enough. See? If you push it, it doesn't crawl back. That's how you know it's not ready yet." I pushed at the dough to show how it lay there, all dead and not ready to rise. Then I poked at mine, to show them how it should spring back.

"Eeuw, it's a giant *worm*——it's the innards of a *clam,* all alive——"

"Don't prod at it like that, Alison. You have to treat it like a friend if you want it to rise nicely. And you, Cecily, don't pout. Sour girls make the bread sour and the ale flat——"

"Yes, mama, and many girls have split from eating the dough."

"Cecily, don't be sarcastic——"

"Lady, lady, come quick, soldiers in the street!" Perkyn the steward burst into the kitchen, his face alight with the news. Bread dough forgotten, we ran to the front door. Every soul on Thames Street was hanging out the windows. We could hear joyful cries as householders ran to hang out tapestries, tablecloths, and anything else handy from the upper windows as a sign of welcome. Down the street came the oddest parade in the world. A good two dozen pikemen and archers from Billingsgate Parish, packs on their backs, still wearing their leather brigandines, marched in ragged order. Behind them was a mule litter and a boy from my father-in-law's estate leading Old Brownie, the most broken down old gelding in the Brokesford stable, laden with chests and bundles. The banners of the de Vilers had been affixed to the litter, although not well, their staffs being at such odd angles as to give them a look of cheerful intoxication. In the litter, reclining like a king, dressed in his long riding surcoat with his leg heavily splinted, lolled my own Gregory, waving jauntily to the faces crowding the windows. Whatever the outcome of the war, no one can say our parish doesn't welcome its own.

All covered with flour, and still in my apron, I ran out to embrace him. Behind me crowded the children, the servants, the neighbors.

"I missed you so," I said, and when we kissed, I could hear them cheer.

"Me, too," he said. Then he gazed about him, eyes glittering with amusement. "Just look at this, Margaret. Last summer I departed as a no-account wastrel, and today I return home a hero. Such is the power of war to transform men's opinions." People were trying to touch him, to exclaim, to be part of it all. He had a crutch lying across his lap.

"What has happened?" I said, looking at the bad leg.

"Why, nothing so bad at all. I'm in high favor with the Duke— and just damaged enough so that I don't have to go back when he returns to Calais with King John. I'll see him at Leicester Castle when he returns and catch everything up. I couldn't be luckier." At the talk of dukes and castles, everyone was awestruck. He turned to the postilion on the lead mule. "Put the mules in the stable with Old Brownie tonight—Margaret, I said we'd keep them here until we can send them over to the Duke's stables at the Savoy tomorrow—" Peregrine had clambered up into his lap, and grinned happily as his father embraced him. I heard a woman whisper, "See the banners? That's the only heir to the Brokesford estates." The sound in her voice made that tumbled-down old manor house seem practically as big as Leicester Castle itself. A good thing she's never seen either, I thought.

"We've no feed—I—I sent the horses to the country—" I told him. Peregrine was crowing, "Papa, papa home." How odd, he wasn't shy at all about hugging his son, stroking his head, admiring him. That wasn't like Gregory, so stiff and formal with children.

"—to save money, eh? Well, nevermind. We'll have some sent in. And have Perkyn send to the bake-house as well for some joints and a spitful of fowl, these fellows with me are all invited to dinner. Set up the tables in the hall, Margaret, I'm home."

"But—"

"Margaret, quit worrying. The Burgundians are paying for this supper. Right, boys?"

"Right!" they chorused.

"And fetch your sweethearts and old mothers. We'll all go home drunk tonight."

"Sir Gilbert, you won't be walking far. You'll already be at home."

"So I am obligated to be the drunkest of all, then," Gilbert proclaimed, extending his arm in a grandiose gesture.

"Right again!" they shouted.

"Margaret, take Peregrine and help me get down." As he leaned on my shoulder and took up his crutch, he said, "and here are my two hellions. How many waiting-maids have you frightened away since I left? You both look prettier than ever. I imagine soon you'll be ladies." The two girls looked knowingly at each other. "Ha! I'm glad to see you unchanged. It would be a great disappointment if you had become meek and mannerly in my absence."

"What on earth has happened to you?" I asked as he leaned on me while I helped him over the threshold. "You seem so—changed." All around him people were crowding, to exclaim, to hear more. More about the war, about the duke, about the king, about battles and sieges, about royal favor and the rise of fortune.

"Happened? Oh, I was hit by lightning."

"Not really," I said.

"Oh, yes, and I had the oddest dream."

"How brave, how modest!" I heard a someone exclaim. "Wounded in a mighty conflict with the wicked French lords, and he won't even boast of it!" Muttering and cheering spread through the watchers, and I could sense the envy of those invited inside as the steward tried to shoo the crowd away so he could close the door behind us. Even so, by the time my returning lord was seated in the hall, we had received three invitations to dinner from the most prominent families in the ward. His leg propped on a stool, his son on his lap, his stepdaughters pressing attentions on him, and his comrades-in-arms scouring the house for comestibles, he looked more content than any king on his throne. But I, I was happiest of all.

"Margaret, you're doing it again."

"What, my own dear heart?"

"Glowing—all pinkish orange around the edges. How very odd. Did you know for years I never noticed you did that? It's not respectable, you know."

"In my own house, lord husband, I'll glow as much as I want," I said, as we kissed again.

"Where's my ink? I thought I had more. I distinctly remember sealing the stopper with wax, so it wouldn't dry up." Gilbert was rustling around in his things, seeing if they were where he'd left them. "And here's my *Garin le Loheraine,* not in the chest, and—ugh, there's crumbs between the pages. Have the girls been reading it? Little savages. Someone should teach them manners. That's no way to treat a book." He brushed away the crumbs. "Whatever happened to that fierce Madame creature that Master Kendall had teaching them French? Now there was a woman who knew how to keep order."

"And I don't?"

"Margaret, the proof is plain. Crumbs in my book, and a whole bottle of ink most likely used up drawing fantasies. And my paper—if those girls aren't in bed sick, they have the whole household topsy-turvy all the waking hours of the day. They must learn to ask permission—"

"They're good girls—"

"I never said they weren't good—just disorderly. Admit, with all that you do, they've got beyond you."

"I *told* them to wash their hands before opening a book—"

"And so they followed the letter of the law, and not its spirit. They washed their hands and ate while reading."

"But the ink's my fault. I let Master Will renew his supply, and the paper—"

"Margaret, it's very clear. They need to be sent to some great household for polish. They haven't a bit, that's obvious, and here they're getting to the age of betrothal and I've never seen two less marriageable girls. Now that I'm standing in good favor with the Duke, I'm sure I could arrange something."

"I can't bear it, I just can't. To have them so far away? Suppose they were ill treated? Suppose they got sick? Here in the City, they have position, their godparents are nearby, they are well regarded. But in the house of a great lord—no, I just can't bear it, I can't."

Gilbert looked thoughtful. "I see what you mean," he said. "Still, it's not proper, keeping them at home. Maybe just a while more— but still, Margaret, you need to see beyond your indulgence of them. If you love them, they need manners. They *have* to have them. Why, if they can even frighten away a dragon like that Madame—"

"They didn't make her go, Gilbert, you did."

"Me?" He looked utterly puzzled.

"She said it was demeaning enough being reduced to teaching French in the household of a merchant, but if I should so soil an honorable widowhood by remarrying a fortune-hunting copy-clerk who had palmed himself off as a monk to get into the household, then it was no longer decent that she remain." But instead of being offended, as I thought he would be, my husband threw back his head and laughed aloud.

"Perfect!" he said, "absolutely perfect! That's exactly the sort of thing they need to know, Margaret. They need it in their bones. Look at it this way—it's a protection for them. The world isn't like this house, Margaret. Wild women aren't tolerated. But a lady, who can't think like anything but a lady, will always be looked after." I just stared at him. "Let's agree, Margaret. They can stay here, at least for a while more, if you can get that woman to teach them to be ladies. Iron-clad ladies, which is what they need to be."

"But—but we can't. Master Will saw her in the street, and asked if she would consider rejoining a household—ah—such as ours, for example—and she said the disgrace would kill her."

"And what was she doing in the street?"

"Fainting."

"Of hunger? My opinion of her grows higher by the minute. Margaret, I know the type well." He chuckled. "This will be a pleasure. I'll send two of those fellows who had dinner with us in full armor to her door—with a message that *Sir* Gilbert de Vilers, companion-in-arms to the great Duke of Lancaster and general all-around war hero, requests a parlay. Margaret, you just haven't lived in these circles long enough to know the advantage of a title—even a purchased one." He stretched out in the chair, put his hands behind his dark, curly head, and grinned, his brown eyes glittering with mischief. My old Gregory, too clever and too troublemaking to fit quite properly anywhere—not in the university, the battlefield, the cloister, or the court. He'd still be ambling about the City, irritating people with satiric verse, if the wily Duke of Lancaster had not seen his virtues and trapped him in his net. To be made immortal by a poet of stature—it was an agreement that pleased them both.

I watched him as he stretched out like a cat, wiggling his toes in his long leather-soled hose. There was still a lump on the shin of his bad leg, where it had not been set quite straight, though I nearly had it fixed. These days, he had taken to wearing the stained old padded leather gambeton that had once gone beneath his chain-mail around the house. It was his new disguise. Knight, returned from the battlefield. It impressed the neighbors. His eyes would spark with satiric malice when they deferred to him in public places. "Margaret," he said, "I count it as a challenge to recapture Madame for you. One of considerably less difficulty than capturing the Sainte Ampoule."

CHAPTER SEVEN

IT HAD RAINED ALL MORNING AND ALL OF the night before, but now as afternoon shaded into evening, damp mist blew between the old oaks. Rooks cawed in the wet green roof above the bubbling spring. The little rags were plastered with water to the tall rock. Hugh the swineherd, well aware that this was a day no mortal would choose to be about, had chosen the time to check his traps. They were quite illegal, but the temptation to poaching was great, and the fear of a wily fellow like himself being caught was small. Beneath the old hide he had wrapped about him to keep off the wet, he carried a sack with two of the lord's rabbits. Head down, and thoughts on supper, he slogged barefoot through the mud, paying no attention to the rushing sound of the roiling green water. It was not until he was nearly full upon her that he saw the figure of the water devil, all in black in the form of a woman, her face veiled, walking "sunward" around the pond.

"Stay there, you have seen me, and now you cannot leave," she said, her voice soft, but as powerful as steel. Hugh fell to his knees.

"Pardon me, a sinner," he cried, crossing himself. "Just let me go, and you can have the rabbits."

"Rabbits?" she said. "Why would I need rabbits? No, I want something more precious that you have."

"N-not my soul," cried Hugh, in despair.

"No, not your soul," she said, and he felt her hand on him, cold as the green water itself. In the midst of his thrill of terror, he felt a thrill of something else. "You are a fine, sturdy fellow," the succubus said. "Give me your seed." He could feel the icy hands working on him until he didn't know whether he was in heaven or in hell. Gently, the succubus pushed him back into the mud and mounted him. Now he was frantic with desire. It was her powers, her supernatural powers that sucked away the seed from him as she writhed atop him, and he could hear his own moaning mingle with that of the succubus. As he convulsed in ecstasy, he never even saw the dagger come down again and again. . . .

Stripped from the waist down, covered with mud and blood, Hugh listened to the gurgle of the waters as darkness came and a full, white moon rose over the forest. Home, he must get home. His rabbits lay in the bag where they had fallen. Even dying, he was a thrifty soul, and pushed only one rabbit into the green water at the edge of the pond. There in the white moonlight he watched the furry carcass bob in the the shining waters until something, like an unseen hand, seemed to pull it below.

He was never sure just how he had come back, or who had bandaged his wounds, but when the priest came to his bedside, he confessed everything but the rabbit.

"Unearthly desire and ecstasy? All in black, you say, and without a face? Surely we are warned of such things. A succubus, without a doubt. Few have lived to tell the tale. What saved you is the cross you wear at your throat. She has taken your seed to make devils, have no doubt about it."

"Oh, Lord Jesus forgive me. I never wanted to add to the world's store of devils."

"Did you suffer temptation?"

"It was beyond temptation. All entirely against my will. A powerful spell settled over me, so I could not move. You understand that, don't you Father? And yet—and yet, the pleasure was so great as to be indescribable."

"Pleasure? The penance will be heavy for that evil pleasure. Better you had never suffered any but pain. Give thanks to God that you were spared so that you might whiten your soul. You were closer to hellfire than you ever knew that night."

As Sir Roger sat in the little parsonage that night, he grew angrier and angrier. Rumors of diabolical pleasure, supernatural beings, succubuses hot with desire—matters were getting out of control. The pond thing would debauch the entire parish if something were not done, and soon.

"MADAME, IN DEFERENCE to your rank, you would be seated below only myself and Lady de Vilers at table." Gregory the impudent monk peered out of Sir Gilbert de Vilers's eyes to see how he was doing. He had not deferred or begged, but received her like a great lord giving an audience. Indeed, for extra effect, he had hung his coat of arms and several ferocious weapons of war on the wall opposite his crucifix, where they would be fixed in front of her eyes during the negotiations. The battle pennants and the balance of the weaponry he had hung up in the hall, along with assorted wolf pelts and animal heads that he felt had no place in the house of a civilized man.

"She'll need to understand there's been a change around here," he addressed the shade of old Master Kendall, as he had stepped back to admire the cacaphonic effect his decorations made when mingled with the cultivated old merchant's elegant Italian tapestries. "You know why it has to be. Margaret always seems to require these eccentric indulgences, doesn't she?"

In fact, the shade of Master Kendall was very far away, but Gilbert always felt it necessary to address him whenever he made changes in the house. The office, so far, had required the longest apology. It was a quiet place now; there were no apprentices scurrying in and out, no Hansa merchants negotiating a price for Russian sables or Italian velvet, no ship captains demanding payment or crates of luxury goods piled in the corners. Chests of books and papers lined the walls, untidy piles of manuscript lay heaped atop them and on the octagonal writing desk, with its little reading stand perched at the center. The shrewd old merchant had had an eye for a bargain; first he had found Margaret, beautiful and untutored, in the street, laying hands upon the sick, and made her his own. Then, when his life was near its end, he had, in a way, found Gilbert, too, so that his well-beloved treasure would not be abandoned to greedy hands.

Gilbert had propped open the door of the office so he could see into the hall when the old lady made her entrance. He was not disappointed. Escorted by the steward, she caught sight of the pennants, stiffened, and then walked cooly by as if she had noticed nothing out of the ordinary. She's definitely the one, Gilbert said to himself. With satisfaction, he noted her composure as she entered, tall and straight, in her neatly brushed black widow's gown. Slyly, he checked the edges of her sleeves, the elbows, the places where well worn wool goes threadbare and doesn't look as dark as the good part. Yes, she's done it, he thought, pleased with himself for spotting it. She's colored in the spots with ink. Just right. Beneath her freshly starched headdress, her iron gray hair showed only in that tiny spot before the ears. Her pallid, proud face, as white as the wimple beneath her chin, showed no emotion whatsoever as she gave her dignified greeting. Excellent, thought Gilbert. Deferential without being obsequious. An elegant balance that the girls would do well to master.

Now things were going excellently. She had made a ritual refusal of his offer three times, and each time he had offered an added incentive. Now, he produced the one thing he knew from Margaret mattered most to her, her place at the table. Her face remained impassive. A faint smile almost appeared on her pale lips, but vanished before the mind could finish sending the order to the mouth.

"It is a task of almost impossible difficulty," she said.

"Of which no one is aware more than I. They are almost beyond the reach of civilization. They should have been sent away at the age of seven, as I was, but as you recall, there was at the time great turmoil in this house. The critical task of forming their character has been neglected."

"In whose household did you serve, Sieur de Vilers?"

"In that of the Duke of Lancaster, Madame de Hauvill, as both page and esquire. But as you may have observed yourself, the way of the younger son is not easy." Now's the time to get round that promise, thought Gilbert.

"The younger son?" asked Madame, raising an eyebrow politely. Excellent, she's coming around, he thought.

"The de Vilers name, as you are doubtless well aware, dates to the Conqueror, and was distinguished long before that time. Ours is the cadet branch. The family estate is in Hertfordshire." And what's left of it is so deeply in debt from this last expedition I'd be surprised if Hugo ever sees half of it, Gilbert thought to himself.

"My husband's lands were in Lincolnshire," said the widow. She, also, did not mention how microscopic these holdings were, or tell how they were entailed on a cousin, who had promptly thrown her out.

"An excellent place. I have cousins in Lincolnshire."

"Cousins?"

As carefully as two diplomats averting a war, they jockeyed for position with ever more obscure family connections until at last they found that they were related through the godfather of a fourth cousin twice removed. Gilbert the scholar had known all along that this was most likely the probability, since the number of families of good blood in the island kingdom was small enough that all were related in some way, especially if you counted godparents as true relatives, the way the church did. This was the final trick he had counted on to catch Madame and restore order to his family.

"If I had only known," said Madame, placing one hand on the bosom of her gown and breathing deeply.

"I know you must understand my cares," said Gilbert in that tone that walks on the fine edge between hypocrisy and sincerity.

"Yes, a burden. They must never disgrace you."

"I would consider it an inestimable blessing if you might give your gracious consent."

"Sir Gilbert, I am honored," said Madame, inclining ever so slightly from her seat in the second best chair.

CHAPTER EIGHT

SIR HUBERT DE VILERS HAD A TERRIBLE toothache. Shouting at his steward, his grooms, and his useless Frenchified son Hugo had failed to relieve it. "Where's the toothache wine Margaret left here in the chest in the solar?" he growled, himself rummaging around in the chest of remedies. "What's this garbage in here, little dried up things in bandages, and this box of powder? Ugh, it stinks! I don't remember that it was here when I left."

"Lady Petronilla's headache remedy," said her old nurse, who was watching Sir Hubert's rummaging with alarm. Lady Petronilla was hovering by the chest, too, shocked by his unexpected demand to see its contents.

"That was toothache wine?" said Lady Petronilla, who had drunk it under the impression that it was a "female cordial."

"The best going. Full of verbena, she said, and a lot of other nasty weeds that I don't remember. Worked every time. What are these needles doing in the bottom of the chest? I go away, and Brokesford gets all changed around. Well, I want it changed back."

"My lord, I can compound you a remedy for toothache," said the old woman.

"You? I wouldn't take a dog remedy from you. Stick to spinning and whispering in my daughter-in-law's ear. William! WILLiam! Get me Goody Ann, the wise woman. She'll manage something. Well, what are you hovering about me for? Go, you useless women! Go!"

"Goody Ann passed into the next world during your absence," said Petronilla, her face icy as she passed by him. I don't like the looks of her, thought Sir Hubert as he watched her vanish through the solar door. Losing a baby usually makes a woman more distraught, more human. She looks less human than ever.

"Oh, there you are William. Whatever happened to Goody Ann? She knew all about teeth, even if she didn't have a one left herself. I always thought she'd live to be as old as Methuselah."

"My lord, she had an accident. She was growing more and more unsteady, and she tripped and fell downstairs in the dark."

"What stairs? There's not a stair worth falling over in the village."

"Our stairs. The night your grandson, Sir Hugo's heir, was lost. She had come to assist in the delivery. She missed her footing on the way out."

"Damned inconsiderate of her. I need her now. What am I going to do about my tooth?"

"Big Wat could pull it."

"That carpenter? That butcher? When he pulled the miller's wife's tooth, he broke her jaw. No, I'll send for John of Duxbury. Now don't tell me he's fallen downstairs, too."

"No, I hear that he prospers. He married the hayward's daughter from Little Hatford and quit traveling. He has enough custom where he is, and she doesn't like him roaming." Pity, thought Sir Hubert. John's itinerant business of tooth-pulling and bleeding had brought him regularly to Brokesford once a season for Sir Hubert's quarterly bleeding.

"I don't want to wait. You go there, he comes here, it's twice as long. Go have two horses saddled. Hugo! HUGO, you useless numbskull! Ride with me to Hertford, I'm going to have this damned tooth out." Sir Hubert had just remembered there was a former laundress of his there, in the shadow of the cathedral, that he had set up as a brewster. A jolly old girl, and she even brewed well, too. He had decided the best course of action was to service all his needs at once. "Hugo! Hurry up! I've decided to stay over. Fetch my sword!" He thought for a moment of Bet the ex-laundress. She had managed to produce both a boy and a girl, each a square-jawed, boisterous copy of himself. Pity Petronilla couldn't do as well. Maybe next time around. At least she wasn't barren. He'd thought perhaps she was, and was pondering methods of having her put away when the letter about the tragic miscarriage had come to Hugo abroad. He'd had a brief spasm of pity for her then, and arranged to have her sent where company would cheer her. Shouldn't have wasted pity on a creature like that, he mused. As cold as an icicle. Must be the blood. Too narrowly bred, that family. All cousins. "Hugo! There you are. What kept you? Oiling your hair and dousing yourself in perfume? An Englishman ought to SMELL like a MAN! The next thing you know, you'll be BATHING!"

THE WARM SPRING BREEZE was rustling in the pear blossoms above the stone bench in the garden. High brick walls shut out the sounds of the city beyond. Hundreds of bees were at work among the flowers, and the scented canopy above the bench hummed as if it were alive. But soft spring and trees throbbing with life did not affect Madame Agathe, the knight's widow charged with making Cecily and Alison Kendall into ladies, whether it suited them or not. She sat as stiff as a poker on the hard bench, her basket of threads and mending beside her, her needle flashing in and out of a pallid linen shift spread across her lap. There was a sudden flash of black and white feathers among the branches.

"Oh, look, there's the wicked pie!" exclaimed Alison, pointing to the tree with a pudgy finger. Still round-faced at seven and a half, she was above the average height and nearly as tall now as her older sister. The neat braids of her silky red-gold hair, tied at the end with rose-colored ribbons, hung nearly to her waist, or what might have been a waist on another child. Her pretty sky-blue tunic almost brushed the top of her soleless leather slippers. All around her, a litter of shattered, split stemmed daisies from a failed garland gave mute testimony to an ambition that outreached the abilities of her round little fingers.

"Pas en Anglais," said Madame, never looking up from her sewing. Beside her on the bench, a gleaming silver button lay among the reels of thread in the basket. Hidden beneath the sewing things, all neatly wrapped up, were lumps of rock sugar, the most expensive and infallible bribe in Madame's armory of improvement techniques. Alison eyed the basket hopefully.

"What's 'pie' in French?" she demanded of her sister in that language.

"It's 'pie,' same as with us, silly," answered Cecily, superior in her two additional years, her grander French, and the expertly woven crown of daisies that lay atop her flaming, unruly red curls. Fierce combing and tight braiding had failed to subdue that hair, which remained as rebellious as its owner. Her ribbons, snatched up in a fit of fury that morning, did not match; her green wool gown, its hem twice turned down, still failed to cover the bony ankles of her knobby, growing legs. Skinny and intense, Cecily spent her days being blown by gusts of passion; a lost ribbon, a moth hole, a sad song, a short answer, a new puppy, or a stranger's smile sent her flying to the heights and the depths at least fifty times a day and set the entire household into fits. That is, the entire household except for Madame.

"Demoiselles must not address each other thus," said Madame Agathe, in the elegant, alien tongue of documents, treaties, and court circles. "Mademoiselle Alison, repeat your question: 'Dear sister, what is the name of magpie in French?' and you, Mademoiselle Cécile, reply in gracious tones, 'Beloved sister, the word is also pie, but pronounced in the French fashion.' Now, immediately." Cecily's face turned red under its freckles, her mouth tightened, and she began to poke holes with her fingernail in the stems of the daisies that still lay on her lap. Alison's eyes lit up at this sight.

"Dearest sister," she said in tones of sickening sweetness, "what is the name of the bird we call magpie in the French language?" Cecily looked at her sister with eyes that could pierce steel armor, and responded in a honeyed, sarcastic tone, "Beloved sister, the name of the bird is exactly the same in French as in English, it is my pleasure to inform you."

"The demoiselles appear to desire that they be reprimanded with a crack of my thimble on each of their hard little heads. Now, again, in that pleasant and agreeable tone that is fit for young ladies," announced Madame, and the exchange was repeated again to her satisfaction. She shook out the mended shift, folded it, and took up a pair of child's hose, worn out at the knees. Alison looked at the hose, and then at her sister. She wrinkled up her nose, as if to say, "eeew, little boys who wear out their hose scrubbing around on their knees are disGUSting, especially if they are baby brothers." Cecily's blue eyes met her sister's as she received the thought. Agreed, the eyes said, and the two children nodded as if they shared a secret. Madame's needle began to make its way through the russet wool as she spoke again.

"And now, my young ladies, we will review the proper subjects for polite conversation. We never discuss money, amours, or the faults of another person not present. All gentlemen are gallant, and all ladies gracious. People of common rank are honest or good souls. Between respectable men and women, godly topics are best, provided care is taken not to enter into debate. But remember, let no man but a close relative offer you holy water with his fingertips in church—" There was a splendid whirring of black and white feathers as the bird landed on the corner of the bench beside the basket. Cecily and Alison were so still that they scarcely breathed. The bird tipped his head on one side as he took in the scene with his shrewd little black eye.

"—and you, Mademoiselle Cécile, when you walk abroad, must cease to glance about so boldly. Remember, look at your toes. A demure and downcast eye is essential in a girl of good breeding—" The bird paused, spying the basket. It tilted its head again. Lovely thread. A shiny button. The large person's nest was splendidly furnished. The two smaller people were very quiet, looking at each other without moving. The bird could feel thinking going between them. Encouraging thinking.

"—proper activities in company may include games such as chess and backgammon but not dice, and never any game for money stakes. Group singing is a pleasant diversion, and the hearing of old tales of heroism and the lives of saints, but never these dreadful modern stories of galantry and improper relations between the sexes. You are to excuse yourself graciously from the room if such subjects arise. Women do not argue with men, but submit humbly to their superior judgment—never let it be known that you can read, a woman who reads is easy prey to gallantry, and cannot be a faithful wife—oh, Dieu! What's that?"

With a fierce and sudden movement of its beak, the piratical bird seized the coveted button and flew into the pear tree. "My button, my lovely button, that horrible bird has taken it!" Madame stood so suddenly that the mending and with it her precious needle dropped into the grass at her feet. "Ah, the rake there, catch it, catch it, Cecily!" But what amazement! Madame had reverted to English, heartfelt English such as they had never heard before from Madame's refined lips. Cecily stared, her great start of joy at the bird's act converted suddenly into astonishment. Could Madame be an actual person, capable of sorrow? Suddenly she saw Madame's snobbish airs, her desperate dependence, her tiny luxuries in an entirely new way. Madame stood beneath the pear tree, shouting up at the bird, "For shame, for shame! Drop it, drop it, you awful creature! What good is it to you?" As Cecily fetched the rake, the bird flew triumphantly from the pear tree into high branches of the tall elm whose branches overreached the garden wall.

"Its nest, there's its nest! It's gone to hide it!" cried Alison, looking up at the big, untidy collection of sticks wedged high in the branches. But Cecily had already tucked up her dress and was clambering up the ornamental fountain set in the wall. At the top of the wall, she paused only to kick off her shoes, where they fell, plop, plop, onto the thyme-planted walkway by the fountain.

"Come down, come down at once, Cecily," she cried, and then reverted to French. "This is improper! Madame your mother does not approve. I do not approve!" Madame shouted up into the tree. Gray hair had escaped from beneath her plain widow's headdress. Her voice was frantic. Cecily was already halfway up the tree.

"I'll get it back for you," Cecily shouted down from above in

English. "You'll see. I'm a good climber." The thin branches could be heard cracking dangerously under her weight. The bird, having hidden its treasure, was flying at her as she came close to the nest, and she raised one arm to protect her head, clinging tight with her knees and bare toes.

"Come down, come down!" shouted Madame. "Leave it, oh, it's not worth it! Come down and we'll have the gardener climb up with a ladder. No higher! I hear the branches breaking!" In the alley outside the wall, apprentices were gathering to hear the source of the shrieking.

"Hey, I know her! It's Cecily Kendall, stuck up in a tree," one of Master Wengrave's apprentices, who had been passed on to him when old Master Kendall had died, called out happily to the growing crowd.

"Come down, I say come down at once!" they could hear a woman's voice calling in French from inside the garden.

"I—I can't," quavered the skinny, flame-headed figure up in the tree. Bobbing perilously among the frail branches beneath the nest, Cecily looked down at the wall and the ground, so very far beneath her. On one side, the crowd of apprentices was growing, and she could hear them shouting:

"Who's that? Hey, that's not a girl, it's a *very big* magpie. Ho, magpie indeed, it's a cat! Hey, meow, come down!" On the other side was Madame, frantically waving, and there, by the unattended basket, Alison quietly rummaging for the sugar. The ground seemed very hard, it seemed to move and sway. The more it swayed, the tighter she clung. It was so easy going up. Why hadn't she thought of getting down? She'd never thought at all. Now all was despair. She imagined it growing dark, with her still clinging to the branches. Maybe she'd be in the tree forever. Could they send dinner in a basket? Do people never come down, or do they fall out some time and break all their bones? Below her, she could see two apprentices coming from the door to the undercroft of Master Wengrave's great house with a long ladder. And there at the corner of Thames Street and the alley, oh, dear, it was mother with a big basket on her arm and Peregrine by the hand, and Cook behind her, laden with provisions from the market.

"Eeeeeeeemaaaamaaa," came the hideously clear voice of the two-and-a-half-year-old, soaring up over the babble. "Lookit, Cecy's inna *tree. Per'grine* wants to go up inna tree. Lift me up."

"Cecily, come down," called her mother, her firm voice full of common sense. "If you got up, you can come down. Just put your foot where you had it last."

"Can't," shouted Cecily, clinging tighter than ever. More strangers surrounded her mother. Mistress Wengrave, still wiping her damp hands on her apron, had come out of her house.

Down below in the alley, Margaret had already packed off her howling son, and was directing the apprentices where to put the ladder. "Not there," she said, "see how the stone is uneven? Brace it here. We'll need two grown men to hold it. But who will climb? He needs to be agile, but light enough so that the ladder can bear the weight of two." She cast about her in the growing crowd for suitable recruits. There was something about the look in her eye, the look of a falcon, of a commander in the field, that made no man refuse her. Already a bulky fellow, a cordwainer by the look of his apron, had come forward to hold the ladder. Two men on horseback, dusty with travel, had been drawn to the edge of the crowd by the cries and the sight of the bobbing little figure high in the tree.

"Bigod, look there, Denys, it's a girl up that tree," said the older man.

"After that magpie's nest, I swear, the little cat," answered the younger. "And now she can't get down."

"Reminds me of someone," said the older man.

"It certainly *doesn't,* father," said the younger. "I always got down. I put my foot where I had it last."

"There was the little matter of the tower roof."

"That's not the same. It wasn't my fault." The old man inspected the woman giving orders. Unfeminine. Must be the mother. Very

well dressed, for a weekday. That squirrel-lined surcoat, very hand-
somely embroidered. The veil, hmm, it looked like silk. And the
cross hanging, half concealed, at her neck, solid gold, foreign work-
manship. And this street, a very good one, lined with the tall, brightly
painted houses of wealthy mercers and knight-vintners. Quick
judgments of the rank, condition, and cash reserves of those who
stood before him were the specialty of the old magistrate. But the
woman's eye had fixed on them there.

"You," she said to the boy beside him, "can you climb?" The figures elevated above the crowd on horseback had caught her eye immediately. Good cloaks. Swords. Possibly knights? They're good at
climbing ladders. The old one, too heavy, too stiff—gray in his
beard. The young one with the black brows. Fifteen or sixteen, wiry
looking, clever face. He'll do. She fixed her fierce, commanding eye
on him.

"Father?" said the boy, looking at the older man to ask permission.

"Are you the mother?" said the old man, his eyes canny.

"I am. That's my daughter Cecily up in that tree, for reasons of
her own," answered Margaret.

"My son, never refuse a lady in distress," said the old man, giving
his paternal benediction. The boy dismounted from his winter-
coated cob, and unbuckled his short sword, handing weapon, hat,
and cloak up to his father. An apprentice boy ran to hold his horse.

"You act as if you know that girl," said the old magistrate, probing
gently.

"Oh, who doesn't know her here? That's Cecily Kendall. She's
not even ten, and you wouldn't believe the things she's done."

"Ah, then, she'll live and die a spinster. No man will have her."
The old man's eye had a speculative gleam. His son had begun to as-
cend the ladder.

"Girls with a marriage portion like hers never go unwed, Master.
So says Mistress Wengrave, my master's wife, who knows everything." The gray-bearded man smiled. Cecily Kendall, he said to
himself, as he stored away the name. A relation, perhaps, of that

wealthy Roger Kendall who had donated the chantry at St. Paul's cathedral for merchants lost at sea? It was worth looking into. And this was as good as an introduction. . . .

Meanwhile, all eyes were fixed on the ladder, which did not reach all the way. The wiry, agile figure of the boy swung easily from the ladder to the limb above. The branches above are too thin for them both, thought Margaret, and she wanted to shout "No higher!" but was afraid that any sound would distract the climbing boy. Her breath was tight in her chest as the boy paused, leaning up under Cecily's cracking perch. What was he doing? Would they lose them both? The crowd was deathly still. Even the boy's father had put aside speculation and, his eyes on the swaying figures, seemed suddenly pale and drawn.

"You, girl, put your foot down on my shoulder," Cecily could hear a voice beneath her and behind her, but couldn't see the source.

"My Christian name is Cecily," she said, not moving.

"And my Christian name is Denys. Put your left foot down behind you and feel for my shoulder. You won't fall if you hold on." Carefully, carefully, he could feel a bony bare foot brush his shoulder. "Set it down hard. Then the other foot. Yes, that's it. Now keep holding on and work your hands down the branch until you can sit on my shoulders." The boy's voice was calm, as if he knew exactly what to say. "You don't need to be afraid. I'm much bigger than you. I'm holding on tight. If you grab onto me, you won't fall. No, not the neck, don't strangle me. Hold still. I'm finding the branch."

"You're not on the ladder?" whispered Cecily in terror, clutching at the stranger's shoulders, her head resting on his black hair.

"Almost," he answered. "Don't wiggle." Some portion of Cecily's fear had spread from her hard-beating heart to his. Carefully he felt beneath him for the ladder. He could hear a sort of gust from below, a sigh from dozens of throats. He'd never climbed with a living burden before. He could feel her heavy weight shift on him. He had lied to her. He wasn't that much larger, and she was hard to carry. Clinging to the branch, he felt for the next rung, moved his foot down—then a hand, carefully, carefully, lean against the tree, he repeated to himself. Keep the weight forward. The next step. Take time. The next. Now he was entirely on the ladder. Don't get cocky, he coached himself. Take each step carefully, you're still a long way from the ground. The girl's legs were bony and sharp, and her hands were clutched in a death grip around his neck. Rung by rung, he worked his way down. Now one foot felt the hard ground, and many hands relieved him of his burden, and he could feel people slapping him on the back and cheering.

"A hero! A hero!" they cried, and from the back of the crowd a voice that cried, "Someone should give that girl a good birching!" and in front of him a sharp little voice said, "You're not that much bigger than me after all. You lied."

He looked at the bedraggled, barefoot little figure in front of him and said, "Of course I did. You wouldn't have climbed down otherwise. Besides, I was big enough to get you down, wasn't I?" But the curious red-headed creature had burst into tears.

"Cecily," said Margaret firmly, "you must thank Master Denys for saving you."

"Th-thank you," sobbed Cecily.

"Whatever made you want a magpie's eggs?" asked the boy.

"N-not the eggs. The pie stole Madame's silver button and flew away with it, and she was so grieved——"

"Madame your mother?"

"N-no, Madame who is teaching me to be a lady." Denys the rescuer couldn't help it, he threw back his head and laughed until the tears came. Laughter rippled outward. The apprentices and journeymen laughed, Mistress Wengrave laughed, and even Margaret laughed, though she didn't want to. "A lady, haw!" snorted the boy's father. But Cecily had turned as red as a beet beneath her freckles. She stamped her bare foot and shouted, "I am *so* a lady, I shall be a great lady someday, a *ver*-ry great lady!" and everyone laughed even harder, except Master Denys, the magistrate's son.

CHAPTER NINE

I T WAS NOT LONG BEFORE MIDSUMMER'S eve, on the purported date of the blessed Saint Edburga's martyrdom, when Sir Roger led the villagers in procession to her namesake spring, to lay forever at rest the idea that Hretha or any other pagan being was the source of the rushing waters. Ahead of him marched a boy in white bearing the silver cross from the altar itself. Beside him walked Sir Hubert's own chaplain, only semi-drunk, swinging an incense censor. Behind him were the bravely embroidered banners of Saint George and Saint Mark, and behind that, carried on a wooden pallet laden with half-burned candles, the brightly painted wooden statue of Our Lady of the Sorrows, who was reputed to weep on Good Friday, if one were virtuous enough to see it. Behind the six sturdy fellows with the pallet rode the folk of Brokesford Manor, dressed as for Sunday. A foolish venture, thought Sir Hubert, who liked things quiet. But in this, the village priest, though appointed by him, took precedence. It was a religious matter. Folks who disagree on religious matters get reported to the Inquisition. The man certainly has a bee in his bonnet on this one, thought Sir Hubert. Best to go along and let him set up his shrine by the water. What harm could it do? Edburga or nixies, they were all the same. God, now, was different. God was like Sir Hubert and tolerated many things for the sake of peace.

Behind the gentlefolk came a cart accompanied by carpenters, with all that was needful to build a little housed shrine to the blessed memory of the saint. Lovingly carved and painted, the little house stood among the lumber for its foundation, at its center a flat and ugly painting of Saint Edburga in the clothing of a nun. Crowding behind the cart on the narrow path were the villagers, carrying flowers. As the front of the procession entered the forest, the priests began to chant a psalm, *Dominus regnavit.* Deeper and deeper they went, into the green, moss-carpeted summer forest, until they had reached the fearful temple of ancient trees. There beneath the arch bubbled the green spring, source of water and life for the entire demesne. There lay the great rock, dappled with forest light and covered with the flapping, ghostly white remnants of old rags. There the priest took up the aspergillum and sprinkled holy water into the spring, onto the rock, and onto the sunny spot by the water where the shrine would stand.

Village men and lords alike took off their hats and all bowed their heads as the two priests chanted prayers in Latin, prayers, endless prayers. Workmen dug the foundation and the village carpenter supervised the mounting of the little shrine on its new foundation. Hammers rang through the forest, but the people were curiously silent. Sir Roger looked at them, the horsemen, their hats off, the ladies, quiet in the saddle, the villagers, shifting from one foot to another.

"Now shout for Saint Edburga!" cried the priest. The feeble cry from the crowd seemed to anger him. "Shout louder! What's wrong with you?" He stood at the place where the round, light-speckled pond of the spring turned into the stream that watered the manor, filled the moat, gave drink to man and beast. The villagers were looking past him. What was it that was drawing their attention? Suddenly the priest turned, filled with new suspicion. Behind him was the huge stone, all draped and decorated with the faded rags. "The stone is Saint Edburga's stone! She scorns pagan offerings!" he cried, and turned to tear down the strings of rags that wrapped the rock.

The village people seemed to move back in horror; the horses twitched and threw their heads. "It all goes!" he cried. "Every bit of it!" Stripping the lowest strings from the rock, he threw the rags into the pond, where they seemed to be sucked away without a trace. Above his head, the breeze made the pallid rags flutter impudently, just beyond his reach. The highest string seemed anchored at the top of the rock, on the water side. Without hesitation, Sir Roger the priest began to climb the rock. Unerringly, his booted toes and grasping fingers found the narrow handholds that let him climb to the top. The highest string seemed to be fastened down tight by something—a bolt, a nail. He pulled hard to snap the weathered white cord. He pulled again, bracing himself against the rock. Suddenly, without warning, the cord and fastening came loose so fast that he lost his balance and fell backward.

With a cry, still clutching the string of rags, the priest flailed in the air. Women screamed. Then there was a terrible splash, and the crowd saw him scrambling there in the shallows for a foothold, slipping on the mud and mossy rocks at the bottom of the pond. His hand was still tight on the cord, and the wet rags flapped about him as he struggled. Something, an invisible current, seemed to be pulling him.

"You men, get poles, do something!" cried the Lord of Brokesford, but the people were still, huddled together, their eyes wide. Without hesitation, Sir Hubert spurred his big sorrel mare into the shallow water and leaned down to grab the floundering priest's arm. At the very moment that he was unbalanced, arm outstretched, the old mare, normally so placid, shied sideways, sending Sir Hubert into the water. He crawled up sputtering, greenish with algae, his white hair all wet in his eyes. He could feel the thing drawing, sucking him into the depths. Blindly, he reached for the mare's stirrup, and clung tight. Spluttering, filthy, he was pulled from the pond by the terrified mare, and lay gasping at the water's edge. As hands took him up, and tried to brush his clothes and wring out his hat, he turned to look at the pond. There was nothing at the center but a few floating white rags linked by a bit of whitened string. Then there was a bubbling, like a cauldron on the boil, and the last of the rags disappeared. The priest had vanished utterly.

"Get hooks," said the old lord, who was always at his best in a crisis. "Get the long pikes from the manor. Get poles. We'll drag this pond for him if it takes all night." Strong men went scurrying while women and children clung to one another. All afternoon, beneath the sorrowful eyes of the painted Virgin, who stood abandoned on her pallet beside the shrine, they prodded and dragged. At last someone thought to fetch a rope to sound the depths of the spring. It was a very long rope, which they weighted with a rock at the end. They found no bottom to the spring, and the rope itself was pulled so hard that it had to be abandoned, where it vanished with an odd slurping sound. At this, the entire company knew that Sir Roger could never be retrieved. Cart and horses, statue and banners, silver cross and Sunday clothes, they walked mournfully back to the village in the purple dusk.

Late that night, when stars had come out in the midnight sky, and a silvery sliver of a moon had risen to light the way, Sir Hubert wandered sleepless from his tower bedroom to the wide chamber beneath his in the tower, where Sir Hugo and his wife slept in a big, straw filled bed separated only by curtains from the squires, servants, and hounds of his retinue.

"Hugo, get up," whispered the old lord, pulling aside the moth-eaten wool bed curtains. Hugo was feeling content with himself, sure he had sired a son that very evening. Lady Petronilla was turned on her side, spine to him, snoring.

"What is it, father?" said Hugo, irritated by this intrusion on his thoughts.

"I have something I need to do. Get up and ride with me." Sir Hubert had two unlit horn lanterns in his hand. Hugo reached his shirt and doublet off the bar over his bed, where they hung beside his favorite falcon, who perched, asleep, on the same bar. As he slipped them on, he heard his father go through the solar, filled with more hounds and sleeping retainers, down the circular stone staircase to the hall. There, the old man tiptoed past the slumbering bodies on the floor and lit the lanterns from the sheltered embers of the great fire at the center. Above him, hams hung smoking in the dark beneath the roof. Even the chickens were asleep, roosting in various likely spots above the reach of the cats and dogs.

Puzzled, Hugo followed his father to the stable, where they

nimbly stepped over the sleeping bodies of the stableboys in the straw and saddled two horses. Quietly, quietly, they led the horses out of the manor gate.

"Where are you going, father?" asked the younger man.

"Hugo, if you ever had a brain in your head, you'd know," he answered.

Across the meadow in the dark, the two little sparks of lanterns bobbed unevenly, but there was no one there to hear the dull sound of hooves in grass. The sparks progressed under the thin, white moon until they vanished into the forest. Beneath the leafy cover, they rode slowly, softly, on the alert. Beasts were out at night, and not the willing beasts that gave up blood and dinner. At last, they reached the darkest place, and then the clearing. The pond was black at night, but the bubbling sounded louder than ever in the night quiet.

"Hugo, hold my horse," said the old lord. Dismounted, hat in one hand, flickering lantern in the other, he stood at the edge of the pond. Signs of the attempted rescue were all around, layer after layer of muddy foot and hoofprints, leafy poles newly cut and abandoned. A spot of moonlight managed to penetrate the forest cover, and shone, moving and white, like a living thing, in the center of the black, bubbling spring.

"Listen, you, whoever you are," said the old lord. "You've just swallowed up the only priest I could ever find who approved of hunting on a Sunday. Do you know how much trouble I'm in? The Brokesford Stud is dead—the only stallion I brought home is Urgan, and even he's looking sick from that godawful French fodder. Everybody owes me money, and nobody pays. The wheat hasn't come up, the rye's got a blight, and the fruit's all small and has worms. There's a murrain at the other end of the shire and that may just finish me off. On top of that, the plague's come back into Bristol, they say, and if we're not here, you're finished, do you know that? This family is all that stands between you and the merchants. That pushy lawyer has his eyes on your oak trees and I haven't a farthing to pay court fees, let alone bribes. You things that live in the woods, what do you know about lawyers? But they'll have you. These oaks will go, and the yews, too, just to buy peacock feathers for some dandy's hat. It was wrong of you to go swallowing up that priest, but since done is done, the least you can do is give me something back. I need prosperity, I need crops, I need good horses to sell for ready cash to hire some lawyers of my own. Hear that, priest swallower? Pull me out, and I pledge that my heirs 'til I don't have any more will keep your trees. I may need you, but let me tell you, the way things are these days, you need me, too. Nobody else gives a rat's fart, that I can tell you."

"Father, you can't make deals with a thing." Hugo had dismounted to come closer and hear, and he had led the horses up behind his father.

"You heard me, Hugo. If it comes through, you're sworn to keep the trees." Hugo thought a bit. Cash was so handy, and trees—well, so tree-like. They just sat there doing nothing. "Promise, Hugo. Swear by Our Lord." Hugo looked upset. He'd had to make a very long and unpleasant pilgrimage just to get off the last bad oath he'd sworn. "HUGO, you UNGRATEFUL WORM, if you don't swear this INSTANT, I'll DISOWN you!" The old lord's voice rang through the dark forest. Sleeping birds fluttered awake in their nests. Hugo felt his father's big hand pushing him down to his knees. He swore. "AND your heirs," prompted his father.

"—and my heirs, for ever, as long as there are any," added Hugo.

"Good," said his father. "It's entirely fair. The thing in the water and I have come to an understanding. In my experience with the French, you can usually make truce, as long as you offer up something."

"But father, you've offered *me* up."

"Well, after all, you're my firstborn, and the heir. That ought to be worth something to a pond, for God's sake. Besides, Hugo, it's time you learned to keep your promises. It's good for the soul. Aerates it, and makes it easier to remember what you planned to do."

NOW THIS I CAN TELL YOU, it is as sure as God created the itch that everything always happens on whitewashing day. The disorder attracts other disorder the way a dog attracts fleas, and pretty soon you're vowing never to whitewash again, and let chaos reign by degrees instead of all at once.

My lord husband saw the servants scooping out the old rushes from the hall and said, "Whitewashing day? How did it come so soon?"

"You yourself had them take down the tapestries and all those old battleaxes and deers' antlers yesterday."

"But I didn't think it would be *today.* I just remembered I have to go to the illuminator's to see how they're doing with the Duke's book." Thumbs tucked in his belt, he vanished out the door.

Then Adam le Plasterer arrived at the back gate with two burly journeymen and his push-cart full of whitewash at the same time that the men with the new rushes came, and the entire neighborhood could hear them quarreling over who would enter the gate first.

"Everything all gone. The hall is *naked,*" announced Peregrine, who had come trailing in with Mother Sarah and my old dog, Lion, who spends most of his time sleeping under the bed. The dog snuffled around on the bare tile floor, looking for a bone he had hidden in the rushes and then looked up at me with a damaged expression. "Mama, men fighting. Take Peregrine to watch."

"No I won't," I said as I hurried past the kitchen screen to the back door. There in the kitchen courtyard stood a half-dozen donkeys so laden with bundles of rushes you could only see their feet, an abandoned pushcart, and a half-dozen tradesmen shouting insults and close to blows.

"You fool, you've come a day too soon. You can't put new rushes down until the walls are whitewashed."

"All over this city, you are known for your sloth, *Master* Adam. It's you who've come late, and now I can't make my next delivery."

Ah, me, Margaret, I thought. You've made deals with the devil incarnate, you ought to be able to settle this quarrel. But as it usually is with peacemakers, by interrupting them, I took the blame. They decided that womanlike, I had told them each the wrong time, and it was with greatest difficulty that I convinced the rush man to pile the bound rushes in the center of the room where they would not interfere with the whitewashing, and the whitewashers to let them enter first on the grounds that they would be soon leaving.

"This wall," said Adam le Plasterer from the top of his ladder, "whoever did this plastering job? It's coming out in big chips. Why, you can almost see the stone here! He mixed it wrong. You should never have hired him."

"It was done long before my time," I said, standing down by the wood wainscoting that circled the base of the hall, and turning my head up to the rafters.

"Well, that accounts for it. You've let it go far too long. I'm afraid I'll have a big job here, much bigger than just whitewashing." I stood on tiptoe, and scratched at the plastered stone as far I as I could reach. Sure enough, it came away in a big, damp flake.

"Maybe it's the damp," shouted down Master Adam from his ladder. "You could have a hidden leak in your roof. You'll need to send for the roofer if you don't want to loose the next plastering job. I don't think you can go ahead with the whitewash until I've redone the wall." Not a day of disorder, but weeks of disorder now stretched before me, all, of course, accompanied by greater expense.

Madame came down, accompanied by the girls. Prompted by her, they both curtseyed deeply and greeted me as "Madame, our honored mother." Ah, manners. The problem is, if other people have them, then you have to have them, too. I gave them both my blessing and inquired after their progress.

"Madame de Vilers," she said, looking about the chaotic room, and stepping delicately about the bundled rushes, "today we shall take our lesson out-of-doors." She was carrying a large basket. "We shall be learning tapestry stitches and reviewing the desireable ways of behaving at table. And what have we already learned today, Mademoiselle Alison?"

"A person of gentle breeding never wipes his hands on the table-cloth, nor does he blow his nose in the same hand with which he takes meat."

"Excellent," I said. "In these few weeks, you have worked wonders, Madame." She inclined her head graciously.

"Now you, mesdemoiselles. You must thank your mother graciously for her interest in your progress." The girls looked at each other, that knowing look they have, then each inclined her head at exactly the same angle as Madame.

"Thank you, Madame our Mother," they chorused with sarcastic politeness. Madame turned to leave, or, rather, rotated, back straight, as if she were oiled. They did the same. Madame never walked, she glided as if on wheels. As she glided off, the girls glided behind her, heads up, backs rigid, in perfect imitation. Only when she had vanished beyond the kitchen screen did they turn their heads back to see what impression they had made, their eyes brimming with deviltry.

"You don't see girls like that very often," I heard one of the plasterers remark. "So ladylike, and so young."

If you only knew, I thought. Thank goodness the Burgundians are paying for all this. Through the open window from the street came bright sunlight, dancing with shining dust motes, and the sound of the St. Paul's jacks beating nine o'clock in the morning. Another hour, and it would be dinner-time.

"Dame Margaret, where will you have dinner set?" I had been too distracted to notice Perkyn at my shoulder. There was already a crashing and banging sound in the kitchen, as they set up trestle tables for the household.

"For the family? In the solar—"

"A lot of dust here," observed the old man. "Whitewashing should always be done first thing in the spring. Then there's no dust." As if we had a penny in the spring, let alone what all this plastering's going to cost, I thought, but on account of his long service, I bit my tongue.

"They're likely to be here a while, aren't they?" he said, wandering between the piles of rushes and looking at the men on ladders. "Where will you be setting a place for that Madame personage, in the kitchen or the solar?"

"Upstairs—oh, merciful heaven!" There was a terrible crash as the front door was thrown open. With a clatter of metal, a terrifying figure filled the door, booted, spurred and armed, gray hair flying, wild gray beard and massive gray eyebrows like clumps of weeds, clothes dusty with travel.

"Where's the steward! Tell my son we've ARRIVED! Boy, take the horses round to the stable. What IS this wreckage in here? Margaret, this is your doing!" All plastering stopped. All eyes were on the ferocious figure in the door. My heart sank. The perfect addition to the day. My father-in-law, on one of his surprise visits to the City.

"Margaret, WHERE'S my SON?" he shouted, as if I'd hidden him somewhere. Gilbert claims he shouts because he took too many hits on the helmet, and it deafened him, but I think he shouts to create more space around him. Space and terror.

"My lord husband is at the illuminator's," I answered, and stared him calmly in the eye. He'd brought a half-dozen of his favorite hounds with him, huge brindled creatures with heavy heads and slavering jowls, and they bounded in, sniffing and smelling in the corners. The plasterers stayed prudently perched above.

"At the WHAT? What's he fiddle-faddling about with that sort of thing for? Twenty-eight and nearly middle aged and he still hasn't MADE anything of himself! THREE TIMES to France in BATTLE, not even COUNTING the time he ran off to WHIFFLE AWAY his time studying to be some sort of GODFORSAKEN CLERK, and he's NEVER BEEN WOUNDED IN THE FRONT! And what happened this time? He was hit by lightning and his horse FELL on him! He should be well by now! He should be in France with the Duke, not messing around with illuminators and jugglers and who knows what other sort of TRASH!" I noticed Hugo, Gilbert's older brother, was leaning in the doorjamb, arms folded, absorbing the denunciation with great enjoyment. He looked more French than ever. He had on a ridiculous blue-dyed beaver hat with a tiny brim and an immense sheaf of peacock feathers held on with a little gold brooch. The toes of his shoes had grown long and pointed, and the fashionably dagged hem of his tunic had shrunk until it showed his backside. He had on parti-colored hose. I knew for a fact the old man hated parti-colored hose. He said they were for mountebanks.

"He is preparing a manuscript for the Duke's return. The Duke has written a book of theology," I answered. I couldn't help it. The day was already hard, and I was tempted to stir things up a bit.

"Theo-what?" the old man choked. "Even the duke himself is writing about God? I tell you, it's Gilbert's doing. He's a corrupting force."

"Confessions or prayers?" asked Hugo, suddenly interested, as his nose smelled a change in fashion.

"Confessions. And a bewailment of sins classified according to the parts of the body."

"Ha. It SMELLS of Gilbert's influence. I swear, the boy's pernicious," said Sir Hubert, shaking his head in bewilderment.

"Father, theology is very fashionable in the highest circles these days. I was thinking of doing a book of confessions myself one of these days. After I have my poetry written up." Trust Hugo to know the exact way to get under the old man's skin. Too much time together. Poor Hugo; thirty years old and still living at home. The cursed lot of the oldest son, living in dependence and waiting endlessly to inherit.

"YOU? CONFESSIONS? Not only do you wear parti-colored hose, you CAN'T READ AND WRITE!" Denunciation had repaired the old man's brief lapse into doubt.

"No more than you, no more than the Duke. That's why Gilbert writes for him." Hugo was looking smug. I could feel the old man swelling up like a bladder for the next spouting fit.

"That's step-grandfather," I heard Alison explaining to Madame from the far end of the hall. "Watch out for him." The girls, seeing the horses being taken to the stable, had come in with Madame to find out what visitors had come.

"He chopped off our half-brother's head. Right there," said Ce-

cily, and I knew she was trying to rattle Madame with her ghoulish-
ness. "It rolled around on the floor and spouted blood."

"Blood does not spout from heads. It spouts from necks," replied
Madame with perfect calm, speaking French. "Now, in French, if
you please, and politely. Ladies do not describe deeds of chivalry
using butchers' language."

"Who, or what, is THAT?" said Sir Hubert, spying the stranger in
black.

"That is Madame de Hauvill. Allow me to introduce you."

"Me? Introduced to a *dependent*?" His stare was scornful. Madame,
pale and straight, walked straight up to him and stared him in the
eye. The girls watched, wide-eyed. This was battle by single combat.
Who would win? Madame who was "too mean," or step-grandfather,
who was meaner yet? Even Hugo began to take an interest.
Madame's chin was up, her eyes narrowed, and her stare unblink-
ing. Sir Hubert, taken unguarded, blinked first, then grew angry.
"And just who do you think you ARE, woman?" he said, the very
picture of menace. With a gloved fist, he could still strike a man to
the ground, and did it with fair frequency on his own estates. Pallid
and fine boned, Madame looked as if a touch could shatter her like
glass.

"I am *Lady* Agathe, widow to Sir Raymond de Hauvill, and related to Sir William de Vilers through his cousin, Isabelle Payton,"
she said.

"In what degree is this—relationship?" said Sir Hubert, his voice
cold and arrogant.

"A degree that does not excuse your rudeness," said Madame, in
a voice that dripped icicles.

As the girls watched, fascinated, they dueled together, talking the
arcane language of cousins-german, degrees of kinship, quarterings.
Madame's voice was intense, but low. In amazement we watched as
Sir Hubert seemed unable to shout, reducing his voice to a hoarse
whisper to match the level of her even-toned French. The plasterers
had forgotten to keep up even the pretense of work, and from their
ladders, were stock still, listening. In the background, servants

carrying dishes up to the solar stopped on the staircase to stare. The clatter in the kitchen ceased. Faces crowded around the kitchen screen. Who would back away first?

"Well, it seems an introduction is now superfluous. I know who you are, Madame, that is enough." Sir Hubert turned and clapped his hands. "Dinner! Where's my dinner? I didn't ride all this way to STARVE!" The servants scurried again. Scents and sounds oozed past the kitchen screen into the hall once more. The girls were awestruck. It was Sir Hubert who had backed down and turned away first. As if to compensate for his public loss of face, he turned and growled at me: "Margaret, since you have destroyed this hall, where is the family to be served?"

"In the solar, my lord father-in-law."

"And that woman——?"

"Madame always sits with the family."

"Whatever possessed you to bring a despicable creature like that into your household?"

"My lord father-in-law, she instructs my daughters in the art of being a lady. It was Sir Gilbert's idea."

"Gilbert! I should have KNOWN he was in this somewhere—oh, there you are, Gilbert. I was just talking about you. What are you doing, dilly-dallying your time away with clerks? You should have been HERE! What kind of house is it, when the lord is too busy to GREET his SIRE? I should have known your blasted STOM-ACH would tell you when to come home, even if your DUTY didn't!"

Through the open door came the sound of Paul's jacks, beating eleven o'clock. One hour. In such hours, is fate remade.

CHAPTER TEN

L ATE AT NIGHT, VOICES CAME GRUMBLING from the parlor downstairs. I felt beside me in the bed for Gilbert and found an empty space. I pulled aside the bed curtain and found my slippers on the floor. The door had been left open, and a hint of flickering light came up from downstairs. Malkyn was snoring on her truckle bed, but Lion, who is not lion sized, but lion hearted, even if he is old, woke up with a puzzled snort and followed me about as I felt for my big *robe de chambre* on the perch above the bed. Quietly I crept out, blessing the fact that the floor of our bedchamber is furnished with a carpet, like the parlor-room downstairs, and not with noisy, crackling rushes. Following the dim light and the noise, I came upon the girls, naked as frogs, sitting on the middle step of the staircase. They were sitting together on the blanket from their bed and listening silently.

"Mother," Cecily whispered. "Don't make a sound. They're getting to the good part." I sat down on the step above them, and Lion lay down beside me with a wheezing sound, and fell back to sleep.

"No, father, you have drained this estate long enough. I have a son now, and want to leave him something."

"And through whose hand did you GET this estate? Who got rid of the other claimants? Who bribed the judges? Who spied out that the woman was worthwhile and carried her off for you before anyone else could get their hands on that old moneygrubber's tidy little fortune? You owe me this!"

"Your bribes, everything, have been paid a dozen times over, father, and always from the estate. The cash is gone, and for all Margaret has done for you—and for me—you owe her the roof over her head. A roof, I might add, that Master Kendall guaranteed her."

"It's just a mortgage, brother. We've got dozens, and it doesn't concern me in the least."

"A mortgage you have no intention of paying off. What happens to her and the girls, if, God forbid, something were to happen to me?"

"Why, I'd look after them. It's my duty as head of the family."

"Exactly."

"Look, brother, if you stick at pledging the house as collateral, why don't you just dip into their dowries? No girls deserve that much." The girls shuddered as if suddenly chilled, and wrapped the blanket up around themselves, huddling together.

"Hugo, I made a pledge of honor to look after those girls. Do you think as little of my word as you do of yours? A whole year of pilgrimage, and you howled every step of the way. Except when you were chasing *pucelles* with your tales of religious ecstasy experienced in the corridors, outer chambers, and whorehouses of Avignon. Did you ever visit a single relic?"

"Just because the Cardinal sold me a pardon, doesn't mean I'm not just as religious as lowly folk who wallow on their knees in long lines in front of some dead man's bones. You're nothing but a hypocrite who lectures other folks about piety and won't dip his hand into a little bit of available silver to help out his family, that's all."

"Tell that to Master Wengrave, their godfather. All the powers of the City will be brought to bear. He wouldn't stop short of appealing to the king himself if you try to get your hands on their dowries."

"Then sell their marriages. That's within your right, and it's high time anyway. Somebody ought to pay you a pretty penny to get his hands on those dowries."

"Mother!" whispered the little girls, shocked.

"Sh." I whispered back, "I'll never see you married against your will. Keep listening. The more we know about, the more things we can think of."

"I have promised Margaret I will never see them betrothed against their will," I could hear Gilbert's words, terse and firm.

"Their will, *their* will. Two little beasts. Why should their will count against father's trees?"

"Your trees, you mean, brother, because it's you that will get them in the end. I tell you, their will counts because Margaret says it counts, and I keep my word."

"Nonsense, Gilbert. Peregrine's trees. Hugo's wife here is as barren as a stick. Think of your son, Master of Brokesford."

"Master of a manor that needs roofing and hasn't got a single decent fireplace, a moat that needs dredging and breeds mosquitoes the size of hummingbirds, horses whose keep is more than they bring you, an orchard full of worms, and a bunch of lie-about peasants who can't manage to bring up a single crop in sufficiency to keep them next winter."

"That last bit's just temporary. And the trees, Gilbert. The woods, the meadows, the roe deer at dawn, the larks singing in the coppices, the babbling brooks and sighing reeds and the best spring of pure water for miles about."

"The oaks will soon be the lawyer's, and the spring's a holy well that people keep dumping things into. It's a gloomy, good-for-nothing place, father. Resign yourself to losing it."

"Resign myself? RESIGN myself? A de Vilers NEVER resigns himself! Not an inch of land to the enemy, not an inch, I say!"

"Look here, Gilbert, don't send him into another rage. The problem's simple. The Lombards won't accept the land with the oaks as collateral because the lawyer says the title is in question. He's gone and filed a trespass suit against us to be heard at the next assizes, and we've filed one against him. Whoever wins, gets the oaks. But we need the loan from the Lombards to bribe the judge to secure our title to the oak forest against the lawyer's claim. And we mortgaged everything else of value when we went on the last campaign. So if you put up the house as collateral, then we buy the judge, get the land, and it's all settled."

"Except that you have no means to repay the loan and I am saddled with the debt, which I can't repay either. No, I don't have to, I'm pledged not to, and I won't. That's all."

"Can this monster of selfishness be my son? The same one that I ransomed from the French?"

"How odd. I seem to recall, it was Margaret who ransomed me from the French."

"I *would* have ransomed you from the French. You must admit, I had a brilliant plan."

"Well, then, you need a brilliant plan now. More brilliant than pledging land that's in litigation as collateral for a loan to bribe the judge to secure the title to the land. Besides, suppose the judge is honest?"

"Honest? Ridiculous! What judge is honest? Besides, the lawyer has already given him twenty gold florins to settle the case in his favor. I have to better it, or I haven't a chance." We heard a whistle of appreciation.

"Twenty florins! That's a huge sum! Are the woods worth that much?"

"That and more, as lumber. And the yews, too. It'll all go, every bit of it."

"The yews, too?" we heard Gilbert say. "They're kind of nice, in a gloomy sort of way. I was always fond of them, they were so pleasantly melancholy." There was a long pause. "No, it seems a bit excessive, to chop down the yews. Someone planted them, you know, or they wouldn't grow in rows like that. Before the conqueror, before Christianity, before even the Romans, I imagine. That lawyer is a swine."

"Well then, you'll pledge the house?"

"Mother!" gasped the girls.

"Or will you sell the brats?" Hugo's voice, with its high, nasal accent, had never been more irritating.

"Sh. Listen to your stepfather."

"No, I won't. But I'll think of something. You need a plan, a masterful plan."

"You? Gilbert, you were born a bumbler. I wouldn't trust a plan you laid to save me. All books, no sense, that's what you are. I regret the day I ever let you study abroad."

"You didn't let me study abroad, father. If you recall correctly, I ran away."

"Ungrateful *and* a bumbler. You can't expect to save my woods by bombarding the judges at the assizes with poetry."

"Tomorrow, father. Sleep on it, and you'll see I'm right." Before I could bundle the children upstairs, Gilbert's long legs had carried him to where we had been listening, and he narrowly escaped tripping over the dog and spilling his lighted candle over the edge of the stair into the bundles of rushes on the floor below.

"My God, you've been listening," he said, "and now I've just missed setting the house on fire. Margaret, we're in trouble. Father needs a large amount of money." The girls were silent, their eyes big in the candlelight. Perhaps never before had they truly realized how much their whole lives depended on the will of men. There was no escape. I could feel their shock as if it were a solid thing.

"As usual," I said, as if I were unaware how closely the girls were listening to every word.

"I told him I'd come up with a plan. Margaret, as long as I breathe I'll not break my pledge to you. But how do I come up with that much money, without gouging it out of the estate?"

"If I were you, my lord husband, I'd consult Brother Malachi. There isn't a thing he doesn't know about money. Besides, he's got the largest brain in London. He's never failed to come up with a plan yet. Look at how well his plan worked to ransom you from the Comte d'Aigremont."

"Of course," said Gilbert, with relief in his voice. "Malachi, that old fake. He has an answer for everything. I'll sleep easier tonight, just knowing I'll be seeing him tomorrow."

"COME IN, COME IN, Gilbert, I recognize your footstep. What are you here for this time? More complaints about the illuminators? The price of gold leaf? Ah, the hazards of waiting on a great patron. I saw you the other day in a velvet-trimmed surcoat and the damndest hat with a feather on it. I imagine it must have been extra large, to fit your swollen head."

Gilbert had to duck his head to enter the low door into Brother Malachi's laboratorium. The walls still looked a bit smoky from his last accident, but otherwise everything was pretty much back where it was. Brother Malachi never looked up from his task, which was pouring molten lead into little molds. I knew the task from old times, when I once lived in Brother Malachi's household. I even used to pour the lead myself before he got Sim for his apprentice. It is for making seals. Malachi takes a bit of soft wax and gets an impression of a seal he wants, then scurries home to make up a plaster cast and get a duplicate. It's all part of his traveling business, which he undertakes in good weather, and which pays for all the glassware he breaks up in his search for the Stone.

"Brother Malachi," I said, when I saw him pause in the operation.

"And Margaret," he said, "why, I never even heard you! What makes you sneak in on little mouse feet? A state visit from the resident nobility of Thames Street. What has occasioned this glorious condescension?"

"Malachi, you know that father made me buy that title. There was no way out. We needed the duke's patronage if we were going to keep Margaret's house, and the only way I could get it was by using her estate to buy the knighthood and entering his service. They caught me like a rat in a trap." He sighed deeply. "It was all easier when everything I owned was in a bundle on my back. I was happier then."

"I sense from your long faces that you are in trouble again. Now that I think of it, when have you not been in trouble? Sit down over there, Gilbert, and start copying out that piece of paper. I need fifty of them, and you always did have a nice clerical hand. While you're copying, you can tell me about it. There's hardly any problem in the world than cannot be solved by the application of a truly powerful brain."

Gilbert sat down at the work table, beneath the shelf that held Brother Malachi's quite extraordinary alchemical library, all fifteen volumes of rare and forbidden works. Laid out on the table was a plenary indulgence, a stack of blank paper, a bottle of ink, penknife, sand, and row of quills. A little smile crossed Gilbert's long, worried face as he saw the paper he was to copy.

"Still in the forged indulgence business? It does bring back the old days." He inspected the quills for the most likely one, uncorked the ink bottle, and began to write. It has always been a marvel to me how precise the movements of his big hands are as the delicate and intricate lines of writing follow the moving quill. Practice, I guess. His mother always intended him for the church.

"And you're lucky I am. I've just been to Lincoln Cathedral, where I overawed the Canon with the sight of my Papal Bull—so artistically sealed, you know. He let me into the cathedral archives, because of a professed interest in ancient history, and while I was perusing chronicles, he couldn't resist showing me some real treasures. I wrapped the impressions in wet moss and hurried straight home before the heat could melt them."

"It's all a disaster," said Gilbert, never losing his place in his copying. "Courtesy of father, as usual. He wants me to pledge the house as collateral for a loan from the Lombards to bribe a judge in a law case he's involved in."

"Why doesn't he put up his own land?"

"That's the problem. The only piece that isn't already mortgaged is the piece that's in litigation that he wants to bribe the judge over. The Lombards somehow seem to think that's not a sufficient guarantee."

"Now he wants us to sell the girls' marriages," I added.

"Margaret, Margaret, we won't sell your girls. My mind's already at work," said Malachi, setting his molds out on the workbench to cool. "Now, where's Sim, that rascal? Here Hilde's been gone two days at a hard labor in Bishopsgate Street, and I'm fainting for lack of her cooking. I send the boy out for a bird or two from the bake shop, and he vanishes. Probably playing dice on some street corner."

"Let me see what Mother Hilde's left you, Brother Malachi," I said, and after finding only half a loaf of stale bread in the cupboard in the hall, I went out to check the garden. There I found that

Malachi had not bothered to remove the eggs from beneath the setting hens that morning, and there were onions and parsley looking
good in the garden. So I set about making soppes dorre and hanoney,
and as the bread was frying and the omelette stirring, and Gilbert
was copying and complaining, Malachi was resting his round body
on a bench in his laboratorium while he exercised his brain. The
signs of brain excercise are very clear in Malachi. First his cheerful
round, pink face becomes very solemn. Then if it's a hard problem,
wrinkles appear between his brows, and he goes, "Ha! Hm!" After
that, he taps the side of his head gently to make sure his brains
haven't congealed with the effort. I was hearing a lot of "Ha! Hm!"
coming out of the laboratorium as I was cooking, so I knew that all
would be well.

"Ah, Margaret, it's smelling good. Lay aside that work for now,
Gilbert. My brain is wilting. I feel its powers suddenly diminishing.
It needs nutrition."

As we fed Malachi's brain, and also our own, we began to feel
much more cheerful.

"So, Gilbert, on what does this lawyer base his claim?"

"A deed recently discovered in a chest by the Austin friars at
Wymondley."

"Wymondley? Where's that located, relative to Brokesford?"

"Their lands touch the estate the lawyer claims, on the farther
side." Gilbert's voice was cynical. Malachi shook his head and made
clucking sounds.

"A forgery, as clear as day," he replied. "I'd be willing to bet hard
cash that he's made a deal with the monks at the abbey. They'll
probably take a nice little part of the money he gets from selling the
trees. Perpetual prayers, a chantry, whatever. That way everyone
goes to heaven. And the apparently legitimate deed lets the judge
appear, or even be, perfectly honest when he makes the decision.
The twenty florins simply hastens the day of justice."

"I thought you might make something to use as collateral with
the Lombards—like those emeralds, or those gold rings that you
took to France," I said.

"Margaret, after many years of hard experience, which include having to flee some of the greatest cities in Europe, I have come to the conclusion that one must never foul one's own nest. I never use my powers within London itself. No, my mighty skills must be reserved for the unappreciative souls in the provinces, or abroad, depending upon the case. One cannot risk having the emeralds return to their native state while locked in the Lombards' chests."

"Oh," I said, very disappointed.

"Don't be cast down, Margaret, I'm seeing a better way out of this." He reached for the last piece of the fried, spicy bread, and finished it off with a big swig of ale. Then he tapped his temple to loosen up his brains again and get them to working. "Margaret, thanks to your inventive cuisine, my brain is fully restored to its highest powers. Now, when you bring your father back here, Gilbert— and *don't* bring that simpleton brother of yours, we'll need him later—you really must bring along some of that superior brown ale that Margaret makes. The good stuff that you keep upstairs under the bed. I will need to be fueled to my highest powers, if I am to get your doltish father to comprehend my magnificently subtle plan. It will take perfect organization, perfect! And I don't want him ruining it."

CHAPTER ELEVEN

THE SIEUR DE VILERS, LORD OF BROKES-ford Manor, looked about him with deep distaste. No respectable business on earth would have ever brought him to this disreputable part of Cornhill, let alone visit the den of some lunatic alchemist. Worse, he was not mounted, and had walked there, which he considered an almost incomprehensible loss of dignity. He, who would not consider walking twenty feet on his own estate, and had always a horse and a groom waiting for him, had wrapped himself in an old cloak provided by his incomprehensible younger son for a visit to something called "St. Katherine's Alley," where pigs wallowed and laundry fluttered overhead, and displaced peasants who ought to be at honest labor flaunted the liberties that their flight to the City had given them. It had irritated him, taking orders from Gilbert, even before they had left the house.

"Don't wear the sword, father, it will give you away."

"No sword? Who do you think I AM?"

"It's not who I think you are, but who the denizens of the street think you are. You can't go riding in, armed, and not be noticed. We need to be unobtrusive."

"It's not my NATURE to be unobtrusive. Just a couple of grooms, my favorite hounds, and Hugo—that's a very small party."

"Not small enough. No grooms, no hounds, and no Hugo. Brother Malachi has said it. It's part of the plan."

"Then why are you taking Margaret? I say no women."

"We need Margaret. That's part of the plan, too." For a moment there, the old lord thought he might shout to get his way, but then he remembered his trees. Then he thought of Margaret, her pale intensity, her deceptively placid, even-featured profile, and the way her eyes flashed golden, like a falcon's, when she was determined to have her way. And there came into his mind a picture, something like an imagining or a waking dream. It was an image of Margaret betting her life against Gilbert's ransom with a foreign lord, and playing with loaded dice. The minstrels that traveled through Brokesford last year had brought it with them as a song. The whole tale was well on its way to becoming legend. A scandal, really, since a woman's place is in the home, and not trekking off to foreign dungeons.

> *"Then Lady Margaret taken her chest of gold,*
> *and she taken tokens three;*
> *I will never rest in my own soft bed,*
> *'Til my lord in France goes free. . . .*

That Margaret is no lady, he thought, playing dice that way with foreigners, and getting songs written about her, too. It wasn't respectable at all. But then, she was no ordinary woman, either. Maybe he did need her after all.

But the moment he almost burst with rage was when he stepped over the threshold of the tall house on Thames Street.

"Your spurs, father. You forgot them. You can't wear them."

"Can't? CAN'T? WHAT DO YOU MEAN, CAN'T?" A horseman always wears his spurs, except to bed. It shows he has a horse, and is a person of consequence.

"You can't disguise the rest of you and leave the spurs on," said his son, with that damnable logic he always wielded like a knife. The trees, said the old lord to himself, thinking of the wind rustling the leaves of the ancient oaks. Think of the trees first, and see what this sinister alchemist has to say. He took off his spurs and put them in the wallet at his belt, just in case he needed to put them on again somewhere to show who he was.

Now he was plunging from the relative decency of a shabby street into an alley of the lowest character. Ahead of him strode his son, as guide. Beside him, silent and pale, his son's wife, dressed curiously plain, her hood up. A lone goose, standing on a pile of muck in the center of the gutter, eyed him. He eyed it back with his hard, blue eye. The goose, offended, blinked its hard little black eye and wandered off. The second storeys of the old, timbered houses extended over the alley. He looked up, and saw the houses were sagging against each other like drunkards. *I couldn't have ridden anyway,* he thought. *The street is blocked from above. How on earth did Gilbert ever get to know the kind of people who lived here, in heaven's name?*

"What did you say this place was called?" said the Sieur de Vilers, treading carefully about a pile of excrement.

"The common name for it is 'Thieves' Alley'," said his son. "Did you see those caps and hoods out front for sale? All stolen." His son was wearing a vile, shapeless old gray robe of homespun, with the hood up.

"I thought I told you to burn that thing," he said.

"You did. But admit this time that it has its uses," answered the ungrateful boy. *No matter how you work, they revert at the first chance. It's his mother's blood. Freakish, she was. How could he have brought himself to put the fate of his land in the hands of madmen, even if one of them was a family madman?*

"Here we are," Gilbert said, and lifted the brass door knocker, made in the shape of a monkey's head. Slowly, with the precise eye of a hunter, the Sieur de Vilers took in the details of the little room that the newly opened door revealed in front of him, and the humble sort of old woman in the tidy gray gown and white veil that had opened the door. She bowed in greeting, but not low enough, and he saw his son's wife embrace her. The room made his skin crawl. It smelled of herbs and strange, sharp metallic stuff and smoke, and between its bright red rafters, someone had painted the signs of the zodiac, alien creatures and monsters and naked humans with stars at various points of their bodies. He felt the hair go up on the back of his neck. He, who did not fear to be the first to enter a sapper's tunnel or face twenty armed men alone, felt something cold and unfamiliar in his arms and legs. It was another sort of fear, the kind that could come through his unguarded back door when he had so thoroughly fortified the front gate. Fear of the unknown, the ocean of magic and alchemy and evil spirits that lay outside the realm of his sword.

"Gilbert, what do you know about this fellow?" said Sir Hubert.

"Only that I'd trust him with my life. I even have, on occasion. I told you, I've known him for years. You even met him once, though you may have forgotten." Malachi looked unperturbed as he greeted his visitors, his hands folded across his stomach.

"Ah, it's Margaret—and Gilbert, and, goodness, this must be the Lord of the Oak Trees here. Welcome, and come into my laboratorium and sit down. We've work to do."

At the mention of the oak trees, the old man's face sagged into deep lines. He felt suddenly weary as he sat down. This ridiculous fat fellow in the friar's robe was incapable of facing down a slick lawyer and a powerful judge. It was all over.

"Now," said Brother Malachi, "let's get down to work. This lawyer fellow has a deed describing possession of a tract of land which includes your forest."

"He does," said the Sieur de Vilers wearily.

"What have you got?"

"The de Vilers lands are listed in the Domesday book. Unfortunately, the description is not very clear, and in the time since the conquest, almost all of the traditional identifying marks have been lost. Blasted oaks, large stones, the course of waters—all changed since then. I have a spring, he says he has a spring. It's my spring, according to every local tradition."

"Have you no deeds, wills?"

"Only recent ones. His deed goes back to the time of Henry the Second. It describes the lands he has just acquired, one tract of which stands on the far side of mine, and touches the abbey lands. Then it adds on my wood and my spring, as a sort of ungodly bonus.

He counted on me being away at war for my king, while he wormed away with his schemes here at home, stealing my land. This is an evil world, when knights are destroyed and lawyers get rich." He shook his head, too sad even to rage. "Sir Roger, the village priest, was taking testimony from the oldest residents before he was, ah, swallowed up. He wrote them all up, handy-like, so I could bring them with me, but the sharp man of law here in the City that Gilbert recommended said they wouldn't stand against a deed." He'd come to London full of hope, armed with a chest of testimonials and old letters from the manorial records, and fired with the expectation of a hefty loan to swing the deal. Now he'd return to the shire with no case and no bribe. He was beaten. So much for wishing wells.

"Sir Hubert, I have given the matter much thought. The deed, I believe, is forged."

"Forged? FORGED? That dogsbody steals my land with a FORGED deed? I'll denounce him! Praise be to God! We've won!"

"No, you haven't. You have to prove it. And if I know anything about those Austin friars, I know this: it will be an excellent forgery, and hard to prove, particularly if they all swear they found it in the monastic records. The second thing I know is that after the lawyer has done all their dirty work, they'll think of a scheme to snatch his prey from him. Monks are always a-building, and good timber land is not easy to come by, these days. They're a cunning crew, and know what they're about. They can outwait him, they can outwait you. No, justice will come to the lawyer, but it won't do you any good."

Sir Hubert had never lacked a certain native craft and shrewdness. The little man's words made good sense. He looked closer at him. The eyes, they were set wide apart. A good sign of brains in a horse or a hound. For humans, too. The friar's face, round and pink, with beads of sweat shining on the top of his tonsured head, shone with the light of understanding. For some reason it consoled Sir Hubert. Perhaps the owner of a face like that could come up with something after all. "What are my chances?" said Sir Hubert.

"As good as his. Sir Hubert, there is only one way to beat a forged deed. That is with another forged deed, even older. Much, much older. How fortunate that you possess one."

"But I don't, and they know it."

"Ah, but it will be discovered. Searching in the church among the old letters and registers, you will find a letter from an ancestor written before the wars of Stephen. Sir Gaultier de Vilers."

"I have such an ancestor, but he left no letters."

"He has now. This letter will describe how he buried a few valuable papers to protect them in the event the manor house was lost. I take it you have ruins on your land?"

"Nothing much, just some stone hermit's hut near the spring."

"Armed with the knowledge of this letter, you will go in front of many witnesses, including your ignorant and noisy son Hugo, and you will dig in the ruins, unearthing an ancient chest. When the chest is opened, surprise! There is an ancient deed. The most ancient possible. It is the deed of Ingulf the Saxon, ceding to your ancestor Guillaume de Vilers and his heirs forever the mystic sacred spring of what was it? Saint Edburga, known locally as Hretha's Pool, as a reward for saving his life, or some other such thing. Are you sure that Guillaume didn't marry some Saxon woman and settle down, after he came over with William the Conqueror?"

"I do believe he did, according to legend."

"Do you have her name?"

"No, women's names weren't important to keep record of in those days."

"Well, then, he cedes it to his daughter Aelfrida, who marries Guillaume. Luckily, his possession is confirmed by the mighty Conqueror himself, who awards the lands of his old enemy, Ingulf the Saxon, to his loyal servant Guillaume de Vilers—"

"How can that be?" sputtered Sir Hubert.

"In the chest, of course. It is your great good fortune that I have recently acquired an excellent seal of the Conqueror, and your brilliant, if unappreciated son Gilbert happens to be able to mimic any hand. Allow our artistic imagination to supply the chest with its contents, and the rest is easy. The family travels back with you to

Brokesford. Such a large family, Margaret, and you pack so much. Hidden away in her excessive luggage is the chest, which you and Gilbert spirit away in the dead of night and bury in the appropriate location."

"And you?"

"I remain in London, so as not to give the slightest taint to the operation. I am, after all, celebrated in some circles." Brother Malachi looked modest.

Sir Hubert's face regained its color. His white hair, which had been drooping forlornly about his face, stood on its ends once again, whirling about his head like a stormcloud. He stood, he punched one fist into the open palm of his other hand.

"It could work! It COULD work, by God! Brother Malachi, you are a genius!" Brother Malachi bowed slightly from his seat in acknowledgment. But the old man's ferocious eyebrows had drawn together in a frown. "It's too easy," he said. "What is it that you're getting out of it?"

"Any number of things," said Brother Malachi airily, waving a hand in the air as if shooing flies. "First of all, there's Margaret, and though we're not related, she's like a daughter to me. Yes, don't look shocked. She's family, and if I don't send you off satisfied, you'll steal the little security and peace of heart that old Master Kendall, in his indulgence, left her. Gilbert and I have been friends for years, and I know perfectly well he can live quite extravagantly on a bundle of old clothes, a pen, and his golden tongue. Not so with Margaret. She has little ones now. And don't pull that face on me, either. If you want my help, you have to see what you are. A pirate, who'd not stop short of robbing his own family for whatever folly entered his mind."

"You—how dare you!" sputtered Sir Hubert, and rose to go.

"When you say good-bye to me, say good-bye to that property— and to your son and grandson as well, for Gilbert is with Margaret on this, and I'd be delighted to put my magnificent mind to work to see you properly caged up away from them. If you want to go, just do so now. Just put on the spurs I know perfectly well you've got stowed away in your wallet, and swagger off down our little alley that repels you so, and straight into the mouth of disaster. It would serve you right for snubbing men of learning, which you have doubtless done your whole life." Sir Hubert gathered himself up like a thundercloud. Had he worn his sword, he might have used it, but Gilbert had brought him here stripped like an infant. He growled, a long low growl, turned, and strode through the door of the laboratorium. So angry was he that he forgot to duck, and the low doorjamb struck him hard on the forehead. He staggered back, clapping his hand to his forehead and sitting down suddenly.

"Dizzy—what a blow. Even your house conspires against me."

"Take it as a warning," announced Brother Malachi. Sir Hubert thought of the mysterious house, the strange jars and baskets, the eerie smell that made his back crawl, and with his thumping head it seemed all too likely that this Malachi fellow had terrible, secret powers which he had unfortunately aroused. Even worse than that God-forsaken pond that swallowed up Sir Roger the priest before he could finish drawing up the papers for the lawsuit.

"Margaret—" he heard Gilbert say. "Father's head—"

"I can't anymore," she answered softly. "You know what happens when you come home from a long trip."

"Do you mean—?"

"What else? I was waiting to be sure before I told you." The old lord saw his son move closer and put his arm protectively around Margaret. He knew of Margaret's eccentricities from the old days, and he knew what she meant. His head would continue aching, and Brokesford was now due to have a second heir. He also knew that Malachi was right. Who'd have thought Gilbert was such a sentimental fool about things like that? Women's breeding is women's business, until they produce a male heir, when it then becomes men's business. He knew too that he'd keep his headache and lose his son, right there and then, when he'd gone to all the trouble to recover him, polish him up, and make him respectable. He thought of all the things he held sacred: he thought of property, he thought of lineage, he thought of victory—

"What's the other thing?" he asked Brother Malachi.

"I hate lawyers," said Brother Malachi.

"By God, I hate them too," said Sir Hubert, though without his old fire, for shouting would make his head hurt worse. "I hate them like poison."

"Then we're agreed?"

"Let us go forward with this thing, and tangle them up in their own documents. And——" he paused a long time and sighed, "and you'll find I'm a gentleman, and capable of apology. I did put the trees ahead of the little ones' house and happiness. I didn't think it counted."

"It does with me," said Brother Malachi.

CHAPTER TWELVE

O FF TO MASS AGAIN SO SOON, YOU two? The holiness in this house becomes oppressive." Hugo was lying on his backside on the bench in our hall, one hand holding a wedge of Cook's pigeon pie, and the other lazily extended to pet one of the large, ugly hounds that they had brought with them. "Nothing like— mmf, munch—a bite to eat to settle a queasy stomach. I swear that dish of smoked pike I ate last night was tainted."

"If you will eat at the stews, that is what will happen," I said, unpitying.

"I might as well settle in to enjoy myself, while you two are praying up a loan. It's going to take a while." Hugo threw the last greasy remnant into the new rushes for the dogs to fight over. I could feel my back stiffen. My nice new rushes. My clean whitewash. Polluted by these oafish, uninvited visitors. Hugo sat up, one leg, the one clad in blue, crossed over the other, the one clad in red. "Tell me, brother, since you're the family expert in theology, if I have my confessions written out, is it best to be seen frequently at mass before I let it be known about the book, or should I experience a sudden conversion, a sort of bolt out of the blue?" I could see Gilbert grinding his teeth. Then he spoke, very carefully, so that he would not be tempted to bang Hugo over the head with the bench and thus delay our errand.

"Attendance at mass is an excellent strategy, Hugo, but only if you refrain from pursuing women during the elevation of the host."

"Hmph. I don't really see your reasoning. A good-looking

woman is a work of God. Pursuing them is a kind of devotional ex-ercise." I could see the back of Gilbert's neck turning red. I pulled on his sleeve. "The way I see it, since there are no carnal relations in heaven, and since God clearly made us for carnal relations, then it's our duty to do as much as possible while on earth."

"That, Hugo, is called the sin of lust."

"A sin, eh? Goodness, who'd have thought it. And here I had it all worked out. Maybe I should pass on this theology fashion and save my conversion for my deathbed. Yes, that's it; I'll confess everything and repent, and take monk's robes, and everyone will weep. Be-sides, it's much holier that way."

"And just what do you mean by that?"

"Well, I'll have ever so much more to confess by that time, and so when I receive God's grace, it will be bigger than other people's." Waves of rage were coming off Gilbert like the heat over a summer cornfield. I saw him eyeing the bench. I tugged at his sleeve again. He looked at me, a long look, then back at Hugo. Then he growled and turned on his heel.

"I'm thinking that lightning blasted the wrong person that day," he said as we went out the front door.

"Odd, that's exactly what I was thinking," I said, but the door had slammed behind us.

WE WERE ALREADY at Cornhill, passing the Cardinal's Hat tav-ern, before Gilbert quit fuming and talking to himself. The smell of stale fish wafted our way from the Leadenhall Market, as we picked our way through the gutters to Malachi and Hilde's house. One look at our sour faces and we were whisked inside and plied with ale until Gilbert stopped spluttering.

"The heat must have made you thirsty. Have some more of this excellent brown ale. Margaret made it, and there's no better in the City." Mother Hilde beamed as she filled the cups again. She and I had planned to have a delicious time catching up on all the abnor-mal births in the City, while Gilbert and Malachi planned the contents of the letter that would just accidentally reveal the hiding place of the chest with the deeds.

"I am well aware of that, you old thief, since I packed the cask over to you myself."

"Nothing better to lubricate the brain. And by the looks of you, you had better lubricate yours a little. Gilbert, you look like a thundercloud. What have you been doing?"

"Arguing theology with Hugo." Malachi burst out laughing.

"Hopeless, hopeless, and you should have known it! Come, let's go to work. I must show you all a treasure I've found. Get up, Margaret, and just take a look at this." I stood up from my seat, a long, low chest that served also as a bench, and stood aside as Malachi opened it and rummaged through. "Let's see, it's down near the bottom," he said, throwing aside a Dominican habit that was folded up with pennyroyal and lavender. "Yes, here!" He plunged his hand deeper and came up with an old drinking horn. "Just look at this. The ceremonial drinking horn of Ingulf the Saxon. Don't you think it will add verisimilitude to the contents of the chest?"

The horn itself was from some sort of gigantic ox I certainly had never seen. The mouthpiece was in silver and gilt, elaborately carved with twisting lines and set about here and there with small, semiprecious stones. The tip was made in the form of an elaborately carved dragon, whose fangs had a gap apparently made for a chain or cord now missing. It looked very old, crusted with age and neglect, and the silver had turned black.

"Did you age it, Brother Malachi?" I asked. "I've never seen a better job."

"No, it came that way. A fellow alchemist friend of mine was about to reduce it for the metal. But I just had a thought that it might come in handy some day, so I bought it from him." Gilbert picked up the horn and turned it this way and that, a beatific smile playing over his features.

"Malachi, you're an artist," he said.

"Of course he is," said Mother Hilde, her eyes shining with pride.

"Gilbert, don't touch the tarnish. It has to be even all over when it's found."

"I was just wondering. Are these some kind of writing?" he asked, pointing to the elaborate, interwoven, abstract figures.

"If they are, then they're nothing we can read. And if we two accomplished scholars can't read them between us, neither can anyone else. It's just the way the Saxons, or maybe the Danes, did things. Just look at that ugly dragon. It's quite popeyed, and hasn't got a nose worth looking at. Certainly not the way a dragon should look."

"Splendidly barbaric. Even father will be surprised to find this thing in there."

"Surprise is essential. It will give a genuine reaction, and the witnesses will believe the whole thing, because of the fraction of truth in the way they behave. Especially Hugo. Gilbert, I have never been able to conceive of how you acquired a family like that. You must be some sort of freak, like that horse of Caesar's with the toes." Malachi stood, taking his ale with him for inspiration, and headed for the door of his laboratorium.

"I always thought it was the other way around, Malachi—I am an ordinary sort of fellow, and they are the freaks—" Gilbert followed him, ducking through the door, cup in hand.

"On the contrary, Gilbert, they represent the average run of humanity—" The door closed behind them.

"Come round into the garden by the front gate, Margaret. I've beans to pick, and a thousand things to tell you." I picked up the basket from the corner to follow her.

"Margaret, you don't have to do that, you're a great lady now. It isn't proper."

"Mother Hilde," I said, following her around to unlatch the front gate, carrying both of our baskets, "I'm still just me, Margaret. The rest is all—clothing, if you see what I mean. We're just the same as ever, and you'll always be my teacher."

"And doesn't this just remind you of the old days, when Malachi wouldn't let us go through the laboratorium and out the back door, for fear our female essence might undermine one of his experiments?" she said happily.

"Or that our tread was too heavy, and might wiggle some delicate process—as if he had such a light tread himself." Mother Hilde's garden was golden with summer sun, and the fruit hung warm on the trees. In one corner were beehives of twisted straw, and in the other was the shed where Mother Hilde kept her she-ass for milking. Asses' milk and goats' milk are best for babies, she always said, if their own mother's milk fails and the wetnurse can't be got quickly enough. But a she-ass has the virtue of also being able to carry panniers laden with market goods, or Mother Hilde herself, if her feet get tired.

The scent of the roses that climbed all over the shed filled the garden. Malachi may be a genius with metals, but Mother Hilde is a genius with plants. In a sunny corner place by the beehives, she had strange herbs that looked like a tangle of weeds, grown from seeds she had brought back from her pilgrimage abroad, the one she had taken with me when we retrieved Gilbert from that French prison. Beyond the wattled fence of her henyard, amidst the contented clucking, there was a raucous screech.

"I meant to ask you, Mother Hilde, where did you get the peacock?"

"A gift, Margaret, but he's so lovely I can't bear to eat him. And my rooster's jealous of him. Oh, it's a drama these days in my henyard. Let me save a few tailfeathers for your children." As I picked beans from the tall tents of her beanpoles, Mother Hilde let herself into the yard and came out with a handful of feathers. "I don't know whether he just drops them or whether the rooster picks them off, but he certainly has more where these came from." I held them up by my head.

"Look at me, Mother Hilde, now I'm fine and grand." I turned my nose up in a mockery of some court dandy.

"You're fine to me always, Margaret. But my, they are a pretty color. Wouldn't it be elegant if the dyers could color cloth like that?

I'd wear it every day." She took to filling her own basket with the things that had come ripe that day, onions, crabapples, a half-row of turnips.

"I see you're expecting again," she said.

"How did you know so soon, when I wasn't even sure myself until just this week?"

"Well, for one thing, your face is shining and your eyes look happy, and for another thing, Malachi told me," she answered.

"Oh, Mother Hilde, and here I thought your powers were greater than ever."

"Not always great enough. Do you know, Margaret, I was deceived? A wind pregnancy. I'd heard of them, never seen one."

"A wind pregnancy?"

"Yes, and nary a baby growing at all. The goodwife just puffed up on wind. It went on and on. In the tenth month, she started to have labor pains, and they called me. She cried out, she sweated, oh, it all looked so real! But when I'd seated her on the birthing stool, and felt beneath her skirts for the head, there was nothing there. The birth passage was as closed as in a woman who never bore child. 'There's no child here,' I said, and she screamed at me. 'You've stolen it!' she cried. Luckily, there were a dozen witnesses in the room. 'There's no child, there's nothing,' I said to her mother. 'See for yourself.' 'But I felt it moving last week.' 'That is wind,' I said. 'This is a wind pregnancy. Put your head to her belly and listen for a heartbeat. There is none.' She listened, they all listened, and the woman squalled and accused them all. She became a madwoman, Margaret, with eyes like the Devil himself. The labor stopped then and there, and I left to the sound of her howling. I hear now that she is completely mad; she claims she is still pregnant, the wind is still inside, as big as a full-term baby, and she's going on twelve months now. Twelve months! Impossible! But she claims it will be a prodigy, since it is taking longer to grow. God spare me any more wind-children, Margaret. I could have been taken for a witch."

"That is the strangest story I've ever heard. What would make a wind-child, do you think?"

"God. Or the Devil. Or perhaps desire. The woman was barren, and her husband malcontent. Maybe she puffed herself up with some charm or spell." A sing-song humming was coming from the shed, mingling with the buzz of the bees and the chirp of songbirds.

"Peter's in the shed again?" I asked. Mother Hilde was once married, but pestilence carried away her husband and all of her children but Peter, who is not right. He is shaped sacklike and short, rather like a troll, and has odd eyes. He's a kindly fellow who sings and talks a bit, and carries heavy things, but he has no mind. Hilde's other children were tall and handsome and clever, but what God takes, He takes.

"We have new kittens out there, and he sings to them all day. I'm glad to see him so happy," she said, casting an eye at the shed where the roses bloomed in profusion. "When the mother of that wind-child woman asked me what to do, I told her the girl should learn to fill her grief with good works. God sends consolation." Arm in arm, we carried the baskets of sun-warmed garden fruits through the front gate and into the house.

NOW THE ONLY THING more difficult that entertaining relatives unexpected is getting up a family expedition into the country. In the first place, nobody really wants to go, or if they want to go they would rather it be another time, or they don't feel like packing or they feel like packing too much. Then there's hiring the sumpter mules and the drovers which is a great bother. At least we didn't have to ride hired horses which are nothing but trouble, because thanks to the Burgundians who had refilled our empty money chest we had been able to have our horses brought back from the country and could afford to keep them again. Besides, Gilbert's father says there's nothing lower than riding hired horses, and we never would have heard the end of it, all the way to Brokesford.

First of all, we were delayed by Hugo, who complained that he hadn't finished his exploration into the more obscure forms of his worship of God's creations, and that he had heard there was a new woman come into the stews who was a giantess, and he wanted to find out whether she was a giant everywhere and whether she would smother him in passion.

"That's disgusting," I said. "Your appetite gets more abnormal all the time."

"Really, you don't expect me to go back to that dull, demanding woman when I haven't half finished up here." Luckily, Sir Hubert cut short this argument by flinging Hugo across the hall, which gratified Gilbert immensely.

Then there were the girls, who whined, "We don't like step-grandfather's house, Mama. It's all ugly and dirty and broken down, and the rain comes through, and besides, we didn't like it last time."

"It will be nicer this time, and we'll be home before you know it."

"Then why go at all?" said Cecily.

"Yes, we don't like Lady Petronilla. She's a mean, bad lady and she hates us."

"It's much different now. Uncle Hugo likes you now, and step-grandfather will make her be good. Besides, Damien and Robert are there."

"Damien! We love Damien! When will he marry us? We're growing all the time." As only little girls can be, they have been passionately in love with Damien, old Sir Hubert's squire, since they first laid eyes on him. It was his sunshiny smile that won them, and the fact that he was "very, very big, but not old." It was probably also because he had so many sisters and brothers at home that he knew how to deal with them. Unfortunately, their love took the form of throwing things down on him from the windows of the solar, and punching his arm, and hanging onto his leg. It was seeing this that made me first realize that they needed serious instruction in being ladies. "No man loves you back if you hit him," I told them, so they went off and poured water in his boots, all out of sheer adoration. Once again, the magic name did its trick, and they went off to pack—oceans of dresses and hair ribbons and other things designed to win over Damien's affections.

"I take it, I will not be needed on this excursion?" asked Madame, and for the life of me, I couldn't decide whether she meant she wanted to go or she didn't want to go. The only way to tell is by her complexion. It looked very pale. I think she thought it might all be a ruse to get rid of her.

"Now, more than ever, Madame," I answered. "The girls have even more need of instruction in the country than here in the home they're used to."

"The ways of great houses require a deep understanding of chivalry. It is not to be expected that they could have mastered the fine points at their ages." She glided away to pack. That's Madame, I thought. Why don't I always know what to say like that?

Then Mother Sarah complained her bones were too old for travel, and Perkyn said the house would fall apart if I left at such a critical season, and him getting on, to expect him to handle everything.

Gilbert moved in and out of the house, vanishing for long periods, and then conferring with me over the arrangements. Sometimes he whistled to himself, "The Knight Stained from Battle" and other tunes, some religious, some I suspect very bawdy, from his bad old days as a student in Paris, singing drinking songs from tavern to tavern on the left bank.

"What's the arrow chest for?" I asked.

"Malachi's thought of everything. It's for the shovels. If any are missing from the estate or the village, someone's sure to notice. You know what gossips country folk are. So we bring our own, locked up."

"I haven't seen you so content since we were sitting in that awful place in Avignon."

"And Malachi and I were forging alchemical secrets to fund our return home? Margaret, you are sentimental about the most amazing things. But I must admit, there's something refreshing and contenting about putting one over on people who deserve it." He sighed. "I haven't been in trouble for so long, Margaret, it was just getting boring."

"You mean you *miss* writing nasty poems and anonymous denunciations to post on church doors, and getting pursued by inquisitioners and vengeance-seekers?"

"It's the chase, Margaret, the game. Some people like to pursue animals. I like to skewer pompous men of authority."

"Not all the animals are harmless, Gregory."

"Oh, Margaret, will that stay your pet name for me forever? Really, it's embarrassing now that I've risen to the grandeur of a purchased knighthood finagled by father." His eyes glittered with cynical amusement as he spoke. "See it my way. Noble creatures make noble sport. I feel the blood pulsing through my veins for the first time in ages. A lawyer, a corrupt judge, and an entire abbey full of scheming monks! There's a game for you! If we win, father has to acknowledge the superiority of learning forever. Ha! *That* will sting! If we lose, we don't lose much—that gloomy little spot by the water and a lot of oak trees that he might very well take into his head to sell anyway. Either way, the title to the house here stays unencumbered." And he went whistling off to Malachi's place to fetch the brass-bound Saxon chest, made ancient by hanging above the vapors of one of Malachi's glass kettles for the past week.

Of all the people of the household, only Peregrine was truly happy about the trip. "D'ere's *frogs* in the moat," he sang, "frogs, frogs, and teeny tiny baby tadpoles, and Grandfather will give me a horse, a horse, a really truly big one." And he trundled around on his little stick horse shouting orders in imitation of his grandfather. And his grandfather did shout orders: "Take those mules around by the gate! Do you call THAT a packsaddle? Look at that one limp; it's unsound, I say, take it BACK! Gilbert, what in HELL are you taking that arrow-chest for? Oh. I see. That's Madame's luggage? ABSOLUTELY NOT! THAT WOMAN DOES NOT GO! I CAN'T STAND HER!"

"My lord father-in-law, if she does not go, the girls will not be able to go, and if they don't go, I won't go," I said.

"Well," he grumbled, "she does seem to keep them in good order. Not that they aren't a pair of she-devils, mind you."

"You don't want them turned loose in your house without supervision, do you?" I reminded him.

"Right, absolutely right. But keep that woman out of my sight. She makes me furious, the way she thinks she knows everything in the world. I can't be responsible for myself if I see too much of her."

Not that Madame wasn't a good bit of trouble. She delayed everything by checking all the girths herself, and instructing Cecily and Alison on the way a lady should be handed up into the saddle and having them repeat it several times, while everybody fumed. But at last we were mounted and ready, and we made a grand procession. A noisy one, too, for Hugo not only had the latest fashion in dress, he had the latest fashion in harness, and there were little silver bells mounted absolutely everywhere, on the bridle, the saddle, even the crupper on his dandified dapple-gray pacer. With every cheerful little "ring-a-ling" I could sense steam coming out of old Sir Hubert's ears, but he rode, firm and dignified, as the head of a family should, at the head of our caravan, his hounds beside him, and his son and heir behind him.

Gilbert rode just behind the two of them, tall and graceful on the big bay gelding he'd brought back when we came from France, with little Peregrine in his pointed red hat mounted in front of him, clutching the gelding's black mane and exclaiming at every new sight. I just beside them, the picture of female frivolity on my little cream colored mare, with my lap dog tucked up behind the saddle in a big pannier. Hidden in the straw beneath Lion's cushion was the long, flat Saxon chest of unknowable antiquity, filled with the dust of ages, kindly supplied by the mix of fireplace ash and the dust of a big puffball broken up by Brother Malachi as a final "artistic touch." Old as he was, Lion loved his cushion, and no one would dare approach the pannier without his barking a warning. Behind us came the girls, double mounted on a big sorrel gelding, and Madame, straight and dignified on a little black mare. Then came a train of baggage and drovers. Around us, before and behind, were the armed grooms from the manor, without whom no one respectable can hope to go safely, in this world of wickedness.

As we passed by the tall, bright-painted houses and high-steepled churches of the city that I loved, and through Bishopsgate into the rolling, summer-scented countryside beyond the walls, all I could think was, the sooner we're done and away from Brokesford, the better. I'd reason enough not to be fond of the place, even then.

CHAPTER THIRTEEN

BROKESFORD MANOR LOOKED EXACTLY the same, if not worse. Memory had never bathed it in golden light, and time had not mellowed it. There it stood, looming above the village, a miserable tumbledown heap, behind walls left to decay and a moat rotten with sewage. It was horses that had stolen the roof slates and caused the stones to fall from the wall. It was horses that had stripped the walls of all but weaponry and souvenirs of dead animals, set the moths in the chests, and impoverished the village. War and horses, to be exact. Sir Hubert's attempt to breed the perfect English destrier and the fact that every so often those destriers, expensive and delicate as they were, demanding of grooms, feed, training, and arming, had to be taken abroad and slaughtered. True, there was compensation in theory, but it was often slow in coming. So for the sake of glory and his chief passion, the meadows of Brokesford supported nothing that could give him milk, hides, or wool. The fruits and grain of Brokesford went to market for the work of armorers and smiths, and his stables were better kept than his house.

As we rode through the village, it looked as unprosperous and neglected as before. A few women with babies on their hips came to the door of their wattle and thatch cottages, and bobbed their heads in greeting. All the men and women who were able were at the haying, as we could see in the distance. The heat of August lay heavily on the land, and I could feel sweat running from beneath my headdress. Dogs and little boys ran beside us as we passed the church, where a handful of old men sunning themselves in the churchyard came out to

bow humbly and ask the Lord of Brokesford if he had brought them
a new priest.

"Soon, soon," he said, handing them a few quarter-farthings. "I'm
to confer with the Bishop before Saint Austin's Day, and until then,
my own confessor will come regularly on Sundays. You'll not be
without consolations of the spirit." As we took the last leg of the
dusty road up to the manor gates, he said to Gilbert, "as if they were
ever interested in consolation of the spirit before. But ever since Sir
Roger fell into the pond, the moiety of them wish there were considerably more Christianity around here—fasts, flagellations, all-
night vigils—the sort of thing you used to annoy me with—" I saw
Gilbert's jaw tighten. He had always considered his father's attitude
toward religion far too lax.

"The moiety? And what about the rest?"

"Oh, they worship the pond. Just as they always did."

"And where is my loving lady? I expected her to greet me," announced Hugo as he strode into the hall. The baggage had been put
away and the drovers sent back with the mules, and Hugo paused in
the center of his father's great hall, looking at the solar staircase in
expectation. In summer the chickens don't live in the hall, but there
were plenty of hounds lolling around on the filthy rushes. I would
wear pattens in these rushes, if it would not be an insult, but instead
I brought old shoes that I used in the garden. Good things are
wasted in this house. The train of my Sunday dress I pin up so it does
not touch the floor, but only let it down in the chapel, which usually
stands so vacant that even the dogs forget to go and follow nature
there.

Up in the rafters above the hearth, hams and haunches of venison
hang, to get the advantage of the smoke that usually rises up through
the louvres day and night. Folk here think it a treat to reach down
the leg of some long-dead animal, hard with salt and smoke, green
and slimy within and without, and slice it up to eat with rare and
elaborate ceremony. I do not eat dead things, which makes them
think me odd, but the eyes of those pitiful creatures would appear

to me in my dreams if I ate them, and I prefer not to have them on my conscience. Last time I was here, I caused a great argument about the nature of oysters, which was purely theoretical because there are no oysters here. I said if they were, I would not have them, because since they could open and close their shells there might be some hidden eyes that I might not know about, and Sir Hubert said that Gilbert should beat such fancies out of me, and he said no, and there was a disagreement in which furniture was thrown. In other houses they play chess and hear music after supper, but these are not the style of Brokesford Manor. The main hearthfire in the center of the hall was out, and in deference to the heat they were cooking outside in the courtyard, where I heard the squalls of a pig being slaughtered in celebration of the lord's return. I felt my stomach turn, and for a brief moment wondered if they had eaten all the eggs that day.

Not seeing Lady Petronilla, Hugo went and shouted up the solar stair for her. His voice echoed loudly, for the solar stair, being stone and built essentially like a tube or a rising cavern, carries sound well when the doors at the top and bottom of it are open. It is circular, built into the wall, with slots above it for raining down arrows and boiling oil on people whose presence is not desired upstairs. The doors at the foot and the head—heavy, studded oak—are marked with old scars from times gone by, when unwanted guests tried to hammer them down with battleaxes. I myself prefer a pleasant, hospitable home, airy and bright, with real glass windows, cozy wood paneling, and neat whitewashing. In short, exactly what I have, and do not ever wish to mortgage to save any portion of this grim, squalid estate.

As I was seeing to the disposal of Lion's basket and Peregrine, who is too young to know the difference between clean and dirty, was fishing for bones in the rushes, Lady Petronilla's old nurse made an appearance at the foot of the stairs.

"My lady sends her deepest apologies," she said, dipping low before Sir Hugo. "She is in a delicate state, too weak to rise." Behind me, I heard Madame sniff. I knew what she'd say: the lady of the house, no matter if half-dead, should rise to greet guests, and offer to bathe the feet of her husband and possibly any visiting knight with her own fair white hands. If three-quarters dead, she should send her pucelles. But of course, Brokesford had no pucelles. What family would send girls to be educated in a place where there was no great lady to instruct them? Brokesford had no pages, either, for the same reason. I always regarded Lady Petronilla as a woman who wanted her advantages, but never lived up to her responsibilities. And that is the kindest thing I can say, considering what she tried to do to me on my last visit.

"Delicate?" said Hugo, a hopeful look in his eyes.

"Delicate," said Goody Wilmot, the hairs in her chin aquiver with hidden meaning.

"Don't count your chickens before they're hatched," growled the old lord. But Hugo, being the gullible sort, took exactly the meaning that was intended, and went bounding up the stair.

"Where's Damien?" asked Cecily, looking about hopefully as Sir Hugo's squire, the ever-cynical Robert, came in from exercise at the quintain. He smiled a malicious smile. "*Sir* Damien has gone a-courting, the deceptive rogue," he answered. "You will have to make do with me."

"*Sir* Damien?" I asked, hoping to avert the storm.

"Sir, and most unfairly, too, if I do say so. The king asked for volunteers at the gates of Montrouge, for a mission of certain death, and offered instant knighthood in the bargain. Young Colart d'Ambréticourt, curiously enough, could not find his helmet and so declined the honor. I, regrettably, had misplaced my breastplate. Damien the ever-needy leapt at the chance. None returned but him, as Fortuna would have it, and he is now a hero, with the king's favor, a knighthood, and a tidy little property in the bargain. A disgusting turn of events, and entirely unjustified by his native qualities."

"He's got a knighthood, and he didn't come to get me on his white horse?" Cecily was bitter.

"It's me he was coming for," said Alison, and Cecily stamped on her foot.

"What is the name of the lady?"

"Rose, the second daughter of Sir Thomas de Montagu."

"I hate her," said Alison.

"Betrayed!" cried Cecily, "I will never love another! His cruelty has pierced my heart!"

"I'm sure I'm much prettier," said Alison.

"He was supposed to *wait*," said Cecily.

"I'll grow up and *fix* him," said Alison.

"You will *not*," I said. "You'll behave." But both sisters had started to howl. Madame put her cool white hand on Alison's shoulder.

"The usual course that a lady takes, when betrayed by her one true love, is to enter a nunnery," she announced.

"A nunnery?" said Alison. "My hair is too pretty to cut off."

"There's nothing left. I'll *devote* myself to prayer and contemplation," announced Cecily. A strange, ironic little smile flitted across Madame's face.

"So be it," she said, "you must begin by humbling yourself. Possibly picking up your own things would be a start."

"I was thinking more of carrying alms to the poor."

"In you, Cécile, that would be pride," said Madame, her face impassive. "But perhaps you can make a start on it, and help carry the baskets for the lord's almoner." Somehow, the juxtaposition of Madame's idealized view of chivalry and the reality of this place had a certain charm. The visit was looking up.

"The lord has no almoner here," I said.

"Well then, his chaplain, when he takes the *tranchers* to the poor after supper tonight."

"The chaplain is a drunk and a lay-about. The dogs eat the trenchers."

"That is hardly appropriate," said Madame.

"Rose, Rose, Rose, I hate her," said Alison. And suddenly I feared that here in the country, with the infinite new possibilities for trouble that the place presented, and without the spur of adoration to keep them in order, Madame's bridle of fine manners and French might well fail the test. Lord, get us out of here before they do something truly horrible, I prayed silently.

WHEN DAME PETRONILLA CAME DOWN, followed close at hand by her old nurse and the confessor she had brought from her father's house, it was for supper, and she looked very strange indeed. Though it was summer and she no widow, she was dressed in a heavy, furlined black surcoat over a kirtle of green so dark as to be almost black itself. The honey blonde hair beneath her veil was coiled tightly beside her ears in two silver mesh crespinettes. Though younger than I, she had the look of someone who had aged abnormally. Her face was puffy and yellowish white, with strange brownish stains, like very large, faded freckles. Her eyes glittered and darted about the room, catching on this one and that one, then fixing on me.

"Why, *Lady* Margaret, where's your son?" she asked, her smile wide and eerie. There was something coming off her, like a scent or a feeling, that made the hair stand up on the back of my neck.

"The children eat apart," I said. How could the men in the room stand there, so unknowing, not feeling the strange thing I felt?

"Quite right, quite right," said Hugo, "my good lady is nervous in her condition." The others went on talking about hunting, and things that happened in France.

"And you, you have come to flaunt yourself with another pregnancy. I see everything now; I see the secrets people are hiding——" I could feel in her eyes some abnormal, sharpened perception. It was true; she could see what others usually ignore, or are blind to. I could tell, and it made my skin crawl. "——you are a crass little thing, you use your son to climb to favor. But I, I have a son, too. A son more highborn, the heir." She smiled a secretive smile.

"This time, we'll be more careful. Everything will be at your hand," announced Hugo grandly. How could he not know something was wrong? But now her eye caught on Madame, steady and pale in her black gown, who was taking in everything. I looked at her, I saw her eyes, and knew that Madame felt what I felt, too.

"You don't approve of me, do you? Who are you, woman in black, and why do you follow Margaret like a shadow?"

"Dame Petronilla, allow me to present to you Dame Agathe, who dwells with our household."

"You will not sit at the dais."

"Madame is a lady born, and of our family, through distant connections."

"I'll not have a black shadow near me, near me. She will steal the child from my womb. I know, I know, she takes from one and gives to another. That one is mine, mine that is gone, that you took," she said, pointing to my belly where nothing, as yet, even showed.

"Don't you dare touch me," I said, standing to my full height and speaking firmly. Fearing me, she turned on Madame, so frail and pallid, who had to speak and act so carefully in a household where she was dependent.

"You—it's you. Put her out, put her out, I say," she shrieked suddenly, and flew at Madame with her hands like claws, to rake her with her nails. Gilbert and I caught her wrists, and as he touched her, she looked at him with an odd look, something like awe, and became quiet.

"Come now, come now, my sweetest," said her old nurse, who had been standing silently at her elbow.

"Ha! This proves it!" cried Hugo, ever oblivious. "She really is in a delicate condition! Women like this are always a little unstable. Are there any little treats or rare fruits you crave?"

"There's rare fruits I'd taste," she said, looking sideways at Gilbert, and again, my skin crawled. "But I'll get them for myself," she said, her eyes bright.

"My dear one has been frail, since coming home from the Duke's court," said the nurse.

"Perhaps, Madame, it would be best if you rested again in your chamber, and had supper sent up," said her confessor, Brother Paul, a wiry Austin friar, longtime in her family, whose back always seemed slightly bent in a permanent suppliant posture.

"Sound like that's for the best," boomed Sir Hubert, settling the matter. "Madame, you must look after yourself, for the sake of the heir." Was it possible? I thought I saw a bulge beneath her heavy surcoat.

"Oh, yes," she said, looking up at Sir Hubert with a melting look. "That's true. I have more than one to think about," and casting her glittering eyes about the room, she allowed herself to be led back upstairs to the chamber in the tower she shared with Hugo, their hounds, hawks, and body servants.

"YOU *BIT* THAT BREAD, ALISON. That's disgusting, and now it can't be given away. Into the dog basket with it." I watched as Cecily flung away the bread, and Alison picked it out of the basket to inspect it.

"I didn't do that," she said, turning it over several times.

"You did so. Those are your teeth marks. I know them. Besides, they're too small for anybody else's."

"They're yours," announced Alison, "and you're blaming me."

"They're not. My life is far too tragic now to go around biting off bread. Nuns never forget to break their bread off. I'm thinking of taking the religious name, 'Mary,' after Our Lady of Sorrows. My lot is grief, grief forever." Madame's eyes were amused, but I found it hard not to snort.

"Mademoiselle Cécile," said Madame, "your stitches have grown fine enough that you might work with me on embroidering an altarcloth."

"*My* stitches are just as fine as Cecily's. I want to, too."

"They are *not,* besides, your fingers are always dirty—"

"Mademoiselle Alison, you may be allowed to do the plain stitching, but only if you are very, very good," announced the wily Madame.

It was bright midday sun, just after the dinner hour, and Madame was overseeing the packing up of the scraps and trenchers into baskets, one for the dog kennels, one for the poor. It had been the storm of storms, when Madame fixed her eye on Sir Hubert and asked permission to make herself useful in her own humble way by assisting his chaplain in taking the leftovers to the poor.

"Are you questioning my largesse?" shouted my grim-faced father-in-law.

"What?" she said, innocently, "you mean you don't have the trenchers taken away? Well, I suppose in this shire, customs are different. I am so sorry, I am a stranger here. I deeply and humbly apologize, and beg your forgiveness for my crude presumption." He might have calmed down with the apology, but she had overdone with the "crude presumption" part. It smelled of irony, and of the sort of malicious defiance he traditionally associated with my own lord husband, his troublemaking son Gilbert. Since he had to stay on good terms with Gilbert until they found an opportune moment to bury the chest, he shouted at Madame instead.

"I distribute ALMS on FEAST DAYS! I give ROBES to CONVERTS on Whitsunday! The LORD GOD does not command that we STRIP OURSELVES!"

"Ah, I see. You must have many adult converts on Whitsundays." Actually, I believe there was one once. A poor simpleton whose parents had thought he would die, and never bothered to baptize him as a child. It was quite an event. But Sir Hubert was always of making one case into many, when the occasion required it.

"Why would you REWARD the SLOTHFUL?" he shouted.

"What of the poor widows and orphans?" she asked.

"I haven't GOT any! They're looked AFTER!" He knew he was on shaky ground now, so he shouted louder.

"By whom?" she asked.

"By their FAMILIES, as is PROPER!"

"But you do believe in assisting widows and orphans, don't you?"

"Do you QUESTION my devotion to CHIVALRY?"

Having backed him into a corner, she then asked if she could by any chance locate a worthy poor widow or orphan or crippled beggar, could she distribute the trenchers.

"Not the crippled beggars, by God. We'd be having them a-swarming from every village in the shire."

That was as good as permission, and so here she was, instructing the future nuns on their charitable duties. It was a wise course, for it kept them away from Lady Petronilla as much as possible.

NOW THERE WAS a virtue to all those charitable activities that we hadn't planned on, but was very useful. What with all that hurrying in and out of the village church with baskets, and measuring for the altar cloth and checking through the other altar linens and finding them lacking or altogether shabby, our presence became unremarkable. That solved the one problem that my lord husband foresaw with the plan, which was planting the letter that explained all about how the deed had been buried for safekeeping. If it was found in the manor, it might look a bit dubious, but if Gilbert went down to the church and fussed among the records, everyone would know, and that would be dubious, too. But as Malachi said, "You've a brain, Gilbert. Just think of something once you get there."

So one bright morning when we were off to take a posset to a poor, sick, but worthy orphan, Gilbert just slipped the letter into my hand and said, "You know, today is a good day, while you're measuring linens and all, to count the candlesticks in the big chest where they keep the church records. I'm thinking I might want to donate a silver candlestick in gratitude for my safe return. But if they have too many, I might just donate a paten instead." I knew exactly what he meant and slipped that letter down the front of my surcoat. So even though the nave was aswarm with folk, and Father Cedric was hearing confessions in one corner and the girls were doling out leftover white bread to the toothless old men that usually snoozed in the churchyard sun, nobody even noticed when I slipped down the stairs and into the narrow vault below the altar to count the candlesticks. I opened the big chest where the old parish record books were mildewing gently in the damp, and took out that nice, aged, pre-mildewed letter and slipped it in among the pages of the oldest looking register. At the sound of footsteps on the stair, I shut the chest lid and exclaimed, "Three candlesticks! He'd be better off giving the paten!—Oh, Madame, there you are. How can I help?"

"The girls have distributed the bread. Where did you set the posset?"

"Upstairs with the children's smocks the girls sewed." So there you had it. As swift as Reynard the fox takes the best hen, and is never seen again.

"Dame Margaret," said Madame, as we walked down the only street in the village, "there is something I must apologize to you for. It has weighed heavy on my conscience these last few days." Beyond the village, the brook rushed and sparkled in the summer sun.

"Dame Agathe, you owe no apology that I can think of."

"Madame, there was an unpardonable rudeness when I last left your house. I had thought that your lust drove you to your husband's clerk. But I know now from the chaplain that your marriage was forced."

"The old man wanted to get his hands on Master Kendall's money," I said.

"Your husband has an honorable heart. I misjudged him. I misjudged you. And yet you in your charity offered me a place at the high table. You are a true Christian, Madame, and I apologize from the depths of my heart."

"But, Madame, you have greatly uplifted the morals of my daughters. For that I am very thankful. If forgiveness is needed, I freely offer it." Madame looked very relieved. Then she inspected the girls capering in front of her, and watched as they quickly glanced back before they took off their shoes and began dancing in the water of the brook, steppingstones forgotten.

"As for the uplift, that is temporary," she said, "but one must make hay while the sun shines."

"Madame, did you have children?"

"Why, yes," she said, watching as the girls were joined by the poor cottar's children, half naked, that they had come to clothe. Shrieking and splashing, they galloped about in the water. "I had four girls and three boys. Two died as infants. Only one lives now. She is a nun; her father did not wish to provide for her." Madame looked away from me as she spoke. What could I say? How does one go on?

Madame's petty tyrannies, her threadbare decencies, all made more sense than ever to me now.

"When I see you with your lord husband, and what has grown between you, I understand that you created love out of duty, and that such things are possible, and I respect you for it."

"One must do what one can on this earth," I answered, not knowing what to say. We were stepping across the rushing green brook on the stones. For a while we were silent, until we stood on the other bank.

"Dame Margaret, is it really true that you ransomed your husband by wagering your virtue for his freedom in a game of dice, and then used loaded dice?" Her face turned surprisingly pink for her, and it was clear from the expression on it that she had been dying to ask me that question for a long time.

"It is," I answered.

"Oh, Dame Margaret," she exclaimed, "where on earth did you get the dice?" We were laughing very hard, when we reached the little hut where the sick woman lay.

The woman was the daughter of Goody Ann, the midwife, who was without land, and without a living now that her mother had died. She earned a bit of bread sitting with the sick and washing the dead, and sold bad remedies made of herbs, for she had not absorbed enough of her mother's wisdom while she lived. I knew the illness well, not fatal, nor of a danger to any but herself, but her legs were swollen up and she was weak and thought herself ready to die.

"Bless you, bless you, great ladies, so different than the she-wolf that reigns in the manor house." We shook up the straw in her bed and made her comfortable. As we poured out the posset she began to pour out talk, and at last, thinking she was on her deathbed, asked us to send for the priest and told us the secret that had been languishing inside of her. Her mother, she believed, had not slipped in the dark, but was pushed off the high outer staircase of the manor tower. "Sure footed she was, and I was walking right before her, holding her things at the bottom. And I swear I heard footsteps leaving, even as she cried out, 'Jesus save me!'"

"Why, that's a terrible thing," I said. "Who would push her off like that?"

"That is the secret they wanted no one to tell. When they called her to attend the lady of the manor, they made me wait outside the door, but I heard it. I heard my mother say, 'This is no child.' I tell you, it was a monster born that evening. A devil with horns and cloven hooves that they strangled in secret. Then she took to wearing black and pretending grief, all the while trying to bring another devil to this earth." Promising to call the priest, we backed out of the low door of the hovel to join the children in the sunshine. There were Cecily and Alison, still wading in the brook, trying to catch dragonflies in their hands.

"If it were a devil, everyone would know. They'd have to get rid of the body, wouldn't they?" Madame asked, her mind full of good sense.

"What she heard the midwife say was, 'This is no child.' The rest might well be what she imagined from hearing that. Dame Agathe, I think it was a wind-baby."

CHAPTER FOURTEEN

J UST BEYOND THE MANOR MALT-HOUSE there is a little garden of herbs and roses, which I found sadly neglected at my first visit, and set to going again. Now on a fine summer morning I was down there repairing the remains of my handiwork, having taken the children with me to show them some of the wisdom Mother Hilde taught me about plants. Tall white clouds were blowing across the sky, and when one of them passed, a shadow would cross over the little garden, and then vanish, leaving it in sun again.

"Oh, look here how big the sage has grown. That's good for melancholy and sweating sickness." Peregrine, in a baby dress and old leggings cut off at the ankle, was intently digging the dirt by the comfrey plants, which had managed to reseed themselves in a big clump. His gaze was intent as he turned up a little rock, a worm, a bug with many legs that hurried away.

"This one's fennel, mama," said Alison, breaking off a little branch of it to chew on. She was barefoot, wearing nothing but a summer smock, her red-gold hair shining down her back. Someday she will be a beauty, I thought.

"Me, too," said Peregrine, looking up, and Alison broke him off one.

"It can grow there because the sun on the wall makes the spot warm," I said.

"Mother Hilde talks to plants," said Cecily. "Is that why hers grow better than anybody's?"

"I don't know. I suppose anybody can talk to plants, but that doesn't mean the plants listen. That's where Mother Hilde is different. She can talk to just about anything and it seems to understand her." While I spoke, I started tying up an espaliered vine that had slid from its moorings and was growing all along the ground in a tumble.

"Look in the clouds," said Alison, pointing up. "They look like things. See? There's a roast duck, and there's a pile of oatcakes and a bee-hive."

"I see a horse and a lion right up there in the big one," said Cecily.

"No, that's the oatcakes."

"I see a green lady," said Peregrine.

"Clouds aren't green," said Alison.

"The lady is green," said Peregrine. "She has a dress all weedy-wet. Her nurse needs to get her a dry one."

"And does she ride a pink horse with wings?"

"No horse, just muddy shoes, and fishes that swim in her toes."

"If she's wearing shoes, then her toes don't show," said Cecily.

"Yes they do," said Peregrine, and went back to digging in the dirt with the garden trowel. A shadow seemed to cross us, and I looked up. It wasn't a cloud, it was the old lord, looking at us intently, silently. He had come upon us as quiet as a cat, and just stood there for I don't know how long.

"Dame Margaret, take the trowel from him." But when I went to take it, he set up a howl.

"Peregrine," said the old lord, his voice not yet fierce, but a storm clearly on the horizon, "lords do not garden. Lords ride. Peasants garden."

"Peregrine digs and finds things. Where's my bug? Mama, get me my bug, I want to show gran'papa."

"Your bug's run away, Peregrine, now put down the trowel for your grandfather."

"When you're bigger, I'll take you badger-hunting. We'll dig and find better than a bug," said the old man. I don't remember when I'd ever seen him so mellow. The shouting storm I'd anticipated seemed to have blown away.

"Come to the stable-yard with me. I've got something for little Peregrine," he said, and astonished, I watched as he hoisted the baby

up on his shoulders. I could feel the irritation of the little girls behind me, as they watched him stride past the paddock. Hugo and
Gilbert were leaning on the top rail, inspecting a yearling being
cantered on a lunge line.

"I don't like his action," Gilbert was saying. "See where the hind
foot strikes?"

"He's the best father's got this year—"

"Maybe when he's shod—"

Their head turned in astonishment at the sight of their ferocious
sire, with the curly-headed boy mounted on his shoulders.

"Did he ever do that with you?" asked Gilbert in amazement.

"Not that I recall," said Hugo, "but he did throw me downstairs
once."

"That's not the same," said Gilbert, as they abandoned their post
by the rail to follow us.

"John, bring out the SURPRISE," the old man roared from the
center of the stableyard.

"Gran'papa, my horsie," said Peregrine when he saw the groom
lead the little mountain pony from the stable door. Black as pitch
and round as a barrel, its short legs close to the ground, the creature had a wily little face with a blaze down the front, and a single
white foot. But it was not the pony that astounded, even though the
old man had always made it clear he would never have anything less
than fifteen hands on his place, it was the saddle and bridle, a tiny
duplicate of the old man's own war harness. There it was, high cantle
and saddle bar, brass embossed leather breastplate and crupper, the
most indulgent gift I had ever seen given to any mortal child. I
could feel my jaw drop. I turned and looked at Hugo and Gilbert.
Their jaws had dropped too. The old man mounted his crowing
grandchild on the pony while two grooms held the bridle. Then he
stepped back and folded his arms to admire his handiwork.

"No more scholarship, no more damned bells. My grandson will
be a *knight*," he growled, looking sideways at his sons and smiling
with a certain grim triumph. "John, take the boy out to the paddock

and lead him around. I want to see how he takes to it. Sit up STRAIGHT, Peregrine, yes, that's IT! See that? Not even three years old, and he sits like a KING!"

As we all followed the pony to the paddock, I could hear Cecily sigh. So did Gilbert. He looked down from his great height at the unruly red head with its fuzzy braid. His dark eyes were knowing.

"It's not *fair*," she said, her face turned down, her bare feet treading in the dust. I remembered her request to Brother Malachi.

"Cecily," he said, sighing equally deeply, "there's not much that's fair on this earth."

"I like to ride, too," she said.

"I'll ask father if you two can take Old Brownie," he said. "The good thing is that he won't be fussy about him, and you can go where you like."

"I s'pose that's good enough," said Alison, interrupting.

"Father," said Cecily, "I embroidered that altar cloth for hours, I've said prayers every morning and every night, and carried all those baskets down to the church and been polite to everybody. I've been *good,* father, and I haven't climbed trees or *anything*."

"I know exactly what you mean," he answered, his voice grave and understanding, "I've been good, too." Two grooms were leading the pony around in a circle, while his grandfather shouted orders.

"Heels DOWN, boy, don't hold on!" Peregrine beamed, and the loafing peasants who always seemed to turn up when anything interesting was going on applauded and cheered.

"Hurrah for the little lord!" they cried. Above the paddock loomed Brokesford's single tower, flat topped and round. At the narrow window, a flash of something caught my eye. It darted away, and then was there again. It was a woman's face, white with hatred.

LAUNDRESSES WERE BOILING the linens over the courtyard fire when Lady Petronilla stormed past. One was stoking the fire while another stirred the heavy, wet stuff with a stick. Margaret had just sent the girl up with the empty basket for the tablecloths. Her old dog, a little creature that looked like a mound of animated, unravelled rope, had followed her out, wheezing, and now trailed at her hems.

"Not them, too," said the woman with the stick.

"Everything," said Margaret. "I swear, you haven't done them since the last time I visited—oh, where's she going like that?"

"She does that when she's angry sometimes. She just rides that mare of hers until it's nearly dead. Well, better the mare than me, I say. She'll take that little whip of hers to anyone when she's in that mood."

"Where does she go?" asked Margaret, as they stood and watched her vanish in the direction of the stables.

"Here, there, and everywhere. She's the ridingest lady anyone ever saw. She outrides her grooms—oh, look, here comes her confessor. He doesn't want her riding alone. He'll follow."

Brother Paul was following with long, lithe steps. Curious, thought Margaret, he's usually all bent over from all his bowing like that untrellised vine. Awhile after the first furious burst of hoofbeats sounded out the main gate, they heard another horse.

"Oh, here's the napkins," said Margaret as the girl with the basket came back down the courtyard steps. "Just throw them in the boiler with everything else, they couldn't be any nastier." At that moment, the woman with the stirring pole could not decide which she preferred. Lady Petronilla was violent, but she was easy, and never noticed anything but what she wanted at that very moment. Lady Margaret, now, was even-tempered but sharp-eyed. She was always poking and prying and cleaning up. You'd think she was mistress, the way she ordered things done and the old lord let her have her way. Still, she'd soon be gone and they wouldn't have to do the linens for another year or two at least, until Lady Margaret came back.

Dame Petronilla rode astride at a full gallop, her veil, tightly pinned to her knotted hair, flying like a pennant, her skirts up to her shins, showing her soft leather hunting boots. Her bay mare was heavily lathered as she left planted land and crossed the meadow. At the far side of the meadow, lounging along in the middle of the brook, was Old Brownie, carrying two barefoot redheaded girls on his broad, bare, swayed back. Every so often he would tug on the reins, and put his head back down to drink. Behind him, a groom mounted on a little cob waited for the girls on the sandy bank.

"Look, there goes Lady Petronilla," said Alison. Cecily pulled up Old Brownie's head, and quit letting him slosh along in the brook. As he climbed the bank, she said,

"Alison, quit *pinching,* I'm going to be black and blue."

"I'm sitting on the fat part, do you want me to fall off? There's no place to get on again. John will have to lift me, and he'll grumble."

"John, where's she going so fast?"

"I don't know, but her confessor's right behind. See there? It's not right for a lady to ride alone. That old nurse, and that confessor she brought from home, they look after her like a baby. If you knew what I knew——"

"We know already. She's crazy mean. Let's follow." Petronilla slowed to a walk at the edge of the woods, and they saw Brother Paul catch up with her. For a moment they talked, then, much to their surprise, instead of riding on together, Brother Paul rode off in the direction of Wymondley, and Petronilla went on alone.

Ahead of them, they could tell by the new hoofprints in the soft, leafy earth which direction Petronella had taken.

"Look at that, she's going to the spring," said Cecily.

"You girls know the spring?" said the groom, surprised.

"Of course we do. When we were here last, mother used to cart down the water in barrels for making ale. She said it was cleaner, and gave a better taste." Dappled sun poured through the green leaves of the oak canopy above them. Old Brownie's hoofs made a soft thudding sound, and the smell of rotting leaves and growing things rose to them, mingling with the damp, sweaty smell of the old horse's coat.

"Well, it's not cleaner *now,*" said the groom, in a knowing voice.

"It's never that clean," said Cecily, who refused to acknowledge knowing less that a groom.

"Yes," said Alison. "Fishes live in it. And do you know what they do? They *pee* in it. That's what you're drinking. Fish pee. Unless you turn it into ale." She was disappointed to see that the groom was unphased.

"There's more than fishes in there now," he answered with a sly grin. "There's a *dead body*. And they dragged the pond with hooks, and couldn't ever get it back." But rather than engendering horror in his listeners, the groom had aroused macabre fascination.

"Really? Whose body?" asked Cecily, her voice nonchalant.

"A *priest's*. He took down the rags on the rock, and the pond just *sucked* him in out of vengeance."

"Oh, so that's where he went," observed Alison. "Noboby would ever tell us. They just got quiet."

"Did he scream and gurgle?" asked Cecily.

"Oh, yes, and cried out prayers, but all were useless, in the face of that devil in the pond."

"There's a *devil*? Is it red and fiery? Did you see it?"

"Nobody sees it. There's some as worships it, but I put my faith in Jesus Christ and stay out of the pond, though I have to drink the water. We all do. When we get our new priest, we'll have him do an exorcism. Then the pond will be clean again."

"Listen, I can hear it. She's there." They paused behind the gray, overgrown ruins of the old stones by the yew temple. Quiet as cats, the little girls slid off the horse and handed the bridle to the groom. Silently, they crept over the dead leaves and hid behind the great stone at the edge of the pond. It was bereft now, without the faded rags flapping all over its surface. It was a light, spotted gray color, with a bit of a sparkle where the sun hit it and shaped like a huge ovoid. It had not been stood upright on its broader end by the hand of nature. At the center of the green pond, the spring bubbled up with force, like a cauldron on the boil. At the edge of the spring stood Lady Petronilla, chanting something incomprehensible. Her eyes were starting in her head; her skin had gone bad again, yellowish brown, her face looked swollen. Loose strands of her hair were flying around her face, though her veil, attached with long pins to her hair, had not fallen away. The words seemed to be English, but they were all mixed up, meaningless, and sung in a toneless howl that made them difficult to decipher.

Then as she began to walk "sunward" around the pool, the girls shrank back so as not to be discovered. Something about her, something like a scent, made the hair stand up all over their bodies. At the far side of the pool, Petronilla knelt down. She was drinking—no—kissing the waters, pouring them down her bosom. The girls peered at her, fascinated. Beyond the stones, the groom saw her, too, and shuddered at the sight, crossing himself.

She stood, her mouth and dress dripping, and they saw her take something from the wallet at her waist, next to the dagger she always wore. With a fierce gesture, she flung it into the water. It floated far into the pool, on top of the water like a little boat, and swirled around the roiling water at the center of the pool.

"Take it, take it!" she cried, eyes blazing.

"Look Cecily, it's Peregrine's *shoe*," whispered Alison. "The one mama made. She'll be very angry."

"What do you want? Money? Blood? Oh, yes, you shall have them, have them all." Lady Petronilla began to laugh wildly. She took her wallet and turned out the copper coins in it and flung them into the water. They plashed and vanished onto the bottom. Suddenly she turned on her heel. "Betrayer!" she shrieked, and fled to her tethered mare.

"I'm getting that for mother," said Cecily, stepping into the shallow water near the great stone. Peregrine's shoe was growing waterlogged now, the light, soft doeskin grown dark and heavy. It swirled in the eddies beyond the upwelling waters, tantalizingly just beyond reach.

"Cecily, it's deep," said Alison. "There's a hole in the middle."

"It's not deep here. Hand me that branch, then hold onto my dress." Carefully, she felt with her bare feet. The soft silt squished up between her toes. Yes, there was bottom here. She took another step. The little slipper was soaked through now, but it still drifted on the surface as if something were holding it up, tempting her to step farther. Cecily took another step. The watching groom dismounted, abandoning the horses and running to the side of the pond.

"Come back, it will suck you in!" he cried.

"Got it!" shouted Cecily, neatly hooking the little shoe with the branch, just as it began to sink.

"God be praised!" cried the groom, as he saw her pull back from the bubbling depths.

"Look at all the money and little things in here," said Alison, who was wading in the shallows and peering down beneath the surface, where she could just barely see her feet through the green.

"Don't take them, they belong to the pond," cried the horrified groom from the shore. Not for all the money in Christendom would he have set one foot into the pond, with its deceptively tranquil surface and ever-boiling center. It had sucked down a priest, and now it had sucked away Lady Petronilla's mind, just as sure as could be.

"The pond hasn't taken them," cried Alison, "Here you are! Here you are!" Laughing and shouting, she scooped up the little offerings that lay in the silt and flung them toward the center of the pond. Then she began to dance in the shallow water, arms up, spinning and singing.

"It's cool and nice!" cried Cecily, who had tied the little shoe around her wrist so she wouldn't lose it. Then she, too, began to run and dance. "Come in with us!" Green water splashed up at every step, wetting their light summer smocks and gluing them to their bodies. Shafts of light piercing the green leaves above shone on their flying hair, making gold lights wherever it touched. Birds called from the dark temple of yews. Then they scooped up water and drenched each other, laughing and shrieking at each other.

"Stop, stop!" cried the groom, who had grown up at his grandmother's fireside, and had heard from her the secret of the pond. The pond was the source of all that grew. No one, no one, dared set foot in it since ancient days, except . . .

The bubbling at the center stopped. The groom fell to his knees and crossed himself, praying.

"Look Cecily, it's quit gurgling," said Alison, pointing to the center. The waters were still, very still. The two girls stood, dripping wet, the green water lapping softly at their knees. Something was moving from the center of the pond, something dark and smooth, swimming with a long, undulant movement.

"It's true," whispered the groom as he saw the shadowy shape. "It's all true."

"Look, Alison, it's the biggest eel I ever did see," said Cecily, pointing to the swimming shape.

"Hold still, it's swimming all around us. Look, I can see its eyes. Ooo. It's swimming around my legs. It tickles."

"Will it bite?" asked Cecily, as the huge eel swam around her ankles.

"It didn't bite *me*," announced Alison. The groom scarcely dared move. He felt his breath stopping in his throat. He watched the dark shadow ripple across the pond, just under the surface, and vanish. A few little bubbles showed at the center of the pond, shining half-circles floating up, reflecting dark yews and specks of light on their shining surfaces. Then there were more bubbles, and more again. The center of the pond made a sound like, "blorp, blorp," and began once again to boil and bubble as if it had never ceased.

"Look, now it's started again."

"The eel must live in the deep part. I can't see him at all now."

"The sun's very low, Cecily, do you think we've missed supper? I saw them making leche lombard this morning." Looking about, they saw the groom still on his knees, saying his beads, and the horses straying.

"Look, John, the horses have gone away. Did you forget to tether them?" With a start, he looked up at the two dripping, barefoot little girls, the sun caught in their shining hair.

"Don't tell anyone," said John the groom. And thinking that he meant them not to tell that he had forgotten to tether grandfather's horses, they agreed. After all, John had caught them soon enough, and they didn't want the Lord of Brokesford to take away the use of Old Brownie in a fit of temper.

EACH MORNING, just as the stars were leaving the sky, the Lord of Brokesford Manor rose, pushed aside his bed curtains, and then shouted at the grooms who slept at the foot of his bed to bestir their lazy, slugabed bodies. There were two perches on either side of the head of his bed. One held his favorite falcons, the other his clothes for the day, in fact, for every day, since he did not change them much. On the wall opposite the bed were two more perches, on which chain mail hung, just as if it were laundry set out to dry. Beneath them was a long, low chest on which stood his helmet and sword, just in case there had been an invasion of the manor in the night, and the tower needed to be sealed off. That was where his father had kept his helmet, and his father before him, and his father before that, and he saw no reason to change, just because the likelihood of invasion had diminished.

While one groom took down and brushed his clothes, the other took out a footcloth and laid it on the rushes between the bed and the window. Then the old lord, naked except for his nightcap, would stand in front of the glassless window breathing deep of the new air of dawn. Winter or summer, it was the same. Sucking the icy, damp air into him, he'd say, "Ah, fresh air. It makes a man strong. What an excellent new day." And then, while breathing, he would give thought to all his plans, to victory, to manipulating his kindred, to ruling his tiny kingdom. At this point, or perhaps while the grooms knelt to put on his hose or fasten his points, his no-account sons, roused by the crowing of the rooster, would enter his chamber, kneel before him in order of age, and kiss his hand in greeting and obeisance.

"Late again, you whelps," he growled, as Hugo knelt before him, still half dressed, and Gilbert ducked beneath the low stone arch that framed the door. The air had not smelled as sweet this morning; it had not brought as much new life. He had thought of his trees, of the treacherous canons at Wymondley, and the perfidy of lawyers, who never faced a man to his front, fully armed, but snuck around the back like some venemous serpent, striking in with poi-

son and treachery. Ah, now, it was Gilbert's turn. Why did he always irritate him so? It was his mother's long nose, and that arrogant, ironic way she had about her, that she'd passed on, along with
her height and dark hair. Hugo, now, he was more in the pattern of
a man, that is, in the pattern of himself before he had turned gray:
blonde, square-set, vigorous, and not overburdened with reflection
and useless wool-gathering. At least, that had been true until this
latest turn Hugo had taken, dressing like a fop and preening himself
like a dancing master. Ugh. The old man shuddered with distaste.
Gilbert rose from his knee, and the look on his face told the old
man that he'd seen his displeasure. Well, too bad. It would do him
good.

"Heigh ho, now I'm off. Want to come with me, Gilbert?"

"Where are you off to?"

"They say there's a succubus off at the pond. I'm off to hunt
her up."

"What's this?" growled the old man, as he popped his head
through the neck-hole in his undershirt.

"I'm collecting earthly pleasures in anticipation of my deathbed
conversion. And nobody, absolutely nobody, gives more earthly
pleasure than a succubus. I've checked with that fellow in the village. Unspeakable delight, taking the very substance out of a man,
at least temporarily."

"The succubus tried to kill him."

"Ha! He was only a peasant. I'm prepared. But that's why I
thought you might go along, Gilbert. Sort of insurance. You can
keep your sword ready in case she tries to slay me with pleasure.
Oof! Ha! What a death! But of course, then I couldn't take the habit
and repent my sins."

"Hugo, I refuse to be a pander for a succubus."

"Hey, now, it's not at all like that. What's a brother for?"

"And what, if anything, do you plan to do with the rest of your
day if you fail to find this creature?" said the old man, as the groom
straightened out his tunic and held up the surcoat for the old man to
put his arms into.

"Oh, I think I'll ride off to Mistress Bet's brewhouse. A man's got needs, you know, and that wife of mine has been useless ever since she got into that 'delicate condition.' " And with that, he was off down the stairs of the tower, his cheerful whistling echoing back up the stairwell to them.

"Gone all day, eh?" said the old man, eyeing his second son.

"Exactly my thought," said Gilbert.

"Wat, go and have John saddle up our horses. We're off for the day ourselves."

"Business with the Bishop about the new priest," added Gilbert, though it was hardly necessary.

CHAPTER FIFTEEN

LION BARELY LIFTED HIS HEAD WHEN Gilbert reached under the bundles for the two neatly wrapped ones, sewn into heavy muslin cases as an extra precaution against tampering.

"Too old for a watchdog, you ought to put him down," said Sir Hubert.

"Margaret would never hear of it. She loves that old dog."

"Margaret this, Margaret that. You indulge that woman too much. She's spoiled."

"How spoiled? She hasn't demanded a place at the Duke's court and then given it up in a huff, she doesn't order new dresses that no one can afford, and she's as brave as a tiger when it comes to looking after her own." Gilbert hoisted the flat, rectangular package to his shoulder. His father took the long, flat one, two shovels wrapped with a board to disguise their shape.

"She doesn't discipline her servants. That so-called Madame creature is a monster." They were half-way down the solar steps now.

"Madame's hardly a servant. But even you must admit, Madame is training the girls admirably," Gilbert felt a strange sense of gratification. His father seemed absolutely benevolent in his presence. At long last, they were doing something together, not snarling and ripping at each other like hounds at a dogfight.

"Cecily Kendall, that little beast, sewing an altar cloth. Who would have ever thought it? Ha!" His father threw back his head and laughed. It was a fierce laugh, somewhat between a bark and a snort, and not long. Gilbert's long, intelligent face was unchanged, but inside, he could feel his heart was expanding. He was having a vision of his father, seated in his big chair on the dais, his hawks perched behind him on the wall, and his hounds all lying down under the table at his feet, saying to guests, "My second son's a scholar. This learning stuff, it has its place."

TOGETHER THEY TOOK the main road toward Hertford, then doubled back secretly by roundabout ways across scrub and uninhabited wasteland, entering the woods by a route known only to them. A doe, startled, leapt before them and bounded off, seeking to lead them away from her twin fawns, cowering in the bushes nearby. But this was not a hunting day. In a tree above the path, rooks were having a parliament. What a lot of squawking, thought Gilbert, just like the real one. He looked over at his father, riding straight and square, and saw from his eyes that the old man was thinking exactly the same thought.

"The Duke will be coming home in the fall or winter sometime, before the meeting of parliament," said Sir Hubert.

"If the French can raise the rest of the ransom for King John. Until then, he sits in Calais."

"Sits in style," harrumphed the old man. His face was weathered, his beard and hair nearly all white now, but he could wield a two-handed sword as if it were a feather, ride all day in full armor and keep watch all the night after without nodding. His eyes were of that pale blue that has seen much death, and dealt it out, too, without ever a pang of conscience. His very passing shadow inspired terror in peasants. Ice-hearted and strong, he seemed to be without weak spots, until now. How curious, thought Gilbert, that oak trees would be the way to his heart. Oak trees and Peregrine.

But they had passed from the mixed forest into the oak forest. It was not an accident that only oaks grew here. Centuries of culling, long before memory, had removed everything else. Above them, birds sang in the airy canopy, and at their feet, the shadow and sun spread ahead of them on the path like a dappled carpet. In the distance, they heard the rushing sound of water, and they approached the pond from the far side of the temple of yews, tethering their horses beneath it while Gilbert scouted to see if anyone was at the spring.

"Don't bother," said his father. "Ever since it ate my priest, most people have abandoned it utterly, except at the full moon, which isn't for another week and a half."

"Margaret won't go, either, and she used to come to get water for brewing. She says she doesn't like to think she is drinking a priest."

"There's a foolish woman for you. No matter where she gets the water, everyone's drinking him, at least, if they use the brook. And washing in him, and wading in him." They hoisted the boxes from behind their saddles, and slashed open the wrappings. "The people say he's gone, sucked into the underworld. That keeps them from having fantasies about hauntings and staring eyes like that woman of yours who won't even eat oysters." Within the outline of the gray, weedy ruins, they found a likely spot and began to dig. "But I have a different notion," Sir Hubert went on. "There's the damndest, biggest eels that ever lived down in that hole. I think they eat up whatever, or whomver, is sucked up by the spring. All those chickens and cheeses and offerings. I fished up a big one out of that hole for my pond last year, but the otters ate it. And now those monster eels have gone and eaten Sir Roger, I wouldn't have the stomach for one of them. It would be like eating him, at second hand, you see, and it wouldn't be respectful." The old man paused, astonished that he had revealed so much of his inner thinking to anyone. Gilbert paused, too, amazed that his father, in fact, had thoughts, and such calculated and sensible ones, too.

As they lowered the box into the hole they had dug, Gilbert thought he heard a scrabbling sound coming from the direction of the pond. Silently, he put his hand on his father's sleeve, and made a gesture toward the pond. There was a scratching, crackling sound of brush being broken, and the soft sound of a four footed beast treading on the carpet of oak leaves. The sound was receding from the pond.

"Some deer, coming to drink," said his father. How interesting, his father seemed to hear perfectly well out here alone. It was only with people he seemed not to hear a word, especially when those words displeased him.

They finished burying the box, trampled the ground, and spread some of the heavy stones on the site. Riding out of the forest the way they had come, they returned home by the main road from the opposite direction, feeling full of satisfaction.

WELL, THEY'VE GONE OFF with it, I thought, and now that it's planted, we can go home and let it sprout at leisure. This is the shortest visit we've ever had here, and I hope it's the last. At least everyone is satisfied now. Sir Hubert gets the rights to the spring and I get my house, and things can go back the way they were. Madame took Cecily off to help her polish the altar silver in the Brokesford chapel, Mother Sarah took Peregrine and her spinning off to the orchard, where he could hunt for worms in the early fallen cider apples, and I took Alison to help me find all the children's scattered things in anticipation of packing.

"Mama, I want to go ride Old Brownie," said Alison.

"It's not fair, when your sister is working, for you to play."

"Yes it is fair, because when I go with her, I always have to ride behind because she says she is the oldest. I want to ride in front, where it's not so slippery."

"You should take turns."

"She says there's no reason to take turns. She's the oldest, so she says when to take turns, and I can't ride in front. Mama, why did you make me be second? I wanted to be first. If I were first, I would share more than *Cecily* does."

"I didn't do it, my love, God did it. First or second, I am very happy you're mine." We were in the solar, hunting about. I found Cecily's shift stuffed behind the little trundle bed the girls shared, and one of Peregrine's shoes.

"Mama, my birthday is a whole month ahead of hers. I've been waiting to catch up. If I am very good, will I be older than her next year, when my birthday comes back again?"

"It doesn't work that way. Goodness does not change time. Even though your birthday is in an earlier month, every year you will be the same number of years behind her. You can't catch up."

"Not ever?"

"Never." Alison sighed deeply. "Alison," I asked, "where is Peregrine's other shoe?"

"Cecily put it in your little chest under the bed."

"What on earth did she do that for?" I said, and fumbled under the big, sagging old bed that Gilbert and I shared. All our little family, Robert the squire, and the personal retainers slept in the solar, but only we had bed curtains, in deference to Gilbert's status as a son of the house.

I wouldn't really call that cold stone room a solar, for the narrow, high windows never caught much sun. It was a long, large room, the entire second story over the hall, and its stone walls were so thick that at the base of each window opening, two parallel window seats, facing each other, were set in the depth of the wall. There were two round rooms in the tower, the uppermost where Sir Hubert slept, along with his body servants, hawks, hounds, and whatever vermin cared to climb that high. Beneath them, at the level of the solar, was Hugo and Petronilla's chamber, from which a connecting passage led to the solar. The ground floor of the tower was the chapel, though you could not get there directly from the tower above, for the long wooden stair from the upper rooms wound around the outside of the tower to the ground. Beneath the chapel lay the dungeon, where Sir Hubert could lock up people, old wine tuns, or loot from some campaign, and no one would ever be the wiser. Comfort and privacy were not part of life in this house. The roof leaked, the rats bounded over the rushes in search of trash the dogs had left, and in summer, it had a damp, repulsive smell from the sewage-clogged moat. If it were my house, I'd begin by having a stone pit built beneath the privy that was set in the wall of the solar, so that everything wouldn't just drop down the shaft into the moat. Then I'd have the pit cleaned out regularly, the way they do in good houses in London, so that they stay better smelling.

After that, I'd change the rushes and whitewash, yes, whitewash everything so that it was clean and decent, no matter what anybody said. Then I'd sell off half the horses and get some decent tapestries. Sir Hubert would die of apoplexy.

But enough of remaking the house, which always comes to mind whenever I'm there. I opened my chest to find the shoe and tie the pair together.

"Alison, what have you two been up to? The shoe is all dried out and stiff, as if it got soaked. It wasn't that way before." Alison got that sly look on her face that she gets when she's been pilfering sweets, and she said,

"We weren't supposed to tell, so that we could keep playing with Old Brownie, but Dame Petronilla took it and threw it in the pond. She was singing and dancing about like a monkey, and then she threw the shoe and went away. We think that's where she always goes when she goes riding. She makes wishes there. We followed her, and she never saw, she was so mad. So Cecily just fished out the shoe with a stick, and we brought it back." My heart stopped suddenly, and jammed itself in my throat.

"But she rides with a groom or with her confessor. I'd think he wouldn't approve of a pagan ritual."

"Oh, that sneaky old Brother Paul? He rides to the abbey, and lets her go on alone."

The abbey? The abbey full of Austin friars? Exactly like Brother Paul? Suddenly I saw him, his sinister eyes and pliable facade, in a whole new light. How many years had he served this crazy woman, covered up her tainted soul to keep her wed into this family while he plotted with his order to relieve Brokesford of timber and water land? And Lady Petronilla? Dear Jesus, she'd gone off riding this very morning, the minute the men were out of sight. Everything would be known.

CHAPTER SIXTEEN

I T WAS STILL TWO DAYS UNTIL THE GUESTS would arrive, and the manor was entirely engulfed in the preparations for the great feast in celebration of the investiture of the new priest the bishop had found for the parish church. A massive pit, lined with stones and equipped with a huge spit, had been prepared for the ox who would be put to roast on the morrow. A stream of peasants, bringing pigs, chickens, and sheep came and went through the great manor gate. Margaret, sweating and fussing, rushed from the bakehouse to the brewhouse, supervising the conversion of a cartload of new milled flour into the fine, high white rolls and bread for which she was celebrated at the very same time she was inspecting the progress of barrelsful of new ale she had brewed with that splendid, rich taste which couldn't be equalled in the bishop's own palace. With her came Alison, who never missed an opportunity to taste anything, while Cecily, more convinced than ever by the splendor of the preparations that she was meant to be a nun, had gone with Madame to starch and iron the church linen.

It was to be a great occasion. Not only would the bishop's representative come to install the new priest, but afterward, the long awaited new altarcloth and a splendid new silver paten would be dedicated for the use of the church. How worthy the younger son of the house was, said the pious old ladies of the parish, to give such a gift in thanksgiving for his safe homecoming from France! And his stepdaughters, the heiresses from the City, had not been too proud to embroider the cloth with their own hands. Then, even though the bishop himself wasn't coming, he was sending as institutor a canon from the great cathedral itself, a man reputed to be so holy that he once caused a plague of grasshoppers to remove themselves by simply preaching God's word to them. The event promised to be altogether uplifting.

"You'd think the bishop would have come, being a cousin and all," old Sir Hubert growled as he passed by the great pit on horseback, accompanied by his two sons, a half-dozen armed grooms, and an oxcart manned by a couple of peasants and their boys. They were off to Hertford to select and bring back the wine, which seemed entirely too much trouble for the lord of Brokesford if the bishop himself weren't coming.

"It's all the better. If the bishop had come, you'd have to order twice as much wine, father," said Sir Hugo, and the old man made a grumpy noise, which might have been decoded to mean, "even if you do cover your harness with gewgaws, occasionally you make sense, Hugo."

"Vintners, never trust 'em," said Sir Hubert aloud. "If you don't taste every barrel, they'll pass off vinegar on you. There's no one like 'em for bribing the stewards of great castles to accept short measure. Only lawyers are worse."

"Priests follow not far behind. Who have you got for ours, father? Not some stiff-necked troublemaker, I hope."

"Ha, nonsense. I've got a cousin, of course. Not one I've ever met, mind you. One of Sir Philip's by-blows, raised up for a priest by his uncle the abbot. The bishop assures me he's young, poor, and pliable, and the abbot paid me a nice little sum for the place— hence the wine. Bad priests and bad wine, I refuse to let either get past me."

"It does depend on what you call bad. Easy penances and Sunday hunting are not the sole measure of a priest. What about his care for the souls in the village?" The old man's eyes narrowed as Gilbert spoke. His irritating second son was reverting to that priggish, annoying tone he had. *He thinks he has me by the nose because of that damned deed faked up by his shifty friend. Puppy.*

"He'll get on famously. He's only one step up from a peasant himself. No pretentions. He'll plow his furrow like the rest, and I'm throwing in a mule with the position."

"Well, then, the mule settles it, doesn't it?"

Needs taking down a peg, thought the old man. But I can't heave a bench at him until after this thing's over.

As they rode through the gate, a yellowish, furtive face appeared at the tower window. Lady Petronilla, "ill" in her room, had ascertained that the masters of the manor had departed, leaving her, the ranking lady of the place, mistress of the house.

"I'm stifling up here, I need to take the air," she said to her old nurse. "Help me put on my riding habit, and then go and tell the grooms to saddle that little pacing mare Dame Margaret brought. I've been wanting to try her out."

"But lady—"

"No buts. I am mistress here now. Dame Margaret must lend me her Burgundian mare, whether she wants to or not."

"I mean, my lady, that Brother Paul is not here to accompany you." Her nurse took her hunting surcoat from the chest, helped her strip off her silver embroidered surcoat and settle the green one over her shoulders until it covered her black kirtle.

"Who would dare touch me on this estate? My belt and dagger, now, and hurry." Her eyes seemed to roll in her head so that the whites showed along the tops, her complexion seemed to puff and swell, eerie brown spots becoming visible on its pallid, unhealthy surface.

"But, my sweet lambkin, the appearance—" The old nurse was kneeling at her feet, attaching her little sharp spurs to her soft leather hunting boots.

"I'm not your lamb or anyone else's. I can look after myself," said Lady Petronilla, grabbing up her riding crop and a bundle in a linen sack from the open oak chest that held her things, and striding from the room. Behind her, something eerie, like a scent without a scent, seemed to linger in the room. It made the nurse's eyes widen, and the hair go up on the back of her neck.

"Another of her spells, and Brother Paul not here to help me.

God knows, it will end ill. I should have claimed my age, and remained behind at my brother's house, sooner than travel to this house with her. But without me, what would she have done? What will happen when they discover the truth? Lord, lord, spare me, I am an old woman, and what I have done, it has been for love of the dear child she once was." She went to the chamber window, and peered down from the tower. It gave a wide view of the courtyard and the fields beyond the moat. Beyond the gate she saw a tiny figure on a cream-colored mare, dashing away at full speed on the narrow path that led away from the village and to the meadow, and beyond it, the woods. "Sweet Jesus, send her the son she requires, before she loses her mind entirely," muttered the old woman.

MARGARET STOOD AT the low door of the thatched roof malt house, the sweet smell of ferment surrounding her like a cloud, and setting the peasant delegation outside all wild with anticipation. Alison stood behind her, barefoot in her blue smock, her red-gold hair streaming down her back like liquid. Several village matrons, clad in russet, their hair done up in cheap kerchiefs, stood, equally barefoot, in front of the group. Nervously, they eyed one another. How to begin?

"Mama, mama, all done!" cried Cecily, working her way through the little crowd, with Madame right behind her. "Every piece so nice and white and smooth, and not a bit singed! You won't see finer linen in the cathedral!" Madame smiled and shrugged a little, as if to say, forgive her exaggeration. The peasants turned to look at the little girl with the fast wilting rose tucked into her fuzzy braid. They eyed her almost hungrily. Ordinarily, Margaret would have noticed, but she was too frazzled with the preparations, and too tired from the early part of pregnancy, to be as alert as she usually was. "Mama, can we play now? We want to go riding."

"Grandfather took Old Brownie with him this morning," answered Margaret. The peasants seemed to shift and look at one another. Something had been resolved. They pushed a spokeswoman forward, the old midwife's daughter.

"Good Dame Margaret," she said, "we can take them riding. Let them come with us for the afternoon. We've games in plenty for these little dames."

"Very well, but you must have them back an hour before sunset," answered Margaret.

"As safe as if they had been in church the whole time," said the midwife's daughter, and the little crowd all nodded and murmured their assent. Margaret, who saw among the crowd many to whom she had given her aid and trust, was relieved to think that her girls would be amused and out from under foot. There was genuine relief, then hilarity among the group that escorted the little girls from the brewhouse door, and one of the older women broke into song. The others joined her, one by one, and then the girls, too, as if they had learned it from them on some other jaunt to the village. They sound so happy, thought Margaret, returning to her work. But Madame, who trusted no one, noticed something. The song was not in any English she had ever heard, not in the north, not in the south. It had a curious tune to it. Something that sounded very, very old. Madame's eyes were like the eyes of a lioness; her nostrils flared. She remembered the pledge she had made to Gilbert de Vilers. As quiet as a shadow, she followed at a distance, letting no one see her.

By the time she had reached the village, she held back, waiting behind the wattle fence of one of the gardens as she heard cheering. The girls seemed in their element, vain and pleased with themselves, as the old village women brought out circlets of bright summer flowers to put on their heads. She heard the sound of lowing, and saw the men leading a snow white heifer, garlanded with flowers, down the main street of the village. A dozen hands lifted the girls up. Madame's heart nearly failed her as she saw the girls mounted double on the heifer, waving and smiling to the people surrounding them. A strange village, strange customs, God alone knew what could happen, and she was all by herself. Madame knew of the savage roots of the ancient world that lay deep beneath the reach of the church, of the Anglo-Norman overlords. As a child at the fireside she had been regaled by tales of secret pagan sacrifices, and brave bishops who faced vile heathens with fire and sword. Her insides froze as the parade headed off across the fields in the direction of the woods. She knew what had happened to the priest. It was as clear as clear to her that the girls were being taken to be offered as human sacrifices to the hideous pool, and she had no way to send for help.

Desperate, Madame hurried on behind the sinister procession. She got a stone in her shoe, and started to limp. Oh, wretched shoes, too light for this long walk, she thought, sitting down on a boundary stone to empty out her shoe.

"My lady, they have left you behind, too?" said a little voice beside her, and she looked down to see a peasant boy with club feet laboring along with the aid of a crutch.

Sweat was rolling down Madame's pale face, and her gray hair was straggling from beneath her headdress. One of the pins had dropped from her kerchief, and it was crooked, but she hadn't noticed, although she was usually so precise that she could feel any displacement of correct dress. "I'm too old to keep up," she said, hoping the boy would leave.

"They are going the long way," said the boy, "and all the singing slows them down. I know a shorter way, where there's no path. That way we won't miss the best part."

"And what is this best part?" asked Madame, fully expecting for the boy to show a row of sharp, cannibal teeth when he smiled.

"It's the petitioning to the pond-thing, and the offering of the sacrifices." Madame kept her face impassive.

"What sacrifices are those?" she asked.

"Oh, every family in the village has made a little offering, a bread dolly baked at the hearth, all painted and wrapped up. We're giving the pond-thing a chicken, too."

"Why are Mesdemoiselles Cécile and Alison riding there on the heifer?"

"Oh, they have to go. Since the midwife died, there has been no one with the power to call the sacred eel—until they came. We thought we were ruined, without a priestess of the pond."

"The sacred eel?"

"Oh, yes. The eel is how the pond speaks, and lets us know it will grant our petitions. Oh, lady, if you only knew the trouble that has fallen on this village. The apples are almost lost, there's a blight on the rye, and now there's a murrain in the next shire, and we could lose all our beasts. How will we plow, if the cattle are gone, lady? We'll starve."

A great suspicion had begun to grow in Madame's mind. The suspicion that the girls had become involved in a prank whose enormity boggled her mind. The disappearances on Old Brownie, the growing numbers of grooms anxious to accompany them "for safety," the curious enlargement of Alison's figure due to the honey seed cakes old women pressed upon her when she visited the village, all were explained. Then there was the wonderful pair of shoes made from a vixen's skin, dyed green and all embroidered and pricked about with strange designs, that had been presented to Cecily. Those little devils, she thought. How shameless! How wicked! They've been extorting things from these poor, desperate, ignorant folk. All the while they sewed on that altarcloth with innocent-seeming faces! Pure fury strengthened Madame, and she stood up from the boundary stone.

"Show me that shortcut immediately," she said.

By the time Madame had reached the sight of the temple of dark yews, the pathless "shortcut" had taken its toll. Madame's light slippers were shredded, and her feet sore and bleeding. Her gown had snagged and torn at the worn places, and the branches had snatched away her kerchief several times. Her gray hair was wild around her face, and she had given up on the remaining pins, which she stored at her bosom, retying her kerchief like a peasant, for security. But where it was a matter of propriety, she would never give up. And this, she was sure, involved nothing but the deepest of improprieties.

As they came within sight of the strange, gray ruins of an old stone hermitage, she saw a white mare wandering untethered in the woods. Margaret's little mare, that she'd brought up from London, all stained with sweat, and blood at her flanks. How strange, thought Madame, who had not seen Lady Petronilla ride out the gate. Margaret never wears spurs. She caught at the horse's reins and lead it away to a concealed brushy spot, tethering it to a straggling branch that dipped down from an ancient oak.

"You see?" whispered the boy, exactly as if they were in a church, "I told you we'd get here ahead of them." Together they walked between the strange columns of the yew-temple at the far end of the pond. Madame recognized it immediately for the pagan place it was, and disapproved. But because she was not at her full strength, the strange tree-temple and ever-flowing spring began to work on her. So these are the trees that the Sieur de Vilers does not want cut, she began by thinking. They are monstrous ugly, and should be sold off as soon as possible, and something wholesome built here. But as the whispering leaves and the sound of the rushing water soothed her senses, the deep, woody smell of the forest seemed to call up something in her that she did not want to acknowledge. At her feet, a patch of sun shone on a clump of wild grasses by the stony ruins, and she saw the tiny blue faces of forget-me-nots peeping up at her from their hiding place among the weeds. In the distance, a bird sang—long, liquid trills that made her heart ache. I have been so long without love, she thought. Duty, you are a cold bedfellow.

"My lady, hide!" whispered the boy, tugging at her sleeve, and together they ducked into the ruins.

"What is it?" she whispered back, as she looked out across the huge, ovoid rock and spied movement in the clearing at the far side of the green waters.

"The succubus. Oh, lady, she has returned. She'll destroy them all." The figure across the pond swayed and danced. Her face was veiled with a black veil, and she wore a black cloak over a black gown. The hems of her garments swirled about her bare, white feet as she danced. Narrow, slender white arms reached from the whirling black garments toward the sky. The thing bowed and dipped toward the water, and they could hear tuneless, mindless chanting. The boy crossed himself, but Madame smiled a very strange little smile indeed. As the creature had bowed and whirled at the edge of the water, the veil had slipped away for a moment from the face, and Madame had recognized her.

"What does this succubus do?" she asked, and the boy marveled at her self-possession.

"Gives men pleasure until they die," said the boy.

"She can hardly manage a whole villageful at once," said Madame, her voice frosty.

"But my lady, she is an infernal creature, from the realms of hell itself. It is she that has blighted the pond, and blighted our crops. The priest told us, before he, well, went away."

"Hmm," said Madame, thinking. That explains the spurs. What a nasty little trick, taking that mare when the lords are gone. That woman envies everybody everything. And why not envy Margaret most of all? Margaret has everything, money, love, beautiful children, the respect of all. Sometimes I'm even a little envious of her myself. What did she ever do for all these good things? I know well she must have started life as a poor girl, not of good family, like me . . . Madame stopped herself suddenly. Envy, you ugly sin, get away from me, she prayed silently. Angels of heaven, strengthen me. This story is not over yet, and I have sworn to keep those girls safe. She looked down, and hidden behind a fallen stone at her feet, she saw a spot of white. Curious, she pulled at it. It was a linen bag with something bundled in it. The angels have answered, she thought. I'll just keep this bag.

But ahead of them, she could hear the faint sound of singing, and the crash and clatter of people coming through the forest. The black thing at the water seemed oblivious to these first faint sounds. The boy recoiled in horror, but Madame poked her head up above the level of the ruined wall, fascinated by the impending confrontation. First there was a cry, "The succubus!" and several tall lads burst out from among the trees with their knives drawn. The figure in black started and turned. A little boy darted out and threw a rock which hit square in the middle of the veil, and the black thing recoiled with a cry.

"It's mortal, kill it!" a woman shrieked.

"Death to the bringer of blight!"

"Slay it, slay it!" The cries were fiercer now.

"Protect the little ladies from it!" cried other voices. Swift-running boys tried to surround the thing as it fled, pelting it all the while with rocks. Covering its veiled head with its arms, it outran them, but as they watched, they could see a red stain trickling on white.

"It bleeds, it bleeds!" and while the little boys pursued it until it vanished, the village matrons led the white heifer to the edge of the pond.

That woman certainly can run when she wants to, thought Madame. And she's chased off in the wrong direction, too. I doubt she'll dare come back for her horse and bag while this crowd remains by the water. She looked about her, and realized her little guide had departed for the other side of the pond.

Cecily and Alison had dismounted, looking rather annoyed at the disturbance of their splendid festivity. But then one of the boys returned, carrying a knife.

"Look, little maidens, you've frightened off the evil spirit. She dropped her knife, all red with the blood of her victims. Now her evil spell is vanquished." Two peasant men took the knife, and, bowing deeply, presented it to the little girls, who accepted it with a knowing smugness that made Madame, all the way across the pond and hidden in the ruins as she was, nearly burst with fury. But there was no knight to aid her, and the crowd of peasants clearly did not want their little goddesses hauled away by their disrespectful little ears.

Madame's anger boiled and bubbled nearly as fiercely as the spring in the center of the pond as she watched the little girls step into the water, holding a garland and singing. She bit her lip in pure fury when she heard the song, a very ancient *chanson de toile* which she had taught them herself in French. This old ballad, used to while away the time by the ladies of great chateaux as they wove, was an entirely secular love ballad. Those unholy little brats know full well these peasants do not understand a word of French, especially old French, and think it's some sacred invocation in an ancient language.

Oh! No wonder they quit complaining of being bored of late! Sir Gilbert warned me about them, but even he could not convey the absolute *shamelessness* of their conduct to me! It's beyond the bounds of language! How could I have been so blind! They've deceived me! They've deceived their mother!

Now the girls offered the garland to the pond, and as it floated toward the swirling green waters around the boiling center, they loaded up their hands with the offerings the peasants pressed on them. As they waded into the water, the crowd around them shouted, "Preserve our beasts! Restore our crops!" and the girls flung the offerings as far out as they could toward the center of the pond. The little fools, thought Madame, if they go any farther, they might get sucked in. But just as she was thinking that thought, something happened that made her blood run cold.

The fountain made a sound like, "glub, gulp, glorp," and coughed a bit of muddy stain, then stopped boiling and pushing up fresh, sweet water. A dark, horrible shadow slipped through the silent green water toward the girls. Without even thinking, Madame found herself reciting the Paternoster, over and over again, as the shadow swirled and swam about the girls' knees. Madame couldn't make out what it was, but the welcoming shouts of the crowd made it clear that it was the sacred eel. That must be the biggest eel in the whole world, she thought. How old is it? How long has it lived in that hole? What on earth does it eat? Good lord, she thought. It lives on bread dollies, and chickens, and the occasional priest. Her skin crawled with horror. How could the girls let it near them? She thought of Cecily, fearless in the tree. Too young to know what to be terrified of, she thought. They have got into a dangerous game now. Even the peasants don't dare step into the water here.

But now the dark shadow quit swirling around the girls's shins and silently undulated toward the center of the pond.

"We're answered!" cried an old woman.

"Saved!" the peasants cried, as Cecily and Alison got out of the water, the hems of their smocks wringing wet. Madame noticed that Cecily had the knife tucked in her belt. Then the most curious thing happened. There was a happy sort of glub, glub, glub sound, and garlands, floating chicken carcass, and all the other trash that had been tossed into the pond was sucked to the center and vanished. Then, with a gurgle, a spit of water danced into the air, and the spring at the center of the pond resumed its boiling, bubbling activity.

Having seen enough, and having reassured herself that the girls were in no immediate danger, Madame limped off, carrying the bag, to find the hidden spot where she had tethered Margaret's horse. I'm older, she thought, and it will do that woman good to walk barefoot back to Brokesford Manor. Before mounting, she peeped into the bag, and found exactly what she thought she would. Two sharp spurs, a pair of soft leather boots, and a beautifully dagged and embroidered green hunting surcoat. Hmph, thought Madame. I wonder how she'll explain that black veil when she gets home. What antics! I can't believe they've tolerated her this long. A houseful of men, led by the nose by a crazy woman. As she rode through the golden light of the late afternoon, Madame thought of what she must do while she took great pleasure in the easy, pacing gait of Margaret's little mare. It had been a very, very long time since Madame had ridden a fine pacing palfrey, and she was enjoying every minute of it.

THE LONG SHADOWS of the ending day were lying across the outer courtyard when Lady Petronilla staggered in through the gate. Madame was long since returned, her story told, and Margaret's horse in the stable. It was Petronilla's misfortune that the first person she met was Margaret, all wrapped up in her big apron, and carrying a very large ladle. Behind Margaret was Sir Hubert's steward, a man of good family although not of legitimate birth, as well as several men and women fresh from the malt-house. Lady Petronella had tucked her black veil about her hair, but nothing could conceal that she was barefoot and bleeding from a cut on the arm and one on the forehead. Her eyes were wild, and her breath came in uneven gusts.

"Your vicious horse threw me," she snapped at Margaret. "I want its throat cut immediately. It is a menace. Do you hear me? I order it! Now!" Margaret looked at her with calm, disdainful eyes.

"My horse not only threw you, it changed your hunting surcoat for that black thing, and stole your boots in the bargain. Very clever for a horse. I give orders, here and now, that mare of mine is not to be touched until the lord of the manor hears this case."

"And who is mistress here? I say, find that horse where it is wandering, and bring it back and kill it."

"And I say, no creature alive can be condemned without a trial. Sir Hubert can hear my mare's case at the next manorial court."

"And I'll show my wounds—my condition," cried Lady Petronilla.

"My dear lady sister-in-law, if you pardon me, your 'condition' is slipping. This morning it rode high, and this afternoon it's as low as a nine-month pregnancy ready to deliver. I would not be surprised if your condition, this time, is a pillow."

Lady Petronilla fell on Margaret with a horrible shriek and had to be pulled off her to the scandal of the gathering crowd at the gate.

"What's wrong?" somebody said.

"Lady Petronilla was thrown by Margaret's horse."

"Thrown? What if she loses the heir?"

"Lady Margaret said the heir was a pillow, and then she fell on her." In the scramble, Lady Petronilla's black veil fell off, and her hair was scandalously uncovered. Margaret pulled herself away, disgusted and horrified, as the frantic madwoman crouched before them, the whites of her eyes gleaming as they rolled.

"Kill the white mare, kill the white mare," the black bundle chanted.

"My pet, my baby, she's ill," cried her old nurse, who had rushed from the tower at the sight of the crowd at the gate. But, as cold as ice, Madame stopped her before she could press through the retainers to her lady.

"I tell you now," said Dame Margaret, standing with great dignity before the lunatic woman, "my little mare shall have a trial, and at that trial, I shall produce evidence that you took her without my leave, that you rode without escort, that she went for you willingly, and that you dismounted peaceably to engage in practices no honest woman could imagine. My horse is in the stable——"

"You see? It's possessed! There's a devil in it, that stole my son from me!"

"——and I have possession of the knife you dropped in your unholy ritual." At this the old nurse recoiled, and Madame looked at her with a frozen face.

"Peasants can't testify against me——I'll have them tortured."

"Just wait and see who testifies against you," said Margaret, hoping by her calm to bring sense back to the disordered mind.

"Who is mistress here? It is I, I rule, I, I, I," said Lady Petronilla, her eyes glittering, her skin pallid, spotty, and fishlike. She stood up at her full height, looking at the circle of cold, accusing faces. "You don't dare touch me. No one does. Make way for me now." As she turned to go, Margaret spotted a flash of white on the ground beneath her hem, and put her foot on it. Lady Petronilla swerved like a drunken thing, and her "pregnancy" lurched from her belly to her knees. All eyes were on the bandage beneath Margaret's foot. With a shriek, Petronilla clutched the bundle to her thighs, doubling over as she pulled away. Margaret removed her foot, and the black clad madwoman scuttled through a silent crowd that parted before her.

"A pillow," said Madame in a cold voice, looking at Margaret. Margaret nodded silently in agreement.

"My chick, my dear," cried the old nurse as she hurried after her.

"And tied on with a bandage," said the steward. "Look at her clutch it, while the bandage trails behind her."

"Pitiful, just pitiful," said a woman.

"Lock the tower room door behind her," said Margaret to the steward, "and do nothing until your master returns home. Post a guard on my mare. I don't want any accidents in the stable." That night the entire manor heard the screams from the tower room, the frantic rattling and banging at the door.

CHAPTER SEVENTEEN

MARGARET, WHAT'S HAPPENED TO your mare?" asked my lord husband on returning from fetching the wine. "There's a groom sleeping in front of her stall day and night, and her sides are all cut up. When we asked what was going on, he just said speak to you." As grooms unloaded the cart in the court, rolling the kegs into the hall to be stored in the cellar, he bounded into the great hall looking fresh and pleased with himself, and handsomer than ever. I knew I looked like a fright, with circles under my eyes from worry.

"Where's your father?" I asked. "We have to speak to him. Hugo's lady has gone mad, and is locked in the tower room. She has a notion to have my horse killed for causing her to lose her son. The son was nothing but a pillow, tied on with bandages." I must have sounded weary. He shook his head, as if he couldn't really understand.

"She's been pregnant with a——a pillow?"

"Exactly," I said. He took my hand and stroked the back of it tenderly.

"Margaret, Margaret, the minute I leave, everything always breaks loose around here, doesn't it?"

"That seems to be how it always happens. It's the genius of this house. You know how I feel about visiting here."

"No different than I do, Margaret. And just think, I was *born* here and I can't stand it."

"But, my lord husband, we have another problem. The girls are in the solar."

"Well, that's good. Are they doing another piece of church linen?" I sighed deeply.

"No, I mean they're up there and can't go out until you and I figure out what to do."

"What have they done this time, put frogs in someone's bed again?"

"No," I answered. "They've made themselves priestesses of a pagan cult and have been foxing the villagers out of gifts and enough honey cakes to make themselves both sick." At this, Gilbert put his hand to his forehead and sat down heavily on the bench that ran the length of the hall under the wallfull of deer antlers that his father had collected.

"Oh, my God," he said, "the Inquisition." He shook his head. "Let me think a moment," he muttered. "My mind's overwhelmed."

"Mine has been ever since you left."

"Have any of the priests here got word of this?" asked Gilbert, speaking very low.

"No, your father's confessor is drunk, and Lady Petronilla's confessor is off betraying your father's cause to the Austin canons at Wymondley. There's no village priest until tomorrow, which is half the problem. They wouldn't have turned to the old cult if they'd had a proper, godly priest. Everyone in the village knows about Lady de Vilers. There won't be any hope of hiding it. She was found dancing about the pond, disguised as a succubus. But they'll never tell. Just as they'll never tell about Cecily and Alison. Gilbert, have you any idea of what they were doing? Parading about on a white heifer and pretending that French songs were an ancient invocation? Commmuning with sacred eels? These peasants have corrupted them almost beyond redemption. My lord husband, we have to get the girls out of here as quickly as possible. And we don't dare punish them before we're long gone from here, or the whole village could rise in revolt."

"Revolt? Hardly. Burn a few haystacks, perhaps."

"Gilbert, they've lost their crops, they're afraid of losing their animals to the murrain that's coming closer all the time, and they just don't care any more. They think the girls are the key to their salvation. You can't put them all to the sword. Your father needs live peasants, Gilbert, or he'll just try another way to gouge funds out of you."

"But Margaret, I do owe my family something." At this, I just sank down on the bench beside him and put my head in my hands.

"I can't stand these people, Gilbert, why, oh, why, did I ever consent to come here?" Gilbert put his arm around me.

"For the house, Margaret. Remember? The canon comes tonight, the ceremony is tomorrow. We'll put on a brave front, see the new priest installed, and leave to let nature take its course with the deed. What is it about father that always entangles me so? My life is clear, neat, and orderly until he steps into it. Every time, Margaret, every time—"

"There you are, woman, THERE you are! I've just come from the kennels, and WHAT do you think I found there? ANSWER ME THAT! I swear, I'm going to make that ghastly little dog of yours into a HAT!" Sir Hubert, his traveling clothes still dusty, strode through the entrance to the hall with his rolling, horseman's gait. Behind him followed Hugo and several retainers, all highly amused. "MY FAVORITE BITCH HOUND! How DARE you?"

"Well, Margaret didn't exactly do it, father," said Hugo.

"Don't interrupt! You know what I mean!"

"See what I mean?" said Gilbert in a low voice, turning to me, his face all doleful.

"I see exactly what you mean. I'd have run away myself, if I were born a son of his."

"Stand up and LOOK at me, you WHELP! My favorite bitch! It's a disgrace! I'm going to drown them ALL!"

"I take it, father, she's had a litter?" said Gilbert politely, raising himself from the bench to stand before his father.

"A litter? A LITTER? A hideous spawning of misbegotten things ALL MISSHAPEN and COVERED with PREPOSTEROUS white CURLS! YOUR DOG did it, Madame. That THING that sleeps all the time!"

"Don't you dare touch my puppies," I said, suddenly furious.

"That's exactly what I mean. You DID do it."

"I can't help it if you insist on bringing all those huge, filthy hounds when you come to visit my house. You had them pissing in my nice clean new rushes the very minute they were laid down, and spreading their dreadful fleas everywhere."

"Pissing and fleas are nature, Madame, and you might as well get used to it," said the old man, planting his hands on his hips.

"And so are dogs humping dogs, so get used to it yourself," I said, feeling my own face get hot.

"Two months to the day, Hugo," said Gilbert cheerfully.

"Imagine the difference in *size*," said Hugo dreamily. "If one must be made into a hat, it should only be for the sake of a *worthy* experience." Hearing them all, I could feel my fury rising. Too much work, too much trouble, and too much Brokesford had loosened my mind from its moorings. Small wonder Lady Petronilla, bad as she was, had gone completely mad.

"Don't you dare touch a one of them," I said. "I'm *tired* of the way you wade around in blood all the time."

"Madame, those things in the kennel are useless mouths. They're all freaks, not suited to be hounds or fit for lap dogs either."

"My Lion is not a lap dog."

"No, he's a lie-on-the-pillow dog, and I don't propose to allow any more such in the world." But when I saw that nasty old white haired man turn to give orders to the groom, all that I had suffered at his hands just rose up in my throat.

"If you even touch those puppies, I'll—I'll tell the canon *everything*. I'll shout it from the rooftops. I'll tell that horrible Brother Paul who's off selling you out to the Austin friars right now—" The old man's eyes bulged, and before anyone could stop him, he'd grabbed my shoulders and shook me until my teeth rattled.

"What do you MEAN, he's selling me out?"

"He's off with the canons at Wymondley. What do you think? And the whole world knows Hugo's wife is a madwoman who's been dancing around the pond as a succubus, and has filled the medicine chest with witchcraft charms—"

"The succubus, my wife? Damn!" interrupted Hugo.

"And what were you planning to do, look her up by the pond some night, you dirty-minded man? No wonder she tried to make a baby with a pillow."

"My wife? Gilbert, you have no idea what a disappointment it is. I've given her everything—"

"Father, don't you dare touch Margaret—"

"Lay hands on ME, will you, you miserable excuse for a son! I'll KILL you!" It is very hard to describe the storm that was going on around me, and all the shouting voices, especially since I was being rattled back and forth between Gilbert and his father, while one said don't touch her and the other said I'll touch whom I like, I'm master here, and so forth. The noise carried out all the windows and, they say, caused people to stop all the feast preparations and gather in the forecourt just to listen. It also carried up the circular stone stair to the solar, and before I knew it, poor old Lion had fastened onto Sir Hugo's heel and there were the high pitched squeaks of a little boy crying "Don't touch my mama," and the sound of a girl howling while somebody, possibly Cecily, belabored the entangled bodies at random with a distaff. Then there came the cool, clear sound of a woman's voice, cutting through the melee.

"Gentlemen! Remember chivalry." Gilbert looked up and took his hands from around his father's throat. "The canon and the priests of the church are at the gates." Gilbert's father took his hands from around Gilbert's throat. I disengaged myself from between them, and smoothed down my veil and wimple. "For shame," said Madame, standing all pale and straight in her shabby black gown, now so damaged that it was impossible to mend, despite all her efforts. Hugo looked down resentfully at Lion, who had not let go his heel.

"That's a *very* expensive shoe," he said, his voice full of resentment.

"Don't touch my dog," I said, my voice still full of menace.

"I don't like you, Gran'papa, you're *mean*," said a little voice. Sir Hugo looked down where the little boy had been pitched on his backside by the struggle.

"I am master here," he said, drawing his fierce white eyebrows together like stormclouds.

"But *he* is the greater gentleman, and him not even three years old," announced Madame. "For he would have given his life for his lady mother at this very moment, when you wished to strangle her over a litter of puppies." Something about her coolness, her preciseness of description, stopped them short.

"I am ruler in this house," said the Lord of Brokesford, in a last attempt to establish his correctness.

"God is ruler in every house," said Madame, gazing straight at him with her cool blue eyes.

"God has a perfectly good house down in the village. He should stick to that," growled the old man, backing down. Madame smiled. A very tiny, faded smile that perhaps only I noticed.

"And God's representatives will soon be within our house, stopping for dinner on their way to Wymondley to stay the night."

"By God, they're all in this together," said Hugo, amazed at the thought.

"Father, you'd better think twice before you lay a finger on Margaret. You need her still," Gilbert reminded him.

"Madame de Hauvill. You look like a street beggar. How can you greet a prince of the church like that?"

"I am not ashamed to meet God himself in this gown. I am cloaked in righteousness," answered Madame. "Such injuries to my poor dress as occurred, came from my service to my two little charges, who might well have been slain by the madwoman at the pond." I had to admire her. It was not really precisely true, but it might very well have been true, and it was certainly enough to stop the old man short.

"If that is so," he said, "then you have done a service to this house. You shall not be shamed before the princes of the church and our high guests tomorrow. Margaret, go to the long, iron-bound chest that is in my room in the tower, and see her clad new, from head to foot. It is my will. I am still Lord of Brokesford." Hugo and Gilbert looked at each other, their jaws dropped. Cecily and Alison stared, the household stared, and outside, as word came to the folk beyond the windows, they stared at each other too, as I heard later. The old man's hatred of Madame had already attained mythic proportions on the manor. Surely, he must be the greatest, most Christian gentleman that drew breath, to make her a princely gift all in a flash like that, despite all her contumacy.

I could tell that Sir Hubert knew exactly the impression he had made. On the world, on his family, and even on himself. The smug look on his face told me that he considered himself still as far above this little world as God was above the great one. His beneficence rained on the righteous and unrighteous alike, just as God sends rain even to heathens. He might as well have shouted, "Ha! Take that! Now who knows most about chivalry, you sharp-tongued old lady!" He folded his arms, managing to look both arrogant and satisfied all at once, as I turned to lead Madame upstairs to the chests in which he kept his French loot and the folded clothes of his long dead and little lamented late wife.

"Father," I heard Gilbert say as I left the room, "there is a great deal that has happened since we left—"

"Whatever has happened, has happened. I expect you two to help me keep a lid on everything until after the ceremony. The most important thing from this moment until the guests depart is that Brokesford Manor must not be shamed. I refuse to be a party to a scandal that promises well to live in legend—did I hear your wife say a pillow . . . ?"

CHAPTER EIGHTEEN

THE BRIGHT MORNING SUN OF LATE summer glinted on the gold embroidered banners of Brokesford, on the shining harness of the finest horses in the stable, on the rich silk attire, invisibly mended, of the manor folk. They had gathered on the dusty road at the edge of the parish in a great parade, followed by the village folk in their Sunday dress, to greet the procession of priests and deacons, the canon of the cathedral, and the new priest as they rode from the abbey. Never had Sir Hubert and his sons looked more imposing, their handsome surcoats embroidered with the family arms, their eyes scanning the road for the first signs of the ecclesiastical party. Someone critical, perhaps, might have noticed a new, embittered look on Sir Hugo's face, or a sort of strange, flitting anxiety on Sir Gilbert's. No one was so unkind as to comment upon the absence of Sir Hugo's wife among the ladies at the rear of the mounted party. Instead, they remarked with admiration how little Peregrine, sobered by the grandeur of the occasion, rode his own pony, led by two grooms on foot, beside his grandsire.

"That is the only heir," they whispered. "Look at him, so young, to sit so straight."

"See the pony's harness? Tom the saddler made an exact copy of Sir Hubert's own war saddle, on the lord's own command."

"What of Sir Hugo?"

"There's no chance anymore, not unless he puts away—you know—"

"He'll just be warming a place for his own nephew."

"It's just as well, I hear he's a terrible spendthrift—"

"Why is the boy called Peregrine? That's not a family name."

"He was born abroad. That's what the name means, they say. They never expected he would be the only son of the house of de Vilers."

"Ah, he looks like a little knight already. God spare him, he will be a great lord some day."

The talk was too far to the rear to be overheard by the menfolk, but some of it carried to the sharp ears of the little girls who rode behind the women. And even though they had been mounted singly for the occasion, and Old Brownie left at home, their ears burned. Malachi had better hurry up with that philosopher's stone, thought Cecily. I'm getting tired of being at the end of every parade. Alison squirmed with irritation, then scratched at the top of her head, setting the wreath of flowers atop her hair at a cockeyed angle. It was hot, and dull, and simply hours of prayers lay between her and the feast, and she was itching for trouble.

Luckily for all, the itch was not to be satisfied at that moment, for rounding a clump of trees the canon's party was seen at a distance. The canon met every expectation of grandeur. Even from here, they could hear the jingle of the silver bells on the harness of his white mule, and spy the elegant crimson of his miniver trimmed robes. Beside him rode two priests in plain attire, and behind him were three deacons on foot. Then, behind them, oh wonder of wonders, rode the Abbot himself on a chestnut palfrey, surrounded by monks on foot, carrying the banners of the abbey and chanting as they went. The prospect of so much holiness all at once sent the villagers into raptures, sending all thoughts of springs and eels and spells in the night flying off, forgotten, into the ether.

When the two parties met, and Sir Hubert's chaplain handed over the keys to the church to the canon for the formal presentation to the new priest, there was only the tiniest of mishaps, one that hardly marred the greatness of the occasion. In the pleasantries exchanged, the canon managed to compliment Sir Hugo on his fine-looking son. As the new priest cringed inside, thanking God a

thousand times over that he had not made the remark, Sir Hugo remarked in a voice constructed of a thousand icicles that the boy was
his brother's son. But the canon, who was both iron-sided and brass
bound, boomed that it was no matter, his lady wife would soon
cheer him with a son, he was well acquainted with her father's
grand-uncle, and it was a most prolific family. "Babies like rabbits,
that family, sometimes two at once." Seeing the red color mounting
up Sir Hugo's neck, his usually tactless father averted the coming
explosion by waving a heavily gloved hand in the direction of the
manor.

"Lady de Vilers is ill in childbed at this very moment," he said,
and the new priest cringed again.

"What did I say? Like rabbits, those de Broc women! I'll drop by
and give her my blessing after the service. You did say she'd be at the
feast?"

"If she is well enough," said Sir Hubert, calmly guiding his anar-
chic family into its place behind the church procession as the canon
spurred his mule ahead.

Everyone agreed that nothing so fine in the way of a procession
had been seen in the village since the burial of Sir Hubert's lady
some twenty or more years before, and even then there had not
been as many chanting monks. Then the old ones of the village re-
called how the good lady's coffin had given off the aroma of roses in
token of her sanctity and good works, and also in token of the con-
tinuous solitary praying in the icy manor chapel that had sent her to
her death. After that, all were silent again, for the contrast with the
current Lady de Vilers who was locked in the tower room seemed
almost too cruel to mention.

"Sir Gilbert looks just like that blessed lady," remarked one old
codger.

"She had him marked out for the church, that she had."

"Just as well he didn't stick at it. Otherwise the manor would
have fallen into the hands of strangers."

"Or that abbot," said his companion, jerking his head in the direction of the abbot, an imposing fellow with several chins and

what all agreed was a greedy eye. The lot of the peasants on the abbey lands was known to be a hard one, for monks keep better records of tithes and duties and labor days than the lax, open-handed, and often absent Seigneur of Brokesford.

The little church was packed with holy folk, and the prayers satisfactorily long, both before and after the keys were handed over to the new priest. Of course, all the women inspected the new priest very carefully, and remarked on his honest, coarse face, his youth, his large feet, and the quality of wool which had gone into the making of his robe. Of his stole, nothing good enough could be said, since it was known to be a gift of his old mother, and worked with her own hands. All this, and a mule, too, went the whisper. Some lucky girl could live well as his "housekeeper," even if she could not have the inestimable benefit of marriage itself. The new priest sang the mass in Latin most indecipherably, and therefore most holy, and the canon himself handed him the glorious new silver paten with the holy wafer on it. All in all, there was enough to discuss about the ceremony to keep everyone happy at least until Michaelmas, and here the feast hadn't even begun, with its promised combination of good food and good scandal.

TABLES WERE LAID in the courtyard, and more tables crammed into the hall, and cooks' boys in plenty ran in and out to fetch ale in infinite supply and take away the empty dishes. At the high table, the sons of the house themselves did honor to the canon and the abbot with the precision of their carving, and the ladies' table, safely removed from the holy men, was ablaze with chatter.

Outside, the peasants roistered and sang and cheered the lord, the new priest, and the heirs of the house. The wine at the high table was pronounced exquisite, and the roasted, gilded swan on a bed of paste combed to look like the waves of a lake was praised as a masterpiece. Margaret's breads were of a magical lightness, the crusts of the lark pies heavenly flaky, and the entertainments provided by the hired minstrels between the courses were sprightly and witty.

I may live through this after all, thought the Lord of Brokesford. Just let them get out of here convinced that we are rich, powerful, and happy. Especially that abbot. I don't like the way his eyes seem to be counting the number of silver dishes on the table. Damn, I wish I had twice as many. He could see the guests admiring the fine falcons on his perches, the antiquity of the battle axes on his walls, and the size and magnificence of the dozens of hounds that lounged beneath the table, gnawing on the disgarded bones of the veritable herds of swine and sheep that had been sacrificed for the occasion. Little do they know, he thought. Freaks in the tower, and freaks in the kennel as well. My life's a shambles, thought the lord of Brokesford, and somehow, I'm not sure how, it all must be Gilbert's fault. Loudly he ordered more wine. The drunker they are, the less they'll notice, said Sir Hubert to himself, as he drained wine cup after wine cup himself.

It was just after the third course, when a gilded peacock was being served with a genuine flourish of trumpets, that the Lord of Brokesford looked up from his trencher to see a horrible sight. Sir Hugo turned white, and Sir Gilbert's mouth tightened, and the chatter at the ladies' table stopped. As if at a signal, all other talk in the room stopped, except for the religious guests, who did not quite understand what was happening. A woman in black had appeared at the foot of the stair that led upward to the solar and the interior passage to the tower.

Lady Petronilla's face was swollen, misshapen, and white, her eyes surrounded by dark circles. The braids of her hair had come unpinned, and damp, straggling hair was matted around her face. She had discarded the black veil of the succubus and made some attempt to fasten on the fine, white linen veil she had brought away from the Duke's court. It trailed disconsolately from the ruin of her hair held by a single, random, pin. She had donned her silver embroidered black surcoat, but it was as crumpled as if she had slept in it, and stained with something yellowish and crusty. Her eyes darted around the room, and her mouth, an unnatural brownish red, seemed distorted from endless howling.

"Where is my seat of honor?" she said. "Who has taken my seat of honor?" There was absolute silence in the great hall as the ghastly figure advanced on the table at the dais.

"Hugo, she's yours," said the old lord in a hoarse whisper. "Get her out of here. And find out who unlocked the chamber, and I'll have his head."

"But—but, I can't. Just look at her—why, she's possessed. It will make a terrible scene."

"It's a terrible scene now. Play the man instead of the fop and get her out of here." But Petronilla had already come to the abbot's seat.

"This is my place. Remove yourself and go lower," she said.

"Hugo—" said Sir Hubert between his teeth. But at the word "possession," so loosely uttered by Sir Hugo, the canon had perked up. Possessions were a specialty of his, and he loved to display his knowledge.

"How fat you are," said the ghastly figure to the abbot. "Are you pregnant, too?"

"Possessed," said the canon. "Hear the devil within her speaking?" The abbot turned in his seat and looked at her, insulted.

"Oh, no, I've made a mistake, I see," she said. "You're pregnant with poor men's geese, and pheasants from woods which are not yours."

"Definitely, definitely possessed," said the abbot, drawing back in disgust. "Only a devil could speak in such a fashion."

Oh my Lord Jesus, thought Margaret, trying to make herself invisible in her place at the women's table, don't let her spy me here. Two strong grooms, summoned from the kitchen, had come up quietly behind Lady Petronilla as she spoke, clutching the high, pointed back of the abbot's chair. In a flash, they grabbed her, but she bit them hard, and slipped out of their hands like quicksilver. Their blood ran out of her mouth, and she licked at it, as if the salty taste pleased her. As lightly as wind, she ran to the end of the hall, pursued now by a half-dozen grooms, one of whom carried a length of rope, and another a fishnet.

"Don't kill her now, I want her back in the tower," said the Lord of Brokesford, giving commands. But again, Lady Petronilla eluded them. Now she stood at the serving side of the ladies' table, directly in front of Margaret.

"It's you that did it, you witch. You stole the child from my womb, and bore it as yours. And now you've stolen the new one. I'll chop it out of you—" with that, she snatched up a carving knife from a dish of capons, and lunged across the table. Margaret dodged the blow, but as the bench she was seated on was set against the wall, she could not escape. Petronilla leapt upon the table, as Margaret dove under it, sending the hounds fleeing. Gilbert dashed to her side as Petronilla, wild eyed and brandishing the knife, tried to pursue her by dashing down the center of the table, while the grooms attempted to get at her from the floor. It was at this very moment of maximal confusion that Madame, with great calm and ladylike demeanor, stood, removed a skewer full of partridges in a savory sauce of ginger and verjuice from the large silver platter before her with the right thumb and two forefingers, and without ever dampening her fingers beyond the correct first joint, directed the tip of the skewer with swift precision right into Lady Petronilla's exposed ankle. With a shriek, the madwoman leapt away, falling from the table directly into the hands of the grooms and their net.

All eyes were on Lady Petronilla as she struggled and howled in the net, and the grooms attempted to remove her without being bitten or kicked. All eyes but one pair. The Lord of Brokesford, who never missed any detail of a skirmish, watched with fascination as Madame, her face calm and pleasant, wiped the tip of the skewer neatly on a napkin and replaced the partridges in their dish. He saw her then reorder the tablecloth with a swift gesture and send a boy to replace the trenchers on her side of the table, for Lady Petronilla had stepped in them. Oblivious to the disorder about her, she could have been presiding at a king's banquet. That is a woman who knows how to keep order, he said to himself. And much as he disliked her, he had to give her credit for it. A lady all the way to the bone.

At the same time, the canon was discoursing to the other men of religion. "I would suspect more than one devil, watching her now.

There is, perhaps, one that speaks, and several more that animate. The biting, for example—Sir Hugo, would you say that she spoke in her natural voice?"

"Oh, definitely much lower and more unnatural," agreed Hugo. "Her real voice is high, delicate, and ladylike." To be wed to a mad-woman made him feel lowered, an object of mockery. But to be married to a woman possessed of not one, but possibly legions of devils, was a thing that brought a certain standing in the world. After all, a woman had to be especially desirable for devils to wish to possess her, and a man can't really expect to compete with devils for a bride. He felt noble and tragic now, instead of like a fool. "Tell me, is there any hope?"

The abbot shook his head. "One devil, perhaps, and there might be a chance. But who among us is powerful enough to cast out le-gions of them?" The devil theory suited him, too. What she had said was mad, absolutely mad, and made no sense at all. The devil theory was gaining rapidly in the hall. It made sense. It made drama. It promised wonderful ecclesiastical drama, just when the grand feast and celebration would be all finished, and dullness would settle back on this little country place.

The canon shook his head gravely. "I have never done an exor-cism of more than five devils at once. It is a risk, a deep risk, for whoever undertakes to cast out these devils." Hugo flung himself at the canon's feet in an ecstasy of religious fervor.

"Ah, save her, save her, you holiest of holy men!" he exclaimed, deliciously conscious of the way that all eyes were fastened on him. The ladies especially, he was sure, were admiring him for his self-sacrificial love, his newer and more devoted side. Even while he was kissing the toe of the canon's grubby shoe, he was warmed all over imagining his new self, the tragic not-quite widower in need of feminine consolation. "My wife, you know—I've tried everything— I cannot abandon her—I can promise you only my adoration—" I'll get rid of all those bells on my harness at once, he was thinking.

The canon was deeply gratified. A battle hardened knight, grov-eling at his feet, begging to be saved. I'll stay several weeks, and go at it in stages, he was thinking. I'll be celebrated throughout all of Europe. A vast, pink cloud of mutual conceit and contentment had enveloped Sir Hugo and the canon. It was invisible to all the watchers of the drama, except for one.

"Gilbert, look yonder at Sir Hugo and the canon. It's almost as if they're in love." Gilbert looked up from where he was assessing Margaret to make sure she was entirely unhurt and directed his cynical gaze at his elder brother.

"I do believe you're right, Margaret. I sense he's about to take up a new fad. Remember when he decided to walk in the steps of the troubadours? His poetry nearly killed me. I wonder how this new one will turn out. Something tells me I will only be able to bear it if I consider it a penance."

"Well, whatever it is, it will involve chasing women," said Margaret, smoothing down her gown over her growing abdomen.

"I need to get you away from here, Margaret. I don't want to remain here for the exorcism. Or for the pilgrims who are going to be flooding the place the minute the word gets out. I tell you, they'll be prying up the doorposts as souvenirs."

CHAPTER NINETEEN

PRIESTS, PRIESTS EVERYWHERE. I'M PRAC-
tically stepping on them. You can't leave me now,
Gilbert, I need somebody who speaks their language.
God alone knows what they're capable of if there's no one to
check up on them."

"But that's exactly why I should go, Father. They're suspicious of anyone who reads, let alone reads Latin. You'll do
better without me." I could tell that Gilbert was losing the
argument, and my heart sank. "Besides," he went on, "Margaret needs to go home and rest. She's found it very disturb-
ing, being chased with a carving knife, and wants to be away."

"Rest? Rest? She can rest here. The city's an unhealthful
place. All that fetid air. Think of the woods, the fields, the balmy
breezes! All good for women who are expecting. Besides, it's
Hugo's fault that woman got out. He forgot to lock the door
when he retrieved his chest and his birds from the tower room.
It won't happen again. Good, that's settled. Now, Gilbert, one
faction's saying they should hold the exorcism in the chapel
and the other in the church. What should I tell them?"

"Have them hold it in the church. Otherwise you'll have
thousands of gawkers in the chapel, all demanding the hospitality of the house. Tell them the church is holier, and you
hate to sacrifice the convenience and honor, but you understand that it's a very difficult process and there's nothing you
wouldn't do to rid the lady of Brokesford of all those devils."

"The lady of—the shame, Gilbert, the shame." The old man
paced up and down the solar, shaking his head. Madame and I
continued our sewing, pretending we weren't listening, but

the girls were frankly gawking. "Can you imagine? The care I took selecting the bloodlines. I looked at the sire, I looked at the brothers. All sound. But I've come to the conclusion they're inbred, Gilbert. There's a taint. They hid the mother from us—said she was sick. Then, at the betrothal feast, she looked well enough, but pale, pale and puffy about the eyes. Nothing much. A little weeping over her brother killed in France, they said. But I recognize it. I swear I do. It's the same look I saw in the daughter's eyes at the feast. Damn! Damn! Why did I never suspect? A family of great wealth and lineage like that, to ally themselves with an heir of modest livelihood in a distant part of the country—they were passing off damaged goods on me, Gilbert. I'm humiliated that I was deceived. Devils indeed. It's bad blood."

"Don't say that again, Father. Stick with the devils. It makes everyone happy and frees you of embarrassment."

"Devils it is, then. Hundreds of the little beggars. Tragedy, not stupidity. A rarity. Unusual. Even fascinating in a ghoulish sort of way. Already they're coming, Gilbert. Pilgrims with googly eyes, priests with nothing to do, old ladies whose faces light up at disaster. I see them in the village, asking directions. They've overrun the abbey guesthouse, and I turned half a dozen of them away from the front gate this morning. Why in the HELL does it have to be MY house that gets infested with devils?"

"If I were Brother Malachi, I'd suggest you charge admission."

"HIM. It's HIM that got me in this tangle. Worries I have, WORRIES. And now devils, on top of it! I swear, I WILL charge admission! I'm OWED something for all this, I'm OWED!"

"I DON'T SEE WHY I have to be present at this, Gilbert, I really don't." We had met the canon and the new priest and the swarm of deacons at the gate, and were now in solemn procession, complete with an immense crucifix and a reliquary with a hair of John the Baptist's beard, to go unseal the tower room and fetch Lady Petronilla off to the church.

"The canon said you had to, since the devils had taken a particu-

lar dislike to you, and might be coaxed to say more in your presence. Besides, I'm here, and you have another lady to support you.
Madame is very cool-headed in a crisis." Madame nodded agreeably
at this acknowledgment. Where once she had been stiff and shabby,
she had now acquired a look of quiet elegance in the rich, dark kirtle and surcoat she had selected from Sir Hubert's chest. The hems
needed to be taken up and a few small moth holes mended, but
when she put them on, the garments flowed in dignified folds about
her small-boned, erect body, as if they were meant for her. If anyone
could put devils in their place, it was Madame.

At the door to the chamber, two armed guards stood. Two new
brackets had been mounted outside the door to hold the bar that
sealed the room shut from the outside. Sir Hugo himself lifted the
bar, and the canon, clutching a calf-bound volume inscribed with
the title *Manuale Exorcistarum,* threw open the door. The stench that
greeted us was almost unbearable. "Aha," said the canon, his eyes
brightening, "the *foetor diabolicum.* There is definitely more than one
in here." He had come prepared. Behind him stood two deacons
with candles on long poles, a crucifer, another deacon with a pot of
holy water and an aspergillum, and a fifth with an incense censor,
giving off heavy, sweet fumes. I put my sleeve over my nose, and saw
the others were doing the same. When we stepped into the room,
we could see no one, but the source of the smell was clear. The
walls, the chests, the bed itself had been smeared with human dung.
Pools of vomit lay on the floor. The smell of incense mingled sick-
eningly with the stink of the room, making it worse than ever.

"By the power of the mighty name of Jesus Christ, I bid thee appear," said the canon, putting his right hand up. We could hear a
faint growling, and a scrabbling sound, and a pair of glittering eyes
peeked up from behind the head of the bed. Lady Petronilla was un-
recognizable: her hair was matted and filled with filth, her face
swollen, spotted with strange stains beneath the skin, and criss-
crossed with abnormal lines, or indentations. She wore nothing but
a filth-bedaubed black kirtle, unlaced and nearly falling off, below
which showed a shift that she appeared to have shredded with her

own hands. "Have your grooms catch and bind her," said the canon to Sir Hubert, who obliged with a wave of his gloved hand. They pulled her, screaming and squalling, from under the bed by the feet, calling for assistance when she began to convulse, foaming at the mouth and trying to bite anyone who touched her. She seemed to have the strength of ten, and it was a long time before the crowd of burly grooms finally bound her securely to a board, for transportation to the church. Screaming imprecations, demanding justice, hissing and growling, she was hauled forth into the sunlight of the forecourt, where a substantial crowd of gawkers had gathered.

As a groom held my mare at the mounting block for me, I couldn't help thinking of contrast with the grand parade of the week previous. No banners, no children, and for a centerpiece, a screaming woman on a plank. I noticed many strangers there, their eyes missing nothing. Some were counting their beads, or crossing themselves. Clearly, this ranked among the edifying religious experiences, almost as enlightening as watching a heretic burn. Ahead of us, I saw Sir Hubert lean from his big destrier to speak to Sir Thomas, the new priest, mounted on his little brown mule. "Don't forget what I said," he whispered in his ear-shattering whisper. "There's a new roof in it for you, and we may get a wall mural or two out of it." I saw Sir Thomas nod, and thought I heard in reply, "—just as you said, my lord, with double for places on the floor, an offering, entirely voluntary—" before the breeze carried the words away.

Fearful she would break loose, they laid her, plank and all, before the altar. Exhausted from her struggle against the ropes, she moaned and panted while the priests sang prayers and censed the space before the altar. The canon, feeling the beginnings of an undesirable pity mingling with the ghoulish fascination in the room, called for holy water, and sprinkled it on her.

"It burns, it burns!" she screamed. "Let me go!" Appalled that holy water could burn, the crowd gasped.

"Ah, yes. They are all still in there." He opened his book, and had the crucifer hold the crucifix directly above her. "Devil or devils, I conjure you by the mighty power of Jesus Christ, tell me your names!"

"You know my name!" shouted the madwoman. "You know it!"

"Ah, that will be the woman demon, Xanith, who lived as a succubus within her."

"Really, how do you know?" asked Sir Hugo.

"Because it is in a female voice," said the canon. I could see Lady Petronilla's unnaturally bright eyes taking this all in. They darted back and forth. She held very still. I could see her mind working. She wanted to be unbound.

"You know me," she said in a high female voice. "I am Xanith, and I crave your body, priest. I will tempt you to sin."

"*Exi ab ea!* I exorcise thee, thou unclean spirit! Pray, good people, pray the paternoster!" As everybody mumbled and prayed, he made the sign of the cross on her forehead and she screamed and writhed. Then he extended the holy wafer to her, and she began foaming at the mouth. There was a terrible, heartrending scream, and she vomited, the greenish slimy stuff from an empty stomach. "That is the first, leaving the body in the form of vomit, but not the last," announced the priest to the crowd. "When she can accept the wafer, all the devils will be gone."

"We will never leave," said the madwoman in a deep bass voice. "We are many and powerful."

"I know you," he said, leafing through his book. Turning to the new priest of the church, who was awestruck with his powers, he explained briefly. "I discern there are four devils in there, now that the she-devil is gone. They are Leviathan, Balam, Iscaron, and Behemoth. Behemoth gives evil thoughts, Leviathan sets the soul in conflict with itself, and Iscaron causes impious actions during mass."

"And Balam?" asked Sir Hugo.

"Balam causes inappropriate laughter. Have you noticed when the lady laughed?"

"Whenever the sermon was on humility and duty," answered Hugo. "Other than that, nothing much ever struck her as funny—oh, except once, during a hanging and quartering."

"Exactly. The book is infallible. But you must understand the great danger. As we remove each devil, the others become more powerful and crafty. It may take days, even weeks. Say, for example, we free her of Balam and Leviathan. Then she will be freed of conflict within herself, but wholly given over to Behemoth, that is, evil, and not a sign of inappropriate laughter. It is the intermediate stages that hold the most danger."

"My lord canon, I am so grateful for your high wisdom," said Sir Hugo, rolling his eyes heavenward. "I cannot tell you how this breaks a devoted husband's heart. My vows before God, you know, they are ever before my mind——"

"What's that?" I heard Sir Hubert whisper to Gilbert on the other side of me, "weeks? I'm telling you, we may get a stained glass window out of this. The wretched woman is worth something, after all."

But I was watching Lady Petronilla. At the pious remarks of her husband, her eyes nearly started from her head in rage. She turned red and began to scream again.

"Monsters! Hypocrites! Liars! I know what you do! I know all! You stole my place of honor! I tell you, this house will fall! It will be barren, and its lands and titles given to strangers! Brokesford will be struck to the ground, her courts and gardens covered in black stone, and peopled with smoke-belching demons!"

"The spirit of prophecy. That is Leviathan speaking," said the priest, thumbing to the proper place in his book.

"I was beginning to be worried," whispered Sir Hubert, "until the bit about the black stone and the smoky demons."

"Sh!" warned Gilbert.

"I adjure thee, o unclean serpent, by the judge of the living and the dead; by the Creator of the world who hath power to cast into hell, that thou depart forthwith from the body of this woman. Get thee gone, vanquished and cowed, o vile Leviathan, when thou art bidden in the name of our Lord Jesus Christ who will come to judge the living and the dead by fire——" The canon leaned close over the madwoman's face, his eyes glittering with a strange fire. She spat in his eye. He cried loudly and drew back. "It burns! My

Christ, it burns! It is the seed of the demon. The demon flies free! I am being crushed!" He staggered back, clutching his heart, to be supported by his deacons. "I see it now, vile, monstrous, spouting a thousand flames. It soars in the room!" A horrified sound came from the watching crowd, and they drew back, crossing themselves. "Now, oh, despicable, it slips back into the woman through her ear. Leviathan, the most dangerous of all!" I could see people putting their hands over their ears. The madwoman, however, seemed to have been seized by a fit of inappropriate laughter.

"That one is Balam," I heard them muttering. Balam indeed, I thought. She has them. She can play this game as long as she likes. She and that canon are partners in deception, and everyone loves the game so well, they are playing it, too. She's twice as clever as any demon I've ever heard of, and sneakier, too. God preserve me from this lady, I thought, Lord God take me and mine from this place in safety. Heavenly father—

"Look at her, just look at her over there, that woman who calls herself Margaret," came the voice of the madwoman. "See the light shining on her face? The light of hell, deceptive and evil. She has stolen what is mine, and death is what it will bring her. I will turn her days to dust and ashes." People turned around to look at me, but the shock had doused the faint orangeish pink light, and they didn't see anything. Thank goodness ordinary people don't have as sharp sight as crazy ones.

"This one must be Behemoth," murmured the crowd, just as if they were identifying shields at a tourney.

"Leviathan has nearly been knocked loose," said the canon. "We will continue to exorcise him until sunset, but if the others be not gone, we will continue tomorrow."

"Very well then," said Sir Hubert, looking content. "Such monstrous beings must tax even your mighty powers. I am full of gratitude that our realm possesses such a defeater of demons."

They worked away all day except for pauses for refreshment, and at last Leviathan came forth in the form of a stinking black turd, which fascinated everyone. Then the canon said he would have to examine the madwoman's body in private for demonic marks, since they often choose to leave by a slit under the nipple, and Lady Petronilla, filthy, disheveled, and with her skirts up, gave him a wolfish grin. Oh, lovely, I thought. Just get me out of here.

It was as we were returning for the third, and what would turn out to be the next to the last, day of public exorcism, that we were greeted at the church door by Sir Thomas. His simple face was alight.

"Sir Hubert, Sir Hubert, I've found the most valuable letter among the church records!" he cried, producing the filthy, crumpled sheet from Malachi's little workshop. There was a grand company of witnesses there that day: peasants, pilgrims, two visiting lords, and the abbot himself with three monks, who had come to inspect the canon's technique.

"Don't wave it at me, I can't read a word," said Sir Hubert. "Just tell me what it's about and ask this good canon, here, to read it to me. I have the highest regard for his powers of reading." The canon simpered at this. He had become a hero in the past two days, and children and old wives followed him everywhere, begging for his touch, his words of wisdom, for exorcisms of rats, worms, and other pests. He had also collected many side payments for praying over the wealthy pilgrims who had gathered to watch his miracles. The church was well on its way to a real stained glass window, if not at least a splendid wall-painting, and everyone was greatly content with the goings-on except me, for my great desire to flee, and Lady Petronilla, who had never been content anyway.

"It is a very old letter, from the time of the wars of Stephen, written by one Gaultier de Vilers."

"Ha! An ancestor of mine. That will be a curiosity worth having." The abbot looked disturbed. I could tell he was dying to snatch the letter.

"It is more than that. My lord canon, read the letter for Sir Hubert, if it so please you." The canon hemmed and hawed and squinted at the antique handwriting, then slowly deciphered it.

" '—and being in fear that the manor be burned to the ground by

our enemies which surround us, the greatest treasures of Brokesford we have buried in safety—' Then, my lord, there are instruc-
tions as to how to find the burial place. In the eastward corner to
the north of the hermitage of St. Edburga. Is there such a hermitage
on your lands?" I could see the Abbot's eyes narrow. Fury was written in the slits.

"Why, nothing really. But there are some ruins—" Sir Hubert
looked thoughtful and stroked his beard.

"The fountain, the fountain!" shouted Hugo. "Father, we must go
dig there immediately!" I could see the abbot watching Hugo, and
his thoughts were as transparent as water. Hugo the fool, he was
thinking. He's incapable of pretending. Whatever it is, he doesn't
know a thing about it.

"Hugo, this holy man must proceed with his duty. Ancient treasures are nothing to the treasure of the spirit." He cast an eye on the
monks, who seemed anxious, suddenly, to depart. "But I will send
my steward and a guard to the place, until we can search there—
perhaps tonight." The peasants who knew of the manor's troubles
all shouted, to the hermitage! To the ruins! A great secret is hidden
there! But Sir Hugo held up his gloved hand to quiet them. Lady
Petronilla, furious that she was no longer the center of admiration,
began to writhe and hiss on her board.

"I am full of many devils," she said. "Spirits of hell dance about
me. And I speak with the voice of prophecy. The thing in the ruins is
false, false, false!"

"Hmm," said Gilbert. "The demon speaks. What purpose does it
have in trying to keep us from digging in the ruins?"

"You have a point there," said the canon. "The demon is very wily.
We should do exactly what it says not to." The abbot was vibrating
with irritation.

"Oh, I could never delay the saving of Lady de Vilers," said
Gilbert, looking shocked.

"Come to me, speak with me! Inspect me for marks. Oh, look
again at my white body, priest!"

"I will proceed with the exorcism," said the canon, whose word ruled. He looked at the abbot, and misread the signs of his impa-tience. "But tomorrow," he continued. "The demon is troublesome, and needs to be cooled down." He gestured to his deacons. "Soak her there in the village fish pond until the demons are humble again, then return her to her place." Screaming imprecations, she was removed, and the canon shook his head. "They seem stronger today. Definitely stronger. They need to be weakened before I go to work again." The abbot gave him an evil stare as he mounted his white mule. Already, peasants with shovels were running across the fields in the direction of the woods.

With a great show of reluctance, Sir Hubert tore himself from the churchyard and mounted his horse. Madame, who stood beside me, looked at him, then looked at me. My face was a blank. So was hers. Then she looked in the direction of the church, and then into the distance, as if she were thinking. For an instant, a little thought flitted across my mind. Had she seen me plant the letter? No, cer-tainly not, I thought, as I let the grooms assist me to mount.

"More things go on at that spring in the woods," observed Madame.

"They certainly do," I agreed, thinking of the scandal of the girls, and how glad I was that she had helped conceal their activities from all those priests and possible inquisitors. "I rely on your discretion," I said.

"You have it always," she answered, as we rode out of the village.

CHAPTER TWENTY

THOSE OF US WHO WERE MOUNTED AR-
rived first at the spring. Even so, it was a strange
rabble, ranging all the way from peasants on donkeys to the curious churchmen on their mules. Even now, the
abbot had an angry, suspicious look, which was distinctly out of
place for one who had ostensibly no interest in the land claims
of Brokesford Manor. But there were already strangers there,
standing beyond the great stone, surveying the strange temple
of yews with their backs to us. At the crashing, trampling
sound of the motley crowd bursting through the trees, they
turned, with some surprise. I couldn't tell who they were, except one was wearing a long gown that had the dignified look
of a lawyer, and the others, in coarser clothes, had the hard,
assessing eyes of tradesmen—or timber factors. I was certain
that I had guessed right, when I heard my father-in-law say in
what was, for him, a low tone, "The ENEMY. Oh, God, that it
were France and I had my good two-handed sword with me."

"Steady, father," said my lord husband, spurring his horse
ahead of the old man's so he would put away the temptation to
charge them. He and Hugo cantered around the broad border
of the pond and planted their horses between the strangers
and the tumbled ruins.

"Why, greetings to you, Sieur de Vilers, my lords. What
brings you here to my lands?" asked the man in the long gown.
His body indicated deference, but his tone of voice was almost
sarcastic.

"Our lands, you mean," said Hugo, putting his hand on the
hilt of his sword.

"There has been a discovery in the archives of the church," said Sir Hubert. "Priest, read out the letter. You there, with the shovels, dig as he directs." The lawyer cast a look at his ally, the abbot, whose face was as hard as iron. Too many people, too many armed men. The lawyer couldn't oppose them. He bit his lip. I held my face as sober as at a funeral. But inside, my heart danced. What an astonishing moment, that by the whim of God, the rival claimants themselves would have to serve as witnesses to the unearthing of the chest! And how clever Malachi was to leave Hugo in the dark. He was everywhere like a puppy, giving orders, contradicting himself, and, in general putting on a show that all who knew him understood could not be deception.

"Nothing, nothing!" he cried. "The letter played us false!" Clumsily, he spurred his horse into the margin of the crumbled walls, interfering completely with the digging. "Try here, try here," he said, pointing to the ground beneath his horse's hooves. His antics made even the abbot impatient.

"They will, Sir Hugo, they will, if you remove yourself."

"Oh, well, of course. Yes. What do you think it will be? Gold? We certainly have need of it these days."

Very softly, I could hear the abbot grumble to himself, "I do not need the powers of prophecy of the great demon Behemoth to tell me it will be a land deed."

At last the digging serfs struck something with a hollow, metallic sound, and the crowd pressed close, silent with awe, as they unearthed the ancient chest. All eyes turned to Sir Hubert where he sat like a statue on his tall palfrey. A strange, secret smile seemed to hover, almost formed, on his lips. His stormy brow was calm, for once. "Pry it open," he commanded. "But carefully." The abbot and the lawyer, sage at reading hidden expressions, were eyeing his face. I don't like it, I thought. He's just not very good at pretending. If that awful Brother Paul has suspected a thing—it couldn't be written plainer on his face for the world to see—he knows already what he'll find. He'll give it away. But that is where the cleverness of

Malachi made all the difference. Within the chest was something the lord of Brokesford had never seen before.

With a groan, the old hinges gave way, and all present could see, in the dappled sunlight beneath the trees, that the chest contained papers. Papers and something else.

"What is that thing?" said Sir Hubert, dismounting suddenly, his face astonished. "Give it here. By the saints, it's a horn! Such an ox has not been seen since the beginning of time! Think of the size of the beast! It was a hero who felled this wild ox." There was not a bit of dissimulation in his face. The crafty look of his half-lidded eyes had vanished. They were wide open with surprise and genuine admiration. The expression could not be misread. The abbot seemed covered with confusion. Sir Hubert beckoned to the canon. "What do you make of this stuff around the rim? Here in the silver?" he scratched at the ancient tarnish, revealing the odd carving. Its high ridges shone dully against the black where his eager thumb had rubbed it. The canon squinted, and rubbed some more.

"It is ancient writing, I believe. But I cannot read it. No man is left alive who can read this. I have seen it before, on a brooch discovered by a plowman at Salisbury. The clerks gathered around the horn, to try to make out the odd figures, but none could.

"The parchments, father, have them read the words. Maybe they tell what it is," said Hugo, clutching up the papers from the box.

"Careful with those, boy, you don't want to ruin them before they're read." As the canon unfolded the heavily sealed deed of the great Duke William, conqueror of England, the abbot's face was dismal.

"My lord, this is a grant of all the lands of Ingulf the Saxon to one Guillaume de Vilers, loyal servant of William the Conqueror. It confirms him in the heritage he has by marriage to one Aelfrida, Ingulf's daughter, and adds to it another tract previously belonging to Ingulf's son, deceased."

"This tells us nothing we didn't know already," said the lawyer, frowning.

"Why, it certainly does," announced Hugo. "I've never heard of this Ingulf fellow, but I'm sure he lived long before Henry the Second. Prepare for defeat, fellow. We'll be seeing you at the assizes."

"But it says nothing about the boundaries we don't know already," said the lawyer, who had pushed up and was eagerly reading the document over the canon's shoulder.

"The horn, doesn't it say anything about the horn?" said Sir Hubert. "Read on, read on, I beg you, lord canon. Look at the other document."

"This one is written in the ancient clerical hand, by a priest who writes for Ingulf the Saxon. He has given his daughter Aelfrida and her heirs in perpetuity the ownership and custody of the holy well of Saint Edburga, together with the sacred yew trees and the land containing the sacred oak forest marked by the boundary stones at Lesser Beechford and Hamsby."

"Well, then, that's done. Property can't descend through the female line."

"No, master lawyer, Aelfrida's property becomes the de Vilers property, by Norman land grant. Yes, it's clearly this place. It describes that big rock there, and the hermitage of Saint Edburga lying directly by it. Aha, here's your part, my lord. It describes the horn. It says in token of saving his life, he has given to Sieur Guillaume de Vilers his own drinking horn, passed down from ancient days, to be taken possession of only after his death. He bids him hang it in the place of honor in his hall and drink from it once a year in his remembrance." My goodness, that's a flourish, I thought. Gilbert must have got carried away. I looked over at him, where he stood by his horse, away from the crowd, arms folded, his face impassive as he watched the play unfold.

"The HORN of INGULF THE SAXON!" exulted Sir Hubert, holding the great horn aloft. "The mighty Ingulf HIMSELF gives us our SPRING!" There was a cheer from the peasant onlookers. Sir Hubert took the horn in the crook of his arm as if it were a baby, and began to stroke it. I looked over at Gilbert again. He looked aghast. Would he be the one responsible for sending the old man off into the realms of lunacy? I could feel the guilt coming off him in waves as he watched his father cradle the great drinking horn. "Every year—ah, God, how many years have we neglected to drink to your memory, you honored ancestor. And yours was a race of heroes. Who else could drink all the ale this great horn could hold without once setting it down?" Then he turned to Hugo. "Hugo! Every year on this date I will drink to Ingulf the Saxon, and I expect you to do the same at my death!"

"Ugh, father, really. That thing's very filthy. It's probably full of insects."

"How DARE you, you UNGRATEFUL BRAT! The blood of the mighty Ingulf runs THIN in you!" The old man's eyes blazed, and he raised his arm with the very first weapon to come to hand—the drinking horn which he was already holding.

"Father, father, don't hit him with it. It's old, you could shatter it!" said Gilbert, dropping his aloof pose, and running directly into the fray. Clever, clever, Malachi. He had read them all correctly. They never could have behaved so genuinely in front of witnesses if he had not planted the horn. But the surprise was Sir Hubert. I'd never seen him in such a mood as this. His beard, his eyebrows, seemed to quiver with triumph as he planted himself square by the open chest.

"My ancestor, I FEEL him here!" he announced. "He stands beside me, bloodied in defeat, but still a hero! His life and lands were saved by the great father and founder of the de Vilers. His noble daughter transmitted the blood of heroes!" Sir Hubert looked into the air by his shoulder. I had never imagined he had a mystical bone in his obnoxious body. "I see him, I see him!" cried Sir Hubert, and all the world was convinced he did. "His beard is white, his noble brow is furrowed by a great scar! He has a helmet, a helmet with a fierce mask of iron, tilted back upon his head! He holds a mighty battle axe! His voice is like thunder. He says, 'WELL DONE. My oaks must stand.'" Behind us, the rippling, bubbling sound of the uprushing waters at the center of the pond sounded almost like laughter.

It was an astonishing moment. To the day that they died, almost every soul that witnessed the happenings there would never doubt that the claim of the de Vilers to the spring was confirmed by law, by custom, and by the ancestral ghosts conjured up by the horn of Ingulf the Saxon. The peasants rejoiced, the pilgrims looked at each other, nodding and gossiping, the neighbors folded their arms and looked triumphant. Only the lawyer looked like a dark cloud had descended upon his brow. And the abbot—well, the abbot looked inscrutable.

THE NEXT MORNING, Lady Petronilla looked about from her board with great irritation. The crowd had thinned considerably, and the abbot and chanting monks had gone. The demons in her had been considerably chastened by the frigid soaking they had undergone, and they had acquired, as well, a serious head cold. Everyone was singing the praises of Ingulf the Saxon and discussing the contents of the wonderful box, and who would go to court to bear testimony to its discovery, and how angry the lawyer had looked, and all the rest of it. Whether Lady Petronilla held two, six, or a hundred more demons seemed to interest very few, except for the canon, who was determined to finish the job.

"Achoo! I speak with a mighty voice from hell—" Ring-a-ring, went the silver bell.

"Begone, noxious spirit!"

"Aren't you even—sniff, sniff—going to ask which one I am?" The canon opened his book to read the formula for getting rid of Behemoth.

"*In nomine Patris et Filii et Spiritus Sancti! Hel, Heloym, Sother, Emmanuel, Sabaoth—*"

"Achoo, achoo, achoo!" The incense set off a sneezing fit.

"It is the demon Behemoth, departing in the form of exudate from the nostrils! *Agia, Thetragrammaton, Agyos!*"

There was a horrible scream from the board. "Why isn't anybody watching? How dare you gossip when I am being exorcised! I tell you, I'll have your tongues cut out, every one of you! I come from a great family! I deserve more than one miserable canon and a clodhopper priest! Where are my chanting monks? I warn you, I won't do a thing more without my chanting monks!"

"Aha," said the canon. "There goes Balam in the form of impious speech." He waved the censor over her and set off another sneezing fit. Then he gestured to the village priest for the holy water, and asperged the possessed one liberally.

"Quit sprinkling me, you oaf!" Lady Petronilla shouted.

"Now, take this down," he said to one of his deacons, who was seated with quill and paper nearby. "On the eve of the feast of Saint Bartholemew, on a day damp with an unnatural heat, the last of four great devils was cast out in this, my most difficult case—"

"You wretched, self-seeking, pompous cretin—"

"A haze of sulfurous fumes lay about the altar, as the last of the demons shouted impious imprecations—be sure to take down the imprecations—at peril of his life, the bold canon—"

"You pawed me all over, you lecherous beast, and you didn't even bring back my singing monks!" Lady Petronilla seemed to me, at least, to have completely recovered herself.

"Wait, wait!" said the canon, raising one hand. "Balam is not yet fully exorcised. Hear him there, mouthing filth? *Agyos, Otheos, Ischiros. Exorciso te immunde spiritus!*" Lady Petronilla laughed bitterly. "Aha, there he is!" cried the canon. "I knew you were still in there, Balam! You have revealed yourself."

"I have indeed," said Lady Petronilla. "Every inch of skin, and what have you done for me? You're a eunuch, Sir canon. As useless as that husband of mine. I tell you, dogs make it last longer."

"Begone, demon of vile speech!—Don't take that last bit down, you—begone! Hear thy doom, O devil accursed! Thou art discovered, O Balam, and sent back to the realms of the infernal!" He sprinkled more holy water, and Lady Petronilla blinked and sneezed.

"Definitely, the demon has exited in the form of snot. Pass me the wafer—now, this part, write down, 'tempted by unholy phantasms, and weak with fasting and prayer, the canon at last extended the holy wafer in his trembling hand—'"

"You charlatan. You always win, don't you?"

"Of course I do. I am, so far, undefeated by—how many demons was it?" The scribe leafed through his book.

"Eight hundred and thirty eight, that's including these four, your reverence."

"Undefeated by eight hundred and thirty eight demons, including yours. Now take the wafer and show that you are no longer inhabited by the forces of hell." Lady Petronilla opened her mouth. But the thing was not to be done so quickly. There had to be a number of prayers, invocations, thanksgivings, eucharistic, and otherwise. As we sang the responses, Lady Petronilla became more and more impatient, and her eyes rolled wickedly. Definitely, she was back to herself. Whatever demons inhabited her were entirely her own.

After she had received the wafer and made a great show of swallowing it, they untied her, and she sat up on the board and had another sneezing fit. I seemed to see her hand go to her mouth, and an impudent, malign look cross her face. Definitely, she was spitting something out. As she stood, she wiped her hand on the back of her ruined, stained kirtle.

"Woman, thou art made clean of demons. Kneel with me now in thanksgiving."

"First up, then down. I want a new dress. Send for my sewing women."

"It is clear to me, thou art clean of demons, but not of the impudence and sin of your sex. Small wonder that the demons found your soul a pleasant abode. Now, kneel and pray."

SIR HUGO WAS NOT THERE to take her back to the manor, because he was off having a new surcoat made "in the style of the ancient Saxons"—whatever that was—and having a mask of terror graven on the face of his helmet, to the degree that this could be accomplished. Sir Hubert was off with his steward and his replenished chest of documents, conferring with lawyers and filing new claims. So it was left to me and to Gilbert to take her home. As I escorted her out through the church porch, she said, "It *would* be you. I don't have to touch you if I don't want."

"Then don't," I answered. But when she saw Gilbert waiting with the horses for her, she let out a scream of fury.

"How *dare* you!" she cried.

Her saddle and bridle were on Old Brownie.

"The other palfreys are all gone," said Gilbert, his face bland.

"Where's my hunting mare?"

"She's cast a shoe. I felt you wouldn't wish to ride a mule."

"I would not be *seen* on a mule."

"Exactly," said Gilbert. "So this is what's left."

"Then I want the white mare."

"That's Margaret's. And you cut her up. I really can't have you ruining the horses we brought up from London."

Lady Petronilla let out another dreadful cry. "You swine!" she shrieked.

"Say, canon," said Gilbert, looking over to where the canon was pulling on his riding gloves and preparing to mount, "are you sure you got all those devils out of her?"

"Absolutely sure," said the canon, looking professional. "I've got it all written up. Numbers Eight hundred and thirty four to eight hundred and thirty eight. Removed from a barren, middle-aged lady of good family, with a strong native constitution and a naturally vicious personality. A difficult, a very difficult job. There were moments I thought my own soul was at risk."

"Middle-aged? I'm nowhere near thirty yet! My body is still beautiful! You *snake,* you *toad,* you——"

"The family of de Vilers owes you a worthy reward," said Gilbert, his face pious and deferential, but his eyes bright with suppressed, cynical humor. Ah, Lord, I prayed. Just when you got the devils out of Petronilla, you've gone and put the devil back in him. The deed, the horn, the whole thing, they've gone and puffed him up. Keep him from bursting out, good God. No satiric verses, no trouble-making theological broadsides, no practical jokes. Give us peace, Lord. And get us out of here as soon as possible. But of course, that's not how God works.

CHAPTER TWENTY-ONE

W HAT ON *EARTH?*" GILBERT'S HEAD turned at the loud, bustling, yapping noise. The children were playing with the new puppies in the corner of the great hall, but the noise wasn't from them. At the sound, Mother Sarah looked up from where she was sleeping with a snort, and even Madame, mending in her hand, ducked her head to keep from laughing.

"Haven't you seen Petronilla's new lap dogs? How could you not have noticed before now?" It was Petronilla who had passed, her nose in the air, followed by not one, not two, but three little spotted spaniels with curly hair and bulging, idiotic eyes.

"It's not the dogs, it's the gown. Margaret, it's a *sight.*"

"Perhaps the canon forgot Lilith, the demon of bad taste in clothing," I said, looking down into my sewing.

"Margaret, you made that up," said Gilbert, his voice full of pretended reproof.

"I thought you liked ray cloth."

"There's ray cloth and there's ray cloth. That stuff, that mustard yellow and bile-green, it's uglier than a sick hound's leavings."

"It's the latest fashion, Gilbert. The draper from St. Alban's who sold it to her said it was 'subtle.' You may be assured that she has let every female within ten miles know how far advanced she is over their low, provincial tastes."

"Subtle, indeed. Stripes the breadth of a man's palm are hardly subtle. It looks like some lackey's livery." In the background, I could hear Madame chuckle.

"But what has brought you from the tiltyard, my lord husband? I thought you and Hugo had a bet on."

"Well, I was on the point of winning, when the word came, and I wanted to share it. Hugo was just as glad to leave off, and now he claims he was on the point of winning, and gallantly let me go to save me from shame. But however it was, the news is splendid. Remember the justice that the lawyer bribed? It's all waste and vanity. The lawyer's so terrified of defeat that he ran straight to the abbey and had the abbot pose as a peacemaker and petition the King for a private settlement. Now the King is sending a royal magistrate out from Westminster to inspect the documents. We've got them, Margaret! We're bound to win, once they see what we've got. Father's ecstatic. Our connection with the Duke, our terribly ancient charter with specific mention of the spring, all those testimonials from old residents—it's all easy now. Margaret, do you know what he said? He said, 'Well, maybe every family ought to have a scholar. Not more than one, though. It isn't altogther a waste.'" I was just on the point of saying something sharp about the selfish, grudging nature of old Sir Hubert, when I saw the look of utter happiness on Gilbert's face. It's not often a second son gets any praise at all, even grudging. And especially Gilbert. So I didn't say anything, so as not to spoil his moment.

"Where's my silver-gilt belt buckle that I brought with me from France, Gilbert? The one with the amethyst mounted on it. Have you seen it? I swear, things just keep vanishing around here. I've hunted in every chest, and I just don't see it." One person who never feared to interrupt and spoil any pleasant mood was Hugo. He came striding down the solar stair shouting.

"Why on earth would I know where you put your buckle? It's always been on your dress swordbelt in your big chest in the tower room. Besides, you don't really need it just now."

"She said you'd say that. She said you probably had it."

"She? You mean your lady wife, Hugo? Brother, I would never take something that was yours." I looked at Hugo, all flaming with indignant wrath, and thought I should point out the obvious.

"Think again, Hugo," I said. "Think ray cloth and new morocco leather shoes, and velvet cloaks with silk linings, and a shiny new silver cloak-pin the size of an archbishop's pectoral."

"What's that your wife is saying?" said Hugo, pulled up short.

"Margaret, you're cruel," said Gilbert, but he didn't look sad to see his brother's unjust wrath diverted.

"Lilith the demon of vulgar clothes has been annoying me lately."

"Margaret, what are you saying?" Hugo had decided to loom over me menacingly as I sat. Loom away, I thought, my Gilbert is here, and you don't dare try to shake me, as you'd like to. I just looked up from my sewing as if he were a more irritating sort of horse-fly.

"I'm saying that instead of beating grooms and threatening to chop the hands off serving women and trying to strike your own brother, you should try to imagine where someone with no money would acquire the funds for three new French lap dogs brought over from Calais, and an entire new wardrobe."

"But she told me—she told me—"

"That the dogs were from her father, and her dear old auntie just sent her a little cash."

"How did you know?"

"Balam, the demon of inappropriate laughter, has been making a few visits lately."

"That, that—deceptive, lying, conniving—I was *fond* of that groom I sent away—" Hugo stormed back up the solar stair.

"Well, well, there goes Hugo to pound on Asmodeus, the demon of excessive spending."

"Margaret, I'm shocked. Have you turned to learning demonology?"

"No, I just made that up, too," I answered.

"It was a mistake to let her out of that room. She's everywhere all at once, and as hard to lay hold of as quicksilver."

"Speaking of that, my lord husband, look behind you out the window—no, not like that, just from the corner of your eye, or she'll see you."

"See what I mean? Like quicksilver. How did she get there?"

"She went up to her room, then out down the tower stair."

"But why? She didn't know Hugo has just gone up looking for her."

"Because she is going to make another grand entrance while you're here. I saw her planning the first one. Don't you know she's trying to attract your attention?"

"She *has.* That awful gown. Those noisy, pop-eyed dogs. Yes, you're right, here she comes again." There was a sudden increase in the yiping and yapping of the little dogs.

"Oh, my poooor little sweetsie Doucette, does 'oo wants 'oo's mummy to pick 'oo up?" Petronilla had paused directly behind Gilbert, where he was facing me on the bench. Odd, how in this comparatively sane state, she was more irritating than ever. Gilbert's eyes opened wide in horror. I just looked down at my sewing and smiled.

"'Oo's *crying.* Is there something sharp in 'oo's tiny paw?" Gilbert's eyes spoke volumes. What shall I do to get rid of this ghastly woman, was what his eyes were saying. I made a little gesture with my chin that said turn around. She won't leave until you speak to her, I mouthed silently, as she fumbled over the dog she had picked up. Gilbert turned, a look of acute distaste on his face.

"Oh, Sir Gilbert, there's something sooooo terribly sharp in my pooooor dear little baby Doucette's paw, could you find it with your big, manly hand?" I tried so hard to keep from laughing that tears started to run out of my eyes. I looked over at Madame. Her face was turned to the wall, and her shoulders were shaking. Gilbert turned quite crimson. In the embarrassing silence that followed, he fumbled until he found a rose thorn in the dog's paw, and drew it out. "Oh, you are so *clever,* Sir Gilbert. I do *admire* a clever man so," said Petronilla, looking up through her eyelashes at him. Gilbert looked appalled. Still clutching the little dog under one arm, she turned so that she managed to bump against him, then put her hand on his arm to steady herself. Then, just in case he didn't under-stand, she ran her fingers lightly down his arm. Then, disengaging her hand, she sidled off, casting a backward glance of smoldering passion through half-lidded eyes.

"Oh, my God, I need to wash," said Gilbert.

"Don't do it in this house. She'll leap on you in the bath," I answered.

"What on earth is going on with her?" he asked.

"It's easy. She can't get what she wants at the pond anymore, and you're the current choice."

"But, Margaret, that's—that's disgusting. What shall I do?"

"Well, when you're not with me, I suggest you keep company with Hugo—she does everything to avoid him."

"The cure is as bad as the disease," he grumbled.

"My lord husband, there's nothing she wouldn't stop at, this I know. She put that thorn in the dog's paw herself. I saw her pause at the door to do it. She is infinitely more dangerous now that she's been let out of confinement and cured of all those devils. Watch her—her mind is sparking like flames in the wind, she has become as swift and sly as the devil himself."

"Well, I did notice her speed."

"Her mind is working that way, too. Swift and wild. We need to get out of here, Gilbert—"

"I thought I heard those despicable little dogs down here," said Hugo, coming in the front door of the hall. "I've looked every-where—has that wife of mine come through?"

"She's gone right up the solar steps." From the corner where the children were playing, sharp, sarcastic little voices came.

"Oooooh, Sir Knight, my tiny, 'eeny, little sweetie puppy has made a big poopie. Can you scoop it up in your big, manly hand?" At this, Hugo's eyes rolled, and he bounded off in hot pursuit of his errant wife. Gilbert, on the other hand, seemed rooted to the spot for an instant. He turned purple, his eyes started, and then, sud-denly, burst into action, reaching the corner in a few big strides.

"Gilbert, don't you dare," I called after him. "They have good reason not to like her either, you know."

"Sir Gilbert, justice must be tempered with mercy," said Madame, drawing at his sleeve with her narrow, pale hand. But her face for once was most becomingly pink, and I myself had seen her wipe the tears of laughter from her eyes with the back of her sleeve.

"Madame, they must learn not to mock their betters."

"It was not their better that they were mocking," said Madame very quietly.

"Father, we're sorry, sorry, very sorry," said Alison, who was always quick to look after her own advantage.

"Father, she's very false," said Cecily. "You aren't going to wear her favor, are you?" Gilbert looked horrified.

"Whatever made you think a terrible thing like that, Cecily?"

"Well, that's what we're learning about chivalry just now, but it seems very wicked."

"And so it does to me, Cecily. You know I'd never wear any favor but your mother's. God didn't send me back from France to be false."

"I'm glad, father," said Cecily. "Stay away from that lady. She's tricky and bad."

"That I shall, even at the cost of seeing more of Hugo than I'd like."

"See Peregrine's puppy, papa. His eyes were all closed. Now they're open, and he can walk. Papa, were my eyes closed like that?"

"When you were born? No, they popped right open. I saw it myself. People aren't like puppies, you know."

"Oh, too bad," replied Peregrine. I had put down my sewing and come to look at the puppies, too, where they tumbled about Sir Hubert's favorite bitch hound. They had been given to the children, all four of them, to take away "as soon as possible, if not sooner."

"They aren't so bad, if you don't think of them as dogs," said Gilbert, cocking his head to one side to inspect them.

"I think they're lovely. They're going to look just like Lion, only bigger."

"That's exactly what I mean. I have never seen the use of a dog that looks exactly the same at both ends."

"Well, *he* seemed to know the difference," I said, picking up one of the puppies.

"Margaret! In front of the the children!" I couldn't help smiling at the shocked look of reproof on his face. Something about my Gregory had never left the monastery, even after all this time.

CHAPTER TWENTY-TWO

THE CHAPEL AT BROKESFORD MANOR was very cold and gloomy, for being one of the oldest parts of the house, it had stone walls twelve feet thick and was lit by the narrowest of cruciform slit windows, designed to keep any stray arrows from penetrating the sanctuary. Whatever whitewash or holy paintings it once boasted had in some previous century fallen victim to the oozing damp in the walls. And though it was attached to the great hall, the alterations in the ancient stonework made to accommodate later extensions of the hall had left the chapel connected by a narrow and inconvenient stone corridor that cut it off from the general traffic to and fro in the hall and increased the general sense of isolation of that chamber.

This tall, circular room, its ceiling blackened by candle smoke and its flagstone floor colder than a sheet of ice, contained little but a stone altar decorated by a cloth gray with antiquity, and a couple of cheap iron candlesticks. But in compensation for this lack of sacred furnishing, it was used for storing old furniture, harnesses in need of mending, and what paper and writing implements the manor possessed. It had also once possessed a ghost, but even she had given up on the place. The Lord of Brokesford liked his chaplains drunk and his penances light. This meant that every so often he lost one, usually to the steep outer tower stairs or the fishpond in the dark, or sometimes just to that overbalancing of the bilious humor which turned them yellow and rendered them incapable of further service. But the general effect of this turnover in spiritual advisers was that the chapel tended to be neglected, which made it gloomier still.

Madame, with her passion for renewing altar cloths, had thought the place a worthy project. But the village church was so much more cheerful and it was so much more delightful to sit in the sunny garden to sew whatever was needed, that the chapel rarely echoed to her footsteps. Margaret, having paid a perfunctory visit, suddenly remembered all the gloom and grief she had once experienced there, and decided that she would worship God in Nature, except on Sundays, when the village church was full of joyful comings and goings.

Only Gilbert frequented the place, and he rarely, coming just to renew his paper, ink, and sand, for he was deep in the throes of creation. It had come to him in the middle of the night, a powerful inspiration for a lament in the old style, concerning a Christian knight held captive by Saracens. It involved a whole series of new thoughts that he, a master of satiric verse and theological polemic, had never entertained before. These thoughts involved a very complex and delicious self-pity, and why they had come to him during this visit to his father's house, which he considered the very antithesis of art and learning, escaped him. Margaret was very happy to see him mentally occupied, for he was at his best when inspiration struck. It made his eyes bright and his face rapturous. People who didn't know him thought he was in love.

At this very moment, in fact, Gilbert was penning the line, "sorrow is my only companion save you, Christ Jesus—" and practically tearful thinking of the poor captive Crusader when his quill went splutter, splut, and he dipped it into his inkhorn only to find it empty. Damn! Completely preoccupied with holding the rest of the inspired and tragic line in his head, he jumped up from the window seat in the solar and hurried down the circular stair two steps at a time. In a flash he was in the chapel where he dove down behind the altar where the chest with the old vestments and writing things were kept. He had just laid hands on the ink bottle when he heard a voice above his head.

"Look up, my bold lover, and see what I am offering you." First he looked at the ground and saw two bare feet beyond the chest. Then he looked farther, and saw bare ankles, and after that bare knees. He kept looking, and he saw all of Lady Petronilla, quite naked and covered with gooseflesh in the chilly air of the chapel. He observed that her arms and legs were covered with unpleasant, bristly hair, and that hair went all the way up her belly to her navel. Her skin was pallid and froglike in the dim chapel light. She had kept on her headdress and earrings. It was the most unappetizing and irritating sight he had seen within remembrance. Furious at the interruption, he kept repeating his last line to himself, so he wouldn't forget the end of it. "I see your color changing. The fierce blood of warrior cannot be restrained," said his brother's wife in a seductive half-whisper.

"Can't you see I'm *busy*?" he said, still on his knees in front of the open chest.

"Put down that ink bottle and put your hands on something more *exciting*," said Lady Petronilla, running her fingers through his dark, curly hair.

"Get your hands out of my *hair,* you floozy," he said, standing up abruptly and still holding the ink bottle.

"Who better than a brother, to make up for what a brother lacks? Together, we will make the true heir of Brokesford."

"You're as crazy as ever. I'm going," said Gilbert, turning on his heel to stride from behind the altar.

"You do, and I'll ruin you. I know your greatest secret. Aha, now *that* makes you turn your head and regard me! You'll go to jail for ever and ever, and so will your father, when I tell what I know."

"What makes you think you know anything?"

"*I* know, *I* know who buried the chest that day out there in the ruined hermitage by the spring. I saw you do it. And I have kept my secret so that you would love me."

"I have no desire to make love to you," said Gilbert.

"Ah, but you must, you must. Hugo's seed is no good. I need a man, a man, don't you understand? I must regain my seat of honor."

Lady Petronilla's eyes were wild. She looks more like a frog than ever with her eyes popped out that way, thought Gilbert. I'll try to calm her down by reasoning with her.

"His seed's perfectly good. He has bastards on two continents. What more proof do you want? Stick to Hugo and quit bothering me." But there was no reasoning with a crazy woman.

"Oh, no, I know that you love me in secret. You crave my white body. I know—the signs—your eyes are bright with hidden desire—" She put her hands on Gilbert, and he jumped back, horrified.

"Get off, get off!" he cried, and as he leapt backward he tripped over the altar step. Sprawled backward and unpleasantly bruised on the stone, he was doubly exasperated that the madwoman took it for an invitation and leapt on him. Oh, curses, he had lost his *line*. Wretched interruption. Rudely, he pushed her off and scrambled to his feet.

"I swear, I'll ruin you. I'll tell the world!" she cried.

"Tell and be damned. No one will believe a madwoman," he said, looking back over his shoulder. But as he stormed out, he saw he was not alone with the desirous Petronilla. "Oh! Madame! Have you been here all along?" Before him, standing in the doorway of the chapel, stood Madame, firm and disapproving. In her hands were a pair of attractive, wrought iron candlesticks. He looked back. Behind him was Petronilla, naked as a plucked chicken. My God, he thought, what will Madame tell Margaret?

"I have been here long enough to know that you are a man of honor," said Madame, who smiled faintly when she saw that he was still clutching the bottle of ink. "Your ink, is it broken?" He looked down and saw the slow drip.

"Oh, I've ruined my doublet. What will Margaret say?" he said, feeling rattled and foolish.

"She will say that a woman who strips herself naked and leaps on her brother-in-law behind the holy altar of the family chapel ought to be confined again," said Madame. There was an awful shriek from Lady Petronilla.

"You'll never, never do it. I'm *cured*. I had four devils. I'm a marvel. No one will ever consent." Petronilla's screeching echoed in the
chapel as Madame accompanied Gilbert down the crooked little
stone passage. While he walked, he was transferring the ink from
the bottle to his inkhorn, which was a fairly complex undertaking,
involving asking Madame to hold the cork for him.

"Dressed or undressed, that woman is preposterous," said Gilbert,
beginning to be absorbed back again into his *plainte*. The line had
come back, and he was imagining how it would sound set to music.
"Oh, the cork. Thank you, Madame. I'm glad you heard everything,
otherwise who on earth would believe me?" Amicably, they walked
through the great hall, beneath the ham and venison laden rafters,
and Gilbert was so relieved he never stopped to ask himself what
else Madame might have heard, if she had heard everything that
transpired behind the chapel altar.

"AHA, THERE YOU ARE, Gilbert. Ink down your clothes again,
just as I was beginning to have hope for you! Oh, and Madame.
Have you any IDEA how many of his clothes he ruined before he
ran off? The idea that he would ever CONSIDER trying to enter a
Carthusian monastery—when they go about in WHITE! Ha!"
Gilbert's ears turned red and he bit his lip. Sir Hubert turned again
to glare at his ungrateful spawn. "You revert, you REVERT, Gilbert!
A hiding would do you good!" The lord of Brokesford planted himself directly in front of his second son so that he could progress no
farther. "STOP daydreaming and LISTEN! I need to take counsel
with you privately." Irritation, irritation, thought Gilbert. Why does
the world conspire against my creative inspirations?

"Well, don't try the chapel is my only suggestion, Father. It's full
of Lady Petronilla dancing about naked."

"Not AGAIN! What did I pay that canon FOR, if not to get rid of
all those devils? Pah! Never mind. We'll go outside." And grabbing
his second son by the arm, the old knight led him to a place where
wildflowers grew in the grass, and no ears but the Brokesford mares
and their foals could hear.

"Listen, I need your opinion about something. We're both into this thing up to our hips now. The lawyer has given up his suit."

"Well, that's good isn't it?" Gilbert hoped to brush him off quickly, before his *plainte* dissolved again into the divine ether from whence it had come.

"Good except for one thing. The abbey has purchased his deed."

"Well, that means the abbot thinks he can win the case when the lawyer cannot. It probably means he can mount an even bigger bribe to win over the king's magistrate."

"Oh, you think so? Then I'm relieved. I thought maybe he knew something—had guessed something. If he can prove our deed's forged, then that Westminster magistrate that's coming here for the settlement might well open us to retribution by the King himself. Think of it, Gilbert. An abbot with lands that would be bordering ours, and the the family in prison, and unable to defend—"

"He can't prove a thing, no matter what he guesses—or wishes. Malachi's the best in the business."

"Malachi, Malachi! Thanks to you, you daydreaming mooncalf, I've put my life and lands in the hands of a lunatic alchemist! What on earth could have led me to such stupidity?"

"But, Father, you're no worse off than before, when you had no case at all."

"I *was* better off! We have more to lose now! All I needed was a better bribe for the judges at the assizes, and you were too selfish to mortgage the house you got by marrying that London widow!"

"Margaret is not 'that London widow,' she is my wife that I have pledged to God to care for, and I would *never* mortgage her house, because I can't pay it back!"

"That's what I mean! Selfish to the bone! You don't need a house! You can always live here!"

"I can't imagine a worse fate! Shut up with a dancing lunatic and a family that doesn't know Aquinas from Hob the Plowman! Every time I get my life in order, this place catches me in its claws!"

"So now you despise the manor where you were born and bred! I see the depths of you, Gilbert, and they're not pretty! You have set me up to be betrayed to a King's magistrate. Is that how you reward me for my paternal devotion? I tell you, I should wring your head off your shoulders this very moment!" At this Sir Hubert dove after Gilbert, intent on strangling him. Gilbert stepped back, and the attack failed, merely knocking him to the ground.

"Father," he gasped, as the heavy weight pressed the breath out of him, "get off, or *I'll* betray you." Gilbert's father grabbed him by the throat and started banging his head on the ground. God, my *plainte,* passed through Gilbert's mind. The blue, cloudless sky and tall grasses whirled above his sight. He could hear the "crack" every time his head hit, and he couldn't breathe. I can't even hit him back. Fathers, you can't touch them. So this is how it ends.

"What in the HELL do you mean, you unnatural beast?"

"Can't—talk—kill me—you stand—alone—"

"What is going on in that malignant, overgrown brain of yours?" said Sir Hubert, removing his huge, ham-like hands from his second son's throat. Spying the new look of bitterness in his son's face, he was somewhat taken aback. He stood, and Gilbert got up, dusted himself off and rubbed his neck for a while.

"Lady Petronilla says she saw us bury the chest."

"Well then, that's no problem. She's a lunatic. She was possessed of multiple devils around that time, and posing as a succubus to boot. We'll just say we didn't do it. Whose word counts more, two men of good family, or a crazy woman?"

"If you succeed in killing me, father, people of sense will assume you're getting rid of the only witness who could testify against you."

"Who's talking of killing? We just had a normal little disagreement, that's all. It's always done you good, a bit of discipline."

"It's never done me good, and if you ever touch me again, you will never see me or my family again. My door will be closed to you in this life, father."

"Family? Family? *I'm* family."

"Margaret's my family. Peregrine's my family. Those little girls that Kendall left are my family."

"Nonsense! Nonsense, my boy! Why, we'll pull through this to-gether!" Sir Hugo put his arm around Gilbert's shoulder.

"I *said,* don't touch me, Father," he said, pulling away. "The time for that was long ago, and it has passed by."

"Without a doubt, you are the thorniest, most obnoxious, most conceited and self-centered excuse for a human being I have ever encountered. It's all from thinking too much! The mind works on itself. Entirely abnormal! You'd have been better off born with an extra nose than too much brain! You're exactly like your mother!"

"We won't go into that, Father. I just don't want you to touch me again."

"Neither did *she,*" grumbled the old man as they walked toward the stable together.

CHAPTER TWENTY-THREE

L OOK, MAMA, PEREGRINE'S *HELPING*." I looked down to see Peregrine clutching a handful of smashed rose petals. He opened up his fist, and there they all were, all scrunched up.

"Why, that's just right. Put them in the basket right there." Along one section of the ruined outer wall of the manor, wild roses had grown, climbing among the tumbled stones in the breach and showing their flat, sweet-scented faces to the sun. Nothing finer for rose-water and for a special jelly I make of the rose hips that captures summer in a pot for the short winter days. Madame and the girls, Peregrine, and I were all laboring there in the sun, all of us in big straw hats that hardly began to cast enough shade. Madame and I cut off the hips with little knives, while the girls managed the big baskets of rose petals.

"I'll put 'em in Cec'y's basket. Then it will be more," announced Peregrine.

"I don't want scrinchy-scrunchy ones in mine, so there," said Alison.

"Sing again, Cec'y," demanded Peregrine. And Cecily started the song over in her thin, high little voice:

> "Gabriel, from Heven-King
> Sent to the Maide sweete,
> Broute hir blisful tiding
> And fair he gan hir greete:"

Then Alison joined the song, her voice sweet and graceful,

and Peregrine followed, still unable to carry a tune, with nonsense words that mimicked the girls:

> *"Heil be thu, ful of grace aright*
> *For Godes Son, this Heven light*
> *Wil man bicome and take Fles of thee, Maide bright . . ."*

Madame pushed back her hat, and wiped the sweat from beneath the edge of her kerchief with the back of her sleeve. "I do so love the country," she said, and I could see her face soften as she watched the children.

"I wish I loved it more," I said, "but since my lord husband and his father quit speaking, it's like living under seige."

"Sir Gilbert has the noblest heart in the whole world," said Madame. "His honor is whiter than lilies. His father is the one who is in the wrong. He should take pride in a son like that. It is just that he has lived too long as he pleased—like these roses, here. He wants a bit of trimming back." I couldn't help but chuckle secretly a bit at that. I had a sudden vision of Madame, armed firmly with a large pair of clippers, trimming up that wild old man, making him shave properly and wash decently and comb his hair every day. A little training and a nice trellis would do him good.

At the clatter of hooves on the wooden bridge over the moat, we looked up to see two Austin canons on mules entering the main gate.

"Oh, look, mama, visitors. I wonder what they want?" Cecily pointed at the two robed figures vanishing into the courtyard.

"I wonder that myself. Let's finish up here and take everything in-side. Then we can find out."

But by the time we had got everything and everyone together and come into the forecourt, things were already well under way. Sir Hubert was standing at the top of the stairs, whip in hand and hunting horn at his belt, clearly irritated at being delayed. At the foot of the stair, grooms holding horses and milling dogs impeded the further progress of the friars, who had to shout up the steps to be heard. Behind Sir Hubert, in the shadowy arch of the doorway, I saw Hugo. Gilbert, of course, was nowhere to be seen.

"Tell that old woman in skirts up at the abbey that he can take his private settlement and use it for ARSE WIPE!" the old man was shouting.

Madame and I looked at each other. One of the monks tried to say something, but we couldn't hear it. Neither, apparently could the old man. The monk shouted, then, too, "—he has said he would hate to so disgrace an old family as to see father and sons in jail for forgery—"

"Ha! Go tell that vile stable sweeping that we know he extends this offer because he knows we'll WIN! Our patron is the MIGHTY DUKE OF LANCASTER! Tell him THAT!"

"It's a pity the Duke is in Calais, and none knows when he'll return. The case will doubtless be settled before you can even get a letter returned from the Duke to the magistrate—"

"Words! WORDS! You sniveling toadies! You tell that snake, that swine, that so-called abbot of yours that WE will bring suit against HIM in ecclesiastical court—for theft, for lies, for forgery, for leveling false charges! He'll never see the sun again!"

"Very well, you have been warned. Our abbot has sent for his own experts from London to verify the seals on your so-called charter before the King's magistrate himself."

"Verify my seals? Verify away! I CHALLENGE him! Those are the true seals of the conqueror himself, granting MY ANCESTOR possession, and NOT a crowd of cringing, whining, psalm-singing MONKS! Now OUT! Out of my courtyard, off my land, and back to your KENNELS!" The old man strode down the stair, brandishing his whip before him, and the Austin canons turned and ran toward their tethered mules.

"Oh, dear," I said to Madame. She only sighed in response. Little does she know the whole of it, I thought. Then I caught sight of her eyes. She did know. Everything.

CHAPTER TWENTY-FOUR

"ASK FATHER JUST WHAT THAT CROWD of riders is coming in at the gate," Gilbert shouted to me. I was standing in the middle of the hall, watching a groom get down one of the smoked quarters of venison from the rafters with a hook on the end of an extremely long pole, and thinking that I had seen corpses hanging on gibbets that looked more savory. Perhaps, I thought, it is eating all that carrion that makes this family so ill tempered. It had been almost two weeks since Gilbert and his father quit speaking, and the general burden on the household was getting unbearable. Gilbert in fact was standing far closer to his father than to me. They were both a half dozen feet apart at the end of the great hall, beside the wormy, battered old oak screen that shielded the hall from the open front door. They had turned their backs to each other. My father-in-law turned his head in my general direction and shouted back into the hall, "Lady Margaret, tell that useless oaf of a husband of yours that they are coming in response to my challenge."

"Margaret," shouted Gilbert again without turning his head, "tell father that he's too old for tourneys. He'd be better off in bed."

"Margaret," shouted Sir Hubert, "tell that IDIOT Gilbert that if he knew his NAVEL from his NOSTRIL he would know that this is the day I vanquish that flea-bitten excuse for an abbot in front of witnesses. These are the clerks from London, come to verify the seals. I issued a challenge to the abbot to bring on his experts. This day he will be confounded and covered in humiliation." The old man folded his arms and smirked. Gilbert spun about and looked at him in horror.

"You've done *what*? Father, you senile fool, he'll bring false witnesses, and you're undone. By God, what did I ever do to deserve a father like you?" His father, content with having forced Gilbert to be the first to break into direct speech, gave Gilbert a superior look.

"I often wonder that myself, with respect to you. But if you must know, I have had the foresight to notify the magistrate, and ask him to send a clerk from the royal archives in case of dispute. We've even made parlay at St. Alban's, he and I, not that you deserve to be informed."

"And just *how* have you got the king's magistrate entangled in this thing?"

"That's my own business. But they'll take the sworn depositions here before witnesses. And if the abbot sends a liar, he'll be finished off."

"So *that's* why you've had the dais and tables set up as if for court day. Ah, God, I'm getting a headache." Gilbert smote his brow.

"Run off, run off. There's nothing you can do for me. Bigod, three times in France, and never wounded in the front."

"Father, the last time I was hit by lightning," said Gilbert, and I could see the back of his neck turning red with wrath.

"That's exactly what I mean," said his father. "Never in front. What will you do next time? Trip over a worm?" At this, Gilbert turned with fury on the old man, and as I raced to separate them, the steward brought them to order by informing them that the first of the guests had dismounted, and that the delegation from the abbey was just entering at the gate.

Now here is what the surprise was. While I did not know any of the clerks, and knew the abbot only by sight, I knew the king's magistrate that had come from Westminster very well indeed. It was Sir Ralph FitzWilliam, the father of Denys the rescuer. He was dressed more grandly; his long velvet gown was lined with miniver, and he wore a great gold chain. But his shrewd face, dignified and calculating all at once, was exactly the same.

"Why, Dame Margaret, what a pleasure that we meet once again," he said, after he had been presented to me. "And how is your charming little wench, Cecily Kendall? I hear she has made much progress in becoming a lady. I myself stopped at the village church on the way here to inspect the famous altar cloth." I'm afraid my jaw must have dropped, and I was silent too long for politeness. Where had he learned all of these things? A horrible suspicion began to grow in my mind.

"Why, I'll have her called, once we've settled this thing," Sir Hubert broke in. "There'll be plenty of time then for pleasant discourse. I've a rare cask of wine in the cellar you might have a taste for." The tone of his voice, the look on his face, made the suspicion grow greater.

But now the grooms had brought the locked chest from the tower room, and the abbot and his clerks were inspecting the locks, while the magistrate's clerks brought out a sheet of drawings of all the known seals of William, Duke of Normandy, conqueror of England, and his servants. Then there was a stir in the doorway, and the last of the swarm of monks that had accompanied the abbot entered, escorting a frail old man in the black habit of the Benedictines, bald as an egg, with a skull as thin as parchment and pale eyes that seemed almost sightless.

It was a curious scene in the great hall, with the officials and clerks clustered at the dais with the abbot and Sir Hubert, Austin canons and blackfriars milling around the ancient old man seated at the bench by the door screen, and Gilbert and Hugo, looking military in their arms-embroidered surcoats, leaning against the wall with their arms folded. Madame and I sat obscure in a corner, Madame with the alert, quiet look of a cat inspecting a new place. Lady Petronilla, dressed in the odious ray-cloth gown, had demanded that a special chair be set up for her, set apart from the women's bench. But even this was not enough, and now she flitted in and out of the room, up and down the staircase, in a vain attempt to call attention to herself, while the most sinister figure of all, her confessor Brother Paul, scurried between the canons, their abbot, and the strange blackfriars, his smile ingratiating, his backbone flexible, and his whispers inaudible from our corner.

Now they all crowded around as the triple locks on the steel bound chest were opened, and the documents brought forth. They laid them on the table dormant on the dais, before the magistrate and his clerks. My heart started to pound. Oh, Malachi, I thought, I hope they can't see the slight blurriness from the impression of an impression. Then I thought of the Papal Bulls, the royal orders, the thousands of indulgences that Malachi had created so well you couldn't tell them from real. How easy it had all seemed before. They have a false document, we'll have a better false document. But they weren't looking at the deed with all the scrutiny they were giving this. And suppose someone had bribed them? The abyss seemed to open in front of me. The clerks nodded, and pointed at the documents, and I thought my heart would stop.

"Ha, hm," they said. "Yes, there's no doubt." I held my breath. "Definitely, the seal is genuine." I breathed again, a big deep breath. "Therefore, we must conclude that this grant predates the deed you have purchased, your reverence." The magistrate looked at the abbot with eyes brimming with false sympathy.

"I am afraid," he said, shaking his head gravely, "some scoundrel confounded the lawyer with an invalid deed. How could such a thing have happened? Oh, there were wretches in the time of Henry the Second." The abbot was sizzling with rage, his own clerks counfounded and helpless. With an avuncular look, the magistrate leaned from his seat and said, "This is a terrible, an embarrassing thing. In such cases I recommend that the parties agree to the quiet, private settlement that I offer in the name of the King, to avoid the cost and time of going to law. And, of course, the disgrace and humiliation." Beneath the sympathetic tone was the ring of hard iron. The magistrate had every intention of finding against the abbot. Beware of damages and penalties, said that secret clangor.

"Wait," said the abbot. "I have more proof that this is all an elaborate hoax. There was another object in that box besides this Norman document. Who doubts that the high and puissant Duke

William gave the family of de Vilers their lands? But it is not the lands as a whole that are in dispute, it is the extent of those lands. And in this, the sealed document is silent." The abbot paused, and pointed to the second document that lay on the table.

"There lies a document in Latin, purporting to be written on behalf of one Ingulf the Saxon, and it is the only actual description of the property in dispute. The description is accurate. Uncannily accurate. And the document is not sealed. How can a document not sealed be official? It is this document that has been inserted among the true documents, and I have means to show that it is false." He turned to the cluster of monks at the end of the hall. "Bring forth Brother Halvard." The frail old man, supported by two monks, was brought to the center of the hall. I looked at Gilbert, and he had turned as white as a linen tablecloth. I looked again at the ancient man with the pale, clouded eyes. Suddenly everything was clear to me. This was the weak link. The monks had found a man who could read runes, or worse, who looked as if he could, and would lie for their advantage. It was over.

Petronilla, in one of her journeys up and down the staircase, paused at the foot of the stair, a wolfish, unpleasant smile on her face as she listened to the abbot speak: "Recently, through good fortune, we entertained this group of holy blackfriars from the far lands of the North beyond the sea. Most generously, they have agreed to make pause on their pilgrimage to the shrine of the blessed martyr, Thomas of Canterbury, to assist us in unravelling this great mystery. This great sage, Blind Halvard the Wise, has deciphered many strange and ancient inscriptions in our possession. He may shed light on the original possessor of the last object found in the box." As he spoke, they cleared a place for the ancient at the table immediately below the dais, and brought pen and paper to record his words.

If the abbot had expected to shatter Sir Hubert with the news, he realized, somewhat to his consternation, that he had done nothing of the sort.

"The drinking horn of my HEROIC ANCESTOR!" cried the old

knight. "It will bear witness! See there where it hangs, in the place of honor in my hall! Ingulf, thy spirit lives! Come forth and save thy daughter's dowry, thy holy spring!" Everyone looked at one another as if Sir Hubert had gone as mad as his daughter-in-law. And yet, every soul there knew he was not capable of dissimulation on such a grand scale. Sly, he was, but an actor, never. Somehow, he had got it all into his brain that it was all true, the discovery, the chest, the ancient drinking horn. He actually believed in Malachi's madcap invention, the legendary Ingulf the Saxon. I wanted to cry. Oh, Malachi, in all the time I have known you, you have never been able to resist the extra flourish. Why? Oh, why? I had visions of inquiries with torture, inquiries to find out who had concocted the will of Ingulf the Saxon, a lifetime visiting the King's prison in Newgate, bringing food packages to my imprisoned husband. And all because Malachi had found an old drinking horn for sale and couldn't resist that last artistic touch. It wasn't worth it, the house. I could have managed somehow. Now everything was spoiled. I snuck a glance at Gilbert. His brow was furrowed, and he looked a little green around the mouth. I knew what he was thinking. Prison was nothing, compared to facing the wrath of his father when he found out that Ingulf was a figment of an alchemist's imagination.

But already Sir Hubert had summoned grooms with a ladder to take the drinking horn down from above the row of dented shields adorned with various versions of the de Vilers coat-of-arms. A faint draft agitated the slashed and battle-damaged pennants that hung on either side of the great horn. "Be careful up there!" shouted Sir Hubert, "It's old! If you crack it, I'll crack your heads!" At last, the immense horn was laid on the table.

"Look at the size of it," people muttered. "There's nothing with a horn like that nowadays."

"How could you let such a person as that pretend to read?" said Gilbert to the magistrate. "Look at his eyes. He can hardly see."

"I hear the voice of youth, reminding me that the sight of my eyes has faded in my old age," spoke Blind Halvard the Wise in a high, cracked voice. "But this I will say; as the sight of my eyes has faded, the sight of my fingers has grown in power. Put my hands upon the runic inscription." I saw Gilbert shake his head in horror.

"Ah, a drinking horn," said Blind Halvard, stating the obvious as he felt the length of the horn. Good Lord, I thought, he's even blinder than he lets on. Then he ran his fingers several times over the carvings at the mouth of the horn.

"These are corrupt runes," he pronounced. "They are difficult to read." Not only blind, but a fraud, the thought flashed through my mind.

"They are forged, then? Meaningless?" said the abbot eagerly.

"No, they have meaning," said the ancient sage. "They are corrupted, that is all. These are corrupt Saxon runes, not the true runes of the Norse. Here, for example—oh, this is interesting— the maker tried to make bind-runes, and did them wrong. These Saxons were a degenerate people, sunk in ignorance."

"How DARE he speak of my great ancestor as DEGENERATE! By God, if he were not such a useless old piece of dried bacon, I'd chop him up into meat fit for stewing for saying that!" Sir Hubert stormed up and down, his hands made into fists, his big white eyebrows drawn together and his face glowering.

But the old man was humming something unintelligible, as his fingers traced again around the designs at the mouth of the drinking horn. Then, after a pause, he said, "The sacred runes have spoken."

"Sacred runes, oh God, when will this charade end?" muttered Gilbert, who had plunked himself down on a bench by the wall, and was holding his head in his hands.

"This first," said the old man. " 'Thorwald.' "

"Thorwald, not Ingulf. Do you hear that?" said the abbot. "The horn is false. Therefore the deed of Ingulf is false."

"Who in the HELL is this Thorwald? Where's Ingulf?" the Lord of Brokesford shouted.

" 'Thorwald made me,' " said the old man, stroking the carvings. The magistrate gave the abbot an evil glare.

The ancient man hummed some more. " 'Ingulf owns me. May

Ingulf own me. God, God strike dead and curse forever he who takes me from Ingulf, if Ingulf does not give me freely.' Thus speak the runes. This is what they often say on drinking horns. Particularly those made with precious metal. Ah, I feel stones here in the carving. And here, on the dragon. Yes. This is rare and valuable, as it was then. Now I am tired. Show me a place to rest. I have traveled too far for my age."

"Show this VENERABLE SAGE my own bed!" cried Sir Hubert. "You wonder! You have brought the words of my ancestor to me! What gift can I give you?"

"A rest," said the old man. "And then a little apple-wine. Doe you have apple wine here?" Sir Hubert cast me a glance. I nodded yes, and he hastened to assure the old man that apple-wine would be his. "And after that, more runes," said the old man. "We'll do what we can," announced Sir Hubert. "These are all I have right now, but I swear, we'll search the countryside. Runes it is! Hundreds of 'em! If there's another rune within twenty miles, I'll have it out for you! Oh, blessed, saintly Blind Halvard!"

But now Petronilla was whispering in the ear of her confessor, clutching his shoulder with fingers like claws, and pointing to Gilbert. As grooms helped the ancient translator up the stairs, she shrieked, "He lies, he lies! I saw them bury the box, I did, and they have brought that old fraud here to lie for them!"

"I assure you Madame, neither they nor I had any inkling that this good abbot, here, had found a reader of runes," said the magistrate to Dame Petronilla. "We have all heard quite enough here. Sir Hubert, what ails this woman?"

Sir Hubert tapped his forehead. "My daughter-in-law. Quite mad from the loss of a child. Why, only last month a canon from the cathedral itself exorcised four devils from her. It was the scandal of the neighborhood, you may ask anyone here."

"You fiend, you are the devil!" Petronilla shouted.

"You see? She fantasizes. Her word is not to be trusted. Why, not so long ago, she announced that the manor would soon be covered by a sheet of black stone, adorned in white lines, where smoky demons would congregate. Humph!" said Sir Hubert, folding his arms and staring directly at the madwoman.

But Petronilla had turned directly to the women's bench, and pointed at Madame, who sat straight and quiet beside me.

"*She* knows," she cried out. "That pale faced harpy heard everything in the chapel. She knows it all." I looked at Gilbert. His face had grown pale again. He knew that Madame knew.

Madame looked at Petronilla. She raised one eyebrow, as if she had never seen such a disgraceful sight, and would not reveal feelings that were beneath her.

"Tell them, tell them!" shrieked Petronilla. "He refused me, he had the *front* to refuse me! I swear I will bring him down!"

"I haven't got the slightest idea of what you are talking," said Madame. "Contain yourself, Lady de Vilers. These ravings embarrass your lord and bring disgrace on his house."

There was a loud shriek of laughter. "You, too!" cried Petronilla as she vanished up the stairs.

"That one's Balam, the demon of inappropriate laughter," said Hugo, leaning confidentially toward the magistrate. "The canon didn't quite root out all of him." Gilbert sat gasping on the bench at the other side of the room, wiping the sweat off his forehead with the back of his hand.

But now everyone was milling cheerfully around, shaking hands, and talking as if they were old friends, except, of course, for the abbot and his canons.

"—rest assured, I will petition the king again—" I could hear him saying.

"—not advisable at all—" the magistrate was replying, while Sir Hubert was shouting:

"If you DARE to show your FACE in court, I'll have experts examine YOUR seals. Henry the Second! A newcomer! If it IS from the time of Henry the Second. Our own good Edward is more like it!"

"—the Duke will return, you'll never prevail, so you'd best pack up before we prosecute *you*—" Hugo was saying. But Gilbert, usually so full of opinions, was utterly silent. I went to him, and stroked his hand, and said, "My good lord husband, all is saved."

"Margaret, I don't understand how——" he said, shaking his head. "Malachi couldn't have known—maybe the man who sold it to him knew—Ingulf, who would have thought Ingulf? I was sure he'd made it up." Gilbert's voice was faded and weak.

"Gilbert, I am beginning to think I may know," I answered. "No matter what the runes or seals said, our case was bound to be victorious."

"Why, Margaret, you are as pale as a ghost. I've never seen you look so ill, all at once."

"My lord, I am sick at heart. I am sure your father——"

"Why yes," the Lord of Brokesford was shouting in a jovial voice. "John, go bring down the little maid from the solar. Sir Ralph, you'll find her as sprightly as ever, but much improved in manners."

"——your father has gone behind our backs and sold Cecily's marriage to the magistrate."

"What? That monster! He hasn't the right! How dare he!"

"Oh, you'll collect the fee, Gilbert. But your father has his court case, today, tomorrow, next year, whenever he wants. How can you refuse him and bring down the magistrate's wrath upon him for the loss of Cecily's dowry? All the triumphs of today would be reversed in the twinkling of an eye. Can you refuse your consent, knowing that it could send your father to the king's prison, or worse? Can I refuse, knowing the same could happen to you? He has us, Gilbert. He's outfoxed us for a wretched piece of land, and sold my girl." I just couldn't help it, I started to cry.

"——tears of joy, Sir Ralph, tears of joy. I was saving it for a surprise. You know how women are——" Sir Hubert was saying.

"Ah, yes, emotional. They hate to see their little girls leave home."

"She's been much too long underfoot, I say, it's about time."

"My clerks, I must say, left no stone unturned. The dowry was even better than you represented it. She even has half interest in a ship, the *Stella Maris,* in addition to the property you mentioned.

Never before in a dowry negotiation have I ever met with a gentleman so noble he understated his case."

"It is the de Vilers blood you ally yourself with, Sir Ralph. The oldest in England."

"So I have discovered. An honor, Sir Hubert, an honor to have made your acquaintance so conveniently."

"Sir Ralph, the times are changing. Even an old curmudgeon such as myself sees the virtue in allying a family of the land with a family of the law. The boy does well in his studies, you say?"

"Without a doubt, he will be magistrate after me—the lad has talent—well, look at that, Dame Margaret has redoubled her weeping. Even more joyful, Dame Margaret?" I wiped my face but everything I saw out of my eyes looked blurry.

"Cecily—Cecily must give her consent," I said between sniffles. "She's not old enough, to, to—marry."

"Why, she's very nearly ten, by my calculation," said that despicable old knight. "Many a girl's betrothed at that age! An heiress with a ship? You let her go far too long without an arrangement. You should be thinking of cultivating Alison's advantage. Ah, there they are, Sir Ralph. You've made a good choice. You wouldn't have wanted the little fat one—besides, you'd have to wait longer for heirs." My blood ran hot and cold with hate and horror. There at the foot of the stair, with the groom between them, stood my girls, as beautiful as the day, with those two ghastly old men smirking and nodding as they inspected them with their eyes, the way you'd look at a prize sheep. Cecily was wearing her tawny, blue embroidered silk surcoat over her green kirtle that she had almost outgrown, and she had a circlet of daisies on her head. Her fuzzy braid had been combed out by the nurse, and it fell in long, bright red waves to her waist. Her blue eyes were huge in her narrow, serious face. I thought my heart would break. She looked like a human sacrifice.

"Don't cry, mama," she said. "I have talked with step-grandfather."

"Why, of course, of course. A very sensible little maiden she is. She said she would give her consent this very day," boomed Sir Hubert.

"You mean all that we have arranged rests on a child's consent? This is preposterous," Sir Ralph FitzWilliam leaned toward Sir Hubert as he spoke. The bad old knight spoke low in response, but I could hear him:

"Shh. It's all a show for the mother. It's her consent you'll be wanting. Gilbert's a stubborn ox, and if he gets it in his head his wife doesn't want it, he'll be quite despicable."

"Just tell her she has to obey," said the magistrate.

"You really don't want to cross Margaret. It's hard to explain just now, but only the girl can convince her it's right." Then he spoke aloud, shouting to Cecily where she still stood at the foot of the stair. "Tell your mother that you find this betrothal agreeable, and give your consent," he said.

Cecily set her jaw tight, the way she always did when she had made up her mind about something. I could see she was pale with determination, and her voice sounded unnaturally old and serious as she spoke: "I have written out my conditions," she said. "I give my consent if you accept them." And with that she fished in the bosom of her surcoat and pulled out a rumpled little piece of paper and held it out to the magistrate, whose eyes bugged out in astonishment. Never, never, in the history of the earth, had such a thing been done.

Sir Hubert exploded: "Conditions! You miserable little cat, I'll beat your conditions out of you! Who in the HELL gave you this accursed notion!" As I leapt between Sir Hugo and my darling to take the blow from his upraised hand, Gilbert grabbed his father and spun him around, and I snatched my baby away from those awful men.

"Hold, Sir Hubert," said the magistrate, who had unfolded the paper and was reading it. "These conditions are not without good sense, and neatly written, too. Mistress Cecily, if you were a boy, you would have made an excellent lawyer. Instead, someday, perhaps, you will be the mother of great magistrates. Who taught you to write like this?"

"My mother taught me to write, but Brother Malachi taught me what to say," answered Cecily.

"Brother Malachi! That damned, interfering—QUACK!" Sir Hubert stormed.

"Cecily," I asked, "how did he know what to tell you?"

"I asked him," she answered. "When I was talking to him about the philosopher's stone—you know, mother, when I wanted my special favor and he didn't quite have it yet. I asked him what if my marriage was arranged before the Stone was ready, and he told me the law says no one can be married without their consent. He said if I was determined, I could oppose fire and sword for my maidenly crown." I sighed deeply.

"That sounds exactly like him," I said.

"And he said if I didn't want to oppose fire and sword, I should make conditions. He told me how to do it. It was my idea to write them out."

"I suppose now the deal's off," said Sir Hubert, sitting down heavily and holding his head. "Now that you know what she is. Unnatural. Wild. I doubt there's a convent in England that could hold her."

"You forget, Sir Hubert, that I first saw her at the top of a tree."

Cecily came and sat beside me on the bench. For the first time, I noticed the shoes beneath her long hems. The awful, barbaric green ones the villagers had given her. "Cecily, what's in that paper?" I asked.

"Let me read it to you, good Dame Margaret," said Sir Ralph. "And I assure you, I am ready to consent to every condition, provided that you and Sir Gilbert will do so as well." I nodded silently at him, too choked to speak.

" 'Condition the first: Cecily Kendall will not be wed until she is at least sixteen years of age.

'Condition the second: If Cecily Kendall is so changed in body as to be unsuitable to be wed, she will not be married.

'Condition the third: Cecily Kendall will only be wed to one who loves her above all others.' You must admit, Dame Margaret, these are very sensible conditions." Oh, Brother Malachi, you wretch, I thought. What have you planted in her mind? I know Cecily. She thinks sixteen is unspeakably ancient, and will never come. And she fully expects to be turned into a boy long before then, and she can wriggle out of marriage. That's why she was willing to tell Sir Hubert she'd consent.

"Cecily, is this really what you want?"

"I don't like embroidering altar cloths very much, mother. So I'm giving up on being a nun. And if I'm not changed by sixteen, I'll be too old to get the good of it, so I might as well be married. Denys is better than Walter or Peter Wengrave."

"*I* want to be betrothed, too!" wailed her sister.

"Be quiet!" I said, "or you'll get your wish——" But I was halted by an unearthly scream from the solar. Before anyone could rush up the stairs, Mother Sarah, her face pale with horror, came running into the hall. "It's Lady Petronilla," she cried. "She's stolen the baby!"

CHAPTER TWENTY-FIVE

LADY PETRONILLA COULD FEEL THE GOOD thing coming, the quickness, the mind that flashed a thousand thoughts at once. So much better than the slow time, the despondent time, like swimming in heavy syrup, when she curled up in a ball, craving only death. Now lights flashed, ideas flashed, and strength poured into her. Ah! She could hear downstairs, ponderous arguments, women weeping. She could hear outside, people, horses. She could hear the birds in the orchard. Ah! She was inside them, looking for worms in the bad fruit, then she was a worm, looking out of her hole at a great black eye and pecking beak. Now back in a flash, her own body. What was that rippling, murmuring sound? The spring, always the spring. A woman green with pond slime, the white of her eyes flashing from deep sockets, her mouth a cavern whispering secret things. Hear her singing, singing. She is calling.

The old woman was asleep. Yes, there he was, the little idol, pushing a little wooden horse on wheels and singing tunelessly. Would you like to visit the green lady, little boy? The green lady with watery toes? he answers, and the old dog tries to bite her but she kicks him away with a powerful blow. But before his yelping can rouse the old woman, she has thrown her black cloak over the dirty little manling and scooped him up like a bundle. Someone far away is shouting, but the swift time has come, and many voices sing whirling songs in her mind, and with great strength she scurries down the tower stairs bearing the squirming, howling bundle slung over her shoulder. There, almost at the stable door, she sees the saddled horses of the visiting dignitaries waiting. Meant to be, meant to be, sing the voices, and she flings the bundle across the nearest saddle bow and grabs up the reins. Oh, wonderful, wonderful, to feel the wind in your face and blood pouring through your body like molten light. The world sparkled and glistened, and the green lady beckoned with her sweet, rippling voice.

"WHERE DID SHE GO, where did she go?" Margaret cried, shaking the nurse by the shoulders as Sir Hubert and his grooms rushed upstairs to the solar.

"Oh, forgive me, I didn't see her!" wept the old nurse, "She was so fast!" A dreadful thought filled Margaret. Petronilla had not come through the hall. She could only have fled down the outer tower stair. If she hasn't killed him by dropping him from the tower, then there's only one other place a person as crazy as that would go.

"The spring," said Margaret, as she flew past the screen and down the front steps without further thought. Behind her came Gilbert, and even as the others, slow to comprehend, were searching the solar and tower rooms, they had taken two of the clerks' little saddled cobs that stood in the courtyard and were off at full gallop through the gate, past the fields and into the meadow at the edge of the oak wood. There they thought they saw a figure in a flying gown on the magistrate's big bay gelding vanishing among the trees, and they followed, slower now, their little horses, no match for the bay, dripping sweat and breathing hard. By this time the hue and cry had been taken up at the manor, and the rest of the grooms and manor folk were in pursuit.

But as Margaret's horse crashed through the underbrush into the clearing, she saw she was too late. Petronilla had ridden directly into the spring, the black, wailing bundle still thrown in front of her saddle. Green, bubbling water flowed around her knees and the horse's belly. The crackling aura of high madness came from her, her eyes were bright and lunatic, and her smile a crazed grimace.

"Ah, I wanted you here," she cried. "The water devil has sent you here at my command so that you will know what I have done. See my sacrifice! Everything that was yours now is mine!" And before they could reach her, she flung off the bundle into the center of the bubbling pool and then whipped the bay so hard that he lept in a single bound to the muddy margin of the pond, scrambled up the bank, and then headed back into the woods. Before Gilbert could drive his horse to the center of the pool, the black bundle had vanished utterly.

By this time, the rest of the household had caught up with them, and what they saw was a terrible sight. Gilbert on horseback, circling the bubbling center of the pool, searching for any sign of the child, and Margaret, dismounted, fetching a long stick to try to probe the depths. The Lord of Brokesford gave a terrible cry, a cry so great that the birds stopped their song and the trees themselves trembled. "Look, look," said one of the grooms to the magistrate, and as they stared, they saw the great stone by the side of the pool was oozing red blood.

"She's thrown him into the center," said Gilbert, his voice cracking. "I can't even see him. He's gone." But the Lord of Brokesford was no longer there; he was off in pursuit, and all they could hear was the crashing of his horse through the underbrush.

The magistrate and the grooms had dismounted, milling about looking for something, a pole, a hook, anything. Even though they knew it was hopeless, they couldn't give up the idea of doing something, not just standing about like fools. But Margaret had waded out into the pool, carrying her long stick, her eyes blank and unseeing. "For God's sake, Margaret, stop! Don't go any closer, I can't lose you, too!" cried Gilbert.

But it was then that everyone saw the strangest thing, the secret talked about over peasant hearths on winter nights, the awful thing that no one who saw it could ever forget, or ever speak of aloud. There was a strange sound from the center of the spring. It went, 'glorp, gulp.' And then the waters ceased to rise, and the pond was deadly still. In the eerie silence, Margaret cried, "By the holy mother, I charge you, give me back my child!" The sound of it echoed through the woods, and then there came a strange rustling, like a breeze in the yew temple. Down in the green, still depths, something moved and floated. A bit of black, unwinding, down in the shadows. No one on the bank moved a muscle. Gilbert's horse stood stock still in the shallows. Something was drifting, drifting softly below the green. A bit of red, a child's smock, too far to reach. Then a face. Was it a face? Bloated, white, silent, the eyes closed, it drifted peacefully in the green depths, then turned away, as if to descend again.

Margaret was on it like a flash. She waded deep, too deep, past her waist, past her shoulders, and grabbed at the drifting red of her baby's smock. Now she was too deep to recover, but Gilbert had ridden out and grabbed her by the hair, beneath her kerchief, pulling her through the water as she clutched at her baby's smock. As they reached the shallows, he grabbed at her shoulders to set her on her feet, but she said in a harsh, alien voice, "Don't touch me." Her eyes were glassy as she strode from the pond, her clothes and hair wet and every inch of her dripping with green pond slime, her kerchief lost, drifting in the water.

She held her child by the foot, and water gushed from his mouth and nose. She squeezed him by the middle, and more came out. No one dared touch her. Something crackling, like light, like the bright shine that reflects from water, was moving all about her face and hands. She laid the baby out on the ground, and leaned over it. What was she doing? No one could see, no one dared speak. They could hear her gasping horribly, then saw her fall over the child as if struck dead. Gilbert grabbed at her and turned her over. She was sheet white, as if her heart had stopped beating.

"Margaret, Margaret!" he cried. "Oh, God, she has been struck dead with grief. Why did you spare me?"

"No, no, my lord. Look. Look at the baby." Gilbert looked, and saw the strangest sight he had ever seen, though he had seen much. A faint pink color was creeping into the still, white face. He put his hand on the little chest. It was moving up and down. He put his hand on Margaret's chest. It was moving up and down, too.

"Is she alive?" asked the magistrate, kneeling down beside them, his face twisted with concern.

"Something, something," mumbled Gilbert, "she's done something." Then he heard a sound, a soft sound. Margaret moaning. "Mother Hilde," she said. "Where is she?"

"She's not here. I'm here," said Gilbert.

"Get my ladies, get my ladies. I'm losing the child I carried," she said, and tears squeezed silently from her eyes, tracking through the green slime to find their way to the ground. Tenderly, Gilbert wiped her face.

"Don't cry," he said, "oh, please don't cry. Peregrine is breathing."

"I thought so," she answered, her voice barely a whisper. "I have given birth to him twice. Lord keep him, I think I can never do it again."

THE LORD OF BROKESFORD pursued the faint sound of hooves and the crashing of brush with all the skill he brought to the pursuit of a fleeing stag. At length, at a distance, he saw Petronilla, her horse at full gallop across the scrubby waste at the edge of the woods. His jaw set as grim as death, he pushed his horse through the dead leaves, over ditches and the through the rippling brook itself to cut her off. She was a fleet rider, with the shining brilliance and daring of one who is truly insane, but Sir Hubert was fired with deadly determination that gave him almost a foresight of how she would move. Now she galloped across the meadow, and still he pursued, getting closer. Then seeing that he was closing the distance, she turned, riding hard past the coppices and slowing only to re-enter the woods, where she hoped to lose him. But every secret path she took was known better to the old knight, who had hunted in these woods since childhood. No matter how she tried, she could not shake him off. Branches grabbed at her headdress, tearing it away, and her braids came down, tangling as she doubled back through the underbrush. Her horse was dripping sweat now, and slower. She cut past a formation of strange looking rocks, poking up through the forest floor, and Sir Hubert knew he had her. He turned away, and she thought she'd lost him, and slowing to a walk, she followed a little deer trail that was strange to her, but looked as if it led to the abbey land. He'd never touch her there, on sacred ground. The abbey, and safety, her voices sang to her.

But the trail led to a damp, brushy spot enclosed on three sides by a stony rise of ground too thickly overgrown to pass through. And as she saw she was enclosed and turned to ride out again, she saw the Lord of Brokesford waiting on the path by which she had come. He sat immobile there, blocking the narrow, overgrown path on his great horse. His eyes were the hard eyes of an executioner.

"Let me pass," she said.

"You will never pass out of here alive," said the Lord of Brokesford.

"Oh, you must let me. I carry the only heir. Did you know? I shall bear a son now. The pond has said it. It took my sacrifice. The green woman loves me."

"I intend to put you down," said the Lord of Brokesford. "You are no different to me than a rabid dog or a horse with a broken leg."

"You can't do that. I'm a lady," said Petronilla.

"You are no lady," said the old knight, "and no decent woman, either. But you are a human being with a soul, so I will give you leave to say your prayers first."

"What have I done? Oh, find it in your heart to understand me and my suffering. If you saw things as I do, you would let me pass."

"I have no heart. I have no eyes. You have stolen them away," said the old man.

"But surely you're a Christian. You have to forgive. I can repent. Let me go, and I swear I'll enter a convent and pray every day, every hour—"

"Pray now. God knows how to forgive, but He is greater than I. If I could take your life twice, thrice, a hundred times, it would not make up for that little boy." At that very moment, Petronilla, with that quicksilver perception that comes with madness, saw him weaken at the thought of Peregrine, and his eyes drop. In a flash, she tried to push her horse past his and to freedom. But the old man was like a cat, who has paused only the better to spring forward, and as her horse leapt past him, he grabbed her by her loose braids and pulled her out of the saddle. In a single swift motion he dropped his reins, pulled the long knife from his belt, and drove it into her heart. "Monster," he said, looking down at her, where she lay face up against his horse's shoulder, tethered by her long, honey-blonde hair. And as the life's blood oozed from her mouth and down her breast, she rolled her eyes upward to his face.

"No greater than you," she said. There was no horn to sound the mort.

WHEN SIR HUBERT re-entered the clearing by the pond, he saw that they were finished cutting branches to make a litter, and he thought that they had guessed what he was about. He was leading the big bay, with his daughter-in-law's corpse thrown face down across the saddle. There was blood everywhere. Blood soaked her gown and flowed down the saddle. Blood stained the front of his garments, his boots, and his sleeves, where he had lifted her up. But then he realized no one was looking at him, and as they tied the litter between two horses, he saw that the litter had not been prepared for Petronilla; it was Margaret they were lifting up. Margaret with Peregrine thrown face down over her pale corpse. And then he saw that he had been right, and cutting down Petronilla a hundred times would never give him back what he had lost. How could he not have known, not have understood, what he had once had? His second son's tall form, hunched over in agony, was silent. We'll never speak again, he thought. Was all of it my fault? He heard from somewhere a dreadful sound, and realized then that it was himself, sobbing. How could it all have come to this? But then Sir Ralph was at his side, his voice concerned. "Sir Hubert, Sir Hubert," he said. "They're not dead yet. Both are breathing. What is that you've brought?"

Sir Hubert took a deep breath. He didn't believe the magistrate, but he had rehearsed what he would say, there in the depths of the woods. "Lady Petronilla committed suicide out of remorse," he said. The magistrate glanced quickly at the old man's besmeared garments, and then at his knife hilt. Not a spot of blood on it. But at Petronilla's belt was a knife. And it was smeared and bedaubed with the blood that was running down his own good saddle. Good enough, he thought. But I want her off my saddle before the blood stains are too hard to remove. But Sir Hubert felt confused. He shook his head. "Did you say they are living?"

"She—she went into the water and pulled him out," said the magistrate. Sir Hubert looked at Sir Ralph's white face, and then he surveyed the shocked look on the faces of his grooms. Some were still on their knees in the mud, their eyes rolled heavenward, reciting prayers. She's done something, thought the old man. She's done another one of those things.

"I told you that you'd want her on your side," said Sir Hubert.

"I think I know what you mean," said the magistrate. "Are the daughters the same way?"

"Not that I know about," said the old knight. There was a merry gurgling and burbling sound as the water gushed up from the spring. Sir Hubert looked at the rock. It was dry, with a faint sparkle of crystal here and there. "I think you must be right. They are alive. The rock's dry once more."

"Did you always know about the rock?"

"Never saw it before. Thought it was a fairy tale," said Sir Hubert.

"And the spring's started up again," said the magistrate, still looking rather pale.

"You mean she stopped it?"

"Yes," said the magistrate. "She told it to cough the boy up, and it did," he gave a long, shuddering sigh.

"I always thought that was a fairy tale, too. Pity I didn't see it."

"I wish I hadn't," said the magistrate. "I liked my world the way it was. Orderly."

"Ha! Lawyers! The world never works like it does in books! Especially law books!" announced Sir Hubert.

"It ought to," said the magistrate.

"Why so? Then I wouldn't have my grandson back again," said Sir

Hubert. But as he surveyed the mournful procession that set off for the manor, he didn't feel his old self-content at getting his way come back to him. Something else, something agonizing that he had never felt before, was gnawing at his insides. Remorse, bitter remorse, had stormed the high walls of his citadel.

CHAPTER TWENTY-SIX

BY THE TIME THE PROCESSION HAD AR-
rived at the manor gate, it was accompanied by
crowds of silent peasants, and the village priest.
Someone had set the bell in the churchyard tolling. Margaret
and her son lay as still as death, and as the word spread that the
little London widow, the one with the fancy shoes and city
ways who married the second son, was gone, there was moaning and shrieking among the women of the village, for she had
done much good among them. Then the word spread that it
was not she that was dead, but Sir Hugo's wife that had taken
her life, and that gravediggers were already digging outside
the churchyard for her burial, and the people of the village
shuddered with horror. It was the last and most terrible thing,
to be refused burial on sacred ground.

As the violet twilight gradually faded into dark, the cluster
of folk beneath the window of the solar grew into a crowd,
milling about by the light of a half-dozen torches.

"What are they doing out there?" said the Lord of Brokesford, who was sitting on one of the window seats set into the
solar wall. It was dark, there, in the recess of the window, and
only a few cold stars shone through. The old lord had his head
in his hands. He had been that way for hours, unmoving.
Across the room from him, Margaret and the boy lay in the big
bed, with her old dog, bleeding and bruised, at her feet. The
bed was surrounded by all of the dozen candles in the manor,
and his son Gilbert knelt beside it, deep in prayer.

"They are singing prayers to the Virgin," said the groom,

peering out the window. "Every soul on the demesne must be there."

"Everything—everything in ruins. My plans. How can I go on? What does a man live for? Glory—my family name—and now, look at them there. Is it my fault?" For a minute, a flicker of realization floated tantalizingly near him. Somehow, somehow, might it have been a chain, a very long chain of consequences, that was rooted in his own frozen heart, his own lovelessness? But as he tried to sieze at it, it floated beyond the reach of his mind, and was lost forever. He tried to comfort himself with the thought of how wicked Lady de Vilers had been, and how he had meted out justice with an iron hand, but somehow that didn't seem to work, either. Something heavy was pressing down on his chest, something that hurt. Now it was going through him in waves, and he felt wrung to pieces by it. He had risked his old, hard heart on the tiny little creature that lay in the bed, barely breathing, next to his mother. And now it was broken. Outside, he could hear the voices rising beneath the stars:

> "My sweet lady, hear my prayer,
> and pity me if it is your will——"

All useless, thought the Lord of Brokesford. How many times had the highest ranking priests in the land called down the blessings of God, of Jesus, and of the Blessed Mother on the great enterprise in France, and what had come of that?

> "You arise like the dawn,
> which separates day from dark night;
> a new light sprang out from you,
> to illuminate the world——"

Whenever would they stop that useless singing, he thought. It's all gone. Don't they know any better? New light. Where is my new light? Who has lost as much as I?

"Take pity on me, sweet lady,
and have mercy on your servant——"

Pity, where is pity? he thought, looking out at the dark. A sliver of a moon had risen, but shed little light. A sliver of a thought came to him, with that rising moon, and began to form in the depths of him. She had a son, that heavenly lady, he thought. She risked all. And she lost Him. Surely, she must know how my heart is dying inside me now.

"Bring us, lady, to your home,
and shield us from the vengeance of hell——"

Ah, God, is this what it feels like? Damnation? Is hell composed of endless sorrow, of infinite and unmendable regrets? I never thought it would be like this; I have always scorned pain, pain of the body. But this stuff, this came like a thief, and cut away everything within. Take pity on me, take pity sweet lady, queen of heaven. Pity on me, your servant. . . .

DOWNSTAIRS, A CAPABLE HAND had taken over, when that of the lord seemed paralyzed. Madame had called the midwife's daughter to wash and lay out the body of Lady Petronilla, and she had shamed Sir Hugo out of drinking himself into a stupor by telling him that he was expected to pass the night in prayer. With a firm word to the steward, she had sent all of Lady Petronilla's servants packing, on foot, into the ending day, and she herself had stood at the door and checked their belongings to make sure that they took away only what was theirs. Then she had given orders to the gravediggers and sent to the village for a pair of strong, lively girls to help her with the nursing. Up and downstairs she went, an indomitable figure, with her candle in her hand, supervising at once a funeral, a disastrous childbed, and a household too crippled by tragedy to offer proper hospitality to the assortment of guests that had remained: the magistrate and his clerks, their horses too exhausted by the chase to travel for days, and a very ancient old blackfriar who spoke almost no English and who could not be removed from the best bed until all the apple-wine in the cellar had been drunk.

Beds and linen, supper, a shroud, extra boys to walk the horses dry, poultices and herbal brews, and blankets warmed before the fire had to be provided. Madame comandeered the servants, she comandeered the villagers, and she comandeered the little girls, who suddenly seemed sober beyond their years. And as dark drew on, and the household dropped with exhaustion, only Madame persevered. Up and down and in and out she went, with her candle, checking up, making things work. And every time she passed through the solar, Sir Hubert looked up and watched her. As the night passed, he saw things he had not seen before, or rather, not seen aright. Her hems rustling about her feet, her straight, unbending back, her ever-vigilant eyes seemed to him the very soul of order, the order that brings rightness and civility to a house, even in the face of chaos and disaster. Looking at her through grief-swollen eyes, he saw other things, a profile like the paintings of saints and angels, a complexion pale and smooth in the candlelight. And such wrinkles as remained in its flattering glow seemed to be signs of character. Maturity. The outward image of her inward competence. He saw capable hands that brought cool, wet, towels, and hot fomentations. And he saw that she never, never gave in, which was a quality he could appreciate, since it was one he believed himself to possess.

At last, in the hour before dawn, Margaret gave a terrible cry. And although the women had pulled the bedcurtains, the old lord, still keeping his vigil at the far end of the solar, watched numbly as the nurses carried away a basin with all that remained of his second grandchild. It was almost with relief that he looked up to see Madame, her guttering candle in her hand, in front of him.

"My lord, your daughter-in-law is well, and will recover," she said.

"And my boy?" asked the old man.

"The little boy breathes, he is sleeping quietly."

"Has he ever waked? Has he spoken?"

"Not yet. But he seems to be dreaming. He spoke once, but his eyes weren't open and no one understood what he was saying."

"What did he say?"

"The green lady has a very wet hall." The old man puzzled over this awhile. Then he asked, his face troubled,

"Is his mind right? Will he be as he was?"

"That is God's will," said Madame, but Sir Hubert could see the tears shining in her eyes, and understood suddenly at what cost she had bought her untiring energy of that night. The cost of unshed tears, of grief deferred. It was a price he understood.

"Madame Agathe, you have been very good to us," he said.

"It is my duty," said Madame, suddenly turning away her face.

THE NEXT MORNING, as he sat down to dinner with the magistrate, they both watched as Madame ordered up a meal to be sent to the solar, gave orders for pallbearers, and set about arranging for a funeral supper of the exactly correct level of simplicity for the sort of death that one does not talk about, and Sir Hubert said:

"She manages things very well, doesn't she?"

"You can always tell good blood," said the magistrate. It set Sir Hubert thinking.

As the bell tolled, and the funeral procession started from the gate, Sir Hugo turned to his father as they followed the corpse on foot.

"It certainly is a relief to know that Madame is back there making things work. It's been hell, never knowing what I'd come back to find in my chamber. Did you know my wife slashed my new doublet in the Saxon style? And after I'd taken such trouble with it, too." Sir Hubert, who had felt the first few unpleasant gnawings of guilt, found his heart suddenly lightened. In the new space that had been made, the idea he had been contemplating grew even larger, and took on the form of a brilliant inspiration.

That afternoon, with Hugo's wife safely interred, and a few extra prayers had been said to keep her spirit from walking, Sir Hubert went to take counsel with his younger son, the only member of his tribe who seemed to have had a worthwhile experience in certain matters.

He found Gilbert sitting on his wife's bed, holding her hand. Margaret was propped up on many pillows, and her color was coming back. The baby wasn't in the bed any more, and at the sight of the empty place, he grew alarmed.

"Father, it's excellent news. Peregrine woke up as good as new while you were gone. He was making so much noise I sent him off with his new nursemaid to find something to eat. And look, I've made Margaret smile."

"That wasn't a smile," said Margaret. "It was a grimace. You make the very worst puns in the world."

"It's an art," said Gilbert, his voice serene. Even now, with all this, they are very happy together, thought Sir Hubert. Is that how it's supposed to be?

"Gilbert, I have an idea," he announced.

"Oh, no," said Gilbert very softly, and his face turned white.

"Not again," said Margaret, under her breath, and Sir Hubert noticed little lines on her brow which hadn't been there before.

"It's a very good idea, and I have come to take counsel with you as to how to best accomplish it. I can't make any mistakes. And you know how touchy *some people* can be."

"*Some people?* You mean Hugo?"

"No, I mean that, well, Madame. That is, Madame Agathe, you know."

"Oh, really, what have you in mind?"

"Well, um, you know how this place needs fixing up—" Margaret's eyes flashed irritation.

"And I've noticed lately that Madame is a very competent woman. That is, even though she doubtless has no marriage portion, she has excellent personal qualities—that is, her blood is good and it would be no disgrace—"

"Father," said Gilbert, his face turning pink, "do you mean you are thinking of proposing marriage to Madame?"

"It does—well, it does seem sensible, doesn't it? A sort of partnership. I mean, a younger woman with a dowry might seem better on the surface of it, but she might not have the strength of mind, that is——"

"You mean the strength of mind to put up with you?" asked Gilbert, a wicked smile crossing his face. "Why, father, you have my blessing."

Margaret's eyes were open wide with alarm. This old man was the most interfering, marriage-crazy creature she had ever seen. First her Cecily, and now Madame. Really, someone ought to warn Madame of the horrible notion he was hatching up in his mind.

"Ah, then you think it's a good idea. I knew it," announced the old knight.

"Be careful how you ask. I've had experience with Madame. You have to be very tactful," said Gilbert, but his father had already dashed out of the room.

Sir Hubert found Madame at the head of the cellar steps, giving orders to several girls armed with brooms down below among the casks and boxes. Dust was flying, and there was a chittering and rustling as all the creatures which God made to live in cellars were being put to flight. A mouse whizzed by his foot like a furry round projectile.

"I've sent for a couple of big cats," said Madame.

"Cats?" said Sir Hubert. "I hate cats."

"You'll like it far less if the rats that infest this place gnaw through your casks," she said. "Stamp them out, stamp them out," she cried down the stairs. "Especially the little nests and the egg sacks!"

"Well, then, I suppose cats have their place," he said.

"Everything has its place," said Madame. "But some things have no place in a decent house." Sir Hubert squirmed and struggled. How best to bring it up? Suddenly it seemed a touchier matter than before.

"Madame," he said, "some people are not in the proper place."

"What on earth do you mean?" asked Madame.

"Well, um, for example, you manage very well around here."

Madame looked at him, her eyes suspicious. "I think, well, I've been thinking—" Madame looked again, wishing to make very sure of what she was hearing. Oh, my, thought Sir Hubert. This way isn't working very well. I'll start it over again. He harrumphed.

"Madame, you are a woman of formidable principles. I appreciate those principles. I propose an honorable partnership." Madame stared at him, and her jaw dropped. "I mean, I mean, not housekeeping. Um, don't mistake me. I propose an honorable marriage. You are just the sort of person to put this place in order again." Madame stared at him a long time, and her face grew paler.

"I will have to think it over," she said.

"GILBERT, GILBERT, for God's sake, what do I do now? She's turned me down!" Sir Hubert had entered the solar wild-eyed, and now that he spied his son, he hurried toward him, oblivious to the fact that he was reading aloud to Margaret. The two little girls were sitting at the foot of the bed to hear the reading, and at Sir Hubert's approach they tried to make themselves as invisible as possible, so they would not be sent away.

"What exactly did she say when she turned you down?" asked Gilbert. The little girls' eyes were huge, as they took everything in.

"Ghastly. How dare she? Perhaps she mistook my motives. She said she'd have to think it over." Margaret tried very hard to suppress a laugh, and it came out a hiccup. Sir Hubert glanced quickly at her, but saw only a face composed along the most tragic and sympathetic lines. So he turned back to his son, where he sat on the bench with Brokesford's big book of household stories and recipes across his lap, and spoke again. "Why do you think she turned me down? I have everything—a title, this beautiful manor, the very finest bloodlines in England, a great patron, why, she has nothing. She should be grateful I even thought of her."

Gilbert looked at his father with a sober face and shook his head. His voice, as he responded, was slow and serious. But his dark eyes were glittering with amusement.

"If my own experience with Madame can be any guide to you, you will have to be prepared to propose three times," he said.

His father spluttered. "Three times? You mean a woman that age can still be coy? I'd think she'd snap at my offer."

"If she was the sort of woman who'd snap at your offer, she wouldn't be the sort of woman you'd make an offer to, now would she?" said Gilbert. The old man nodded. He had to admit Gilbert was right about that one. How had he gone and got so subtle about women? It was practically indecent. "I think, given what I know of Madame, you will have to be prepared to offer conditions," Gilbert said, his voice thoughtful.

"Conditions! This is worse than negotiating with the French!" The little girls turned toward each other, and Cecily gave a knowing nod. "Gilbert," said the old man suddenly, desperately, "what sort of conditions do you think I should offer?"

"Offer the things you think a lady would like, not the things you want yourself," said Gilbert.

"I was thinking of a new saddleblanket and her own falcon," said Sir Hubert.

"That's exactly what I thought," responded Gilbert. "You'll have to do some more thinking."

"Ladies! What do they want? Dresses, frou-frou, useless gifts to priests, minstrels and dancing, wasted time and money!"

"If you put it to her that way, father, you might as well save your breath. You'll be proposing until doomsday."

"But what do I say, what do I say?"

"You have to say it in your own words, father. You'll have to think it over before you speak, or all is lost."

IN THE NEXT FEW DAYS, Sir Hubert had plenty of time to think. Time spent riding to and from the coroner's inquest concerning Lady Petronilla's suicide. What did women want? What did women want? How to say it without making it an insult? Oh, God, he wasn't some perfumed dandy with a snake's tongue. Why couldn't she appreciate that? The inquest was of the most perfunctory. Sir Hugo testified that his wife had often threatened suicide, saying death was better than being married to him. And then after being liberated from all those devils, albeit imperfectly, she had often been despondent, saying she'd be better off if she cast herself down the tower stair. Sir Hubert explained how he had caught up with her and remonstrated with her for throwing the baby into the pond, and she'd said they'd never try *her,* and stabbed herself, and the magistrate, who had departed the manor after the betrothal arrangements had been signed and sealed and cast in bronze, had returned to say he himself had seen the lady's bloody knife. Who was anybody to doubt the testimony of such important men? I'll have to find some wandering grayfriar to confess this all to, thought Sir Hubert as he rode home in Hugo's company—preferably one who doesn't speak English. I don't want a secret like this floating about the shire. Then he turned to Hugo, who had bought a new hat with a tiny brim in the latest style, and had an elegant black velvet doublet stitched up from one of his late wife's dresses so that he would catch the eye of any woman who might possibly turn up at the inquest.

"Hugo, what is it that women want?" he asked. They were still far from Brokesford. The first leaves of autumn were beginning to dry and shrivel on the trees, and there was a hint of chill in the morning air. Summer, generous summer, was coming to a close. The old man was growing to hate that feeling, when his bones could tell that winter was not so far away. The house will be so cold and empty, he thought. The little boy will be gone, and Margaret with all her bustling and interfering, and even Gilbert, who wasn't turning out so badly, though he had certainly taken his time about it.

"Why, women want a man who can renew his passion five times a night or more, like myself," Hugo said. "They're just ravenous. You have to satisfy them constantly, or their vital fluids all migrate up to the brain, and make them insane. I've given it great thought. Since men can't be interested in one woman only, it is impossible to satisfy a woman within the bounds of marriage, since a man must always share his attentions, while a woman must concentrate on her own husband only. So a man shouldn't marry, unless it is to several wives, for the stimulating variety, like the Grand Turk."

"Hugo, those fluids have got to your brain, too. Christian men are required to cleave to one wife only. Or at least, one at a time."

"True. That's why I need a little rest from marriage. Oh, the tragic black of a handsome young widower. Did you notice how many women have offered to pray with me lately? My consolation goes on apace."

"Hugo, what made you such a beast?" muttered the old man.

"Why, father, I've always modeled myself exactly on you," answered Hugo, his voice cheerful. Old men, they always get so morbid. Father would doubtless soon start walking with a stick and complaining about his rheumatism and sitting in the sun like a lizard. Ah, life's mysteries. Luckily, nothing grotesque like getting old will ever happen to *me,* thought Hugo.

"But women, Hugo——"

"When you think women, think passion," announced Hugo. "It's all their tiny little brains can hold in the way of a thought."

When they arrived home, after Sir Hubert had seen to the horses, he went up to his chamber and had his groom bring a little bronze mirror in which he studied his features. Not bad, not bad, he thought. Not young, but lines and the scar look noble, well-tried. But perhaps, to please a lady, I might need a bit of barbering up. Then he had the groom fetch scissors, and trim his wild white beard and the grey wisps that grew out of his ears like smoke. Then he looked again at his image. There is, he thought, a difference between making oneself more presentable to feminine company and entirely removing all signs of *character.* So he contented himself with having only the long, protruding hairs trimmed off his stormy white eyebrows, rather than having them slicked down like some gigolo. He then slathered his hair down flat with goose grease and parted it neatly in the middle. "I look like a damned dancing master," he grumbled to himself.

Attired in his Sunday best, he went off to seek Madame, who was in the bakehouse with the little girls and several of the manor women, popping generous, big round loaves into the ovens on long handled wooden paddles. When they saw the old man, Cecily and Alison, without a word, took Madame's paddle from her and untied her apron in the back, so she could slip it off unobtrusively. Together Sir Hubert and Madame went into Margaret's little herb garden, where the climbing roses on the wall were dropping their petals, and the little red rose hips shone among the briars like ripe fruit. There was the smell of sage and thyme, and all the good things that can be dried for the winter.

"Madame," said Sir Hubert. "I am a persistent man. I have come to offer you my hand and my heart." Madame looked at the ground, silent.

"I will arrange for a lady-companion of your own choice, so that you will not be without worthy company of your own sex," he said. Madame looked at the ground still, but he could hear her breathing heavily. A good sign. "This house—this house has been empty of pucelles and pages, since it has had no lady," he said. "It could be full of merry, youthful company that would delight your heart." Madame looked up at him, taking in the neatly trimmed beard, and the goose grease. It's working, thought Sir Hubert. But she hasn't said yes yet. So he forged on. "You shall always have a fine palfrey at your disposal." Madame was silent, and looked back at the ground again. "And two new dresses a year—ha, hm, not counting one for Christmas," Sir Hugo added hastily, and Madame looked up again. Her face was very pale.

"And every year, a trip to the City—no, two trips." He distinctly saw Madame smile, a faint smile. Sir Hubert could feel the blood beating powerfully in his veins. Madame looked at his eyes very closely as she answered.

"You shall, of course, have to apply to my sister's husband as head of the family. I do not believe he will make conditions," said Madame, her voice even. "My cousin deprived me of my dowry lands, and my sister's husband has always found it odious to support me."

Sir Hubert looked at her, astonished. His eyebrows grew stormier than ever, and his face turned red. "The man's a fool!" he shouted. "Why, you're a treasure! What gifts! What elegance! I tell you, if he makes the least peep, I'll challenge him to single combat!"

It was then that an amazing thing happened. Madame blushed. She turned pink to the roots of her hair. Her smile was authentic, and her eyes deeply admiring. Sir Hubert, to his dying day, would never forget that look. His heart expanded and he was sure there was no gentleman in England, no, the whole Christian world, that was more joyful than he was at that moment.

"Mon seigneur," said Madame, "you are my one, my true knight."

"JUST THINK, GILBERT," said Sir Hubert when he came to consult with his son after the Great Event, "you were WRONG! I only had to ask her TWICE!"

Margaret was propped up in bed playing with Peregrine when Gilbert brought the news to her. "Oh, my goodness," she said, "I suppose this means we have to stay until the wedding is over. Let's see, posting the banns, at least two weeks——" she started counting on her fingers. "And Gilbert, don't be surprised if your father asks you for a loan for Madame's wedding dress."

"Her dress?" Gilbert was puzzled.

"Of course. She hasn't got one, and this is one time he won't be content with one out of the trunk. He'll want to cut a swathe, you know."

"Well, Margaret, I suppose it's entirely fair that the Burgundians pay for a wedding. Maybe if the Duke likes the manuscript when he gets back, he'll make it all even out."

"Gilbert, I think it's all evened out anyway. Give thanks to God, who orders all things mightily."

"I do, Margaret, I do," said Gilbert, and very tenderly he kissed first his wife, and then his baby, who pulled his nose and insisted that he pick him up and carry him.

CHAPTER TWENTY-SEVEN

I WILL NEVER KNOW WHAT HAPPENED BE-
tween the time that I walked into the water and the time
that I woke up in bed in that ugly solar of my father-in-
law's manor, with all the hounds snuffling around the bed and
the mice chittering in the corners. My hand was between my
Gregory's two big ones, and my little boy that I had brought
home from France in a basket, with such care and pains, was
lying beside me, his face as pale as the sheets, and his brown
curls all tangled and wet on his head.

"Push him closer," I said, "I need to feel him breathing." A
round, warm thing was heavy on my feet. I saw my old dog,
wheezing and snoring, with blood matted on his coat. "What
happened to Lion?" I asked.

"He tried to rouse the nurse when Petronilla stole the baby,
then bit at her legs and she kicked him. He looks as if he'll be
fine, now," said Gregory. "I saw to him myself. Besides, I have
mended my opinion of him. I must say, for a ridiculous looking
dog, he is very gallant." Lion opened one eye at the praise, and
thumped his tail languidly on the coverlet.

"Lady Petronilla," I said, "don't let her in here. Promise me
you won't let her in here." I felt suddenly agitated, terrified.
"She hates me, there's nothing she wouldn't do."

"She's not going to be let in anywhere, unless it's in through
the gates of hell. She has committed suicide."

"Suicide? Her? Not likely," I said.

"Father has sworn it at the inquest."

"Then he did it, Gregory. Just like he'd drown a sackful of
puppies he didn't want."

"Sh, Margaret. What he says is what is. But this much I know, I've never seen him look so bad over something. He's looking quite hollow eyed. For once, he's got a bad conscience over something."

"Not hollow eyed enough, as far as I'm concerned. He's cost us our new little one, without ever giving it a second thought."

"It's not his fault, Margaret, it's my fault, all my fault, for not listening to you and taking you away as soon as you asked me to."

"Why is it that whenever your father misbehaves, you always get the bad part of it? And now you're taking his blame. Don't you dare. He did it, not you, with all his quarrels over deeds and money and—and ancient drinking horns. And he's sold my precious girl's marriage for his own advantage, and even talked her into it behind my back. And *she's* such a baby she agreed because she thinks Brother Malachi is going to turn her into a boy before the wedding night. It's all, all your father, this trouble, every bit of it. Wherever he goes, he makes trouble."

"But he couldn't help it—"

"Oh, yes, he could. If he were a better manager instead of a spendthrift, none of this would have happened."

"But, Margaret, there's nothing to manage. When all is said and done, he doesn't clear a shilling off this land—"

"He would if he had sense. Madame says that if he raised sheep instead of horses, they'd be bringing him money instead of eating it all up."

"Sheep? That's ridiculous. A knight doesn't raise sheep."

"Why not? Knights sell fish, knights import wine. Why shouldn't knights raise sheep? It's better than skinning the French for a living. Besides, then he'd quit trying to borrow money from you."

"Oh, Margaret, Margaret, I refuse to argue with you, even if it is making your cheeks pinker. Father would rather sizzle a thousand extra years in purgatory than do anything practical, even if I do grant you that you are theoretically in the right."

"Theory's not good enough, Gregory mine. How do we get Cecily untangled from this betrothal? I don't want to have that scheming, money hungry magistrate in my family. Besides, that boy of his is a spineless toady who's as ambitious as his father. Cecily needs someone more thoughtful, more appreciative of her, someone with a nice family—like Walter Wengrave."

"Well, we'll have to be patient. Seven years is a long time, and the boy is older. He may find some other girl and break the engagement himself. In the meanwhile, I want you to be nice to the magistrate because he's promised to pry that awful old monk out of father's bed and take him back to the canons at Wymondley when he leaves. The old fellow's drinking up all the apple wine and just lies up there in the tower room singing in some language nobody understands—"

"Madame is wrong. Your father shouldn't raise sheep, after all. He should convert this house into a lunatic asylum—he's got a good start on it already."

"Margaret! You're being rude!"

"Not as rude as that awful old father you have. Something has to be done about him."

"Now, now, Margaret, we'll manage," said my lord husband, stroking my hand and then feeling my forehead, as if I were somehow delirious and could not be held responsible for anything I had just been saying.

That night I was feverish, and as I sweated and turned in the stuffy, damp bed, I had a very strange dream. I was back at the pond, hunting between the columns of the strange old yew-temple for something I had lost, but I could not remember what it was. Was it a thimble? A little silver boss from my best girdle? It was very important to me, and I had knelt down to the ground, all puzzled, scrabbling around but finding nothing. Then as I was hunting, I saw two watery feet, ebbing and flowing, all green in front of me. I looked up, and what I saw surprised me so that I sat back on my heels. It was a woman, all green and mossy, clad in a wet gown green with pond scum. Her hair was dark and shadowy, like water-weeds seen at a depth. Her eyes were hidden caverns, where fish could swim in and out, and she flowed and swirled like the tides. Behind her, clinging to the hem of her gown, was a little girl with a high, white forehead, and curling black hair. Her chin was pointed, like mine, and she had my Gregory's sorrowful, intelligent brown eyes.

"You don't have to look any more," said the water woman. "I've kept her." And then I knew that I had not been looking for a lost button or a shoelace or a ring, but my own heart's delight that could never be held in human arms. "She was fading so fast, so fast, and could never have lasted long enough to be yours—and I was lonely. Centuries lonely," said the water woman. And as I looked longingly at the little girl, taking in every feature with my hungry eyes, I saw that she seemed very frail, and held together with water weed and dreams, and that only the magic of the green woman was making her live.

"Be good to her," I said. "She is very clever, and will be mournful without her mother. You must make her laugh."

"Oh, I have thousands of beautiful things in my green hall," said the water woman. "And I'll love her like my own. We'll play and tell jokes and spin fishes here beneath the yews. It's not your fault that your little light was not strong enough for two."

"I thought it was, I thought I could will it so," I said. "I was greedy, and I was terribly punished. But how could I make a choice, and still have a mother's heart in me? And now my light's gone, and I have to pretend to be the same as ever."

"Why do you need to pretend?" asked the pond creature, and the caverns of her eyes were curious.

"Because I wish it were my turn to fly free to heaven, but I have children to raise, and a husband to look after, and I need to free my Cecily from that wily old fox of a magistrate."

But the water woman laughed a laugh like golden ripples on the surface of a river, and she said, "Is *that* all?" as if it were nothing in the world. She sat down beside me and put her watery arm around me while she held my baby on her lap. And this is the curious thing: her green arm was warm and liquid, and smelled sweet, like the heart of growing things, and it flowed all around me as if I were swimming. "Don't worry about those girls of yours," she said. "They'll always manage. Alison has made herself quite fat on my honey-cakes, and Cecily wore my green shoes to her betrothal. I promise you, if the man she marries doesn't meet all of her conditions, there isn't a river in all of England that won't reach up and drown him."

"You are in all the rivers?" I asked, suddenly curious.

"Oh, no, I never travel from my own place. But we waters are all related. That's how we were made by the Great Creator." She laughed again, like the gurgle of a brook over stones. "And you," she said, "be merry again. Your dream-child will sing sweet music in my hall—a lot better, I might add, than that tuneless *kyrie* that boring priest keeps humming—and besides, look you there: your little light was just resting, and it springs up again. See? It was worn out." I looked down and I seemed to be underwater, with my clothes all floating out in billows around me, and deep under my skin, like the glow of blood, a faint tinge of orangeish pink was shining and flickering, like a candle coming to life after a cold draft.

"Ah! There it is! That's how I first knew you—by the little light, all soft and warm. You used to come and dip up my water for beer."

"And very good beer it was, too," I said.

"Aha! I said to myself. I have made little frogs and fishes with shining scales, but never before have I made beer. Not good beer, at any rate. I thought to make your acquaintance, but you went away."

"I don't live here, ordinarily."

"So I found out from my cousin the Thames, and he said, 'why do you want such a little one?' And I said, 'I had a man with a cold blue light that was so very strong, and he never once listened to me, for all that he lived for forty years in the hermitage beside me. He thought I was the voice of Sin. But now you are listening to me, even if all you ever did was brew and do laundry from me. That's how it is. We women of sense can always come to an understanding. I need you, Lady Margaret. I need you to talk to the shining ones above for me. The Maker who knows all. I know you can. I've heard you do it. You go into the house of stone and I can hear you and see your light brightening, like the pink light of dawn."

Now as you can see this dream didn't make much sense, but it also made all the sense in the world, especially since I had seen what they took away in the basin—a jumble of flesh like liver and a bubble of jelly with no baby at all. When I saw it I knew all at once that my child was only imagining, since she had never quickened, and the soul flown down from heaven to dwell in her, as the priests say happens. Yet in my heart she had been strong dreaming, as strong as the water woman talking in the night, who was real and not real. It was my dream-child she'd kept, as soulless and ageless as herself. My own, but now hers.

So because I was dreaming, I just asked the water woman what it was that she needed, instead of fussing and weeping, and she said she was terribly worried about her lovely green hall and her singing fountain and her sighing yews and oaks that were full of rooks and saucy squirrels. She explained that she *was* them, and if they were all spoiled she'd die, because she didn't have a soul apart from her green and growing body. She said that it really wasn't a horrible pagan, heathen thing to look after her interests, but really more like praying for the sick, which all good Christians are enjoined to do. I was not so sure about this, having already once fallen into disfavor with the Inquisition for doing healing without the proper credentials, which I explained was very frightening, and I almost got burned alive, except that I recanted.

"You need to get them on your side," I said. "Perhaps you should change your name to something Christian."

"Change my name? What an insult! I haven't got a name! Do you know how old I am? I was made just after light was divided from dark. I'm older than names. And don't go suggesting 'Edburga.' That's the ugliest name I've ever heard. Besides, did you ever see that Saint Edburga? A mean-spirited old woman who went around terrifying people with tales of hellfire. She's not my style."

"What about something like 'Marywell'?" I asked, making my voice sound as humble as possible. Wind and water, stars and sea, one should never go around rousing up elementals.

"The 'well' part is all right, because that's what I am. But who's this Mary?"

"The Queen of Heaven. You can't go much higher," I said.

"Marywell, Marywell," said the water-spirit, rolling it around inside her like a current of bright liquid. "Not bad. Maybe she'd help out with my trees and my singing birds and my lovely dark eels and shining fishes."

When I woke up in the morning, the sun was already poking through the deep, narrow solar windows. The sheets were wringing wet, and my hair was soaked through. Everyone was up already, and I could hear the ring of the blacksmith shoeing horses outside in the courtyard. In a panic, I felt suddenly for the place that Peregrine had lain, but he was gone. Then I heard, "woof, woof, woof, woof," and looked over the side of the bed to see Peregrine crawling about on all fours with the puppies, barking like a hound. "Look, mama," he cried. "I'm teaching them to *bark*!" On the bench beside him sat an alert, capable looking young village woman wearing a big apron and wooden clogs. She was spinning and smiling.

"Oh," she said, "I'm so glad to see you're finally up. You had a dreadful fever in the night, and they all despaired."

"I—I've had the most amazing dream. The pond must be renamed 'Marywell.'"

"'Marywell'?" said the girl. "Why, that's a beautiful name. Surely we will all be blessed if the heathen waters are called Marywell. Prosperity will return with a name like that."

CHAPTER TWENTY-EIGHT

NOW HERE IS WHERE I HAVE TO CONFESS that I was wrong about one thing: Gilbert's father did not borrow money from us for the wedding gown. He just borrowed money for the wine, the spices, and the delicacies he ordered up for the wedding feast, which Gilbert said would have been cheap at twice the cost given the new mellowness that had seemed to settle over his father's temper with the benificent influence of Madame Agathe. But in a chest with a number of odd things he had brought back from France in a prior campaign, he had a length of silk all patterned with figures and fit for an empress, though I rather suspected it had been originally intended for some French bishop's dalmatic. So he gave me charge of the sewing women, and Madame herself supervised the cutting of it, and I must say, she had a very sharp eye for fashion, for a lady who had worn the plainest of black for many a year.

"Lady Margaret, you won't harbor any ill will toward me, for taking up this place in the world, will you?" she asked as we sewed on the magnificent gown.

"Madame Agathe, if you can ever tame that old he-bear, you will have done us all a service that is beyond price. I, for one, will be happy to call you mother, and pray for your good fortune always."

Madame seemed relieved, as if it had been eating at her heart for a while. "I do have a few little ideas for improving this place," she said. "After all, a gallant warrior like Sir Hubert cannot be expected to have to worry about tiny details. His mind must be on the affairs of the great world." She looked a little pinker to me as she spoke, and a faint smile seemed to cross her austere face for a moment. Goodness gracious, I thought, who would have believed it? She's actually in love with that horrible old man.

"I'm glad you'll be happy with him," I said.

"How could it not be so? A hero of Poitiers, of ancient lineage and high connections, wily with his foes, just in his judgments, a true knight without peer. I could never imagine that the sire of your own gallant husband would be otherwise. They resemble each other perfectly. It is the true blood," she said, and I dropped my thimble from pure astonishment. If I ever thought there were the slightest resemblance in the world between those two, I'd probably go the way of Hugo's departed lady. How could a woman be so steeped in the lore of chivalry that she could be blind to that man's monumental ghastliness? But then, perhaps that is why I'll never be a real lady, I sighed to myself. A kind of selective sight is one of the chief requirements. Cecily, who was working with the sewing women on the trousseau linens, jumped up and found my thimble settled upside down in a crack in the floor, and fetched it to me. A look of understanding and amazement flashed between us.

"I've decided I like those green shoes after all," I said, spying what she had hidden beneath her longest gown. "Have you been wearing them every day, while I was in bed and couldn't forbid you?" Cecily smiled a secret smile.

"They're my favorites," she said.

"Cécile, your stitches are very even and tiny," said Madame, looking at her work. "I commend you."

"Merci, almost-grandmother," she answered, and I could see the pink color rising beneath her freckles.

"Lady Margaret, you are looking so pale. You mustn't overwork for my sake. I beg you, take rest now. You need to renew the blood you have lost, so that your little light will grow back." I looked at her, amazed, and she smiled that quiet, knowing smile of hers. "My almost-daughter," she said, "I could not be a woman and not understand what your struggle with that devil in the pond cost you. Every soul on this manor is grateful that you managed to negotiate an agreement with it." Madame Agathe really is a true lady, I thought. She sees the pond-thing as a devil. Only the uncouth, the untutored, the wild things see the water woman as she is. Maybe some day even the children won't see her anymore. And me, I must be made wrong, for I sat with her, all finny-wet and slippery, and we made discourse, even if it was only in a dream. Lord, Lord, why didn't you make me a complete and spotless lady, too? Then I would see things all aright, the way they're supposed to be. And while you were doing it, great Lord of the Universe, you could have given me golden hair as well, which would have been ever so much more admirable. But God, who is often so enigmatic, didn't choose to answer this time, either.

Now FROM THE MOMENT the banns were cried, there was such a buzz and a stir as was never before seen in the entire shire. Carts and and chapmen with sumpter mules began to arrive, all laden with good things, courtesy of the Burgundians. After them came all the flotsam and jetsam who knew that a wedding meant largesse: minstrels and jugglers and cripples who claimed they were war wounded comrades and soothsayers and wandering friars and pardoners and all the rest of them, and they camped outside the manor gate and infested the courtyard. Then messengers were sent to the grand gentry and to the neighbors to invite them all to the wedding, and those who lived at a distance came with their trains of servants to encamp themselves in all the houses about, including Brokesford itself. Gilbert and Hugo followed their father about, and every time he began to get irritated with the crowds and inconvenience and it looked as if the furniture might fly, they plied him with ale and told him how lordly his hospitality was, until he forgot who he was angry at.

But then something happened that made his malicious spirit beam forth good nature: a nervous messenger arrived from Madame Agathe's cousin, conveying congratulations to the mighty Lord of Brokesford, comrade in arms to the most high and puissant Duke of

Lancaster. And Sir Hubert intimated that Madame's dowry lands might make a very nice little wedding present, and save her ungrateful cousin from the wrath of his many powerful connections, "INCLUDING the King's Magistrate, Sir Ralph FitzWilliam," he bellowed, as he kicked the fellow down the front steps, "JUST IN CASE YOU WERE UNAWARE!"

"Father, you needn't get entangled in another law case so soon," said Gilbert, as he hastened to dust off the esquire sent from Madame's former relatives and to make apologies to him.

"NONSENSE!" shouted Sir Hubert down the stairs after him, "just look how well the LAST one came out! Why, they didn't even dare face us in open court!"

"Hugo, where did you put that ale cup?" said Gilbert, looking quite pale around the mouth.

"Finished it up myself, brother. Oh, Margaret, there you are. How did you know we'd want replenishment? Give it all to Gilbert. His need is greatest."

But after that, all annoyances rolled off the Lord of Brokesford's back just as if it were greased, and he strode about with his eyes fixed on vast distances, with a tuneless little sort of a humming on his breath, the way he always did when he was planning great mischief. "I don't like it," said Gilbert as we sat up in bed that night, with the bodies of dozens of guests crammed into the solar, all snoring and wheezing and breathing. "The last time he was like this, he charged a French position single-handed."

"My lord husband, this time take my advice. The minute the nuptial knot is tied, we speed from here more swiftly than an arrow's flight."

"Consider it taken. We'll get everything packed the night before."

"It's not as if we're abandoning him. Madame will be in charge, though it may tax even her formidable powers."

"Oh, I think not. I saw her qualities from the first. Why do you think I took such pains?"

"Gregory! Did I hear you right? Did you plan this whole thing as *matchmaking?*"

"Well, I didn't *plan*. With father, you can never plan. Let's say, I thought if I gave it the proper sort of push, that is, a meeting would be inevitable, given the way he's always moving in on us, well, you know. I thought it might improve him no end. And you must admit, Madame's credentials as mistress of Brokesford are absolutely impeccable."

"More than impeccable. It was a stroke of genius," I answered. After that, it was Gilbert who went around for the next few days with a humming sort of sound under his breath, and all filled with contentment and conceit about his cleverness.

When at last all the guests and friends and villagers and gawkers had gathered to see Sir Hubert give the ring before the church door, they were treated to yet another surprise. Sir Hubert announced in a loud, firm voice, that his gift to the bride was a lifetime interest in the village and lands of Hamsby, with all the rents and duties pertaining thereto. In the general buzz, Hugo nudged Gilbert,

"What does he mean, Hamsby for life? How does he expect me to live, for God's sake? On the remainder?"

"I hear he's sent south for some sort of especially hairy sheep she admires," said Sir John. "Imagine, sheep at Hamsby. Sheep are suited only for knaves. Gentlemen have horses."

"Oh, I don't know," responded Sir William who had come with his wife and his son Phillip, who had been a squire, long ago, with Gilbert. "My Joan, here, has spinning women who make the finest wool in Derbyshire, and those sheep she talked me into getting are putting in a new gatehouse and paying for my second son's knighthood. You just have to keep them out of the good pastureland. They cut it up."

"I say, when he wakes from this love-stupor and discovers his lands are covered with sheep, there'll be no holding him," responded Sir John. "Ah, the church doors are open. Why, look at that! A stained glass window! How ever did he manage?" The visiting knights looked astonished at the church's new grandeur. I looked at Gilbert, and Gilbert looked at me, and we were silent a long time. I thought from the very first that window was in the worst possible taste, considering what had gone on, and Gilbert thought so too, though he hadn't been able to talk him out of it. Christ vanquishing demons, presented in honor of his marriage. Why not a lovely virgin, or a Christ in glory, or maybe an archangel Michael? Oh, no, demons it was, all pouring out of a woman's mouth and flying away on leathery little wings. Gilbert's father said it was appropriate.

"My goodness, Christ vanquishing demons. Yes, I remember, this was the church of the miracles. I wonder if I offer a candle here, the saint will vanquish those mice in my storage barns." Overhearing the visitors, I suddenly understood all.

"Gilbert," I whispered, "he chose that awful window for the money." Gilbert nodded silently toward the poor box.

"It's been full ever since—well, you know. The place has got a reputation." I hadn't been in the village church since I had recovered from my illness, and I found it much changed. All the statues had been re-gilded, and there was a beautiful new rood screen, and even a little organ, wheezing and thumping, pumped by a sweating little boy while an old friar played tunes. Prosperity shone from it, and it looked good, all crowded with folk clad in their best. At the front, the wedding mass was being celebrated in great style, with beeswax candles of the finest, and incense that was supposed to come from the Holy Land, but probably was just brought in from King's Lynn.

"Quick, Margaret, think of something annoying. Accounts. How much the wine will cost."

"Whatever for? Look, they are elevating the host."

"Margaret, you're doing it again." And sure enough, I realized the room was looking pinkish orange, and Alison was pulling on my sleeve, and Cecily was looking away at the vaulted roof, all embarrassed. What a funny sound it was that I thought I heard then, as I looked down at my hands to see that the light had come back. It was the sound of sunlight on water, of the shining bubbles that dance by the stones in the brook. There in the crowded nave beneath the hammer-beams and the scandalous new window, with the smoke of candles and incense rising toward heaven, I swore I could hear the soft echo of the water woman's laughter.

THE WATER DEVIL
READER'S GROUP GUIDE

ABOUT THIS GUIDE

Amysterious pond in the woods that terrifies and intrigues; a lady possessed by devils; an alchemist who conjures items from the past to help secure the future . . . Judith Merkle Riley's *The Water Devil* contains many fascinating themes that are perfect for discussion. This guide is designed to help direct your reading group's conversation about this last novel in Riley's mystical Margaret of Ashbury trilogy.

QUESTIONS
FOR DISCUSSION

1. "When you think of wars and high talk, Margaret, remember it's all really a matter of money" (page 4). Talk about the role of wealth (and lack thereof) in the novel. How important is money in *The Water Devil*?

2. Margaret, Brother Malachi, and Mother Hilde all inhabit a spiritual world that is in juxtaposition with organized religion—what did you think of this, and how do you think the two ways of life are compatible?

3. Consider Margaret's special gift of healing powers. After Lady Petronilla kidnaps young Peregrine and throws him into the pond, Margaret and the boy nearly drown as Margaret attempts to pull him from the water, and Peregrine hovers near death for days afterward. Why wasn't Margaret able to employ her skills to help her son?

4.   What did you think of Sir Hubert? Did your opinion of him change as you read *The Water Devil*? What did you think Madame Agathe found attractive about him?

5.   Margaret speaks with God, who tells her, "Margaret, for every person who prays for love and peace, there are a half-dozen who pray for war and glory" (page 14). Why would God say such a thing?

6.   Sir Roger, the town priest, muses to himself, "Rumors of diabolical pleasure, supernatural beings, succubuses hot with desire—matters were getting out of control. The pond thing would debauch the entire parish if something were not done, and soon" (page 62). Discuss the roles of Christianity, superstition, and pre-Christian paganism in *The Water Devil*. Why were the townspeople so fascinated by and fearful of the pond and the spirit that inhabited it? Who were some of the characters who weren't afraid of the pond and its occupant? Why weren't they scared?

7.   Discuss Gilbert's near-death experience (pages 25–28). How does this experience change him?

8.   At the behest of Gilbert, with wary approval from Margaret, their daughters Alison and Cecily are taught the ways of

becoming a "gentlelady" by Madame Agathe. What is Madame's definition of a "lady?" Which character in the novel best fits it?

9.   Discuss Lady Petronilla. Was she truly insane, or was there a method to her madness? If the latter, what do you think she was trying to gain by pretending to be possessed by devils?

10.   In Chapter 7 (pages 60–64), Hugh the swineherd encounters the succubus and is seduced by her. Did you think there really was a succubus, or did you realize it was Lady Petronilla? Hugo speaks longingly of encountering a succubus, and attempts to do so: "They say there's a succubus off at the pond. I'm off to hunt her up" (page 143). For such a dangerous creature, why did men in *The Water Devil* find a succubus so appealing?

11.   What did you think of Brother Malachi and his practice of alchemy? Did you think the scheme he concocted to help Sir Hubert regain his land would work?

12.   There are many memorable, even eccentric, characters in *The Water Devil*. Who do you think were some of the most interesting? Why?

13. *The Water Devil* offers many plot twists, especially near its conclusion. Which ones took you by surprise? Why? Were there any that you predicted? If so, what were some clues?

ALSO BY

JUDITH MERKLE RILEY

Discover How Margaret of Ashbury's
Adventures Began . . .

Margaret of Ashbury has experienced a Mystic Union—a Vision of
Light that endows her with the miraculous gift of healing. Because
of this ability, Margaret has become the target of envy. Powerful
bishops want to silence her; only one man understands her gift,
and the possible danger it can bring.

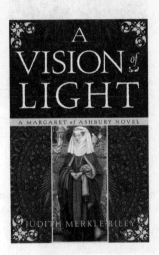

A Vision of Light
$13.95 PAPER ($18.95 CANADA)
ISBN-10: 0-307-23787-7
ISBN-13: 978-0-307-23787-3

When her husband is captured in France, Margaret of Ashbury teams
up with old friends Mother Hilde and Brother Malachi to rescue him.
And thus begins a wild romp across fourteenth-century Europe.
Murderous noblemen, scheming ladies, truculent ghosts, and a steady
stream of challenges plague the journey. Margaret will need not only
her special gift of healing, her quick mind, and her independent
spirit, but also the loyalty of her friends and the love of her new
husband to carry them all safely home.

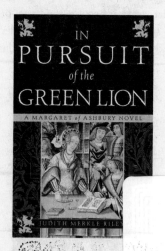

In Pursuit of the Gree

$13.95 PAPER ($18.95 C
ISBN-10: 0-307-237
ISBN-13: 978-0-307-2